THE VAN RHYNES

Bold men and proud women . . . living, lusting, loving across a reckless century . . .

THE VAN RHYNES

With their strong arms, cunning and iron will, they seized the wealth of a raw, restless land . . . built the gleaming railroads . . . whipped a wild continent into a mighty nation . . .

THE VAN RHYNES

A family like no other, a law unto themselves— they'd stop at nothing to win the golden prizes of ambition and desire . . . to carve out of their arrogant dreams . . .

THE VAN RHYNE HERITAGE

VOLUME TWO IN THE AMERICAN DYNASTY SERIES

DO NOT MISS
THE FIRST VOLUME IN
THE AMERICAN DYNASTY SERIES:

THE VALLETTE HERITAGE

THE VAN RHYNE HERITAGE

LOUISA BRONTE

A JOVE/HBJ BOOK

Printed in the United States of America

Library of Congress Catalog Card Number: 78-61601

First Jove/HBJ edition published March 1979

Jove/HBJ books are published by Jove Publications, Inc.,
(Harcourt Brace Jovanovich) 757 Third Avenue, New York,
N.Y. 10017

To the industrial families
that helped make America great . . .

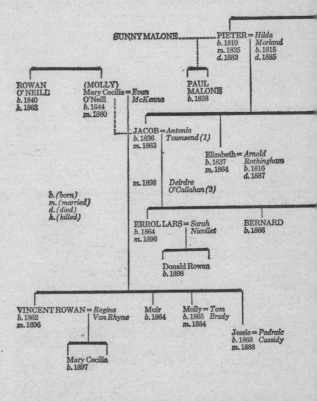

SUNNY MALONE · · · · · PIETER = Hilda
                                    b. 1810 Morland
                                    m. 1835 b. 1815
                                    d. 1883 d. 1885

ROWAN   (MOLLY)   PAUL
O'NEILL   Mary Cecilia = Evan   MALONE
b. 1840   O'Neill   McKenna   b. 1838
k. 1862   b. 1844
               m. 1860

               JACOB = Antonia
               b. 1836 Townsend (1)
               m. 1863
                                Elizabeth = Arnold
                                b. 1837   Rothingham
                                m. 1864   b. 1816
                                            d. 1887

               m. 1898 Deirdre
                        O'Callahan (2)

b. (born)
m. (married)
d. (died)   ERROL LARS = Sarah   BERNARD
k. (killed)   b. 1864   Nicollet   b. 1866
                 m. 1896

                        Donald Rowan
                        b. 1898

VINCENT ROWAN = Regina   Muir   Molly = Tom
b. 1862   Van Rhyne b. 1864   b. 1865 Brady
m. 1896   m. 1884

                                          Jessie = Padraic
                                          b. 1868 Cassidy
                                          m. 1888

          Mary Cecilia
          b. 1897

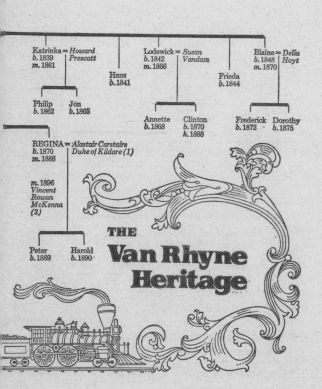

THEODORIC VAN RHYNE = *Wilhelmina*
b. 1758 *m.* 1809 *d.* 1833   *b.* 1778 *d.* 1840

Hendrik = *Audrey*
b. 1812   *Wainwright*
m. 1831

Marta = *Lars*
b. 1814   *Sorensen*
m. 1831

Sadie
b. 1818

Katrinka = *Howard*
b. 1839   *Prescott*
m. 1861

Hans
b. 1841

Lodewick = *Susan*
b. 1842   *Vandam*
m. 1866

Frieda
b. 1844

Blaine = *Delia*
b. 1848   *Hoyt*
m. 1870

Philip
b. 1862

Jón
b. 1865

Annette
b. 1868

Clinton
b. 1870
k. 1888

Frederick
b. 1872

Dorothy
b. 1875

REGINA = *Alastair Carstairs*
b. 1870   *Duke of Kildare (1)*
m. 1888

m. 1896
Vincent
Rowan
McKenna
(2)

Peter
b. 1889

Harold
b. 1890

THE
Van Rhyne Heritage

PART I

1830–1860

Chapter 1

Pieter Van Rhyne steered the great, clumsy periauger with the skill of long practice. It was like the old Dutch canal scows. Loaded with rough lumber, it could still ride the shallow, treacherous waters, the marsh flats of New Jersey, because it was of shallow draft. Its single four-sided lugsail caught what little wind was raised. It could not go rapidly, but tonight Pieter did not care. He had other matters on his sharp mind.

A small fortune, he thought. His uncle Pieter, his mother's brother for whom he had been named, had died and left him a part interest in some canal boats. What could he do with it? Canals were the future, his father had said, remembering his days in Holland. America had finally gotten smart and started building canals; now they would see some progress!

Pieter's large, attractive mouth tightened in the darkness. He was young, and he was out in the world—the bustling world of New York, and he was no longer confined to a farm on Staten Island. He had listened, watched, and picked up information when sharply dressed businessmen rode across to New York on his periauger. He had heard, and he had thought about what he had heard. Yes, the canals would be good for business, but the real future lay in something quite different.

He let the boat bump gently into the dock. Then he sprang ashore and tied it up, his large, sturdy body moving rhythmically. He was six feet, two inches tall, as stocky as his Dutch ancestors, and as strong as a young bull. He had worked hard all his life, first on the family farm, then on the periauger he had paid for with his

11

own hard-earned money. Now he was ready for grander affairs.

"Hendrik!" he called softly, yet imperiously, into the darkness. There was no answer. It was past midnight, yet Hendrik had promised to wait.

He sighed and began to unload the lumber himself, tossing it into neat piles near the dock. He had the boat unloaded and secured for the night and was on his way to the sturdy Van Rhyne farmhouse by one o'clock.

When he arrived there, he quietly let himself in, to find his mother rocking beside the dying fire.

She was large-boned but thin, and her face was worn. Their father's illness had wearied her more than had the births of four children and the still-births of five more.

"The soup is hot," she said briefly, not pausing in her rocking. Then she looked into the Bible once more, her mouth moving soundlessly with the words.

He had taken off his heavy, wet boots at the door, and he now walked in his stocking feet to the kettle. He dipped out some soup, then found the bread and cut off a large piece. His mother had set out some cheese, covered with a wet cloth. So he sat down now at the trestle table to eat and drink hungrily. It had been a long day, beginning at four in the morning.

When he had finished, and set aside the bowl, his mother finally let the Bible rest in her lap. Then she pushed her hair back wearily.

"You should not anger your father," she said placidly, yet with a warning evident in her tone.

"He is no better?" asked Pieter.

She shook her head. He came to stand before the fire, tall, broad-shouldered, straight, his blond hair gleaming, his vivid blue eyes sparkling in spite of his weariness.

"He thinks only of the past," said Pieter, showing the harsh judgment of the young for the old and feeble.

"He is furious that you do not think of buying another boat. Hendrik needs one to increase our produce sales."

"Hendrik does not help me with this boat," said Pie-

12

ter. "He did not come with me tonight, and he did not meet me at the dock to help me unload. Shall I fling away the money on a boat for him, when he does not work with the one he has?"

His tone was flat, precise. His mother sighed again. Pieter had grown up, and he was now twenty in this year of 1830. He had always worked hard and he could not understand his younger brother, who liked to laugh and run off with his friends.

"He will grow up with responsibility," his mother said.

"No matter. That is up to him," said Pieter, with a shrug. "I have my own plans for the future, and I shall carry them out. This inheritance but brings my plans closer to the working out of my destiny."

Wilhelmina Van Rhyne looked at her eldest son in a puzzled manner. He had inherited her shrewd mind, but he had gone beyond her understanding. His father was solid, hard, a farmer who had been grateful to have her dowry of a few acres of farmland. But Pieter was different; he longed for boats, and for a life beyond Staten Island. What did he dream of, that made his blue eyes shine? Where would he go, that made him glitter with bright promise, and set his will against his father's?

She herself had taught him to read and write, and he did both indifferently well. He had caught on to mathematics much more quickly, not on paper, but in his mind. He cared nothing for reading books, yet he would draw by the hour on any scraps of newspaper or butcher paper. And draw what? Engines, and tracks, and more boats!

Strange, foolish matters, she thought.

"Your father is ill. I will not have him disturbed by these arguments," she said firmly. "You are only twenty, but you owe it to us to help out. We raised you; now you help your family."

He bowed his blond head, and thought for a moment. "I will work on the canal for two more years," he said finally. "Hendrik must do his share, however. At the end of that time, he may have the periauger as his

13

own—if he has worked hard. And I shall go off on my own when he is able to help the family. I will send money back to you, but I will not be bound."

"Be bound! Is that how you think of your own family?" she flashed, in a momentary anger. It stirred her plain face and showed the spirit she had had once, as a girl. She had once been pretty, some twenty-five years or more ago, when she was first married. Now her hair was gray, her face worn and thin, her hands reddened and rough. "You are ungrateful!"

"I must be off about my own business," he repeated. "I have dreams, and no one must stop me, Mother. I do not forget you and Father and my family. Yet, I will do what I must."

She looked at the hard, inflexible mouth, and shook her head. "The farm is not good enough for you," she said sorrowfully. "You work at it, but your heart is not in the land. No, you must go off about the boats, and work until you can buy a boat. Now you work all day on the land, and in the early morning and the evenings, you work your boat on the river and the flats. You will drive yourself to death, and for what?"

"For the future!" he laughed, his shoulders shaking a little. "Does not every young man dream of the future?" He stretched, then yawned mightily. "I will sleep now. Wake me at five, if I am not awake before."

She did not need to wake him. He was up long before five, and had eaten and left the house in the darkness before she was up. She roused herself, and then got Hendrik up. "Your brother has already left, Hendrik. You must rise, and help me with the farm work."

Hendrik yawned and rose reluctantly, shivering in the cold darkness of the early spring. He splashed cold water on his face, shuddered, then wiped it dry. He pulled on his shirt and pants over the underclothing he had worn all night.

"Did you speak to him, Mother? Was he angry with me?" he asked eagerly as he sat down at the trestle table for his breakfast of hot tea, eggs, and ham.

14

"Yes, he is angry, but firm. He has his plans, as you know. Why did you not go with him last night?"

"Oh, I went off with the boys," he said, quickly sullen. "Pieter can work all night, if he wants! I worked fourteen hours yesterday, that is enough!"

She compressed her mouth and looked at his handsome features; she knew him to be weaker than his brother. She sipped her tea and said, "He has promised to stay on for two more years. However, you must work with him. At the end of that time he leaves, and you may have his periauger. If you work well, he said."

"Two years!" flashed Hendrik. "But I want a boat now! He earns money for poling the produce across to New York, and the lumber and straw. I know he has some stuck away. Why does he begrudge me the money for my own boat?"

"He earned the money for his own. I suppose he feels that you should also!"

Hendrik finished his breakfast in silence, and stamped out of the house. Nevertheless, his mother noted with relief that he, hoping for that boat, helped more on the land and was more courteous to Pieter.

The two years slid past, then Pieter said, "Hendrik, you may have the boat. I shall be off. Take care of the family, and I will send money from time to time."

They had talked a little about his plans. "Let me come with you," said Hendrik eagerly. "You will have adventures! I don't want to be stuck here with the family!"

"They need you," said Pieter firmly. "Father may not last long, and Mother and the two girls need you. Take care of them, and I will come and see how you do. If you wish to marry, as you said, then you must learn to take care of the weaker ones. You cannot both start a family and be off to adventures!"

Hendrik flushed, for he was already fond of a girl on a nearby farm. The girl had no brothers. Her father had said warily that if Hendrik showed promise, the girl might marry him, and Hendrik could have half of her father's farm as her dowry. Hendrik scratched his head.

15

How could a man marry a sweet girl, and have her farm, and be off on adventures at the same time? He reflected sadly that he did not know how to plan his life as well as Pieter did. Wholeheartedly, Pieter had made up his mind, and his iron will would not permit any changes.

Pieter had been carefully dividing his money, the money he had earned over the years with the extra work on the boat. Now he left half of it with his mother, advising her to put it carefully away where it would not be seen.

"For Hendrik would immediately think of a dozen ways of spending it, Mother," he said. "You will need it for the girls' dowries, and for Father, as he is so ill. I will come to you and see you when I can."

She touched his cheek when he left. They did not kiss; they were not sentimental people. But she looked after him wistfully, standing a long time on the dock in the chill wind, as Hendrik poled Pieter away from the farm where he had lived all his life.

Hendrik left him in New York. "What will you do, Pieter?" he asked for the hundredth time.

"My business, brother," grinned Pieter. He felt as free as the seagulls above them, lazily wheeling about in the air. But he was no bird, he was a man of money and promise!

He had been looking about these past two years, and he had been thinking soberly for longer than that. He had gone to see the canal boats left him by his uncle, and he had directed their use on the canals. But he had no intention of becoming a canal man. He had had enough of boats, at least for now.

He rented a room at a boarding house near the docks. He had stayed there overnight at times, when he had been detained on business in New York. Now the landlady asked, "And how long will it be this time, Mr. Van Rhyne?"

"I don't know, ma'am. I'll let you know in a day or two."

He washed, then changed into his good suit of dark

green wool, and tossed a yellow muffler around his neck. He still wore his boots. He brushed his hair until it lay down, although some curls still rose about his bronzed neck.

Then he went directly to the office of the Grimes brothers. He knocked at their door and stepped in. The two men were seated at their identical mahogany desks. They looked up impatiently when their clerk showed him in.

"Yes, what is it? Foreman or laborer?"

Deliberately Pieter closed the door after him, on the clerk's quiveringly curious nose. "I came to see about some stock in the railroad. I heard it was for sale."

"Stock?" Their eyebrows rose high. They looked him over, in his hard wool suit and his high boots, with his cap in his hands. "Stock? Huh! How much you want, one share?" said one brother, and the other one laughed gruffly.

"How much per share?" asked Pieter. He was still standing, for they had not invited him to sit down in one of the hard chairs opposite the desks.

"One hundred dollars per share," said the other brother promptly.

"I heard it was sixty-two dollars per share," Pieter said, his voice very gentle.

The men looked at each other again. Then they looked back at him. Was he a greenhorn, or no? They looked at the sharp blue eyes, at the big, burly build.

"Sit down, Mr.—ah—?"

He sat down on the hard chair. "Pieter Van Rhyne," he said.

"Mr. Van Rhyne. Ah—where did you hear it was sixty-two dollars per share?"

"On the street, maybe," he said, his face impassive.

"Hum. Well, how much did you want to take?"

"How many shares do you have for sale?"

They did not know how to take him. Businessmen had manners, and they wore high stocks and carried ivory-handled canes. This man looked like a laborer. He seemed to be a tough businessman, it was true, but

17

he was obviously a hard-working man, judging from the look of his big red hands.

"We've got plenty. How many you want?" the quieter brother asked. He pulled a pad of paper to himself, picked up a pen, dipped it in the ink, and looked up, ready to write.

"At sixty-two dollars per share, I'd like one hundred shares—to start," Pieter said casually, his boots squarely before him on the wooden plank floor.

Both men stared now, jaws agape. Pieter would have been amused under other circumstances, but now he only felt impatient. How much time men wasted!

"Do you have the money with you?" they asked.

"I don't carry that kind of cash. If you care to come to the bank with me . . ."

They cared. They both went with him, after closing the office. At the nearby banking office of a merchant, they went in with Pieter and watched as he was greeted with respect and shown into the office of the merchant. They saw him ask for his account, waited while a clerk filled out the forms, and watched as he signed his name in a painful scrawl.

Then he hesitated for a moment. "Ah, I believe I'll take two hundred shares," he said, still as casual as could be.

Both of the Grimes brothers felt rather dizzy. The man must be wealthy! Treating him much more respectfully than before, they signed over two hundred shares of their railroad stock to him and took him to dinner. It warranted at least a steak and oysters, with beer to wash it down, to have sold such a large block of Grimes Railroad Company stock that day.

Pieter questioned them over dinner, asking short, brisk questions that went to the heart of their operations.

"How far along are you? Where is end-of-track? How much do you pay the foremen? How much do you pay the men? What kind of food do they eat? Where do they live?"

They returned to the office with him and took out

18

charts and crude maps and showed him how far along the railroad lines were.

"We mean to join up with the Erie to the north," they said. "That will make our line important, you see."

He saw that and much more. "How much do you pay the foremen?"

They told him. He said impassively, "I'll take a job as foreman for that pay, and one more share of stock per month. I'll live out at end-of-track and oversee the operations. I like to see where my money is going."

They did not like it much, but he had his way. He was a big, solid Dutchman, and they could see he knew what he was doing. And all that money—!

Pieter bought a horse and moved out the next day. He rode to end-of-track with his gear, including a new tent, rough blue workclothes, a pistol and powder horn, and a sharp knife he always carried. Then he got to work.

He was at end-of-track for a year before he went home. He had sent notes back to his mother from time to time. There was one man he trusted, and with this man acting as a courier, he was able to send some money to her along with the notes. Other than that, he worked from one end of the week to the next, and took Sundays off only because the men insisted on it.

He lived out of doors, except for the nights, which he spent in the tent. He became even browner, tougher, harder. He swung an axe with the men cutting ties, and he swung a pick with those digging in the hard earth.

His quiet voice directed the workers even better than did the yells and oaths of other foremen. They knew that when Pieter Van Rhyne said something, he meant it. And he could outwork them, outthink them, and out-figure them any hour of the day.

Most of the men were Irish, but a few were German, and this led to fights regularly, every Sunday. Pieter watched them curiously. To use up such energy in such a wasteful fashion! And he stopped them with a few curt words when they went too far.

"You got so much vigor and strength, tomorrow

you'll dig those roots out with your picks," he said once, separating two combatants, one Irish and one German.

"Listen, he called me a son of a——" the Irishman began.

"Words! So they make scars, do they? You'll make scars in the earth tomorrow, they're the scars you'll make," said Pieter.

"I'm a foreman!" Joe McSweeney blustered. "I direct the men, I don't do no work like that!"

"You do what I tell you, that's what you do," Pieter said, staring him down. He was taller and broader than the Irishman. McSweeney hesitated, then flung himself away to drink from his bottle and grumble in low tones to a friend.

That night, Pieter kept the flap of his tent open. He always slept lightly, with one eye open, as Hendrik used to say of him. Now, about midnight, he heard and saw the shadow that came into his tent.

When the figure had come right inside his small tent and was about to bend over him, he said, easily, "What do you want? The pigs got loose again?"

The man started, yelped, and ran out. Pieter grinned to himself and lay back, laying the small sharp dagger in his hand carefully beside him on the blanket.

He went home again after a year and a half. He went first into the office of the Grimes brothers and reported their progress and corrected their maps. Then he took a boat out to Staten Island.

As he approached the dock, he looked over the farm land. It didn't look bad, and the corn was coming along well. He tied up and went slowly up to the house.

One of his sisters came flying out to meet him. "Pieter! You came!" She clasped his hand and beamed at him affectionately.

"Well, Marta, all goes well?" he asked, clasping her hand in return. She was his favorite sister, for she was quiet and hard-working and good to their mother.

She shrugged. "Oh, Sadie, she is crazy over a boy, and Hendrik grumbles about his work. And Father—he is ill," she said, and her face shadowed over.

He saw his mother working in the fields and strode out to her. "Where is Hendrik?" he asked furiously, without greeting her. She was standing with a hoe in her hand, her face under the sunbonnet looking drawn and brown.

"He is out courting a girl, Pieter. It is good to see you. I stop now and come in to fix you dinner." She showed no surprise, only her fingers went briefly to his cheek. "You look good, Pieter. So much bigger and stronger. You are happy, yes?"

"The work goes well," he said. "How is Father, worse?"

She nodded. "I think he will not live another winter," she said simply.

They went back to the farmhouse together. He listened more than he talked, and learned much. Sadie was crazy about a city boy who had been visiting with relatives on a farm nearby. Marta had been going with a young man, the second in his family, who helped on the Van Rhyne farm at times. Hendrik often came home late, flushed, with the odor of drink on him.

His father lay in bed, thinner than ever, his gaunt face upraised to the ceiling, his eyes sunken. He brightened a little when Pieter bent over him. "Son," he whispered. Theodoric Van Rhyne had always been big and husky, and it was a shock to see him now, so wrinkled and crumpled, like a husk of himself. "You come home to us, eh?"

"For a few days. The work goes fast, and I will be needed again." He listened to the old man's vague complaints, and noted the way his hand pressed feebly to his bowels. He was sick unto death, Pieter thought compassionately. Already his father's mind wandered.

In the kitchen, he talked to his mother quietly. "What does Hendrik do all day?" he asked mildly.

She looked uneasy. "He goes to help at the farm of his girl. He is too tired to help us much here."

"And the boat?"

"He said it was too much work to haul lumber and produce. He sold the boat and bought a ring for his girl,

21

some suits for himself, and a bonnet for me. I did not want the bonnet," she said apologetically.

"Will the girl have him? And her father, does he approve?"

His mother looked relieved at Pieter's mild tone. "Yes, he likes Hendrik; they laugh and play cards together."

"Well, I think all can be arranged." Inwardly, Pieter was furious. "Hendrick needs to be married, I think. And what of little Sadie?"

"She is too young to marry. I told her so."

"And Marta?"

Wilhelmina Van Rhyne looked sad. "She loves a good man, but he has no land, Pieter. He has but his own two hands."

Pieter looked thoughtful. They talked a while longer, then they went to bed. He lay beside his brother in the old bed, and thought. He had never needed much sleep. By morning, his plans were made.

He called on the family of Marta's young man, and liked them. There were eight children, sturdy and strong, of Dutch descent. Her young man was shy, but eager to work, and his eyes went often to sturdy Marta.

"You will walk part of the way home with me, Lars?" Pieter asked as he took his leave.

The women had gone ahead in the carriage, with Hendrik driving. He liked to show off his skill with horses.

"Ah, yes, Pieter. We become acquainted, ya?" Lars was eager, hopeful.

Pieter got quickly to the point. "You like my sister Marta, and she likes you much, I think, Lars." They were striding along the river, and Pieter looked back at the fields keenly. They were well-kept, in neatly plowed rows.

"Ya, very much, I like her. She is the kind of woman I wish to marry. If only—"

"Lars, if you marry my sister, you will have the land. Only I wish you and Marta to make a home for my

22

mother and father, and for my young sister Sadie until she marries. You would do this?"

Lars gaped at him, his honest face shocked. "But—but the land belongs to Hendrik! He says so!"

"It would have, but he does not work the land. Lands belong to those who would take care of them. He cares more to work the land of his girl's father," Pieter said dryly. "I will look to Hendrik. What do you say?"

"I would work my fingers to the bone for Marta. However, I do not wish to cause bad feelings in her family. Whatever will Hendrik say? And the good mother?"

"Say nothing now. I will arrange all before I go. Come tomorrow; it is Sunday, and we will visit. All will be good, Lars. I like you, and you will make a good husband for my fine sister. Let us shake hands on this." He held out his burly, bronzed fist.

They shook hands heartily. Lars drew a deep breath, and began to beam. "I could never believe it would happen! I thought all my life to work for my father and brother—"

"You will care for this land, you will work it well. I make pretty good money now; I will send money for the care of my father and mother. If aught goes wrong, send for me at once, and I will come. I depend on you, Lars."

"May you never regret your trust in me!" Lars said fervently, his face glowing.

"Go home, now, and come tomorrow with your parents. Perhaps at three o'clock?"

They agreed on it. Pieter went home to tackle his sister, then his mother, and finally his brother.

Hendrik was furious. "The land is mine, all of it! You said so! It is mine, and you cannot take it back!"

"You pay more attention to the land of your girl's father than to ours," Pieter said calmly. "I come home to find Mother working the land. She will do so no longer. You will marry your girl, if she will have you, and that land is yours. This land goes to Marta and to

23

Lars, who will care for it, and for our parents and sister."

Hendrik fumed and fussed, and tried to get his mother to take his side. But she had had enough of him and his ways. She had quietly saved money, and Pieter agreed with her that Hendrik should have a sum of one thousand dollars to take to his new father-in-law.

So it was arranged. Before he left, Pieter saw Hendrik married to his girl, and Marta married to her Lars. Lars was installed as head of the household in the Van Rhyne home, and Pieter knew that his parents would be cared for.

Pieter finally set out on his own business with a sigh of relief. Later, he would find a good husband for Sadie, for he had warned Lars to let him know if she began to show interest in someone unsuitable.

Chapter 2

When Pieter returned to end-of-track, more than a month had passed. His assistant seemed relieved to have him back, and told him that the men had become unruly.

"The Germans are threatening to quit. The Irish are more in number, and always threatening to beat them up. Sundays have become hell!"

"Indeed? I will see to it," said Pieter.

He watched the men keenly for the remainder of the week. They were coming to a tough stretch of land, and the men growled over their duties. The route ran alongside a new canal, and when they did not fight with each other, they managed to pick fights with the burly canalmen. By mid-week, half his crew was incapable of working, lying in drunken stupors, or so crippled from fighting that they could not work.

And the route to come was worse. Here at least the ground was level. All the men had to do was cut down wood for ties, smooth the roadbed, lay the ties, fasten them down, and move on.

Now they were coming to hilly, then to mountainous country. The canal had been dug through a notch in the hills, and they had the right-of-way through that notch. The railroad would have to tunnel through the hills, then through a mountain beyond.

Some men would want to quit when they came to the rough parts. They would go off with their wages, and drink up their money. Then they would seek a job with another railroad, one of the many that were being built through the states of New York and New Jersey, and into Pennsylvania. With Irish laborers coming in a flood from the old country, jobs were not easy to find, but a cunning man could find the easiest jobs, if he was willing to work for little.

Pieter thought about it much that week, now that his family was settled. By Sunday, he had decided what he would do.

Sunday morning started quietly. He was up early, as usual, studying the maps the engineer had given him for the next part of the track. He was sitting on a camp chair, at a crude folding table, when the men began to straggle out from their tents, some with bottles in their hands. They were drinking their breakfast, and were red-eyed and cross.

Joe McSweeney was the nearest, and Pieter kept an eye on him, and went on studying the maps. You had to teach these men to respect you, and Pieter knew just the lesson he planned to teach.

Joe wandered around, getting closer and closer to Pieter. He had a bright gleam in his Irish eyes, for he dearly loved a fight. And the big Dutchman intrigued him. He was so tall, so broad, yet he did not fight. Could he fight, or was he all bluff?

Suddenly Pieter rolled up the charts with a brisk snap, and put them in his tent. He folded the table and camp chair, and set them aside. Having cleared the ground, he came out again, and looked about in his deceptively calm manner.

"Well, Joe, you look drunk already this morning," he said, folding his arms over his gray wool shirt.

The words were like a red flag to a bull, and Joe reacted predictably. "Drunk? *Me* drunk? An *Irishman* drunk? No, no, Mr. Van Rhyne. A fool of a Dutchman might get drunk, but no Irishman, no, sir! We can hold our whiskey, we can!"

Men nearby heard the words, and gathered, grinning with anticipation. They had heard that Joe was a bully fighter, skilled in kicking in the groin, twisting a man's neck until he screamed with pain. He had been known to break a man's arm with a little twist of his hands. But they had never seen him do it.

"You talking against Dutchmen?" rolled out Pieter in slow, deliberate speech, his blue eyes bright under his blond eyebrows. "Did I hear you clear?"

Joe beamed. The man was going to fight! He came closer, his red fists already prepared to swing.

"An Irishman is better than any Dutchman, any day, no disrespect to you, Mr. Van Rhyne," he said mockingly. "It's just that we're naturally stronger and faster and harder and smarter—"

"All right, I'll give you a fight. You've been wanting it for nigh a year and a half, Joe," Pieter said bluntly. "Oh, by the way, it's between us two. No others allowed. All you men, stay off. Joe is my meat!"

The men laughed, or grinned, according to their nature. Pieter's thin, lanky engineering assistant emerged from his tent, heard them, and put his hand to his pistol dubiously.

"You'll stay out of it," Pieter ordered him. "This is between me and Joe."

He had scarcely spoken when Joe rushed him, the big bull head held down to butt him in the stomach. Pieter sidestepped, as he had on the periauger when he had seen a wave coming toward him, moving with surprising litheness for a man of his size. Joe rushed past, turned,

26

and in amazement, saw Pieter's fist coming up. It connected with his chin. Joe's head snapped back.

The men cheered. It was going to be better than they had thought. Pieter set himself solidly, and tried to plant another fist on Joe. But the big Irishman merely ducked, and lunged forward. His huge arms closed about Pieter, and he lifted him clear off his feet—no mean task, as Pieter weighed more than two hundred pounds.

Joe threw him, and Pieter landed on the ground on his back. Joe then pounced on him enthusiastically, and proceeded to try to pound him into the earth. Pieter fended him off, but received several hard blows in his shoulders and his stomach.

Then Pieter got a firm grip on Joe's neck, and his arms tightened crushingly. Joe gasped and began to fight defensively against this great grip on him. They rolled over and over in the dirt. The men who stood watching grew quiet, eyes open wide. They saw the fighters roll downhill into the canal, and did not see them again until they came out separately, dripping wet, fighting as soon as they touched land.

Pieter had found Joe's weakness. He locked his two arms about the Irishman's neck, lifted him off his feet, and hugged him in a cruel clasp. He closed his arms tighter and tighter, ignoring the blows Joe aimed at his belly and groin. Pieter's face was so bloody he could scarcely see. But he held on.

Joe went limp. Pieter let him slip carefully to the ground. Yes, the man was unconscious. He picked up a bucket of water and flung it on the man, then on himself, to wash off the blood. Joe needed a second bucket of water flung on him before he regained consciousness.

"Get up, Joe. I ain't finished yet," Pieter said, standing astride him.

Joe lifted his hands weakly. "I'm finished. God, you got a grip. No more!" A faint grin lit his bruised face. "Next time we fight on the same side, huh?"

Pieter let a little disappointment show on his features. "No more fighting? Oh, well—anyone else? I'm just

27

warmed up." His bold blue eyes roamed over the crowd, and the men shrank back in case his gaze should light on one of them. "Anybody else?" he asked again, hopefully.

No one wanted to fight. One by one, they disappeared into their tents, coming out only when Pieter went to his tent to wash and change. He heard the bantering, the joshing and laughter, as some of Joe's friends helped him to his feet and led him away.

Pieter let them alone until after lunch. He ate with his assistant, ignoring the bruises that burned his face and the pain that flared in his groin and belly. Joe had hit home more than a dozen times. But he would live.

Then he came out of his tent and looked about him. Joe was sitting with his friends, having finished a huge meal of beef stew, potatoes, bread, and whiskey. He looked up at Pieter out of two blackened eyes.

"Am I fired, boss?" he asked, with unusual meekness.

Pieter showed a little surprise. "Fired? No, you're a good fighter, Joe, and we'll need good fighters for that!" He waved his hand casually toward the hills and the mountain before them. "No, I just thought I'd tell the men that from now on the wages will go up one dollar a day, because the land will be rougher."

There was a heavy pause, then the men cheered lustily, throwing their dirty hats in the air.

He allowed no one to leave the camp. No one quit and went home. He let them fight on Sundays, but when they went too far, he would approach them and say, "No more now, boys," and they would quit and go quietly. He had earned their respect—as a boss, and as a fighter.

They worked hard that summer. Pieter wanted to get the tunnel through the mountain before the winter set in. And it was hard frost and cold earth that they dug in when they set the last blasts of explosives and tunneled through to the other side. Fortunately winter was late, and fall had lingered.

Pieter walked some on Sundays, gazing at the crisp

fall leaves of red and gold and orange-brown. They touched him, somehow, and made him think of home, and the harvest there. He began to wonder how Lars fared, and Marta, and his mother. He had heard from them several times that summer. His mother wrote when she could, and he received the letters when supplies were sent up to them. But he had a feeling he should go home.

When they had laid the last ties, completing the railroad line through the tunnel, he paid the workers off, and sent them home. Joe grinned at him and stuck out his hand. Pieter took it and they shook hands warmly.

"I'll work again for you anytime, Mr. Van Rhyne," said Joe McSweeney. "You're a good boss."

"You're a good worker, Joe. I'll let you know where the next job is."

"You can reach me through Grimes in New York. I'll keep in touch," Joe said hopefully.

They left by packhorse and mule train; a few of them rode fine horses. Pieter left on horseback, impatient now to get home. He arrived in New York late one night, found his landlady, and was glad she had a room for him. He slept hard, and awakened about ten in the morning, refreshed and ready to go on.

He went to the office of Mr. Jensen, the merchant who kept his money and stocks for him. The man beamed respectfully at sight of the big, solid Dutchman. Mr. Van Rhyne was a quiet one, he had told his friends, but they would hear from him in the future.

"Good to see you, Mr. Van Rhyne. I've got mail piled up for you. Use my office! I was just going out to lunch. Unless you'll join me for lunch?"

"Some other time, thank you. I just ate." Pieter liked the eager young man but was anxious to get on with his affairs. He sat down in the empty office, and opened the packets of mail.

He read the letter from his mother first. His father was very ill. She did not expect him to last through the winter. Could Pieter come home to say farewell?

He read the letter again, then folded it up slowly. He

would take off for a time, put business aside. He would see how the farm did, and the family.

He opened the other letters and read them slowly. He still could not read rapidly, and his impatience with himself hindered him. He read the words again and again, and as their meaning became all too clear, his mouth tightened to a hard line. He picked up the gazettes that had gathered dust, and looked to the stock pages.

Then he put them down, and stared into space. Damn them, he thought grimly. Damn their souls!

The stock of the Grimes Railroad Company had gone steadily upward all through the long months he had been gone. But they had said nothing. They had paid him merely his foreman's wages, though he had done the work of an overseer. And they had paid him on his stock at the old rate of sixty-two dollars. Pieter shook with anger. The stock had gone up to ninety-five several times, before leveling off at around ninety. And it had not gone below ninety for five months! They had tried deliberately to cheat him!

Cheat him! When he had lived in a crude tent, and had done the work for them, while they had sat on their comfortable velvet chairs, behind mahogany desks, eating lunches of steak and oysters.

For a time, he figured in his head and on paper, and became so absorbed that he barely heard the manager return from lunch. The man wondered at the hard, bright blue eyes, and at the taut figure bent over his desk.

"Bad news, Mr. Van Rhyne?" he asked anxiously. "Did you see that your stock went up?"

"Yes, *that's* fine." Pieter managed to smile at Jensen, then gathered up his papers and stuffed them into a carpetbag. "Keep these for me in your safe, if you will, please. I appreciate the use of your office."

"Anytime, sir, anytime. Anything I can do, let me know."

"Have you seen Ted Brady lately?"

"Ted Brady? Oh, the newspaper fellow? Yes. Matter

30

of fact, he was just coming into the Fur and Feathers as I was leaving."

"Good. I'd like to have a chat with him and learn the latest news." Pieter went out, and the manager turned back to his own accounts.

Ted Brady was still sitting at his corner table in the Fur and Feathers when Pieter went in. The thin, red-haired man lifted his hand and waved at him, a grin lighting up his face.

Pieter made his way over to the table, shook hands with the seated man, and dropped down across from him, facing the wall. A waitress came over and handed him the menu. "Sir?" she asked shyly.

He did not look at it. "The same as him," he said, glancing briefly at Ted Brady's plate. He hated to have anyone see how slowly he read.

"Yes, sir, and whiskey?"

"No, just tea."

"Yes, sir."

She scurried off. The man looked in a temper, and he was so huge! She brought his plate, slopping it a little in her haste, but he did not seem to notice it.

"Someone mentioned you were back," Ted Brady said eagerly. "What are you going to do next, Pieter?"

The two men had met casually some time ago, at this very restaurant. Pieter had never thought he would like a man like this, small, red-haired, and weasel-like, with a quivering nose for news. But they had got to talking, and surprisingly, they had found common ground. Brady knew all about the stock market. He always had news of merchants, of ships that had come in, and of auctions to be held. He was a goldmine of information, and to someone he liked, he told what he knew. And he liked Pieter. He admired the big, hard Dutchman, who spoke so little and thought so much.

"I thought I'd go home to the farm for a time," Pieter said slowly, picking up his fork and digging into the beef.

"Home to the farm? Giving up railroading?"

"Winter's coming along, and the next patch will be

hilly. We may not start again until spring," Pieter replied, chewing methodically.

Brady leaned forward, his nose quivering, his voice lowered. "Trouble?" he whispered.

Pieter glanced around, as though he were uneasy. Then he nodded. "It may not last," he muttered.

"A secret?" Brady whispered again. His eyes were bright.

Pieter hesitated, then shrugged. "Everyone knows it in the game. Part of the risks," he said. "So many railroads never make it to the end of their route, never link up. This might be one of them. Chances of the business."

"Oh, gosh, that's a damned shame!" Brady leaned back, already mentally composing a paragraph in his mind. "You can get on with any railroad, though, Pieter," he said, coming out of his trance. "You're known, now. You can get hired."

"Ain't the same as being your own boss. Oh, well. What's the news?"

Brady eagerly gave him the latest, running competently through the items he knew Pieter would be interested in. Jerome Morland had started a new rail line that would go out into Pennsylvania.

Pieter listened intently, storing the information in his sharp mind; he kept everything filed there in its proper place. It would all work into something one day. He rarely put anything down on paper; if he had to put it on paper, he might as well forget it. The important stuff got filed where he needed it, in his mind.

Having told all he knew, Brady rushed off, anxious to get his item in the next gazette. Pieter finished his meal slowly and contentedly. He had done what had to be done. Time would do the rest. He went back to the boarding house, packed his things, and headed for the docks.

He took the next boat home, and alighted, his pack on his arm. As he approached the farmhouse, he was pleased to see Lars working in the late corn fields, the corn standing around him in shocks. The vegetable garden was in neat rows, and the late tomatoes and beans were in brisk patches.

Lars lifted his hand to him and strode in from the fields, a big grin on his tanned face. Pieter met him with a handclasp.

"All goes well, Lars?"

Lars nodded. "Except for Father," he said, his face shadowing. "He will not last long."

"I had the feeling. I have come home to be with him for a time. And Mother?"

"She is well. Marta—ah, she is expecting our child," he added, and the beaming grin came out again, proudly.

"Good, good." Pieter clapped him on the back and the two men went up to the house.

Pieter had tried to put his father's illness out of his mind. Now, as he entered the home of his childhood and saw the sad eyes of his mother and the thin, bony frame of his father, he felt suddenly empty. His old life was passing away. As he looked at his father he saw only a vacant stare. It was, thought Pieter, as though he had already left this world and passed on to the next.

Pieter approached the old man's bedside and took his hand. His father did not know him. His mind wandered most of the time, his mother later told him.

But as the days passed, Pieter observed them all at home and saw there was much to be happy about. His mother, though quieter than Pieter had ever remembered her, seemed stronger and surer.

Sadie had settled down, and Lars was like a kindly older brother to her. Gentler and more thoughtful than Hendrik, he listened to Sadie, observed her beaux, and advised her.

Hendrik came over on Sunday with his new wife. He looked discontentedly at Pieter in his smart, bottle-green coat and highly polished boots.

"Some men have all the luck," he complained.

"Luck has nothing to do with it," Pieter said easily. "A man uses his brain and his strength, and makes his luck."

Hendrik frowned. His wife looked apprehensively at him, as though she often felt his quick temper. She seemed worn and tired. Pieter decided to have a talk with her father. No girl her age should look as weary as she did. She must be doing Hendrik's work in the fields as well as her own housework.

After they had left, Pieter said quietly to his mother, "Let us walk for a time." She nodded, and went to get the new woolen shawl he had brought for her.

In the fields, she smoothed her hand lovingly over the good, strong wool. "A warm cloak for me. Pieter, you are so thoughtful."

He nodded, his mind elsewhere. "Mother, how much money have you saved of what I sent?"

"There is about twenty-two thousand, my son," she said, smiling at the quick surprise in his face. "I was careful, yes? Hendrik has hinted often of what he could do with more money, but you are right about him."

"Yes, with Hendrik, money goes into a well with no bottom," said Pieter dryly. He put his hand under her elbow to help her over a rough patch of ground, and kept it there. She seemed lighter, more fragile than before.

"I cannot help them much. The girl is proud," his mother said with a sigh. "Hendrik must work matters out. He quarrels now with his father-in-law."

"This is not wise. I will speak with him." Pieter walked on more slowly, shortening his stride to match his mother's steps. "Mother, I go to New York for several days next week. I wish to take with me twenty thousand dollars. I will invest it."

He intercepted her surprised look. "You do not gamble, my son?" she asked, then shook her gray head. "Forgive me, I know better than that. Of course, the money is yours."

"It is *yours*. In a year I will return it to you— doubled." She was silent, thinking about it. He did not explain more, and she did not ask. The trust between them was absolute.

He went to see Hendrik the next day, and had an

unpleasant meeting with his brother. If the man did not work harder and treat his wife better, he would lose both land and wife, Pieter told him sternly. Hendrik seemed more subdued, but Pieter decided to watch him closely this winter. He would not return to the railroad until early spring.

Pieter helped Lars harvest the last of the corn, moving the great bundles with ease. It was child's play after swinging an axe and a pick into the stony ground of Pennsylvania. They cleaned out the chicken run, and moved it, setting in new wire. He talked at times with his brother-in-law, liking the man even more as they became better acquainted. Lars was sturdy and honest, good-hearted and open. He made their home better for Marta and his new relatives. He did most of the work himself, but when he needed help, one of his younger brothers would come over and pitch in.

After the harvest, Pieter went to New York with the money in his pack. He went to the merchant who handled his affairs. The young man regarded him curiously. Had Mr. Van Rhyne seen the gazettes? Grimes Railroad Company stock had started to drop. It was down below sixty now. Pieter smiled to himself.

"Mr. Jensen, will you do some business for me?"

"Gladly, Mr. Van Rhyne!"

"I have some money to invest. Grimes stock will continue to drop. When it goes below forty, send a man to buy some stock. Do not tell them for whom it is. Keep the stock for me. Let me know if it goes below forty."

The man nodded and agreed to keep the matter a secret between them. He seemed excited to be in on it. Pieter left the money with Mr. Jensen and went to the Fur and Feathers to find Brady. Again, he sat gloomily, shaking his head over the railroad. By the time he left New York, the stock was below fifty dollars per share.

Pieter remained with his family during November, December, January, and February. On a cold, bitter night in January, his father passed away peacefully in his sleep. They buried him, and a pastor of their church came for the services. Lars and Marta moved into the

35

larger bedroom, and Pieter's mother took their small one.

Meanwhile, Grimes stock continued to plummet. Pieter had Mr. Jensen buy small amounts at a time. When it went down to thirty dollars, he told him to buy a large amount. It slid to twenty-eight, before halting.

He stopped in at the Grimes office, to find the brothers tearful. They could not imagine what had happened, they said. Pieter replied, "Well, it may go up again, do not worry. Perhaps it is the market conditions. Where do we start in the spring?"

They discussed maps and charts, and showed Pieter the engineer's markings. He agreed to go out in early March. By the time he left home again, Marta had had a son—and Pieter owned more than half the stock in Grimes Railroad Company. One brother had dropped out of the company, having sold out all his stock. Pieter said nothing about the stock he had accumulated. He merely went quietly back to work.

Joe McSweeney was glad to see his foreman. He had gone home, stayed drunk until he had used up all his savings, and then had taken odd jobs that had not made use of his great, brute energy. "So, here we are again! I thought we would not have a railroad to work on, Mr. Van Rhyne! You hear the talk in New York, that our railroad goes bust?"

"Winter talk. Now it is spring." Pieter shrugged. "The stock will go back up again, I think."

They had a difficult job to begin with. They had to blast their way through the next mountain. But this time, the blasting powder was of better quality. Pieter had persuaded the remaining Grimes brother to buy good powder. It was worth the higher price.

Still, it was dangerous. The man in charge of blasting had to hang from a rope on the cliff, plant the charge, then yell to be hauled up before it went off. Injuries increased as the men tired. Pieter found himself pressed into the role of a doctor: binding up the injuries, watching for the deadly infections to set in, swabbing out the wounds. He had to send one man home with his arm gone, and with the sight lost from one eye.

He lectured the men sternly on safety, and they listened. He watched over them as anxiously as a father might watch over his boisterous children.

One day, several men were injured in an explosion inexplicably larger than should have been produced by the charge they had set.

Joe McSweeney came to him, fighting mad. "Mr. Van Rhyne, you know what?"

"What, Joe?"

"Them God-damned canal men, *they* set the charge! I know it, I seen them sneaking around at night. *That* was what happened! If they're spoiling for a fight, I'll *give* it to them!"

Pieter rubbed his fist against his chin, and thought. Joe waited eagerly, hands on hips.

"Joe, I think they need a lesson."

"Yes, sir, we'll give it to them, huh?"

"Right. Let me think about it. I'll tell you when I'm ready."

Pieter knew the canal men were both angry and frightened. The new railroad would take business, their very living, away from them. Pieter sympathized. He himself had been a canal man once. But he had seen then and he saw now that progress must go on. No matter what the personal sacrifice, the business of the country must come first.

Pieter had set two watchmen near the river. One came back to his tent at two in the morning. "Mr. Van Rhyne, a dozen men are out there setting charges!" the man panted.

Pieter was up in an instant. He went to the tent where Joe slept with four other men. "Joe, come out, and quietly. Help me round up a dozen or so good men."

They armed themselves with picks, and set out. In the darkness they stumbled to the river to find men climbing the cliffs, setting charges into holes they had

37

dug. A great yell alarmed them all, and a grand melee started.

Pieter had no time to direct, but Irishmen do not need to be directed into a fight. They waded into the river joyously, all fists and kicking boots. One man, then another, was dumped into the river; others rolled in the mud and dirt, pounding away with fervor.

Pieter saw a man in the dimness, climbing the cliff to light a charge there. He climbed after him, caught at the man's legs, and hauled him down. They fell into the water, Pieter's arms hard about the man's body. They struggled, legs kicking away to keep them afloat and to try to hurt each other.

They came up on the bank, and went at it again. Pieter could not see the man's face, for it was darkened by dirt and grime. But the man fought well in the darkness, kicking at Pieter's shins, banging at his blond head that shone too well in the dimness before dawn.

Suddenly a man's voice bellowed in his ears. It was Joe. "Look out, boss!"

Somewhere a charge exploded above their heads, and Pieter was hurled to the earth. Joe fell on top of him and lay quietly.

The canal men disappeared into the darkness, and the Irishmen set up a cheer. When they came to see who was damaged, they saw Pieter struggling out from under Joe.

The foreman bent over the body of his best worker and friend. "Joe? Joe?" He wiped the man's face with a wet handkerchief and shook him. The huge body was limp, the head lolling lifelessly.

They carried him back to camp, but Joe was dead. He had saved Pieter's life by flinging himself on top of his boss as the charge exploded. Tons of dirt had fallen about them, with rocks flying about like bullets, and one of them had hit Joe hard, on the head.

They washed Joe, and dressed him in his good suit and boots. A priest came from a town a dozen miles away, for Joe was a Roman Catholic, like most of the

Irish. He was buried near the end-of-track, in a quiet ceremony that all the men attended.

Afterward, the assistant said to Pieter quickly, "Should we give them a couple of days off to get drunk, Mr. Van Rhyne?"

"No," Pieter replied curtly. "Back to work tomorrow morning."

He turned away, and went to his tent. He sat at the folding table and put his face in his hands. Joe had been a good man, and he had saved Pieter's life. Pieter would remember that fighting Irishman. Back in New York, he must see Joe's folks, and make sure they were well provided for.

That was all he could do for Joe. He rubbed his face and straightened his shoulders and stared down, unseeing, at the charts.

Chapter 3

By late autumn, the stretch of railroad line was linked up with the main line. The men were paid and dismissed. Pieter Van Rhyne returned to New York and went directly to the office of Bill Grimes, who was relieved to see him and to get his report.

"Our stock went up to one hundred ten," Grimes announced happily. "My brother was crazy to get out just because of a scare. Now we run the line well, eh?"

"Oh. Do you *own* it?" asked Pieter evenly, sitting down across from the other man. He was enjoying this.

"Me? No, but I control most of the shares. Some others are scattered here and around. Now, I want you to go out and run our share of the line from—"

Pieter reached into his carpetbag and hauled out the shares he'd purchased using Mr. Jensen as a front man. "I think I own sixty percent of the line, give or take a

39

point," he said, and spread out the papers like a winning hand of cards. An expression of stunned shock came over the thin, greedy face of Bill Grimes.

"But—but they were bought by—" He looked over the shares, noting the name scrawled into the ownership line. Van Rhyne. On each and every one of them. "I can't believe it. By God, how did you get hold of—"

"I bought when the stock was down," said Pieter mildly. "And no man ever cheats me twice. You might remember that for the future, Mr. Grimes."

Bill Grimes stared openmouthed at him, a dull flush coming up into his face. "You going to buy me out?" he managed to ask weakly.

"No. I don't want this line. *You're* going to buy *me* out. At one hundred ten per share, like the market says."

Bill Grimes looked like a fish out of water. "It will break me, I won't have anything else—" he managed to whisper.

"You find the money. I'll wait a week," Pieter said, and deliberately counted out the amount of stock he already knew totalled more than one thousand shares. "It comes to one hundred eighty thousand dollars," he said, as he casually stuffed the shares back into his carpetbag and got up to leave.

Pieter grinned briefly as he went out past the gaping clerk. He could have stayed and taken over the railroad, but he didn't want this one. He wanted a bigger one.

He sought out Ted Brady, who filled him in on the latest stock market gossip. He listened, asked a few questions, and stalked about town. Then he returned to the farm to make sure all was well. He was pleased to find Hendrik a little more sober with his responsibilities. His wife was expecting a baby soon, and could not work in the fields, so Hendrik was forced to do the work, about which he grumbled.

After a week, Pieter went back to New York. By that time, he had decided what to do. He was sitting in the Fur and Feathers when Ted Brady came in with Jerome

Morland. Brady hesitated, then waved, his face brightening.

"Oh, let me introduce you to two railroad men," he said, as though he and Pieter had not set this up the night before. "Mr. Pieter Van Rhyne, this is Mr. Jerome Morland. Mr. Morland, Mr. Van Rhyne. He just finished the Grimes line."

Pieter got up, shook hands with the man, and looked him over. He knew Morland was a Dutchman like himself, and that was one reason he had wanted to meet him. The other was that the man was only in his late forties, and already wealthy. A stocky man, with blond whiskers and sandy-red hair straggling over his balding head, Morland was not nearly as tall as Pieter.

The two men sat down and talked casually.

"How are you doing, Pieter?" Ted Brady asked brightly. "Are you going to stay on with Grimes and run his railroad?"

"No, I've sold out," Pieter answered in a calm, drawling tone. "I'm looking for a bigger line. Does anyone know of someone who wants an investment of about one hundred thousand, and a man who knows his job?"

He grinned as he said it, casually, as though only half-serious. Morland's eyes sharpened.

They changed the subject, and chatted about an auction of silks and boxes of tea from China. They were sizing each other up. Presently Ted Brady excused himself and went back to his office, deliberately leaving the two men alone.

"Why don't you come over to my house, and we'll talk business?" Morland suggested.

Pieter nodded. "Why not?"

They got up, paid the check and left. As they strolled along the wharf, Jerome Morland proudly pointed out a ship he had just bought. "I'm going into the China trade myself," he said. "That schooner will take New England goods to Nanking, load up on porcelain, tea and silks, and nankeen. Then bring it back here, and I'll make a profit of five hundred percent!"

"Is that right?" said Pieter, idly. But his mind was already registering the percentage of profit.

They turned into a neat street lined with white-painted houses. Pieter knew many merchants lived here, near to their countinghouses and the docks. Morland led Pieter up the steps to the corner house. A maid opened the door for them.

They went into a neat, shining wooden hallway lined with several lacquered Chinese tea chests with tall Chinese vases on them, and flowers in the vases. Morland turned right, into the front parlor, and Pieter followed. It was large, furnished with mahogany furniture and with red silk draperies unlike any Pieter had ever seen in his life. He was almost afraid to set his heavy boots on the thick Persian carpet of reds and blues on a cream background.

A girl came into the room. She was short and slim, with pretty blue eyes and a sparkling look about her.

"This is my daughter Nancy," Jerome Morland announced proudly. "Nan, this is Pieter Van Rhyne, a merchant and railroader."

Pieter took her hand gently in his. It was so delicate and white. Her brown eyelashes fluttered over her blue eyes as she gazed sideways up at him.

"How do you do, Mr. Van Rhyne?" the girl asked in a demure tone. He noted the little diamond ring on her finger, and the gold locket at her neck.

They sat down. Nancy brought them tea, and poured for them. Pieter drank it down, and ate some cakes. Then Jerome Morland sent the girl away and closed the door after her.

"Now, to business," he said briskly.

"What's your proposition?" Pieter asked.

Morland grinned slyly. "You're as blunt as I am! Well, we're both Dutchmen. We know what we want. Not like the foppish Frenchmen or the elegant Englishmen, eh? Or like those military Germans with their way of ordering one about."

"Um," Pieter said. He had never liked small talk.

42

"What's your situation, now, on the Morland line? How many own stock in it?"

They talked business in a frank manner. Morland owned forty percent of the stock; associates owned the rest. He wanted to build a line clear out to the Ohio country so that the emigrants would travel on it rather than on riverboats or in Conestoga wagons.

Pieter listened and thought. He read between the lines, understanding the hesitations here and there. Morland had overextended himself. He was short of ready cash. His vanity and eagerness had led him to buy the China schooner before his railroad line was finished.

The house was built and elegantly furnished. Morland had five daughters, most of them of marriageable age. He would probably have to figure on dowries.

"Well, what do you think?" Morland asked presently. "I've done all the talking. Do you really have one hundred thousand to invest?"

"More than that," Pieter replied shortly. "But I want to think about it. I want to see your maps and charts, and figure out whether the railroad will be worth the trouble."

Morland compressed his thin mouth, looking angry for a minute. Then he shrugged his shoulders and laughed gruffly. "You're a hard one! But you're right. Never buy a pig in a poke. Stay for dinner, won't you? Then come to my office tomorrow, on the docks near my schooner. I'll show you the charts then."

By the sly look in Morland's eye, Pieter could tell he had something planned. He decided to watch for whatever it was.

Pieter was the only guest for dinner, but all of Morland's five daughters were present. Four of them were quite pretty. And vain, Pieter thought. He looked them over dispassionately. His mother had spoken recently of his marriage. "Aren't you going to marry soon, Pieter? You're the eldest. If Sadie marries, you'll be the only one without a wife. And you need a wife. And sons, to carry on after you."

He had not thought to marry so soon. But his mind was busy. Morland did not have enough money to give dowries to his five daughters. And one of them wore a ring, a small, sparkling diamond, on her left ring finger.

He looked Morland's daughters over, and listened to their talk. Eyes sparkling, they spoke of dances, and of parties—all but the middle one, Hilda, who sat quietly at the end of the table, where her mother would have sat, had she lived.

Hilda did not look like the others. She was plump, with a snub nose. Every so often she would murmur to the maids, and they would hurry to carry out her commands. Pieter watched her as she ordered one to bring more sauce to their guest.

Hilda wore a blue silk gown that did nothing for her sallow complexion. The silk was good, though, and so was the lace at her wrists and throat. Her hair, sandy brown like her father's, was parted neatly in the middle, and drawn back to her neck in a plain fashion that showed her lack of vanity. The others wore curls to their throats, flirted with their blue or brown eyes, fluttered their eyelashes, and were gussied up with golden lockets or silver trinkets.

"A good meal, Hilda," her father proclaimed, complimenting her as they rose from the table. "My girls do most of the cooking, Pieter, and let me tell you, they learned well!"

Pieter half-bowed to Hilda. "My compliments, ma'am. Never tasted anything half so good."

She flushed, but looked straight at him. "Thank you, sir, I am glad you enjoyed the food. Nan will serve coffee to you in the parlor, Father."

And she departed, beckoning a maid, to attend to the coffee tray. The other girls fluttered around, and sulked when told sharply by their father to go to the other parlor and practice their music.

The two men settled themselves in the deep, comfortable chairs in the left parlor. "I'm paying for the lessons, so they have to practice, right?"

"That's right," Pieter said. He tried not to wince as

44

the music started, pounding out noisily from the piano, whining miserably from the violin and the flute.

Nan brought the coffee, fluttered her lashes, and departed. Pieter was quiet, thinking. Morland looked at him sharply from time to time.

"I'll tell you my chief trouble, Pieter," Morland said, leaning toward him, his cigar ashes dropping on his flowered vest. "I have no sons. I just have five daughters. If only one of them married a man I could trust, I'd treat him like a son, I would!"

"A man wants sons," Pieter murmured, not committing himself. He shook his head at the cigar, and sipped the coffee slowly.

"You understand my position? I'm building an empire, my boy, an empire! This is a new country, a good country, a promising country for a man who is smart enough to reach out and grab his opportunities!" Morland's narrow eyes shone. "But he wants an heir to give it to, someone who's as smart as he is, someone who'll keep on building up the business! Someone who knows how to dicker and deal, a man who's not afraid to spend in order to earn! A man who'll take a business gamble and turn it into a good profit. As I told you, I bought the schooner for the China trade, and it'll turn a five hundred percent profit!"

"If the ship doesn't sink," Pieter shot back.

Morland frowned. "Well—that happens sometimes. But one ship isn't much. I don't have that much invested. One day I'll own a dozen ships! I'll keep them going across to China and back. Then you'll see. I'll be a millionaire a dozen times over!"

Pieter looked around the room. He thought of the farmhouse where he had spent his youth. There the sofa was homemade, of native oak, and the hand-sewn cushions were worn with age. He thought of the wide-planked wooden floor, unpolished, but always swept and clean. The chairs he had helped make himself, along with the stool for sitting near the fire and turning the meat on the spit. There had been no maids to scurry about in uniforms; no Betty lamps on the tables to light

45

one's way up to the bedrooms; no chandeliers with fine wax candles in them.

He drew a deep breath, inhaling the sharp redolence of Morland's good cigar and the mellow aroma of the Jamaican coffee. The candles twinkled overhead. The sounds of the piano and violin weren't so bad when one got used to the screeching and the pounding.

He looked down at the rug. It was so soft and colorful. Somehow he knew he had longed for color in his life, for color as brilliant as autumn leaves, as effulgent as the lights shining in a girl's hair, as radiant as sparkling eyes, as soft as shiny silks and satins, as lustrous as polished gold, as resplendent as glittering jewels.

There was more to life than the carving of a rough living out of a wilderness. There was more than trading shrewdly, than working in icy cold water, than poling a heavy boat through the midnight wind after a day that was twenty hours long. There was more to life than working, with a pistol on the hip and a knife in the belt and eyes in the back of one's head.

There was mellow laughter in a restaurant with friends. There was talk over a shining table with a lace tablecloth on it, and meat served in a porcelain platter with gravy spilling richly over it. There was the comfort of a cigar after dinner, of business talk, of talk about the China trade, of railroads and money—ah, the superabundance of money to be made in this new country! If only a man was smart and quick, and shrewd. . . .

Pieter left the house at eleven, regretfully, and walked back to the comfortless boardinghouse that had seemed so luxurious after the camp in the wilderness.

Mr. Morland had shut the big front door after him, and had winked at his daughter Nan. "He'll be back, daughter, never you fear," he said, with expansive confidence.

Pieter went to bed, only to lie awake with his hands under his head, thinking, thinking.

He went to Mr. Morland's office early the next morning and looked carefully over the engineer's maps and charts. He made some suggestions. "You're gambling here, Mr. Morland, making the road go over the mountain instead of tunneling through or going around. Look, you could aim for a dozen miles south, and not have half the problems of dealing with that mountain."

"You're right," Morland said with admiration, puffing his cigar alarmingly. "I'll fire that damned engineer!"

"He's done a good job. I wouldn't fire him. Did you perhaps tell him to go straight to save miles?" Pieter asked shrewdly. "Tell him to go back, aim for the flattest land, and buy the right-of-way, or get it from the government. Folks will be glad to have rail lines going through their town. That improves a town, you know. Look, there's a village here," he said, pointing with his bronzed finger. "Get the right-of-way right through here. That's what I would do."

"You know your railroading, my lad, that you do," Jerome Morland said, nodding. "Yes, sir, you're a smart man. How much did you say you could put into my railroad?"

Pieter did not respond, but continued studying the maps with a sharp eye. If the line continued to the Ohio country, across those rivers and mountains, it would be a gamble at best. They might go broke venturing it, unless they were careful. But if they won through, it would mean a fortune for them—for both of them, not just for Morland.

He declined an invitation to luncheon, and went to see Bill Grimes.

"Have you got the money to buy me out yet, Grimes?" he asked, strolling in past the clerk.

"You have to give me more time," Grimes said, "or let's make a deal, and settle on ninety dollars a share."

"No, no deal," Pieter snapped, frowning. "How much time do you want?"

"Another month?"

Pieter shook his head. "I guess I'll have to sell out to someone else. Of course, I have sixty percent of the stock. The fellow will probably want to change the name of the line to his own name," he said reflectively.

Grimes shuddered, and wiped his wet forehead. "I'll have the money in a week," he said. "I'll ask my brother. He might buy back in."

"You do that. You have three days," Pieter countered gently, and left before the man could answer him.

He went to the Fur and Feathers and waited patiently. Ted Brady came in, beamed at him, and came over to his table. He sat down, looked over the menu, and ordered rare roast beef.

"I'll have the same," Pieter said to the waitress. He leaned back and studied Ted thoughtfully.

"I hear you're seeing Jerome Morland," Brady said hopefully.

"Um. Brady, you got married not long ago, didn't you?"

Ted Brady looked faintly startled. "Yes, about six months ago."

"How do you court a girl?"

"Court? My God, Mr. Van Rhyne, do you mean—?"

"Never mind what I mean. How do you court a girl?" he repeated.

Brady drew a deep breath. "Well, you bring her flowers—"

"She has plenty of flowers," Pieter said shortly.

"That's not the point." Brady leaned across the table, his thin face eager and alert. This was something different from the trade talk. "You take her flowers, special flowers, to let her know you're thinking of her. You take her boxes of candy. Expensive chocolates, say. And on Sunday afternoons, you ask her folks if you can take her for a walk. About an hour or so, that's all right. Then you pop the question."

"How do you do that?"

Brady scratched his head. "Well, what I did," he said frankly, "I bought a ring, asked her to marry me, and popped the ring on her finger before she could say yes or no. Then I kissed her, and she kissed me back, and we were engaged. But I had to wait a year until I got a raise from the newspaper. It's worth it all, though. She

48

makes the house so cozy and comfortable, and I can talk to her like nobody else. She keeps it all to herself. She's a good sort, Mr. Van Rhyne."

"Hmm." Pieter finished the last bit of food on his plate.

"You can get nice flowers at the shop near the wharf."

"Too expensive."

Brady sighed, and began to talk about the trade, about the ships that had come in recently, and about the prices for tea and silk.

The next day, Pieter went down early to the wharf, where the markets were, and headed for the flower barrows. He picked out handfuls of flowers, and had the woman there put them into five neat bunches.

"You got a girl, Mr. Van Rhyne?" she said, daring to tease him, chuckling into her double chins, as she bound grass stems about the last bunch.

"Five girls," he replied soberly.

"Good land!" She gazed after him. That man, he does deal big, she thought.

He made his way to the Morland house, feeling like a lunatic with his arms full of flowers. He rang the bell, and the maid came. She gazed at him, eyes open wide, as he spoke over the bunches of flowers.

"Are the young ladies at home?"

"Which *one*, sir?" she gasped.

"All of them," he said. She showed him in, and, scratching her head, went for Hilda. The girl came, stared at the flowers, and a faint flush rose to her plump cheeks.

The others came. He greeted them, carefully gave each one of them a bouquet, wished them good health, and departed.

The next day, he brought them boxes of Holland chocolates, one for each girl, all carefully alike, except for the ribbons. To Hilda, he gave the one with the red ribbon.

The following day was Sunday. He came in the afternoon, just after dinner, and rang the bell. Mr. Morland came to the door himself.

"Well, Pieter, my boy," he said jovially, though somewhat uneasily. "Which young lady do you want to see?"

"All of them, sir."

He was shown in, and again the girls came, giggling and trying not to laugh aloud. All except Hilda. She came only to serve tea, then departed to the kitchen.

The next day, Pieter went to Grimes, and this time, got his money. He left almost half of it with Mr. Jensen, and took the other half in large bills. Then he went to Morland's office on the wharf.

He was shown in at once. "Well, my boy, come to see the charts?" Morland asked, standing to shake hands. Pieter set his carpetbag down on the desk.

"No, I came to pay for the stocks." Pieter opened the bag, and casually spilled the paper money out onto the desk.

Morland gasped, called his clerk, and began to count, his hands shaking. Pieter watched him silently. They counted one hundred thousand dollars, to the bill.

"Well, my boy, I think we can buy out the other fellows now," Morland remarked, scarcely able to contain his jubilation.

"That's what I'd like, Morland." They talked of ways and means, and of the time it would take. Then they discussed how the railroad would be continued, and what the best route would be. They talked through luncheon, then went back to the office and continued their discussion till dinner.

They went on the next morning, calling in the partners, and buying out their stock. The partners were curious, but they had had enough of trying to outguess Jerome Morland. Besides, the money was right there, in crisp, clean notes. They took their money, signed over the stocks to Pieter, and departed.

"Well, it's all ours, my boy!" Morland cried.

"We'll call it Morland and Van Rhyne now," Pieter declared. Morland looked as though he might object, but then he laughed and called his clerk to bring a bottle of whiskey and two glasses.

That night Morland took his new partner home to dinner. Hilda sat at the end of the table again, twin spots of color lighting her cheeks at all the excitement. Affection gleamed in her eyes as she saw her father's happiness. The food was superb.

The next day, Pieter came with five more bouquets of flowers, and again, he gave the red-ribboned one to Hilda. The following day, he brought more chocolates. The next day, he brought flowers again.

On Sunday afternoon, he dressed carefully in his new brown suit, his new low boots, and his high silk hat. He arrived at the Morland home at precisely two-thirty.

The maid opened the door, and giggled. "*All* the young ladies, Mr. Van Rhyne, sir?" she asked coyly.

"No, just Miss Hilda, if you will," he said calmly.

Her mouth dropped open, she blinked, and then went to call Miss Hilda.

The girl came, wearing her Sunday afternoon dress of blue silk, with her hair coiled neatly in its usual coronet, parted in the middle.

"Good afternoon, sir."

"Good afternoon, Miss Hilda. It's a fine day. I wondered if you might go for a walk with me."

The brown eyes grew round. "With—me?" she whispered.

"If your father has no objection." They were standing in the hallway, stiffly. She looked up at him, then away.

"Are you sure . . . you don't wish . . . to walk with . . . maybe Nan? Or Margareta?"

He smiled down at her. He was reminded oddly of a small brown robin that had appeared one early spring day near the railroad camp. It had chirped briskly, gone hopping about for worms, then flown away to its nest to feed its hungry little ones. Small, with a vivid, orange-red breast, it had been so bright and eager, with shining eyes.

"With you, Miss Hilda, if you will?"

51

Her father, rather dazed, consented, and they set out. Pieter drew her arm into his, and walked along slowly to accommodate her shorter stride. They strolled down to the wharf. She liked to see the ships, she had said.

Her eyes shone at the fine sight. Five ships were in harbor, idle because it was Sunday. Men lounged near the shops or paced up and down, smoking their pipes and exchanging sea yarns.

"Miss Hilda, do you read?" Pieter asked abruptly, as they paused to gaze into a window of ships' stores.

"Read? Yes, sir. I often read to my father in the evening, when his eyes are tired. He likes the gazettes and all the news."

"And you can add and write and all that?"

"Yes, our mother taught us all," she said simply. "She died five years ago."

"And since then, you have had the care of the house, and of your sisters?"

"Well, they are old enough to care for themselves. Papa likes things just so in the house, so I try to please him."

He nodded to himself, satisfied. They strolled, they talked. She was eager to speak of her father's ship. "I have gone aboard twice," she said. "Oh, I long to see her when she returns with the spices and the teas and the silks. Papa said we may all have new silk dresses when she comes in."

"Your father is a smart man," Pieter said.

"Oh, the smartest in the world," she said, her cheeks pink, her eyes gleaming. He saw how she might be, contented, in a house of her own, bustling about, making everything comfortable.

"Miss Hilda," he said, as they neared a quiet part of the wharf. "I have a question to ask you."

"Yes, sir?" Her arm trembled in his and he clasped it more firmly. His hand went to his pocket, and he drew out the ring he had bought only a few days before.

"I have been thinking of you ever since I met you, Miss Hilda," he said, with quiet sincerity. "I think, well, you and me—we could make a match of it. I like the way you are—if you could see your way . . ."

She halted, making him halt. She gazed up at him. "But—I thought you liked Nan—" she blurted out.

"Nan is too silly for me," he said. "I am a simple man, sober and with hard work to do. My wife would not have an easy time of it, Hilda," he said, gazing down seriously at her. "I would be away for months at a time in the summers. With a girl like you, a man could rest easy, knowing she was taking care of the house, and waiting for him to come home."

She flushed, then went pale. "I—I'm not pretty, Mr. Van Rhyne," she said. "I'm a good housekeeper, that's all. You'd do better . . . you're going up in the world, Papa says. You'd best look to one of my sisters—"

"You have beautiful eyes," he said, surprising himself and her. "They are honest eyes, I think."

He took her hand, and she did not pull back. He put the ring on her finger, then bent and kissed her cheek in the shade of her bonnet. She did not pull back then, either. He liked the feel of her cheek. It was silky-soft, and she wore a faint perfume, maybe lilac or lavender. He kissed her cheek again.

"Will you marry me, Hilda?" he asked again.

The ring was on her finger. She looked at it, then at him, and nodded, very shyly. "If Papa says yes, I will," she whispered, and smiled at him. Her eyes were radiant and shyly amazed.

"I'll see that he says yes," Pieter said confidently. He tucked her hand more securely in his arm, and they strolled on in the autumn sunshine.

Chapter 4

Jerome Morland was not easy to persude. Yes, he wanted husbands for his daughters—four of them. But Hilda! Hilda was his housekeeper, his confidant, his reader, his cook, his everything. How could he part with Hilda?

He held out for a time. He tried to persuade Pieter to walk out with Nan, or any of the others. Hilda went about with red eyes and was even more quiet than usual.

Pieter would not be dissuaded. He brought his mother across the water to meet Hilda. He brought Marta and Lars along too, figuring shrewdly that these three would be the best to introduce to the Morland family. He persisted. He walked out Sunday after Sunday with Hilda, refusing flatly to take one of the others.

"Hilda is the girl for me," he said firmly to Jerome.

"But how will I manage without her?" Jerome Morland wailed, ruffling up his sandy hair frantically. "She—I depend on her! Damn it, man, take any of the others, take two!"

Pieter did not laugh, as the older man had hoped. "I want Hilda," he said, setting his mouth.

On their Sunday afternoon walk, Hilda, holding his arm with more bravado than usual, told him, "Father is angry with me, Pieter. He wants me to refuse you."

Pieter patted her hand, more confident than ever that he had made the right choice. "He doesn't want to lose you," he said tactfully. "But he must give way. You *do* want to marry me, don't you? Hilda, I'll give you a fine house, and all you like, even better than Nan's fellow is giving her. I have found a small house where we could live about two blocks from your father's, until our big house is built. I bought some land on Long Island. We'll have a big house there, with carpets like you have, and a piano if you want it—"

"Oh, Pieter!" She looked as though she would cry, and her arm hugged him briefly tighter. "You're so good to me, but papa . . ."

"He will miss you, but he'll get along. And I need a wife like you, Hilda," he said persuasively. "The giggling girls drive me right out of my mind. I want an intelligent woman, who'll bring up my sons right."

She blushed furiously, and turned to stare, unseeing, out at the ships. Finally she whispered, "I'll talk to papa again, Pieter!"

Jerome Morland finally relented. He gave his consent and they were married the next Sunday. It was a small wedding with just the families in attendance, in the front parlor of the Morland house. Hilda, at Pieter's suggestion, wore a cream-colored dress, with cocoa-brown lace at the wrists and neck, and looked as beautiful as she could, with her sandy hair in curls like her sisters'.

After the simple ceremony, they went right away to their new small house. Pieter had bought it unfurnished, and had coaxed Hilda to fit it out the way she wanted it.

"Buy good stuff, Hilda, so we can move it to our new house when it's ready," he had told her. Her father had given them Persian carpets for the parlor and a fine mahogany set of sofa and chairs.

Hilda had chosen rather timidly, with Pieter's encouragement and good taste, for the rest of the house: a dining table of Caribbean mahogany that shone with polishing, and chairs to match; a huge bed with tall oak posts and a canopy of green silk; a mirrored dresser with matching oak chiffonier; a fine wardrobe that held their dresses, suits, and cloaks.

When he brought her into their house, he was proud of her and of it. He had looked forward to this day for many years, when he would marry and go to a home of his own, with his wife on his arm. He was twenty-five years old, and a man of property. It was time that he married. Besides, his masculine urges were getting rather hard to manage. He had had a few women, casually, in houses along the railroad lines, but no special woman, no clean, decent woman whom he respected.

Now he was married, with his own wife! His chest swelled. Hilda was bustling about, giving orders to their new maid, seeing to the disposition of their valises and a trunk of Pieter's. He sat down on the new brown plush sofa, stretched out his arms and his legs before him, and contemplated his new shiny boots.

Hilda came in shyly, a bright blush on her rounded cheeks. She had never looked so attractive as she did today, he thought. Marta had been so happy for them, and Lars had shaken his hand and congratulated him. Only Hendrik had been his usual sullen self, looking at his unadorned wife and then at Hilda, with the jewels at her throat and dangling from her ears.

Well, Hendrik could feather his own bed, and he would feather his, Pieter thought coldly. He had done what he could for the lad. From now on, he was on his own.

"Dinner is ready on the table, Pieter. Are you hungry?"

"Hungry? Yes, I ate little at our reception, my dear," he said. He rose, and put his arm about her rounded waist. She was so much shorter than he. Her head came only to his shoulder. He leaned over and pressed his lips to her forehead. "Are you happy?" he murmured.

She nodded. "I never thought I would be the first to marry," she said simply.

He smiled. If Jerome Morland had had his way, Hilda would not have been even the last to marry—she would not have married at all. He was reserving her for the role of spinster, the one who would care for him all his days, and make him comfortable. It did not diminish Pieter's pleasure in his marriage that he had taken the daughter that Jerome had least wished to give.

They went in to dinner, and Hilda took her place at one end of the grand table while Pieter took his at the other. In spite of her nervousness, and her blushes at his tender looks, Hilda still managed to keep a sharp eye on the maid, and to direct her in low tones.

Yes, she would be a good housekeeper, a jewel in his home, Pieter reflected.

The dinner over, Hilda spoke to the maid, then carried a tray of coffee to their parlor. Pieter was stretched out as before, his shiny boots planted on the new Persian carpet of brown, wine, cream, and gold. Hilda laid the newspaper before him.

"Do you wish to read it, Pieter? I shan't mind. Papa always liked the newspaper and a cigar with his coffee."

Pieter accepted a cup of coffee. "I don't read well, Hilda," he said quietly. "I went to work early as a lad, and reading and writing never came easy to me. I wish you would read to me, if you will, after you finish your coffee. It would give me pleasure."

She looked startled, then happy. "Oh, there *is* something I can do for you," she exclaimed softly, blushing again. She picked up the newspaper, and between sips of coffee and glances at him to judge his interest, she read the evening gazette to him.

They discussed the news as she read along. He was pleased, but not surprised, to find she had a wide knowledge of the business world. She commented on a ship that had come in, on her captain, and on the goods she would be carrying. She noted the progress of a railroad, and the fight over canal stock.

The evening passed quickly. The maid came in to take the tray and bobbed a curtsey in saying goodnight. Presently, Hilda excused herself, and took a lamp up with her to their bedroom.

Pieter gave her half an hour, then followed. He found her carefully arranged on one side of the huge bed, the covers up to her chin, wide brown eyes watching him as he came in.

He removed his clothes, laid them on a chair, and put on his long white nightshirt, new for the occasion. Then he got into bed, and turned to her.

"Hilda, you have had no mother for some years," he said gently.

"I—know," she muttered.

"Did any woman speak to you about—about marriage?"

She drew a deep breath. "I talked to your mother—and to a neighbor," she confessed hurriedly.

He sighed with relief. "I will be as careful as I can, but you may feel some pain," he told her, taking her into his arms very gently. Huddled in bed, she seemed somehow even smaller and more vulnerable.

Hilda trembled in his arms. He felt sorry for her, and suppressed his quickly rising desires as well as he could. He found, under her nightdress, that she had a sturdy, rounded, and silken body, with soft breasts that he enjoyed fondling. He bent over her and kissed her mouth. It marked the first time he had done so. Her lips were sweet and generous, warm and softly moist.

She cried out when he possessed her, and it dulled his pleasure to find that he gave her pain. He finished quickly and drew back, soothing her awkwardly. She could not fight back the tears. Excusing herself she rose and went to wash, and returned in the darkness to the bed.

"It will be better the next time, Hilda," he said in the hope of giving her comfort. He was happy when she turned to him and put her face against his arm. Turning on his side, he wrapped his other arm about her.

"I know. Forgive my ignorance, Pieter. I want so much to make you happy."

Her cheeks were still wet. He kissed them, and found a quiet delight in holding her against his body. Then they slept. In the morning, when he wakened, he missed her warmth. Hilda had already risen and dressed, and was downstairs talking to the maid in the kitchen.

Pieter stayed about the house all day, thinking about his plans for the future. It was December now, and in the early spring he must go out on the railroad. At that time, too, the ground would have softened sufficiently for the foundations of his new house to be laid. But

58

what to do with the long winter months that loomed ahead? It behooved him to use them for some constructive purpose.

He finally decided to use the time to have Hilda teach him to read and write better. It gave her a sober pleasure to help him do this, and she was a conscientious teacher. He soon found that he could read much better, though he would never be quick at it. Hilda also taught him some bookkeeping. But the tedious arithmetic was harder for him to learn.

Jerome Morland came often to visit them, and stayed to converse. He clearly missed Hilda, and grumbled than Nan was not a good housekeeper, and that she was careless and allowed the maids to be impertinent at times.

The winter went quickly. When they were not busy with lessons, Pieter enjoyed walking out with Hilda to see the ships, or going over by himself to the countinghouses where he had friends and business associates. He would stand quietly and watch the big ships come in, or he would talk to captains and learn of their differing abilities and reputations. In the short, gray days, the prospect of trade with the Orient was something to ponder.

But to Pieter, the railroads came first, and trade with the opening West. He was anxious for spring, and his return to an outdoor life. Being indoors, even in so grand a house, was not for him.

He and Morland discussed the railroad, and decided to link up their line with another to Chicago. The line would extend across Pennsylvania into Ohio, and then north. It seemed a good plan.

Before Pieter left, Hilda shyly informed him that by the following December, should all go well, they would have a child. Pieter was delighted. They had spent many an evening in bed, enjoying their increasing intimacy, with Hilda becoming a little less shy and more open with him.

They were in bed when, blushing deeply, she told him about the child. He pressed his hands to her belly,

59

and asked, "You are sure? How splendid! I have wanted a child. And you?"

"Oh, yes, Pieter, I want your son more than anything."

He smiled in the darkness, and took her in his arms. "It will not be bad for the child, if we continue to do this?" he murmured.

"I asked your mother. She said we might—for now," murmured Hilda, and wriggled when he laughed joyously.

"Oh, so you have thought of that, eh?" he teased her.

"Of course! I mean, it was only right and proper . . ."

He buried his face against her soft, rounded breasts. His hand went over her belly, her thighs, and he thought of the child growing in her. His child! Perhaps a son! How splendid was life!

He drew her closer, and began to caress her with more passion. His lips lingered over the soft throat, over the beautiful, bud-like nipples of her breasts. His hand reached lower, and he moved his fingers gently, until she was soft and moist for him, and he began to enter her. Her hands grasped his thick blond hair, and she caught her breath in a sigh.

He gathered her up in his arms, and held her closely to him as he entered her willing body. He pressed in tenderly, mindful of her condition, and enjoyed the way she responded to him, with gasps, and with soft cries of pleasure.

"Pieter?" She was lying with him, in his arms, her head contentedly on his shoulder.

"Um?"

"Have you—never regretted Nan?"

He grinned. Nan was about to marry her fellow, and was driving Morland to distraction with her demands for clothes, jewels, and household furnishings. Instead of being humbly grateful like Hilda, she demanded more and more as her due.

"Never!" he said emphatically. "Her man is welcome to her. I think she would nag a man to death with her wants."

She sighed as her confidence returned, and rubbed her silky cheek on his bare shoulder. "And I have the finest husband in the world, the handsomest, the best—"

"Keep on thinking that way!" he told her. "I must come first in your life, Hilda. Always first."

"Oh, you do, you do."

He frowned now. He was thinking how he often came home from some business to find Jerome Morland in the parlor, talking to Hilda. And she would always be listening in sympathy. What could they be talking about, that they broke off so guiltily when he stamped in and shook the snow from his boots? Perhaps family matters. Surely Jerome Morland did not confide business matters to Hilda! Even Pieter did not tell her—or anyone—of his future plans. An inborn caution kept him from it.

He left her reluctantly in the spring, having seen the house begun on Long Island. Lars had promised to oversee the workers, and Marta herself took a keen interest in the construction of the house. They would help Hilda also, should she need help, as she became more heavy with her pregnancy. Pieter felt better about leaving things in their care.

When he returned in late autumn, after a long, exhausting six months on the railroad, having driven the men on into the heart of Pennsylvania, nearly to the borders of Ohio, he was pleased to find the outside of the house completed. By November they were able to move in. He wanted his son born there.

And a son came. Jacob made his way into the world, bawling lustily from a seven-pound frame, in early December. He was the small image of his father, blond, with clear, vivid blue eyes, and long feet that signified, the midwife said, that he would be a tall man. Hilda was exhausted by the birth, and had been stretched much by it. But she was so happy about producing a son for Pieter that she could even smile after the delivery.

"A son, Pieter—I have given you a son . . ." she managed to whisper.

He kissed her forehead. "You should be proud of

him," he said, squeezing her fingers gently. "He is so strong and sturdy. You are of good stock, Hilda."

She beamed, and drifted off to sleep. Pieter went again to look at the tiny baby. Yes, he was small. But a fighter, thought Pieter, noting how his newborn son had managed to kick off his covers. A strong, sturdy son, with a look of brightness and intelligence, Pieter gloated quietly.

He went down to the study Hilda had planned for him. At the side of the house, far from the visitors' parlor, it was lined with dark wood paneling. There were two enormous bookcases, which she had filled. Between them was a large mahogany desk, with plenty of drawers that could be locked. Pieter was also pleased to see that a safe had been built into the wall, behind a painting of a canal scene.

A dark leather sofa stood in front of the windows, matched on either side by two leather chairs for masculine guests. And beside each chair was a cigar stand, and a liquor bar stood near the desk. Pieter gave the cigar stand a thoughtful stare. He did not smoke, but his father-in-law did. Had Hilda thought he would learn to smoke, or was that cigar stand for her father?

Nevertheless, he was a happy man. He stretched out on the nearest chair, put his feet on a leather stool, and contemplated his future. It looked very good. They had cleared a profit on the old line this summer of another one hundred thousand dollars. And with freight moving on the new lines, these lines, too, would show a profit within a year. These lines had enabled them to link up to New York, and to a river that came in from the west, the Ohio River. Pieter's eyes narrowed. He would buy a share in a freighting company, and that way he would earn more from the lines. And what next?

A railroad on farther west. To Chicago? Or to St. Louis? He got up, took out his precious charts, and sat down to study them.

That winter he made more plans. He confided in Morland a little, and the man's eyes lit up greedily. "A freighting company—splendid! Let me take care of the negotiations, I know just the man to handle the matter."

Pieter gave his consent. It was just as well that Morland should handle it. Pieter had other, more urgent business. He was consulting with the government engineers who were surveying through the West. The government was eager to have rail lines in areas where no canals could go. It would increase the number of emigrants eager to farm the new lands, and that would help populate the opening West.

Pieter spent the whole of the following summer directing the operations of the new lines to the border of Pennsylvania. They ran into huge mountains, and the blasting and drilling were tedious and dangerous. He was glad to come home in November to spend a month or two with his wife and year-old son. In January of 1837 his first daughter, Elisabeth, was born. Her birth was easier on Hilda. She was blond-haired and eager-eyed, looking a little like Pieter's mother.

He was pleased at how well things went at home. Hilda managed everything with amazing efficiency. She found time to care for the two children as well as the house, and his bookkeeping, which he left to her. He had invested part of his money in some parcels of land in New York, on which he might eventually build offices or houses. As he watched New York spread north, he thought the land would be valuable some day.

Hilda never whined at the long periods of time alone. She was happy to see him when he came, and more confident now, she showed her affection for him openly. He responded with gifts for her, especially with silks for dresses in colors he liked on her—cherry red, cream, green, snuff brown, chocolate—but none in the blues that were bad with her complexion. He gave her jewels: a diamond bracelet, earrings, and rings.

In May, he left again for the mountains, and a long, hard summer. Because of the harsh work, the bitter air, and the distance from any towns and amusements, the men were sometimes surly and difficult. The one place they could go was to a gambling saloon, and there they got drunk regularly, every Saturday night and Sunday.

Because they were so long in one place, Pieter decided to get a room in a nearby boardinghouse. Several widows had started them at end-of-track. They had poor reputations, but he didn't mind. The women must make their living some way.

He was in a saloon one night when a woman came in on the arm of one of the Irish railroad workers, who was rolling as he walked. Pieter glanced up from his poker cards, surveyed them briefly, and looked down again. The woman sat down somewhere behind Pieter, with a rustle of silk skirts. He had noted vaguely that she was a buxom woman, an attractive blond with bright blue eyes and a little fringe of hair on her wide forehead. She was wearing something bright blue, the color Hilda could never wear.

He thought about Hilda, then forgot her again, absorbed as he was in the poker game. He only played for small stakes, but it helped to while away the evening. A man could not look at charts all night.

Finally the fuss behind him attracted his attention. The Irishman was telling the woman she should take him back to her room. She was saying he was too drunk tonight. She kept putting him off, more and more uneasily.

"I bought ye a dinner for four dollars. I bought ye two drinks. My God, woman, what more do ye want? Let's go back to your house—"

The Irishman had stood up, and was attempting to drag her with him.

"No, I will not go! I told you, I wanted only to go out for the evening." Her voice was level and dignified, even in this place, thought Pieter. He laid down his cards and turned around, surveying the situation.

Her blue eyes caught his notice. How very vivid they were, like his own. Her blond hair had a warm honey-yellow hue, and the blue dress was cut low to show the tops of her rounded breasts. A nice-looking woman, but not fast, he thought.

The Irishman caught her arm and twisted it cruelly. She cried out, then compressed her lips and stood up.

64

"Will you let me go, then?" she flared angrily, despite her awkward position with her arm twisted behind her.

Pieter stood up slowly and kicked back his chair. It fell to the floor with a crash. "Let her go," he said, his voice a growl.

"It ain't yer quarrel, me lad," the Irishman blustered. His red head turned warily toward Pieter, and for a moment, he measured the big Dutchman.

Pieter did not lose a minute. He stepped behind the Irishman, caught him around the neck in a powerful grip, and squeezed. A howl of anguish rewarded him, and the woman was released. The Irishman stamped his boots at Pieter's legs, trying to kick back like a mule.

Pieter tapped him on the side of the head with the edge of his big hand, and the man went down like a blown-out candle, and sprawled on the sawdust-strewn floor. The woman stared at Pieter, her blue eyes reflecting how startled she was.

"Ma'am—if you'll come and sit beside me until I finish this game," Pieter drawled, "I'll be glad to escort you home."

He sat back down. She came over to him slowly, and started to sit at his right. Not looking at her, he said, "The other side, if you will, ma'am. That's my gun side."

She gasped sharply. So did someone else. She went around to the other side, and carefully sat down in the chair someone provided for her. She sat beside him, without a word, while he played out the hand. He raked in his earnings, some fourteen dollars, and finally stood up. The Irishman was just beginning to stir.

Pieter escorted her home in silence. They walked along the plank walk that covered the muddy earth and made do for streets in the tent-and-shack town. She paused before a rough frame house.

"This is my place. I thank you, sir."

Still he said nothing. He led her to the door, opened it, and stepped back to let her go inside first. She lit the lamp on the hall table, and he looked about keenly.

"Does that Irishman live here?" he asked.

She nodded. "He took a room here. I have four roomers. He thinks he—well, he doesn't!"

"I need a place to live," Pieter said. "I'd like to move into his room instead of him."

She drew a deep breath, and nodded. She looked relieved.

Pieter moved in that night, hauling his possessions from the other crude boardinghouse to this one. He threw the Irishman's belongings out into the street, and the man evidently came for them and carried them off, because they disappeared.

The other boarders were very respectful to Pieter.

The summer was long, cold, and rainy, with many foggy nights. Pieter began to stay home evenings. The woman, whose name was Sunny Malone, made him welcome in her parlor. Her husband, she said, had been a railroad man, in charge of explosives, and one night there hadn't been enough of him left to bring home in a box.

Sunny Malone was bright, earthy, and amusing, with a little-girl-lost look in her eyes. She made him laugh. Rocking, she would say, "If Mama could see me now! She said I'd end up in a house, with people waiting on me . . ."

"Where did you come from?" Pieter asked her one evening.

"Germany," she said. "My father was impressed into the army. He had to fight, though he was a peaceful man. He came home, broken in body and mind. He thought he was a duke, giving orders!" She laughed shortly, her eyes glistening. "Mama and I would curtsey and say, yes, sir; no, sir. He died two years later, of the injuries to his head. Before he died, Mama and I decided to come to America to join her brother and his family. We thought we'd have to sneak away from the Duke."

"And you married an Irishman."

She shrugged. "I was young and foolish." She

grinned, and held up her glass to him. "If I had known you were coming, I'd ha' waited . . ."

"I'm married," he said bluntly.

"All the nice men are," she said. "But they don't always say they are. Any children?"

"A boy and a girl."

"I never had any. Married for too short a time, I expect. Oh, well, sometime I'll go back East, and find another husband." She could drink as much as he could, and her tongue scarcely turned over, he thought. "For now, I'll follow the railroads."

The days that summer were long and full of work. The nights were long and empty. One night he came home to find the house quiet and empty. Except for Sunny. The other boarders had gone off to a celebration. They had cleared through a big mountain that day, and the men used any excuse to have a drunken spree.

"I'll fix you some dinner. And we'll have some good wine," she said. They ate and drank and talked. They were lonely, both of them. Hilda's letters, months apart, had become reserved. Pieter had become accustomed to sleeping with a woman, a nice, perfumed woman who wanted him, and his bed felt empty.

When they were finished eating, he stood behind her chair, meaning to hold it for her while she stood up. It was a gesture he used at the big house on Long Island when there was company. Tonight they were alone, he and Sunny. He looked down, and saw the form of her rounded breasts, beneath the neat line of lace at the top of her revealing blue dress.

He put his hand on her throat, and slowly moved his fingers toward her breast. As he stroked his fingers lightly over the silky skin, she caught her breath.

"I want you," he said urgently. "I want you. But if you don't want me, stop me now, for God's sake."

She stood up and turned around to face him, her smile tremulous. "I've wanted you since the first time I saw you, Pieter," she said softly. His arms closed around her and he drew her savagely to him. He pressed his hard body to her softness, and the desire

67

sprang up between them so fiercely hot it was like jumping into a fire.

They went to her bedroom and shut and locked the door. He undressed her, not lingering over it, though he had often imagined drawing each thin, whispering garment sensually from her. Tonight he could not wait. He laid her down naked on the wide bed, yanked off his clothes, and lay on top of her.

Tasting the wine on her lips, he pressed his mouth hungrily to hers. Her tongue flicked into his lips, and slithered around in his mouth, startling him with the sheer, erotic pleasure of it. He moved his naked thighs on hers, searching. Her hand came down between them. He thought she was resisting, but no—her hand closed slowly on him, and squeezed. He almost went through the ceiling with the pure, lusty delight of it.

Her arms closed about him, stroking over his back and down to his thighs, as he pressed home. She was big for him, and rounded, all woman, and he mounted her and enjoyed moving against her slowly, teasing her as she teased him back. Her fingers went up and down his spine—as though she were playing the piano, he thought. He got so big, it scared him, for he thought he might be hurting her. He began to draw out.

"Don't—don't—" she muttered, and hugged him tighter. "God, you'll kill me—but you're all man. I've wanted you. I've thought about you until I couldn't go to church!"

He laughed against her mouth, and laughing, he continued to move teasingly against her, and she giggled in his arms and squirmed beneath him, urging him on to more powerful thrusts from his hard thighs. He held back as long as he could, wanting to prolong their pleasure, and she dug her fingers into his thighs and pulled herself up to him.

He let loose, powerfully, and she groaned with delight. She moved languidly under him, her hands moving on him, his body lax on hers, until he rolled off.

"I went too far," he said.

"Don't ever be sorry, no matter what happens," she

said, and turned and buried her head in his hairy chest. She kissed his nipples, and rubbed her cheek in his chest hair, until he wanted her all over again.

She was generous, loving, giving, more woman than he had ever had in his life. The next day he kicked out the other boarders. He wanted Sunny Malone all to himself.

The summer flew past. When autumn came, with its witching fires, and with its scarlet and yellow leaves in the mountain trees, she promised to wait there for him, to be at end-of-track the next spring when he returned. He left her plenty of money to live on, for he could not bear that another man should pay to have her. He fiercely wanted her to be his, all his.

Chapter 5

All winter long, Pieter could not put Sunny Malone from his mind. He thought of her at night as he lay in bed, Hilda asleep next to him. He remembered all the glory and delight of her unbound blond hair spread across his pillow, her generous mouth open to his, her round body moving slowly beneath him, her fingers everywhere. He wanted to see her again. He snapped at Hilda, and walked long miles through the growing city of New York, thinking of the woman who waited for him at end-of-track.

He left early in March, though the ground was still frozen solid. He went out to end-of-track, and Sunny Malone was gone.

"She left right after you did," a bartender said, giving him a curious look. "She went on into Ohio, she did. Said she had some relatives there."

Sunny Malone had told Peter she had no living relatives. He waited grimly, to see if she would return. Had she gone off with another man? No one seemed to know.

She did not return. He took a room in a boarding-house, and began again the hard, rough, dangerous work of blasting through the Pennsylvania mountains. They laid track, blasted, laid more track, cursed and drank through the weekend, and started again on Monday morning. It was the worst summer he had ever had.

When snow came, he went back to New York in a foul temper. Another girl had been born to him, Katrinka, a pretty little girl who whimpered for attention. He had little to give.

Pieter turned his thoughts to the future. His family was growing. He would build a huge house for them on Manhattan Island, above the docks and warehouses, out of reach of the huge office buildings. He would build a grand house, with velvet curtains. . . .

He opened his safe one evening and began to take out papers he had not studied for two years, to see what he had, what property he might use. He scowled and looked again, unable to believe his eyes. The land ownership papers were gone.

He shouted for Hilda, and she came, white of face. "What is it, Pieter?"

"Some papers are gone from the safe, Hilda," he said in an ominously quiet voice. "Do you know anything about it?"

She put her hand to her face. "Oh, Pieter—" She looked so guilty, so unhappy, that he knew at once.

"Your father? Did he dare to come—"

"Oh, Pieter," she said in a rush. "He came to me two years ago. One of his ships had sunk, and he had to have more than two hundred thousand dollars right away. I thought if you were here you would lend it to him—"

He stared at her, his heart sinking to his boots. His Hilda had betrayed him! That was why she had been so uneasy, so terse, writing so sparingly to him. She had felt guilty, she knew she had done wrong.

"Tell me all about it," he said, keeping his voice

steady. He came toward her and she flinched as though he would strike her, but he had never struck her in all their life together.

Her hands twisted in her brown apron. The color had faded from her sallow cheeks. He looked at her curiously. She had never looked so plain. Before God, why had he married her? He had thought himself so sensible and smart, choosing a girl who was a good housekeeper, a good wife and mother. And she had done this to him, putting her father above him. Betraying him.

She explained in a low tone. Her father had come to her, grief-stricken. The freighting matter he was handling for Pieter had gone bad, and he had invested some of the money in a new ship to repay the loss. But the ship had sunk, and he had lost everything.

"He borrowed the money to buy another ship, Pieter. It's due in before long. When it comes, he'll repay you, and with interest. I know he will. He swore he would . . ."

"He didn't have the combination to the safe, did he? You let him into my property?" His voice had risen in anger in spite of his wish to control himself.

"Yes, Pieter. I'm sorry—"

"No, you're *not* sorry!" he yelled. A frightened maid put her head in the door, and withdrew it quickly, running away. "You would do it again, damn it! You put your father first, and not me! I warned you, Hilda. I have to come first! Your loyalty should be to me!"

"I know, I know . . ." she whimpered, but there was a stubborn set to her chin, and her eyes looked more than ever like her father's, cunning and sly. He wondered that he had never seen before, how much she looked like Jerome Morland.

"When is the ship due in?" he flashed.

She shook her head. "I don't know. Soon."

"And you let him have all the property in New York that I bought! Let me tell you, woman, what I was going to do with that property! I was going," he said deliberately, his voice high, "to build you a lovely big house, because this one is getting crowded. I was going

71

to make it easy for you, with more servants and the finest clothes. . . ."

Hilda began to cry, but Pieter was not moved. He closed the safe, locked it, and stormed out of the house. For once in his life he went out and got drunk, and stayed in the bar until noon of the following day. He got so dangerously drunk that everyone avoided him and left the bar, except for the uneasy bartender.

He could not get so drunk that he could forget what had happened. His wife had betrayed him and stolen his money—for her weasel of a father! And she had done it almost two years ago, and never said a word!

Finally he gave up. He sent out for some coffee, and the relieved bartender treated him to a huge platter of ham and eggs. As he sat over the food, he thought sullenly of what he would do. He would not just get the money back, he thought. He would get Jerome Morland in a way that the man would never forget!

No man would ever cheat him and get away with it! After this, he would be so cautious that no man would ever get the chance to cheat him again! He was through trusting men—and women. The thought of Sunny Malone walking out on him still smarted in the back of his mind.

In the middle of the afternoon, he got up from the table and went to see Mr. Jensen. He told the merchant what he had in mind, and the man agreed to put the plan into action. It was an odd request, but he had learned never to question Mr. Pieter Van Rhyne.

They went out together, and found a quiet little office in one of the new Manhattan office buildings. They bought a large safe and moved it in. They hired a clerk, a nephew of Mr. Jensen, who had a crippled leg and a humble, eager-to-please nature. The lad, only too glad of a job, swore that no one but his uncle and Pieter Van Rhyne would ever have access to that office and to that safe.

Then Pieter went home, loaded all of his precious papers, his stocks and bonds and his contracts, into several valises and took them away in a carriage. He did not speak to Hilda, though she hovered about anxiously in the back hallway.

Along with his papers, he took with him a valise full of his clothes. He did not wish to speak to Hilda for some time. He rented a room in a boardinghouse near his new office, and occupied himself with setting up matters the way he wanted them. Then one morning he went down to the wharves to see Jerome Morland.

Pieter came in to Morland's office and sat down, uninvited. Morland, from behind his huge desk, eyed his son-in-law nervously. Finally, he spoke. "You heard."

"I heard you stole my property," Pieter said evenly. "Can you think of any reason I shouldn't press charges and have you thrown into jail?"

Morland flinched. "I'm going to repay you!"

"Damned well, you're going to repay me. What about the freighting venture?"

"There were problems! It wasn't my fault!"

Pieter carefully dug into the matter. It seemed Morland had been too trusting with the contractor, and had given him money and freight and wagons. And the man had run out on him. "You should have waited to pay him when he came back with the goods," Pieter remarked. "It was poor business sense."

"I know that now," Morland admitted unhappily. "For God's sake, boy, are you going to hold it against me, that I borrowed money from you?"

Pieter gave him a cold look. "Getting into a man's safe while he is away, enticing his wife to steal from him—that isn't borrowing, Morland. And the value of that land has more than doubled in two years. I could get twice that now."

Morland flinched, and his face went white. "I've got a ship coming in. We'll share the profits, fifty-fifty," he whispered.

"No, we won't. You bought the ship with my money. I've decided to be generous, and not to press charges," Pieter declared evenly. His anger had drained away, and his mind was working with its usual precision. "I'll figure that you acted as my proxy in this matter. You

73

bought the ship and the goods, and hired the captain for me. And I'll get the profit when she comes in, all the profit."

Morland practically collapsed behind his desk. "You can't do it! Pieter, I have to have the money, I have to have it! I overextended on the railroad I'm building north to Maine—"

"Really? Another railroad? With whose money?" Pieter sneered. He had already heard about the new line from talkative Ted Brady.

Morland bit his lip, shaking his head. "I didn't mean I wasn't going to cut you in on it. You're my daughter's husband. . . ."

"Do me no favors. Just keep your sticky fingers out of my money and my property," Pieter said abruptly. "When is the ship due in?"

"Any time now," Morland answered dully, his head in his hands.

"Let me know." Pieter rose and quickly left the office. He felt somewhat better, though he still burned inside at the way they had cheated him. And his wife! He couldn't get over that.

He slept in the little bedroom at the boardinghouse for a couple of months. He stayed away from Hilda all winter, as much as he wanted to see the children. He was afraid of what he might do or say to her.

She came to see him on Christmas day, red-eyed, wearing black. It wasn't a pose. She felt very badly, he knew.

Humbly, she came into the parlor of the boardinghouse. Lars had driven her in, and he waited in the hallway.

"Pieter, I came to ask you to forgive me. For the sake of the children, if not for me," she said in a low voice. "I did wrong, I know it. I should have been loyal to you, I know it now."

He sat on the parlor sofa, his hands dangling between his legs. He wanted to lash out at her, but he knew it would accomplish nothing. The matter had been settled.

"I've missed the children," he allowed himself to admit. Lars's anxious face peered around the corner of the door, then drew back again. "How are they?"

"Jacob misses you. The girls don't remember you." A tear trickled down her cheek. He thought of how he had left her alone winter after winter, even when he was here, and of how he'd been away all of the long spring and summer and fall. She had stood up to that, and had managed to raise the children on her own. His heart softened a little. "I'm asking you to come back home to them, Pieter. You're a good father, and you were a good husband to me. I did wrong."

She was humbling herself, and he could not hold out. He gave a deep sigh.

"All right, Hilda. I'll come back. I suppose I've gotten over my anger. We must get some presents for the children for Christmas."

Her face brightened eagerly. "You're—coming home?" she breathed.

He forced a smile. "Yes. I'll go pack, and pay my bill. You wait here. Lars, come on in and have a drink. It's a damned cold day." He went out and told the landlady he would be leaving permanently.

She took some tea in to Hilda, and brought some whiskey for Lars, while Pieter packed. He felt good about going home again. He was satisfied that Hilda realized she had done wrong, and had come to admit it. But her father was another matter. He was a businessman, and Pieter would not be satisfied until he had gotten back at him.

Pieter went home with Hilda, and enjoyed the children that Christmas. And in his study, he worked hard on his plans. His mouth had a cruel set to it as he worked on the charts for the railroad. He knew something that Morland didn't know, something he had learned while working on the roads. The main roads were going to Chicago, and not to the Ohio River, as Morland had planned.

It would be work wasted, so far as the future of Morland and Van Rhyne was concerned. The short lines they were building could only be used locally. But Pieter cared little. He had other ideas. Bigger ideas.

He did not go out until late spring, for he had lost interest in this part of the railroad. He oversaw the short lines, and directed the blasting and laying of rails. But his heart was not in the work. He returned in early autumn. Innocent Hilda did not realize why he had come home so early. She thought he had missed his family and could not wait to return.

She had bad news for him. "Pieter," she said, the first evening, after giving him a joyous hug. "I have to tell you about your mother. Lars came over last week. She doesn't have long to live, he said."

His face shadowed over. He loved his mother, with a deep understanding of her long, hard life, her devotion and sacrifice for them all. "I'll go over and see her tomorrow." He picked up Jacob, who was clinging to his pants leg. "Remember me, son?"

The five-year-old lad beamed up at him. " 'Course I do. You're my Papa. I'm not stupid, like my sisters!"

Hilda rebuked him, but Pieter only laughed and swung the boy higher, noting approvingly how tall he was, and how heavy and sturdy.

Jacob was a fine-looking lad, with his father's blond hair and blue eyes, and his sturdy frame and height. He was also bright and quick. Hilda was already teaching him letters and numbers.

When Pieter went to see his mother, he took Jacob with him. They found her sitting on a bench near the vegetable garden, her face tilted toward the sunshine. It was a shock to see her idle, for Pieter had never seen her so. When he came close, he saw how snow-white her hair was, and how thin on her pink scalp. Her eyes, as she opened them, were blurred and misty.

"Pieter?" she murmured, as though coming out of a dream. He sat down beside her and took her tiny hand in his. It felt all bones. Jacob ran away to play with his cousins.

"Yes, Mama. I have come home."

"You're a good boy," she murmured, as from afar.

For a long time they sat in silence. He did not kiss her. They had never been demonstrative with each other. But they were close—close in heart.

Presently she spoke again.

"Pieter, the money I left with you. It grows, yes?"

"Yes, Mama. You want it again?"

"No. I leave it all with you. Hendrik—the money trickles through his fingers like raindrops. If he and his wife are in need, you will take care of them. Lars and Marta will do well, barring accidents. You will watch over them, my eldest?"

"Yes, always."

She sighed. "Your Jacob looks like you, when you were a lad. So strong, so helpful always. Your father would be proud."

"Have you seen a doctor, Mama?"

"No. He would just cut me open. I don't want to be cut. I know when I will go, and that is all right. You will come to see me again?"

"I will come often. The railroad work is done for the autumn. There is no more work until spring." He talked to her of the rails, and of the way West, knowing that she listened only to his voice, to his tone, and did not pay attention to the words. She clung to him with her fingers, as though drawing strength from his big hand.

She died in late November, and they buried her near the house, on the land where she had worked all her life. Marta and Sadie wept, as did Hendrik. But Pieter did not, he felt the grief so deep inside. Yet for her he was happy, that she would never feel pain again. Her last weeks had been nothing but agony.

He had put her money into safe investments. Now he began to invest more deeply, studying the markets that winter and the next. He went out to end-of-track, but his heart was not in it. He returned early, and set to work again on his plans. And he began quietly to sell the shares in the railroad he owned with Morland. By 1844 he had gotten rid of all of his shares, and Morland did not know it. Pieter had even sold some to Morland, through an intermediary who was handling Morland's investments. It confirmed Pieter's opinion that the man was slipping, that he had too many interests, and that he could not keep them all in his head and hands.

Pieter went down to Washington that winter, and talked to government surveyors. Then he bought land where he needed it, right across New York State, into Pennsylvania, through Ohio, and on into Chicago: pieces of land here and there, to fill out some existing rail lines that began and ended vaguely at villages and towns. He hired a surveyor to map out rail lines that would link them all, right to Chicago, which would be the new railhead.

When he told Morland that he was out of their partnership, the man could not believe it. He sat and stared at Pieter, his mouth gaping, his face crimson.

The office was quiet. From the open doors came the brisk smell of the sea, the cries of hawkers, and the chatter and laughter of sailors as they strolled past.

"You don't mean it, Pieter! Tell me you are joking! You would not treat me like this! Who will direct my line? Who will manage it? I am too old to go out to end-of-track!"

"You can hire someone to do it," Pieter retorted indifferently. "I just came to tell you I was finished. I have bought a railroad of my own. I'll call it the Van Rhyne New York and Chicago line."

"Chicago. Chicago!" whispered Morland. "The lines aren't going to Chicago!" His face drained of color.

"Yes, I'm afraid they are. It's going to be a big city, where all the lines will link up," Pieter said. He stood up to depart. "Your line will be useful, I suppose. Short lines will still be needed by the farmers to get their grain to nearby markets. And the line to the Ohio River might be useful. It will take some doing, though, competing with the river traffic."

"Pieter! Don't go! We must talk!" Morland followed him to the office door, oblivious to the curious glances of his clerks on their high perches at the accounting desks. When Pieter looked hard at them, they bent their heads and scribbled in their ledger books.

"There's nothing to talk about. I'm going out to look over some New York property. I might build a house in town someday," he said. "I would have long ago but for the fact that you sold my land from under my nose, you and your daughter."

"You still hold that against me, even now! In spite of the fact that you took my ship and all the profit from it!" Morland was talking wildly at Pieter's broad back, all the way to the outer door.

Pieter shrugged. "That is in the past, and forgotten," he said smoothly. He had looked forward to this day for four years and more, but now it had somehow lost its edge.

He walked out, and instead of going to an agent, he went to the Fur and Feathers. Presently Ted Brady slipped in, more eager-nosed and sharp-tongued than ever. He saw Pieter, but hesitated until Pieter motioned him over.

"How are you, Brady? It's been a long time."

Ted Brady slipped into a chair opposite him, eyeing Pieter dubiously. Pieter Van Rhyne was a striking figure now, in his black velvet coat and smart pantaloons, with shiny boots and a sharp reputation. Brady didn't feel easy with him anymore, though Pieter had never treated him badly.

"Yes. It's been a long time since we last met," Brady agreed, and ordered from the menu, after studying it. Then Pieter said to the waitress, "I'll have the same," and waited until she had left before asking, "Well, what's news?"

Brady thought for a minute and came up with some items. The fur trade was booming, and the trade with China was progressing well. Someone's ship had come in, another's had gone out. All during the time he spoke, he looked sideways at Pieter. "Is it true you're out of business with Morland?" he blurted out at last.

"That's right," Pieter replied. "We're going our separate ways. I bought myself a new rail line, from New York to Chicago. I'll be going out, come spring."

"Your wife's father?" Brady asked dubiously.

Pieter's mouth went hard. "I don't let relatives and relationships stand in my way. Business is business," he snapped. "I know what I'm doing. I like being my own boss."

"Yeah, sure, that's right," Brady muttered. "Uh—did you hear anything about the steam boats going around to California?"

"I've heard a little," Pieter said, glad to change the subject. And they talked on about steamboats and clipper ships for the rest of their meal together. Later, Pieter saw in the gazette a simple, cautious item stating that Morland and Van Rhyne had broken up their partnership in the railroad business.

One afternoon, as he played with Jacob in his study, showing the lad how to draw a railroad line, Hilda came to him hesitantly. He held his young son on his lap, feeling a curious pleasure in touching the flesh of his flesh, bone of his bone. The boy was so sturdy, so quick, with a free laughter that rippled through him.

"Pieter?"

"Yes, Hilda?"

She held the gazette in her hand, and there was a pinched look to her mouth. "Is this true?" She held up the item about Morland and Van Rhyne dissolving their partnership.

"Yes. Your father likes being his own boss. So do I. It's best that we part." He looked down at the lines Jacob was drawing.

She swallowed. "Is it because of what I did?"

"I would have gone off on my own one day anyway," he said. "It's time I managed my own business. Your father can do what he wishes."

"But he'll be ruined," she whispered. "He can't go out and run a railroad line, overseeing the men! Pieter, think of him, he is getting old."

He patted Jacob's head and told the boy to run off and play with his sisters. Jacob, who had looked up at the face of his mother, went willingly.

"He won't be ruined, Hilda," Pieter said, after the door closed behind Jacob. "He'll have money to play

80

with. Maybe that's all he needs. He won't be important anymore, so he'll have to sit tight on what he's got. The rail line won't go anywhere, but lots of lines don't. That's the business."

She seemed about to say more, but taking into account the hard look of her husband's mouth, she turned and left the room. Pieter stared for a long time at the wiggly lines Jacob had drawn, then crumpled up the sheet and went out for a long walk.

He found his thoughts drifting to Sunny Malone, as they often did, these days. Sunny, with her laughing eyes. Would she approve of what he had done? Ach, what did he care! What did he care what any of them thought! He had a hard reputation in the city, but that wasn't against him. He had earned the respect of men, and they did not dare to cross him.

Money and property. These were the important things. He had bought more property in New York. Some day it would be worth a lot more than it was now. The city was creeping northward, with offices and apartments, houses and streets spiraling upward into the island from the docks and wharves of lower Manhattan.

He had also bought some new clothes. No longer did he go around in rough gray flannels and hard boots. He wore smart redingotes with velvet collars and braid, and tight-fitting trousers that strapped under his shiny shoes. His hair had grown full at the sides, and he allowed himself to develop side-whiskers. On Sundays he carried a cane and wore a cravat and silk top hat to church.

For Hilda, too, he bought more clothes. She had no room to complain of his treatment of her. She wore morning dresses of silk in the new style with bustles and many petticoats. Her best pelissé was of mink, and she had a beaver hat. They had two carriages: one that he drove daily into the city, and one for Sundays. They kept a coachman and grooms, and five house servants. It was apparent that they would soon need a larger, grander place in New York.

In the early spring, Pieter bade them all farewell and went eagerly out to survey his new railroad. He was treated with new respect. He was not just the "boss"; he was the owner of the line. Following a judicious plan, he linked up two of his new lines and by the end of that first summer, the line reached the border of New York, extending far north of where he had worked before.

That winter, he dickered for freight to carry on the line, looked over the new designs for railroad locomotives, and talked to some Englishmen who were inventing new types of rails to go over the sharper slopes of the American landscape. He bought some passenger cars that were open to the sky, resembling carriages, and arranged deals with farmers to carry their goods to market.

He worked hard, and gained a reputation for being as tough as his steel rails. In the heavily guarded safe in his office, the stocks piled up, for real estate in New York, and for contracts to build railroads on the rights-of-way he had arranged to get.

One day Hendrik came to see him. He complained to his brother that he had no money to live on. Pieter agreed to provide an allowance, but only if the money was given to Hendrik's wife. This infuriated Hendrik.

"You can't handle money," Pieter told him bluntly. "Your wife is better at it than you are. I gave you money last year to buy new clothes for the children, but you never did. What did you spend it on?"

"I had to buy a horse," Hendrik shot back, his face red with anger.

"A horse for racing? You are an idiot, and you always will be. Your wife will have the right to sign for this money, not you, Hendrik. Or there will be no money at all!" Grumbling, Hendrik agreed and hurried from the grand house. Hendrik, Pieter knew, would always be a nuisance.

Lars and Marta, on the other hand, were a pleasure to be with. They greeted Pieter with homely comforts when he visited; they beamed at him, and welcomed his children as their own. Marta would sing while about her work, the children clinging to her skirts, and she smiling down at them with an expression that resembled her mother's. But Sadie had married rather well, and she ignored them all, flitting from one benefit to another in the city. Yet Lars and Marta, they were good people.

All in all, things went well. Another son, Hans, was born to Pieter and Hilda in 1841, and Lodewick the following year. Then came another girl, Frieda, in 1844. It was a fine, big family, and Pieter began to look over his New York City property for the ideal location for a new house. They definitely needed more room.

He was an important man now. Men took off their hats to him on the street. He was known by sight to the bankers and the real estate men, and on the wharves, to the sailors and the captains.

And his family was large. Yes, it was time to make another move upward, to a grand house on Fifth Avenue in New York City.

Chapter 6

Before he could decide on a house, something else happened to change his life, and that of hundreds of thousands of others in the United States.

The merchants heard the first whispers. Gold—gold—gold! No one believed it, especially the cautious, tightfisted New York bankers. But more stories came, and more, and then a flood of stories inundated the city, and a wave of young men streamed out West to see if it could be true.

Gold had been discovered in California! It was America's new land, for Mexico had just recently, and reluctantly, sold it to her. Gold in the new land! How ironic, how just, how wonderful!

The stories came back East, and made big headlines in the gazettes. Pieter studied them thoughtfully, sometimes getting his lame clerk to read to him, for the man read quickly and clearly.

He learned that gold had been discovered around Sutter's Creek, running freely in the waters of a trace, in the wooden tailrace of a mill. More gold had turned up lying on the ground in great nuggets, free for the picking. Nuggets of ten ounces, twenty, thirty. The stories grew and grew and soon, one didn't know what to believe.

The young men went wild. Farmers left their fields. Store clerks abandoned their counters. Droves of young men with a sense of adventure borrowed a grubstake from their parents and went off—by land across the unknown deserts, by sea around the terrors of the Cape or down to Panama, from whence they traveled overland to the Pacific, where they boarded another ship for the trip north to California. Unprepared for the horrors of wilderness and fever, many died along the way.

Pieter was not a young man. He was now thirty-nine years old, shrewd, clever, and practical. He did not believe any longer in laying rails himself; he hired men to do that. He had promoted several promising young Irishmen to the rank of foreman, and he went out to check on them unexpectedly, at intervals, to keep them on the alert. No one knew exactly when the boss might show up to cast a keen, cold eye on their work and their progress. They knew he knew more about railroading than they would ever learn. He would berate them caustically when they tried to make excuses for poor work. They respected him, and so they did good work, driving their men as he himself would have.

Pieter thought carefully about the California gold strike. A railroad stretching to the West would be a bonanza. Men were paying any amount of money to get a bunk on the deck of a ship going to California. Was it worth it, when they got there? According to rumors, there was no food out there, no clothing, and no picks and shovels. All must be taken with them. What if a railroad were laid out to the California country, and goods could be freighted there? Would this not be better than the wagons that were already going out, loaded to their canvas tops with flour, meat, salt, sugar, picks, shovels, household utensils, and tinware?

Even Jacob, a tall, strong young lad of thirteen, was eager to go West. "Let me go, Papa, I'll bring you back a bag of gold!" he pleaded, while Hilda alternately stormed at him and wept with alarm.

"No, but I think I'll go out there, and see what the fuss is about," Pieter replied.

He bought himself a sturdy wagon with large wheels, took two of his best Irishmen with him, and brought along guns, pots and pans, and some trade goods. He might as well make the trip profitable, even if he didn't strike any gold, he thought.

"When will you be back, Pieter?" Hilda wailed.

"I don't know. I'll try to write. There is plenty of money in the bank under your name for the household. Maybe I'll stay a year, and set up a freight outfit. I don't know yet. It depends on how big the opportunity is."

She wept all night but he was inflexible. His worst trouble came the next morning, when Jacob, determined to accompany his papa, tried to stow himself away in the wagon. He was removed forcibly by Pieter, who spanked him, then, relenting, kissed him.

"You're a good lad, Jacob. You stay here and look after your mother and sisters," Peter said, unable to remain angry for long with the adventurous boy. "One day you'll go West with me, and that is a promise."

Jacob's scowl faded, and he beamed up at Pieter. "Truly, Papa? Then I'll wait," he said. Overwhelmed with joy, he hugged his father about the waist. "Papa," he said, "don't let a bear get you."

Pieter chuckled for a couple of days about that last remark. But he did not laugh for long. It was a difficult, arduous journey. They drove all day and rested by night, rifles at hand. His son's words took on an ominous ring, for there were indeed wolves, bears, and snakes about—and bad men driven desperate and feverish by the thought of gold. They would steal a man's horses, his wagon, anything, so long as it enabled them to go farther west. They must get to the golden land. Men seemed to have gone mad with gold fever.

Pieter and his men got as far as St. Joseph, Missouri, only to find that they must there join a wagon train, as protection against the ferocious Indian tribes that inhabited the vast plains, deserts, and mountains between the civilized East and the beckoning West. They waited a week, till Pieter was able to buy his way into a train. The wagonmaster was glad enough to have an additional three sturdy men with their own wagon and weapons—and with a toughness that suggested they could protect themselves and others.

There were men, women, and children on the train. The wagons were loaded with rocking chairs, horsehide trunks, mirrors, dolls, and every sort of item imaginable. These items began to strew the road as the train progressed farther and farther, and they were forced to lighten the load for the patient, sturdy oxen that drew the huge Conestoga wagons. Finally, only the drivers remained on the wagons; the others walked. Children striding along on their short legs reminded Pieter of his own children, and he thanked God again and again that they were snug and secure at home.

Several children ate berries, got sick, and died by morning. They were buried by the trail, and the wagons went on.

Farther out, Indians were seen hovering in the distance. Lookouts rode far to the sides, front, and back of the train, watching carefully all the while. Their faces grew blackened by the sun, which bleached Pieter's blond hair as light as silk. To protect themselves, they took to wearing great sombrero hats like the Mexicans who had inhabited this land before them.

As they pushed deeper into the wilderness, the supply of food grew short, and their store of flour was depleted. Pieter and his men joined the crew that hunted daily for food, hoping to shoot a rabbit, a deer, or if they were lucky, an immense buffalo that had strayed from its herd.

The Indians seemed content merely to watch them. Relieved by this, the wagonmaster grew careless. And one night the Indians attacked.

Pieter awoke instantly. In seconds, he was behind a makeshift barricade of bales and boxes, firing his rifle into the darkness. He reloaded, caught sight of an Indian flying toward him on a small pony, and fired quickly at the ferocious, painted face. The Indian toppled to the ground. Pieter reloaded, and fired again and again. Finally, with a wild yell, the Indians disappeared into the darkness.

Now the whole camp was a bedlam. Everyone scurried about, counting the casualties. One woman lay dead, with an arrow in her back. Her children stood staring with shock and disbelief. Two men standing guard had had their throats cut.

After that, they took no chances. The guard was tightened, and every night the wagons drew into a circle for protection.

Then sickness swept the camp. Nearly everyone wanted to stop and rest, but the wagonmaster drove them on mercilessly. He kept casting anxious looks before him, toward the mountains, where the peaks were already white with snow.

"We must get across before November, or we're lost," the wagonmaster told Pieter soberly. "We'll all die in the snows, if we can't cross. We don't have enough supplies."

"We'll kill more meat, then dry it in the sun as we go." Pieter set his mouth hard. "I didn't come this far to die from foolishness."

They went out and shot whatever game they could. As they approached the mountains, game became more plentiful. They even found some fat, slow bears, killed and skinned them, and hung the meat to dry on their wagon frames. Pieter thought of his son Jacob, so far away, across the thousands of miles. He was rationing his tobacco now. Pieter had taken up smoking and quite enjoyed it. The others had taken to smoking some

87

weeds they found by the trail, but Pieter hadn't had to go that far yet.

They came to the mountains, and found some passes already filling with snow. "Reckon we'll be the last ones over the pass this winter," the wagonmaster predicted.

"*If* we get there," one man remarked.

"We'll get there," Pieter stated firmly. They had to unload those wagons that were too heavy to go over the icy mountain passes. Cradles were dumped beside the road, along with tables and chairs. Household treasures were cast aside, with only fleeting, backward glances from the sunburned wives. Lives were more important than possessions. Families crowded together. The women drove, while the men trudged through the snow, binding their torn boots together with strips of sheets.

And all the way Pieter was looking, looking at the land. Could a railroad be built across this harsh terrain? This up-and-down land of flat deserts with shifting sands followed by snowy, treacherous mountain passes? Could they lay track here, with the burning sun and the biting cold winds, and think it would remain? If the track were not corroded by the weather, would the Indians tear it up? Must the track be guarded forever?

He observed all that he could, and wrote down notes, busily, though he kept much in his big, solid head. Gold did not lure him. He figured a man worked hard with his hands and earned his gold and coin. He did not put much stock in the stories about men standing in a cool mountain stream, putting a pan under the surface, and coming up with enough gold to last a lifetime. It didn't work that way, he thought. Life was much too treacherous and cruel to work that easily. There was some trick to it.

Scaling the last range of mountains was horrible. They lifted the wagons over the snowdrifts with their bare, torn hands, and they killed the last of the oxen for food. Worn, bone-weary, and shocked for a lifetime from the terrors and deaths, they stumbled down the final pass into the fertile, green valleys of the Promised Land.

A Spanish hacienda lay in the valley. The courtly Spanish don, who chose to remain after Mexico had sold the land to the United States, welcomed them, and made them comfortable.

His wife and children set out mattresses, and his servants cooked food for them in great, smoky piles over the outdoor fires. They had vegetables, fresh and green and glorious, after the months of smoked and dried meat.

"Truly the good God has held you in His hand," the don said in his gentle way. "You went through much danger. But California is worth it."

"Gold?" the wagonmaster gasped, his eyes greedy, his hands shaking with weariness and anxiety.

The man smiled, and shook his white head in negation. "I have heard of this gold. But if God wanted us to have gold, he would have placed it in our hands, no? But here is everything a man could want," and he waved his slim hand out over the lush green acres, the fruit trees, and the white-painted barns with their trim horses and placid cows. "Here is the wealth that is worth the working. Food, clothing and shelter for any man and his family. The valleys are green, my friends, not golden. Here is the wealth. Here is the quiet, peaceful life."

They did not listen to him. They could not believe there was no gold, as they had heard. But Pieter did not forget the don's words. When they were ready to depart, a week later, he tried to pay the man.

But his money was waved away with reproach. "A man does not ask for pay when he does God's work," the don said gently. "If you have money, use it to do good for others of God's creatures, Mr. Van Rhyne." He gave Pieter a keen, understanding look. "You have a hard look. You have lived a hard life. Know, then, that life is short and fleeting, meant to be lived with sweetness and gentleness. God will reward you for your kindness to others."

Pieter was moved by the man's speech. He preferred to pay his way and ask no favors, but he realized that the don would be greatly insulted if he insisted. He thanked the man, shook his hand, and climbed on the one wagon they had managed to save. The don had sold them horses. He had many horses, he had told them placidly.

Would he go with them, they asked. They were still certain they would find gold. Did he not wish to be rich along with them? He smiled and shook his head, no. Was he not rich already? Did he not have a fine wife, three daughters and four sons? He had all he wanted, he said, and urged them on their way.

Looking back, Pieter saw him sitting erect on his leather saddle trimmed with silver, his white hair blowing in the breeze as he waved his wide black-and-silver hat to them.

They drove for many miles, refreshed, thinking eagerly ahead to the gold. Many of their hardships were forgotten, in anticipation of the great wealth that lay ahead of them. Even the children had cheered up considerably, brightened by the thought of this new, green land.

After several more weeks, the weather turned cool and rainy, and they experienced the California winter, less harsh than that back East, but definitely cold. They huddled in their scarves and overcoats, and longed for new boots and stockings.

Then, unexpectedly, they came to the gold. A group of tough-looking men were standing up to their hips in a cold mountain stream. One of them looked at the ragged emigrants, scrambled to the bank, and waved a rifle at them.

"Go on, go on!" he shouted. "This claim is ours!" He was bearded, fierce, and red-eyed from lack of sleep. A shabby bag hung on his belt, heavy with metal.

They drove on through fertile valleys sleeping in the wintry sun. And they crossed many shallow streams. They wanted to pause and look for gold, but someone had heard of a town called Corona. At Corona there

90

was not only gold, but a camp, stores, and houses. They thought that would be a good place to stop and to part from each other.

Corona was reached at last, near the end of December. Pieter got down from his wagon and looked about in vague amazement. Was this a town? It looked like the roughest of his end-of-track settlements. Tents held store goods, huts held a jail and a sheriff. The streets were narrow and muddy. Men went past, hard-eyed, with pistols at their belts. From one big tent came the rattle of dice and the monotonous call of gamblers.

His Irishmen were eager to be off to the gold fields, but they still looked to Pieter for guidance. "We'll find a place to stay first," he decided.

That was not easy. The few frame houses held the sheriff and his family, a gambler and his woman, and a dozen or so miners. Pieter decided to set up a tent at the end of the town and live there. They went into town to buy a tent, and found it cost a dozen times what it would in the East. He paid, grimly.

They were out of flour, out of vegetables, out of meat, out of chairs, and out of clothes. They would pay dearly for all these goods, for they were shipped in from outside, and there was no competition to keep the costs down.

Every night the men trickled into town, then went out again the next morning to their gold fields. They were careful not to be followed, for they feared others would try to jump their claims. Pieter went out with them and watched curiously as men leaped into the water with their pans and tried to find gold. Some came out with gold, only to lose it to the hard-eyed gamblers in the big tent, in exchange for a few games of poker and a bottle of whiskey. The next day they would wake up, hold their heads, get sick, and go out again.

Pieter looked, listened, and decided upon a course of action. He would send wagon trains of goods west with a good wagonmaster, until rails could be built. One day he would lay rails from the East to the West, from coast to coast, but it would take years. The country was not easily tamed. But the profits would be there, though not in the gold of the rivers.

He came into town one Friday afternoon close to Christmas. He was tired, and wanted a shave, a bath, and clean clothes. He went to his tent, and managed to boil some water. His Irishmen had disappeared, going north to some claim they had heard about, where they could get rich in two months. He had shrugged and not followed them.

Dressed and refreshed, he strolled about town in a neat gray suit, his whiskers shaved off. He felt younger, somehow, in this wild frontier town. Once he had gotten over the shock of it, he felt more alive in the heady atmosphere of growing prosperity, of hopes and laughter, of fresh, happy voices of free and eager young men. He did not miss the confinements of home.

He was strolling along the plank sidewalk when he spotted a lady with neat blond hair, primly half-hidden by her blue silk bonnet laden with ribbons. She wore a close-fitting jacket of matching blue silk, and a deeper blue skirt that reached to the ground, plain, full, gathered at the waist, and pleated. She looked, thought Pieter, like a breath of spring—a fine woman, a lady, with lace at her throat and wrists, and dainty boots on her feet.

She lifted her head to thank him as he stepped aside into the muddy earth to let her pass. Her smile faltered, and the deep blue eyes went wide.

"Pieter?" she whispered. "Is it you—Pieter?"

The meeting gave him such a shock that it felt like a kick in his stomach. He stared down at her. She looked the same except that her face was tanned, and thin lines were etched around her eyes. She looked older, yet serene.

"Sunny," he said slowly. Then the old anger rose in him. "Damn it, why did you run out on me?"

He reached out and gripped her elbow. To his surprise, she smiled, dimpling. "Oh—I had an excellent reason. Would you like to see it?"

He stared at her helplessly. She laughed, and he remembered that laughter with almost physical pain. He managed to nod, and turned to walk with her.

"What are you doing here?"

"Running a boardinghouse on the coast. I heard there was money in a house here, so I came and bought it," she said briskly, like a businessman. "I'm planning to rent out four bedrooms. Like one?"

It was like old times, only she was even harder and more sure of herself.

"Is that what you have been doing all this time?"

He had thought of her with other men, under the protection of one man after another—even of her having become a prostitute. And the fury and pain of it had driven him out to the streets of New York, to walk endlessly until he was tired enough to sleep.

"Yes. I took the money you left me," Sunny said, "and moved farther west, with the rails. There was always a place where I could stay—usually in a village or a small town—buy a house, and rent rooms for the summer. Then I would move west again with the rails. I got as far as Ohio and Indiana. Then I heard about California. I enjoyed moving on, so I took a wagon and went west with a train of wagons last year. About the time I arrived, they struck gold, and the men went wild." She shrugged. "They'll pay anything for a decent room with a bed, hot water, and a good meal occasionally."

"Is that *all*?" he growled, his hand closing fiercely, protectively, about her arm.

"That's all, Pieter," she said quietly. They came to a small, white-painted house which he remembered. When he had gone about looking for rooms, the neat little house had appealed to him, but he had found it all shut and locked. Sunny Malone took a key and opened the door. "Paul?" she called.

His heart sank. He almost turned and ran away, thinking she had married, or—worse—was living with a man. Then he heard light, eager steps.

A boy of about ten or eleven came into the room, then paused to stare frankly at Pieter. He was neatly and nicely clothed, wearing a single-breasted, short jacket of dark blue, and plaid trousers of ankle length. He wore slipper shoes, and had curly blond hair. His eyes were a vivid blue.

Sunny's smile wavered a little as her hand went to Pieter's arm. "Pieter, this is my son Paul. Paul," she said, faltering slightly, "this is your father, Mr. Pieter Van Rhyne."

Both of them, the father and the son, caught their breath. They alternately stared at her and at each other. A long, aching silence followed. Finally, Paul smiled an exact replica of his mother's frank, friendly smile.

"Hello, sir," he said. "Mama has talked to me about you." His look was questioning, and eager.

Pieter held out his hand, and the boy's slim hand met his. Then he pulled the boy to him, and held him against his heart. He felt full, choked, stunned.

"This was why—Sunny, why didn't you tell me?"

She was laughing, her eyes brimming with tears. She took off her bonnet, then smoothed back her blond hair. "I didn't want you to feel—obliged," she said. "I knew you were married. So—when you gave me enough to live on—I decided to pull out. Paul was born in Ohio. He was a darling from the minute he was born. We've been good company for each other ever since, haven't we, Paul?"

"Sure, Mom." Paul drew back from Pieter and grinned up at his mother. Pieter could see that the lad adored her. "Do you want me to go fix some supper while you talk?" Paul asked, showing his mother's understanding and an unexpected maturity for his years.

Sunny gave a nod of approval and he flashed Pieter a quiet smile and left the room. The big Dutchman sank into a chair, his legs weak. He stared up at Sunny.

"You never said. You know I would have helped."

"Your wife wouldn't have liked it, Pieter. Besides, I was young and strong. I'm still strong." She smiled, removed the jacket, and hung it up. He looked at her sturdy shoulders, her proudly held head. He ached for her. If only she had told him. He could have taken her back East, set her up in an apartment, gotten a midwife for her. Instead, gallantly, she had endured everything alone.

"I was a widow. I just told folks that Paul was born after his father died—which was sort of true." Sunny was chattering away, as easily as though years had not separated them. "What are you doing here, Pieter? Do you mind if I ask? Don't tell me if you don't want to. I know you hate to tell your business."

"It doesn't matter now. I'll be here all winter. Then, in the spring, I'll take you back to New York with me, you and the boy."

Her hands hesitated as she went to remove her boots. She finally tugged them off, and put on some blue slippers. She sat down opposite him. "Is your wife still alive?" she asked quietly. "Not that you would marry me," she added, managing to smile gaily.

"I would if I could," he said heavily. "Yes, Hilda is alive, and she has had seven of my children. She is a good woman. I cannot leave her. But I can make things more comfortable for you, Sunny."

She shrugged, then smiled. "Don't worry about me, Pieter. I can take care of myself, and of Paul. He's growing into a big boy now. He's already talking about going to the gold fields."

"You won't let him!" he said sharply, possessively. The boy was slim, fine-boned, not big and sturdy like Jacob. He had a look of intelligence in that wide-browed face. "Are you giving him schooling?"

"I taught him to read and write and add," she said. "And he gets more schooling whenever we're in a town with a school. He learns very fast," she added proudly, her eyes glowing.

Paul finally came in and laid the table, smiled at them, and went back to the kitchen. He brought in a huge pot of tea, plates of meat and bread, pickles, even a plate of cake slices and a bowl of apples.

They gathered around the table, the three of them, and talked. Paul listened most of the time, but he joined in freely when he wished, with no self-consciousness, his face smiling and his blue eyes shining like his mother's. He could not keep from staring at his father's face. Pieter wondered if he liked what he saw.

"Where are you staying?" Sunny asked presently.

He shrugged his massive shoulders. "In a tent." He grimaced. "Look, Sunny, let me stay here as a boarder, and don't take in any others. Come spring, we'll go back to New York. I'll get you an apartment, and you and Paul will have it easy. He can go to school there."

"Now, Pieter," she said calmly. "Don't rush me. You can move in, and we're glad to have you. But I can make my own living." She held her blond head proudly erect.

They fought about that amiably all winter. But the winter was hard, with gunfights in the streets, and with several murders out on the gold fields.

One night Pieter's two Irishmen returned from the icy streams, one burning with the fever, the other with a rattling in his lungs. Sunny took them in and nursed them devotedly. They needed milk, she told Pieter, and fresh vegetables.

He went out to buy milk, but couldn't get any. So he found a Mexican with a milch cow, bought it for an exorbitant amount, and took it home. Sunny burst out laughing when she saw Pieter leading the cow.

"Oh, my God, Pieter!" she cried. "Can you milk that thing?"

"I can," he said, with a reluctant smile. "And I'll teach Paul so he can do it when I'm not here."

They milked the cow, and took turns sitting up nights with the Irishmen. Broke, feverish, and fed up with the madness for gold, the wagonmaster came to see Pieter. While the distraught man raved, Pieter listened patiently, calmly.

"God, I wish I had never come here! A man makes a fortune one day, and loses it the next! Do you know what a man pays for a decent meal in town?"

"Are you ready to go back home?" Pieter asked. "If you are, I have a job for you."

The wagonmaster was curious. "What is it? All I know is trailing."

"That's the job. I'm going to set up a wagon supply coming west. If you start early in the spring, and return in the late fall, you can do the trip once a year. I'll stock you, and split the profits with you."

The man was elated, and by candlelight, they worked out the plan at the oak dining table.

It was March, and Pieter was eager to be on the move. He had important business, business that would not wait. Yet Sunny still refused to accompany him back East. Then one day, on the plank sidewalk, Pieter ran into Paul.

The boy's face had turned so white his freckles stood out like pepper. "What is it?" Pieter asked, alarmed. He had become very fond of the lad.

"I'm going home for my gun." Straining to maintain his composure, Paul gulped. "That man—he said things about my ma!"

"What man?" Pieter asked. He had heard the rumors. The wagonmaster had reluctantly told him of the gossip the night they made their deal. It seemed Sunny was causing talk by letting Pieter stay with her, with the boy so obviously like him. "What man?" the Dutchman repeated, his tone rising in anger.

They walked back to the gambling tent. A man lounged in the doorway with a grin on his face as they approached. He was dressed in a black silk suit, with a silk top hat, a white ruffled shirt, and an unhealthy pallor to his face. He straightened as they came up to him, then threw down his cigar.

"So here's the bastard and his pa," he said clearly.

Shoving Paul away from him, Pieter drew his gun, just a shade before the gambler could get his pistol out. Pieter shot the man dead. Paul, sprawled on the plank sidewalk, got up on his hands and knees, shaking.

"Are you all right, my son?" Pieter asked clearly. Men came back from where they had fled as the fight started.

"Yes, Dad," Paul said simply, and stood at his father's side, staring at the neat, round bullet hole in the man's white ruffled shirt. "You got him dead center!"

Pieter reloaded his pistol, then glanced around. "Anyone else have words to say about me and mine?" he asked, iron in his gravelly voice.

No one had anything to say. He and Paul went home, where Paul proceeded to tell Sunny what had happened. The glow disappeared from her cheeks as she listened, but Paul babbled on excitedly. He was so proud of his father, of what he had done.

But Pieter was not proud. He was angry. That night, Pieter told Sunny, "You can't stay here. It's my fault, but your name is on everyone's tongue. I'm sorry, my dear. They should not insult someone as fine as you."

There were tears in her eyes. "I don't mind the talk; I can endure that. But Paul and you in danger! And I can't keep Paul sheltered forever!"

"You'll come East with me," he said, with decision, and that was it. They began to pack up.

As soon as the snow melted on the nearby mountains, they set out in two new wagons. The trek was long and difficult, but this time Pieter had prepared for it. Soon they were joined by more wagons. There were about twenty of them in all, driven by disillusioned gold-seekers: some dudes from the East in shabby tailcoats, and some farmers eager to go home. Unlike the ones Pieter had accompanied coming west, these men were tough and hardened by their experiences. The Indians let them alone, they only watched them pass by. For these men were going back where they belonged, back East.

On that long journey, Pieter had plenty of time to think. During the day, he drove the wagon, or walked while Sunny drove. He learned to know Paul even better, and found the lad had an excellent mind, as keen as his father's, and the gentle sensitivity of his mother. He needed to go to a regular school. And he needed protection from gossiping tongues. They might not shoot you in New York City, but the darts from gossip would be just as deadly to a sensitive child.

He decided to set up a trust fund to take care of Sunny and Paul. No matter what happened to Pieter, they would never know need. And in the fund, he would acknowledge Paul as his son. One day he would tell Jacob, his eldest son, and have him look out for the boy. It gave him pleasure to think the boys might become acquainted, and possibly friends.

He worked out plans for his freight wagons to supply the West. Besides the wagons, he would need plenty of able men. The two Irishmen were interested, now that they had recovered from gold fever as well as the real fever they had endured. This was longer, harder work than panning for gold, but more rewarding, ultimately.

Pieter could already envision the beginnings of a business. Eventually, he would add more wagons, and more men. But to start, they would need at least ten wagons and twenty men to undertake that long, hard trek. And, in the meantime, he would push his own rails west. First to Chicago, then, finally, on to the Far West. One day the whole country would be joined by rails, shining steel rails, running from New York to California.

Chapter 7

Pieter arrived home in New York City in the late summer of 1850. He had been bronzed by the harsh sun of the desert, and toughened by the hard work of trail driving—taking care of the horses and oxen, and striding beside the wagon for long days.

Nights had been the best. He and Sunny had lain together under warm blankets, his arms encircling her. Sometimes they talked softly about the future, or about the past. Sometimes they lay still, enjoying each other's presence. Sometimes they made love, passionately, in the quiet night, coming together with an earthy need that each filled for the other.

It had been good, and he hated to have it end.

In New York, he installed Sunny and Paul in a cheery boardinghouse, paid for their lodging for a month, and gave Sunny the money to go out and buy all the clothes they would need. She protested, but he was adamant.

"You'll never need to work again," he said. "I can't marry you, but I'll always take care of you." He had told her about the trust fund. She had shaken her head, but he had insisted. "Paul must have his education, and be able to earn a living."

"Pieter, the cost will be high," she protested. "He's talking about becoming a doctor!"

"That's fine," Pieter replied, nodding and pleased. "He'll make a fine doctor."

Jacob was more like himself. Tough, hard, a fighter. Even small Hans showed signs of tough strength. They would become good, hard businessmen like himself and like Hilda's father. But Paul—he was different. He needed a special profession, one that would make use of his intelligence and sensitivity, and not hold those traits against him. Business was too rough for Paul, too competitive. He would be a doctor, and a good one.

Pieter saw them settled, then went home. Hilda greeted him stiffly, but the children, all seven of them, threw themselves at him. Jacob was screaming with delight, and demanding to hear all his adventures at once. Elisabeth looked prettier than ever, quite a young lady, at thirteen.

He had presents for them: for the girls, some gold nuggets to be made into jewelry; for the boys, some genuine gold dust in a tiny pouch. There was also a bear hide for Jacob, at which Hilda shuddered. He watched all of them somewhat distantly, then retired to his study, stretched out his legs on his own big chair, and thought and thought, on into the early morning.

Two days later, he was already conducting business. When he returned weary from a long conference with his clerk and merchant, Hilda came to him. Her eyes were red, her voice querulous.

"I have to talk to you, Pieter!" she commanded. He gave her a narrow look, and they went into his study and shut the door.

She sniffled and wiped her eyes. "I heard talk in town. Pieter, they say you brought back a woman with you! And her boy, who looks like you!"

He studied his wife of fifteen years with a dispassionate gaze. She had not grown more attractive with age. She had borne him seven children, and she was plump and short. Her sandy brown hair had grayed, and she still wore it in a tight bun at the nape of her neck, which pulled the hair back from her forehead in a harsh manner. In spite of the many rings on her fingers, and the gold locket at her throat, she looked hard and coarse. He thought of Sunny, with her easy laugh, and the soft roundness of her, and the thick gold of her hair.

"So?" he snapped.

"Is it true?" she whispered, twisting her hands in her handkerchief, and looking everywhere but at him.

"Is *what* true?"

"Did you come back with a woman?"

"I came back with more than two dozen men and a half a dozen women and some children," he drawled sardonically.

"You know what I mean!" she flared. "Don't tease and taunt me, Pieter. I mean to know the truth!"

"Whether it makes you unhappy or no?"

She finally stared at him, her brown eyes round and wide. Her mouth was tight like a purse string, and her eyes looked like marbles.

"What does that matter? I have to know the truth!"

"The truth? What is truth? It's what one man sees and another does not. It's two sides of a coin, four sides of a house."

"Don't torment me! Do you have a woman?"

Pieter leaned back and thought, his face calm and inscrutable. Tell Hilda the truth? That was like handing a child a knife.

101

"She is a widow with one son, Hilda," he said gently. "I'm seeing to it that she has a place to live. Now, do you want to hear about the new house I'm building for you on Fifth Avenue?"

She stared, then gulped. "What—what house?"

"This one," he said, pushing some sketches toward her. "We need a new house, what with the children growing up, and with us needing more servants."

"You're changing the subject, Pieter!"

"You're damned right I am," he said grimly. "I will not be questioned like a fool in a witness box! Now, do you want to hear about the house, or shall I plan it all myself?"

She wavered, her jealousy at war with her greed. The latter won. Her mouth sulked, and finally she said, "Yes, I want to hear about the house. Where is it?"

"I have a big lot on Fifth Avenue, up where the town is growing. I hired an architect today. It's going to be the biggest, finest house he can build, of marble and stone outside, and with wood paneling inside. Persian carpets, mahogany furniture, and with lots of mirrors and paintings—" His eyes were dreamy.

"As big as Pa's house?" she asked.

He came back to earth with a jolt. She still thought in terms of her father, after all these years!

"Your father's house could fit into one wing of this one," he said curtly, "and be lost! Now, look at the plans."

Awe-struck, she crept over to look. He indicated the large central portion, four stories high, then pointed out the two-story wings. "In the back, there'll be quarters large enough for twenty servants, and a carriage house for four carriages and the horses. There'll be a drive sweeping up to the front—"

"Pieter, it's too big," she gasped.

"Nonsense. We have all these children. They'll be growing up. Besides," he reflected, his eyes narrowing, "I'm an important man now, with a railroad of my own. It pays to advertise that one is a big businessman. It makes people realize they must do what I want, or pay the price. You'll be wearing finer clothes, Hilda, and we'll have a governess for the girls. I want the boys tutored until they go off to college."

"College!" she gasped weakly. "What do they want with college?"

"They're going to be smarter than their pa, or I'll tan their hides," he said. "They will have a chance to learn that I never had. I learned by the seat of my pants, and I got cheated. They'll have my experience plus college learning. They can own more than I ever will—though I'm going to be a millionaire before long."

"A millionaire!" She dared to put her hand on his forehead. "Pieter, you contracted a fever from the West!"

"You'll see," he said firmly. Actually, he was already a millionaire twice over, as his clerk had proudly informed him. The value of his land had doubled and tripled. His agent had had offers to buy it, which he, following Pieter's directives, had regretfully turned down. No, Pieter would hang on to it, and its value would double again.

Pieter operated on the principle that the less Hilda knew about his wealth and business, the better. The information would not be handed on to Morland, and so to the world. Modesty, in this case, would be the best policy. Businessmen could look at his new marble mansion and wonder if he had gone into debt for it. He would smile and let them wonder.

The foundations for the big house were dug before autumn, and the walls began to go up. Pieter doubled the work force, and got the house under a roof before the cold and snows came. In the meantime, he had found a grand apartment for Sunny and Paul, only a few blocks from his own new house. She had the whole of the fourth floor of a sweet place, which she promptly made homey with her own touches, with handwoven rag rugs, rocking chairs, a sofa of blue silk and velvet, and tasseled plush chairs. And she's installed a huge bed in the master bedroom, for when Pieter came to see her.

Paul had his own room, a large one, at the back,

overlooking the gardens. And Pieter showered Paul with all the toys Pieter had never had, and that his own sons had loved.

Pieter helped the architect and Hilda to plan their new house. He meant it for a showplace, and the man willingly went along, expecting a huge commission for this job, and more publicity for himself.

A showplace it was, indeed! The front was all gleaming white marble from Greece, with pillars that shone in the sunlight. The front steps were of red porphyry. The inside hallway was paneled with cherrywood, and there were little cupboards where the guests could set their coats and shawls and umbrellas.

The large drawing room to the right of the entrance hall was of green and gold, and had draperies of green velvet with gold pulls. The rugs were layers of Persian carpets, in flowery patterns of soft, delicate shades of green, yellow, red, rose, and blue. There were tables of shining, deep reddish-brown mahogany, and sofas of matching majesty and hue, covered with green plush and gold tassels.

On the left was the long library, with huge bookcases from floor to ceiling. Pieter had stared at it, and wondered how they would ever fill it. But the resourceful architect had ordered crates of books from local bookstores, telling them to include every classic work from Greek to modern, all in fine leather bindings. They looked grand behind the wire screens that held them. A little stairway in one corner led up to the second row, with a balcony all around the room, so one could reach any book. Katrinka, the reader of the family, was thrilled.

Behind the drawing room was the long dining room, in blue and silver. The draperies were of blue velvet with silver tassels. On the mahogany sideboards were set the silver services: huge trays, epergnes for fruit, and utensils for the table. Huge cupboards with glass fronts held the fragile porcelain set from France, of Sèvres ware, with blue borders and silver centers. The architect had ordered the set, with an elaborate, scrolled *V* in the center of the silver, in blue.

Smart. Pieter wished his mother had seen them. She would have been torn between awe and laughter. Their family name, the name of plain, hardworking farmers, had come to this!

There were more rooms: a small parlor for sewing and guests, the kitchens, and the pantries. Upstairs, there was one wing for the girls and another for the boys, with adjoining rooms for their nurses and governesses and tutors. In the central part, Pieter had arranged that Hilda should have a huge front room and sitting room of her own. He took a large back room, with a huge mahogany bed.

Hilda had studied the plans in a troubled way. "You mean you're going to have a room of your own, Pieter?" she had asked tremulously.

"That's right. Of course, I'll be sleeping with you nights, when we want," he said casually. "But we're getting older, aren't we?"

She bent her head and said no more, but her mouth was tight and quivery.

He arranged for a table and desk to be put in his bedroom, matching the huge, ornate furniture. There he could spread out his plans and work until late at night, without disturbing anyone—or letting anyone know what he was working on. He had hired a valet for himself, and a maid for Hilda. His valet was discreet, close-mouthed, and Pieter had warned the man sternly about talking to anyone about what he did. The valet was a younger brother of one of Pieter's foremen, and too frail of health to stand the hard railroad work, but of quick intelligence, and loyal.

Pieter meant to surround himself with loyal men. He would trust no one more than he had to, but it paid to be careful about hiring men.

By the following summer, the house was ready for them to move in. They did, leaving most of the furniture behind in the old house. They just moved their clothes, Hilda's jewels, the children's toys, and Pieter's work. It was a whole new life, and he meant to start afresh. He sold the other house cheaply to a retired, crippled railroad man, who was immensely grateful for it, and who moved his own family in at once.

The wagonmaster returned in the fall with a fine profit, and more orders than he could handle. They split the profits. Then the man went home to his family briefly, and prepared to start out again in the early spring. The Van Rhyne wagon train was doing well. Supplies were much in demand in the West, and Pieter scoured New York that winter for the most wanted goods: chairs, tables, boots, and clothing. And he put in orders for flour, salt, and sugar.

Often, when he was weary, he did not go home to the grand mansion on Fifth Avenue. Hilda had hired a social adviser, recommended by a wealthy matron of her acquaintance, to assist her in starting the heady, upward climb into the heights of society. Pieter did not feel comfortable with the kind of man who'd earn his living as a social adviser and pleading business, he escaped whenever he could to the warm, cheerful apartment of Sunny Malone.

Sunny, with her usual independent spirit, had started a sewing business, and she made dresses for a number of women. The apartment had an extra room that she had set aside for her sewing, and there was usually a clutter of fabrics, threads, and laces strewn about. But when Pieter arrived, she set it all aside, and came to the parlor to visit with him.

Paul was always gently tactful. He would come in from his lessons, and smile. He would hang around for a little while, his eyes fixed worshipfully on his father. He'd listen, and sometimes chat a bit. Then he would say, on a bright day, "Is it all right if I go out and play with Tommy?" Or on a dark, rainy day, "Mom, may I go downstairs and play with Fred?"

Sunny would smile and say, "Run along, Paul. Come back at six for supper."

And Paul would smile, dash off, and be gone for a few hours. Pieter realized the boy knew what was going on between them, but did not mind. Paul loved Pieter as his father, and Pieter could do no wrong.

Pieter would sit and relax with Sunny for a time. Sometimes they just talked or laughed, and spoke of the old days on the trail. Other times, he wanted her, and would scoop her up in his arms, carry her into her bedroom, and shut the door.

She was marvelous to make love with. It was always "with," he thought. She entered into the lovemaking spiritedly, with laughter and passion, holding him in her arms afterward with quiet affection.

She had a wonderful body, and he loved to caress her nakedness. He would lie above her, studying the soft roundness of her breasts, kissing the pink nipples, and fondling the round, smooth thighs. She was tall for a woman, and he liked holding her against himself, thigh to thigh, and feeling her warm flesh as he sank into her. Her arms would rise and cling about his neck, while her long fingers stroked his back as he caressed her. Her blue eyes would half-close, as Sunny, sensuous as a cat being stroked, frankly enjoyed his handling of her. There was no difficulty, no capricious whims or whining. He could kiss her all over, and she would only giggle if he tickled her, or murmur with passion as he aroused her.

On a cold day they would lie in the warm bed, and play under the covers. Her hand would stroke his hairy chest, and she would tease him by twisting and pulling gently at the hairs. They would talk—about the future, or Paul, or the city, which she enjoyed exploring. She could tell him more about New York after a few months there than he had learned in all his years. He knew the business, the finance, the hardheaded men. She knew the buildings, the parks, the shops, the artists, and the fascinating streets lined with immigrants from every country of Europe.

At times, his passion would rise so swiftly that he was on her and making love to her wildly before she was ready. "Oh, my darling, be easy," she would murmur, and it would stop him, or slow him down, until she was moving and indicating her willingness to him.

She satisfied him so completely that he went less and less to Hilda. Only duty made him go to her, and he did not go often. She seemed satisfied with her new social life, for her cheeks would flush with triumph when a noted society matron deigned to leave her card.

One Saturday, as Pieter worked on charts for the next extension of his railroad, Jacob came to him in his study. He tapped on the door and entered, to stand hesitantly in the doorway. "Papa, may I disturb you?"

"Yes, yes, my son, come in." Pieter saw the indecision on the sturdy fair face so like his. "What is it?" He set the charts to one side, and swung his swivel chair about. He was growing his beard again, and it scratched a little on his cheeks. He rubbed at the beard, and studied Jacob's face as the boy came in.

How tall and straight he was! How proud and sturdy! Pieter's heart swelled with pride in the boy.

"I—I wanted to talk to you. But later, if you're busy," Jacob said nervously.

Lord, was it time to tell him about women? Pieter felt acutely uncomfortable, yet he braced himself for it. "Yes, what is it? We can talk now. I leave in another month for end-of-track, you know."

Jacob perched on the edge of a straight-backed chair near the desk. He twisted his big hands, then drew a hard breath. "Papa, I have heard talk. And a couple times I followed you. Do you—that is—Mama said—I mean—do you—"

Pieter's eyes narrowed. "Spit it out," he said.

"Do you—have another—wife? I mean—it is true you have a son named Paul?"

Pieter studied him in silence. He had planned to tell him about Paul someday. But so soon? Yet, how to lie to him? He might as well tell him the truth, Pieter decided.

"I have a woman of whom I am fond," he said ponderously. "Yes, the boy is my son. I have not said this to your mother, she only guesses."

Jacob's blond head bent, and he studied his shining shoes. "I know, really. I—I went to Paul, and talked to him."

Pieter stiffened. "You talked to him?"

Jacob nodded. "I started talking to him. He guessed who I was, and we talked. He calls you 'dad,' you know. We have talked together several times. I—like him, Papa."

"How long has this gone on?" Pieter felt relieved and anxious all at once.

"I went last December, Papa."

"My God—four months ago?"

Jacob nodded. "I couldn't talk to Mama, she drives me mad when she cries," he said frankly. "So I thought I would speak to you. You know, one time you said you would take me west, but you didn't. You took Paul instead! He said you were with him on the trail. And he said you shot a man because he said bad words about Paul's mother."

Pieter tousled Jacob's hair. Jacob was too frank sometimes. Well, he had taught the lad to be honest; he could scarcely blame him for speaking the truth.

"Is that true?" Jacob asked again. "You took him west?"

"No," Pieter said. "He and his mother were in California. I decided it was no place for my—my son. So I brought them both back to New York to live. Paul wants to become a doctor."

Jacob digested that. "But you never took me west," he insisted.

Pieter studied him. Jacob had grown straight and tall; he was almost six feet, and sturdy, with big hands and feet. He was much more slender than Pieter had been at his age, but then, he ate good fruit and vegetables, not potatoes and pork. His face was serious and mature.

"How old are you, Jacob?" Pieter asked abruptly.

"Papa, I'm almost sixteen!"

Pieter suppressed a smile. The boy's birthday was in December; this was March. Sixteen was a long way off—but not to the boy.

"I think I'll take you west with me this summer," he said. "It's time you learned the railroad business. We'll be laying track in Ohio and into Indiana this year."

The blue eyes, so clear and direct, sparked into fire. "You mean it? Me, with you, to end-of-track?" he gasped.

Pieter nodded. "I want you to become a railroad man, Jacob. You need to learn the business from the ground up. There's no better place to start than at end-of-track. I'll fit you out, boots to sombrero, and we'll leave in mid-April."

Jacob was ecstatic, all doubts forgotten, his face radiant. He could scarcely speak. "I'll be r-ready—I can't believe—truly, Papa—you'll t-take me with you—"

"Right. I'll keep you under my eye. And Jacob—you'll do just as I tell you, lad! It's a dangerous business, with the explosives and enemies we make along the track! You'll stay with me and obey every word I say! Understand? Or I'll pack you right back home to your tutor!"

"I'll do it, Papa, I will—oh, may I tell Hans?"

"After I tell your mother," Pieter said, frowning at even the thought of that task. "Wait a day or two."

Hilda heard anyway, and came storming to him. She had been meek and quiet for a time, but this had royally stirred her up. "Pieter, you cannot mean to take Jacob with you! Not with those roughnecks! He is going to college! He is going to be a gentleman, not a railroader!"

Pieter, tired from the long day, spoke up sharply. "Railroading was good enough for me, and good enough for your father! Who do you think will inherit the road? What do you think I will do with it? No, Jacob must learn the business!"

"He is only a child, a mere boy!" she wailed, twisting her hands in the old worried gesture.

"When I was his age, I was working the farm from before dawn until after dusk. And two years later, I bought my first periauger and plied the waters from early morning until midnight, in the cold darkness," he said sternly. "The boy will not be weak and timid, Hilda! He will learn to do the railroad work, and one day he will step into my shoes."

"Leave it to your other son!" she said nastily, her mouth twisting. "You seem so set on spending your time and money on him! He is a whoreson, it will be good enough—"

Pieter stood, towering over her, and she shrank back. His mouth was set so firmly that white lines stood out around it. "Never—*never,* woman, will you ever say such things again!" he hissed in a low tone. "Keep your tongue from matters you do not understand!"

"Oh, I understand, all right!" She managed to brave him, her head flung back, twin circles of color blazing in her cheeks. "You'll work your real sons to death for you—but that other one—that bastard—he'll have it soft—"

He caught her twisting hand, and clamped it so tightly in his that the wrist seemed about to break. "Be silent, be silent, woman! By God, I have never struck you before—"

"Oh, strike me, beat me, kill me! Break my bones!" she screamed hysterically. "But leave your sons to me! Do not force them to join in your hard, cruel life! I want Jacob to be a gentleman, not like you! I want the best of life for him—"

He released her abruptly, and stood back. If he did not control himself, he would take her throat in his hands, and choke the life and words out of her body. He clenched his fists in rage.

She kept screaming at him. Finally, he poured a glass of whiskey, and forced her to drink it down. Her sobs died to gasps from the burning liquor. She sank down into a chair, weakly, and wiped her face with her lace-edged handkerchief.

He poured a drink for himself, and drank it down. She had been nasty and vicious this winter, knowing he went off to visit Sunny, but never had she turned on him like this. She had been afraid of him, afraid he would kick her out of the fine house, depriving her of the social life she adored.

"Now, Hilda, listen to me," he said, so coldly that she stilled her sobbing, and listened. "You will never speak of my other son and his mother again. You will keep still about them. Jacob goes west with me of his own wish. He wants to learn the railroading, and he shall. I want a son to follow me in the business. Yes, he shall have his college education, but he must learn the railroading from the earth itself. No college professor can teach him about that; he must feel it in his bones, eat, sleep, drink, and struggle with it himself. That is the only way, and by God, he shall have it. And in his turn, Hans will learn, and Lodewick, and eventually Blaine. The girls shall have their dowries and marry well. I will see to that. And you will introduce them into society. But the boys, by God, they will be men, and have big shoes to walk in!"

"You will kill them all!" she muttered, twisting her fingers, hanging her gray head.

"That is not my intention," he said bitingly. "My sons are on earth by my will and by my body and loins. They will learn the business I have to give to them, and what skill and cunning I can teach them. And one day they also will be wealthy and sought-after in society—not because they can bow and scrape, and dance a round! But because they can rule men, and direct their own destinies! Their work will be their salvation! And in time, their sons will learn, and work, and build more of this empire!"

"Empire!" she whispered, gazing at him fearfully. "You are mad, Pieter!"

"Empire!" he said with a curt nod. "I shall have an empire to leave to them, by the time I am done on this earth! And my sons will learn the way of keeping it, and building that empire bigger and richer!"

She wiped her face again. "We have strayed from the point," she said, with the wearying persistence of her father. "I am talking of that woman and her son. What

112

do you leave to them, eh? I will not have them in New York—they shame me! Everyone laughs behind my back."

Pieter stood at his desk, his boots planted widely apart, his fists pressed on his big hips. "No one dictates to me how I shall live," he said with terrifying intensity, his blue eyes flaming. "I live by no rules but my own! I form my own life! Society does not dictate to me, nor does any man, or any woman, either. No one ever cheats me, that you have learned, for I will have my own back. And no one tells me how I shall act, or how I shall work, or how I shall love, or what child I shall have! I am my own man, and shall ever be!"

"You will be sorry for it!" she cried. "You will be sorry!"

"Never! So long as I am true to my own principles, I shall never be sorry," he promised grimly. "Now be off, for I have much work to do before Jacob and I go west next month."

She scurried away, but that was not the end of it. She cried, she whined, she persisted. She tried to turn his children against him, until, in desperation, he would stalk off to go to Sunny Malone for comfort and distraction. Sunny could always make him laugh, and bring him back to sanity.

Chapter 8

By early 1856, Pieter Van Rhyne was a millionaire more than ten times over. His railroad had reached Chicago, and was streaking westward hungrily. He still had wagon trains moving steadily each spring out to California, and returning in the autumn.

He had bought five clipper ships, and sent them to the Orient with loads of New England tinware, stoves,

113

and Virginia tobacco. The ships returned with tea, silk, and occasionally even with jewels.

He had built a new office building, and his offices occupied five floors. His chief clerk, the same fellow he had hired to guard his one small safe, now had the only extra set of keys to his private offices. There, a large safe held Pieter's private papers, deeds to real estate comprising much of New York City above Sixtieth Street, trusts set up for Sunny and Paul, and reports on various businesses in which Pieter might one day invest.

Jacob had at last gone off to college, and Pieter missed his eldest son sorely. This lad was the one most like himself, and he had taken to railroading like a duck to the waters of Long Island Sound. He had gone out with Pieter summer after summer, and they had grown close. Now the boy was enrolled in an exclusive college in Massachusetts, where he was learning to be a gentleman. On his vacations, he came home in smart suits, with smart talk of matters Pieter knew nothing about.

Hilda's social adviser, Rollo Shipton, a thin, wasp-waisted and wasp-tongued gentleman with white, fluttering hands, had moved into the house on Fifth Avenue with them. Pieter grimaced whenever he thought of that Shipton, and he walked out of the room rather than talk to the man. Hilda had told him tartly that he could learn much from Mr. Shipton. Pieter had cursed, under his breath, that he had no wish to learn such stuff.

If Mr. Shipton knew of Pieter's distaste for him, he showed no signs. He spent most of his time teaching Hilda and her daughters to be women of society. He tinkled on the piano with his long white fingers, sternly instructing Hilda how to dance and curtsey and bow. Then he would give the girls similar lessons, showing each of them how to be a proper young lady. Elisabeth took it in her stride. She was naturally graceful, and the movements came easily to her. Katrinka still preferred her heavy books in the library to dancing lessons, but she managed to struggle through them. Frieda, at twelve, was still in pigtails, and more concerned with her dolls, but she, too, had her lessons every day.

Pieter rarely came home these days, anyway, except for an occasional meal. He spent much of his time in his offices, while his clerks ran about New York, gathering up information for him, and returning with it, quickly and efficiently. He had joined a club and went to it daily, listening with seemingly casual interest to the business talk. And he kept up his acquaintance with the aging Ted Brady, who had gone to work for the new *New York Times* as a specialist in business news.

Pieter's beard was now full and luxuriant, and reached down to his chest in broad, blond waves. His blue eyes still blazed feverishly, especially when he was intent on some new deal. He was heavier than ever, and his rolling gait, his whiskers, and his blazing eyes were often cartooned in the journals and gazettes. "The great Van Rhyne," they called him. "The fabulous railroad magnate."

He could go nowhere without being followed by reporters, pencils poised in their fingers, pads in their eager hands, hoping for a quotable word or two from the reticent multi-millionaire. He had to duck out the back door of his own home, and take a closed carriage when he went to see Sunny, rather than walk the few blocks to her apartment.

But still he went. He could not stay away. She was his peace, his serenity, his laughter. She made the world tilt back upright, even when he had grown weary of the earth and all it held.

She was making a name for herself with her dressmaking. "Sunny's Designs," she called her ground-floor shop. Every morning, she received her ladies, measured them, advised them, and sewed for them. As her business expanded, she hired and trained four girls to help her with her work.

She was not high-fashion, but practical, and she had a clientele among the upper middle-class women who wanted good clothes.

Pieter had had his portrait painted, and it hung in the hallway of his mansion. Hilda had found the artist, and had pestered Pieter until he posed for the portrait. She

115

had had hers done, also, and the man had managed to make her look quite attractive.

Pieter's portrait was full-length, with his hand stuck into his vest—like some damned Napoleon, Pieter thought ironically. The huge head was lionized, with a great, flowing blond mane. He looked imposing, rather cruel, and important. Was *that* how the world saw him? he wondered at times.

Only Jacob had dared to tease him about it. "You look like some jungle lion, Papa," he would quip, then laugh.

"So I do," Pieter would reply. "Grrrrr!" And Jacob would bellow with laughter. Yes, the boy was like himself. God forbid he should make the same mistakes.

He talked of the business of the times with Jacob whenever the boy was home. Jacob's eyes snapped with keen understanding. He told the lad how to keep from being cheated, how to trust no one with secrets, how to keep everything in his mind and keep his plans to himself. "Don't be deceived by surfaces," he advised. "Keep in mind that the other man may be deceiving you every minute! Never forget, he is out for your money, or he wouldn't be slicking you up. Your job is to out-slick him."

But now Jacob was off to college and Pieter missed him sorely. He wandered about the huge mansion and sighed. It hadn't worked out the way he had thought. The mansion rang with parties—and the laughter of the gay social butterflies with whom his wife enjoyed surrounding herself. If he wanted to talk to important men, he went to their offices, or they came to his, or they met at his club. Yet he felt a contempt in their manner toward him, the contempt of men whose families had been in America for generations, who had gone to universities, who were slick and smooth and suave.

But by God, they hadn't earned anything under their own steam, Pieter thought complacently, puffing the pipe he still enjoyed as they puffed at their big, expensive cigars. He listened to the deals they casually offered him, noted the gleam in their eyes, took what he pleased that would profit him, and curtly turned down the rest. He had the reputation he had earned, that of being a hard, cautious man, one who played his cards close to his chest.

"Are you still dreaming and working in here?" Hilda's sharp voice roused him upright in his chair, where he'd been reading with his feet propped up on the stool before him. She came in, and blinked at him in exasperation. "I declare, you're still in your day clothes, and the guests are coming in one hour!"

She was attired in a splendid gown of gold lace over hoops that spread from her waist to her slippers. It made her look like a fat pigeon, he thought. He preferred Sunny's sensible ginghams and plaids, with their modest lines. Hilda's ears were hung with diamond earrings, her throat choked with pearls and diamonds an inch deep. Her plump arms were stuffed into white gloves that extended above her elbows.

"Guests?" Pieter murmured. He had planned to slip out and be gone an hour ago. I've slipped up this time, he thought, by lounging here dreaming by the comfortable fire in my slippers and loose, comfortable smoking jacket.

"Yes, guests! You know Mrs. Astor is coming tonight!" Hilda said in alarm. "Oh, Pieter, don't disgrace me, not tonight! Mr. Shipton has planned everything. We have one hundred guests exactly, and cases of champagne from France."

Reluctantly he heaved himself from the chair, and made his way up the imposing staircase already festooned with white ribbons and white lilacs. Lilacs—in March! They must have cost a fortune, he thought. He went to his bedroom to find that his valet had laid out his black frock coat, his black trousers with straps at the cuffs to pass under his shoes, his white ruffled shirt, and his diamond studs.

He forced himself into his clothes, grimacing. "Yes, sir," his valet chimed in gently, as Pieter swore. "It won't last longer than four or five hours, sir."

"God," Pieter groaned, in a deep, gravelly voice. "If

117

I had known when I bought my first railroad that it would lead to this—"

The valet suppressed a grin, and managed to look solemn during the rest of the time he was assisting his master.

Pieter went downstairs in time to meet the first formidable guests. He stood in the drafty hallway, with the March wind blustering about his chin and ears, trying to look pleased. Hilda was fluttery with excitement, stammering in spite of Mr. Shipton's promptings in her ear.

They went in to dinner. Pieter found himself at the head of the main table, where his daughter Elisabeth was already eating the food. He beamed at her fondly. She was looking especially lovely tonight. Let's see, he thought, she is at least eighteen. Getting married one day soon? It startled him when he saw her smile coyly at a thin, intense young man seated next to her. Her pretty, curled head bent to the young man, the pearls sparkling in her ears, the pale blue gown demure to her shoulders, but revealing too much of her young bosom, to Pieter's way of thinking.

The food was awful, he thought. Too rich and exotic. Who wanted snails? Only Frenchmen ate those beasts! The guests cooed over them, but he noted that some of the men merely poked at them, and talked over them. Then came some good cold salmon; that was all right, except for the yellow, poisonous-looking stuff, some kind of sauce, smeared over it. He flicked the sauce aside, and ate the salmon.

The next course was steak. They couldn't do much to ruin steak. He devoured his portion, washing it down with good red wine. Then came the cold asparagus, with some strange fish wrapped about it, and he glared suspiciously at it. He curtly refused the weird, flaming, brandied pudding, and drank coffee while the guests quaffed bottle after bottle of champagne.

Other tables were set in the drawing room, in the hallway, and even in his library. Yes, he realized, there must be a hundred guests here, with flowers at the place of every lady, and gold favors for the men—cigar holders and tiepins. It had all cost him a pretty penny.

The meal finally ended. Hilda, swaying from intoxication and the headiness of success—for Mrs. Astor, herself, had come!—led the ladies into the front parlor—now called the drawing room. She poured more coffee, listened to the bright talk, and watched with a dark eye for the gentlemen to return with Pieter.

The gentlemen did indeed return to the ladies, after their port. But Pieter was not among them. Mr. Rollo Shipton showed them ingratiatingly into the drawing room, his white-gloved hands rubbing together in pleasure. He sat down at the piano and rippled off some light, soft melodies, his thin face flushed with pleasure. It was the height of his career, the very peak—but he would carry on to more peaks, and higher ones.

Hilda came to him. "Where is Mr. Van Rhyne?" she hissed, through a taut smile.

"He went out the back way," Mr. Shipton muttered, suppressing an impulse to add "small loss" after that. To his way of thinking, the heavy body and dark impassive face of the man, millionaire or no, cast a chill that few dinner parties could survive. Better if he stayed away altogether.

"Where did he go?" she managed to ask.

"He didn't say."

Hilda went out to investigate, and discovered that Pieter had changed his clothes, and taken the closed carriage. And it was barely ten o'clock! He could be going only one place, and she felt hot with humiliation. To go to that female—tonight, of all nights! She had wanted him to see how sought-after she was, how good a hostess, how she chatted with Mrs. Astor. . . .

Hilda was standing near the door when she heard a gentleman ask Elisabeth about her father. "Is he not here? I meant to speak to him about a business matter."

"Oh, Papa has gone out, sir, I am so sorry. Another business deal, no doubt. He is always busy about them." Elisabeth smiled, casting a hard look toward her mother.

Hilda crumpled. She had to go out to the pantries

119

and wipe her nose and eyes before she could return to the party with her head held high, and with her voice artificially light as well. That he should do this to her! Tonight of all nights! Everyone knew where he had gone! Everyone knew about his—his whore! She had managed not to discuss the matter with Pieter this week, but tomorrow she would tell him what she thought of him!

Pieter, in the meantime, had already arrived at Sunny's apartment. He had found her still sitting up, listening to Paul reading from his books. The tall, slim lad had come to the door, and smiled at seeing him.

"Come in, Dad," Paul said, in his quiet voice. "It's a cold night. Shall I fix you a drink?"

"I've had too much to drink, lad," Pieter said, limping in, for the soft shoes had hurt his feet this night.

"Some coffee, then," Paul offered. "I'll fix it." And he went out to the kitchen, to return a short while later with a battered silver-plate tray and some quaint china cups and saucers.

Paul poured the coffee deftly. He had long, neat hands, careful and skilled. Sunny had told Pieter that Paul was always bringing home a hurt bird, or a cat with its leg broken, or a maltreated dog, and fixing it up, keeping it a few days or a week or two, then turning it loose in the woods.

Pieter sat down next to Sunny. She was curled up on the comfortable sofa, wearing a loose pink wrapper over her petticoats, her slippers kicked off, her feet under her. From time to time, he put his hand on her soft blond hair, pushing his fingers through the thickness. She would smile lazily at him, and lean against his shoulder contentedly.

"How is Jacob?" Paul asked, watching them. "He wrote to me a couple of months ago."

"He's fine. Working hard, I'm glad to say. He'll be coming home in June."

"Will you be going out to end-of-track again, Dad?"

Pieter shook his head wryly. "Too old for that now, Paul. I leave it to the younger men. No, I'll be directing the work from the office. Jacob will be going out, though."

"Jacob wrote that he could hardly wait till summer." There was a sort of hero-worshipping tone to Paul's voice. His eyes sparkled.

Pieter nodded. "I reckon so. He needs to learn more of the work. It'll be Illinois and Missouri next."

They talked about the work for a time, and Pieter began to relax in the warmth of their interest and their calm pleasure in his company. It was past two o'clock when he got up to leave.

"Sorry I stayed so late," he half-apologized.

"Didn't you have a party tonight, Dad?" Paul asked. "I thought I saw something in the paper."

Sunny's quick frown and shake of the head was not lost on Pieter. "That's why I came," Pieter said. He ran his hand over Paul's head affectionately. "Take care of your mother, boy. She's a good woman."

"I will, Dad. Goodnight."

The door was shut after him, and in the cool, dark night Pieter felt uneasy. He rode home in the closed carriage, entered by the back door, and silently made his way up to his huge bedroom. A fire was blazing in the fireplace, and his valet rose sleepily from his seat next to it.

"I told you not to wait up."

"I thought you might want me, sir. It's no trouble." Deftly, he helped Pieter to undress, saw him into bed, and stirred the fire, leaving Pieter to his somber thoughts.

The next day Pieter worked long, then returned home in the early evening. He heard the piano in the drawing room, grimaced, then heard girlish laughter. He paused in the doorway, smiling involuntarily at the pretty sight.

One of the governesses was seated at the piano, playing some light air. Elisabeth was whirling about the room, with Rollo Shipton's arm about her waist. He was dancing properly, holding her hand high, his face intent. Katrinka was dancing with her younger sister Frieda, counting aloud, "One, *two*, three, and one, *two*, three—"

"Shush, Tinka, you shouldn't count, you should not need to count!" her older sister rebuked her, pausing in the dance. Mr. Shipton paused with her, of necessity, and Pieter's eyes sharpened as he saw how the lean arm lingered about her slim waist, how the white fingers smoothed over her back, before he finally released her. He saw the look on the man's face. The girls were fussing, and the governess stopped and scolded them primly, then began to play again.

Pieter went to his study, thoughtfully. He pulled off his boots, gave them to his valet, put his feet in comfortable slippers, and sat in his favorite chair before the fire. The footman brought back a glass of whiskey, and Pieter thanked him absently.

At nine o'clock, he was still in his study, dozing before the fire, when Hilda appeared in the doorway. Her face was flushed. She snapped the door shut after herself.

"I was horribly embarrassed last night, Pieter! You shamed me before all of New York City!" she began dramatically.

"I ate with the right forks," he said, amused. He put his feet on the hassock, and waited for her shrill denunciation.

"You walked out right after dinner!" she rebuked him, her small mouth pursed righteously. "Everyone wondered where you had gone—rather, they *knew* where you had gone, and looked at each other and at me in such a hateful way."

"Why do you want friends like that?" he asked, his eyes half shut. "Seems to me you'd do better to ask Marta over. She's a good sort, never gossips or speaks ill of anyone."

"Oh, your sister—she *has* to be perfect," Hilda whined. "But everyone in New York does gossip, and today they're talking about *me*! Pieter, I want to go away!"

He did not flare up, as she had half expected. "Where do you want to go?" he asked.

"To Europe!" she said promptly, her eyes glistening. "It will still the gossip. And besides, it is fashionable to go to Europe! Mr. Shipton says it is all the rage. We shall have first class accommodations on the ships, we shall call upon the Queen of England, we shall see Paris. And we shall buy some fabulous gowns from the best designers—"

Shipton, again. He waited until Hilda paused for breath. "How much would it cost?"

"How much! What do you care? You have millions, and you do nothing with them! You know nothing about art and fashion, and famous people, and being accepted! You don't care to know!" she wailed.

He thought about that. No, he didn't care. He had all the money he had ever wished for. Yet, strangely, it gave him little satisfaction. He had been more content in the old days, working his periauger across the cold waters on a frosty morning, than he was now, seated before the fire in his opulent mansion.

Hilda shrilled on, complaining about his preoccupation with business, about how he neglected her, about how everyone pitied her. She did not dare speak Sunny's name, but she said everything else.

When she had finished, he still sat silent. "Well?" she half-screamed, her face an ugly red. "What are you going to do about it?"

"Let you go to Europe," he said abruptly. "It's time the girls saw something of the world. We'll leave the boys in school, but you take the girls with their governesses. Miss Hadley speaks French and Spanish, I understand. She can be of help."

She stared at him, her mouth gaping open.

"There is only one condition," he said quietly. "You'll get rid of that pimp."

"What? What? What did you say?"

"That pimp, Rollo Shipton! You'll get rid of him. I should never have let him into the house."

She gave him a triumphant look. "You're jealous of him!" she crowed. "You're jealous!"

"I don't want him for a son-in-law," Pieter roared. "Nor do I want him creeping into Elisabeth's bed. Get him out of here tomorrow, and you can have the trip to Europe."

"Elisabeth—? Son-in-law—? Pieter, you are mad . . ."

"And you are very blind, Hilda," he grumbled sarcastically. "Sure, he wants to advise you. He wants your money. But I can see his face when he looks at my eldest daughter, and by God, he shan't have her. I have better plans for her than that—that dancing master!"

This took the wind from Hilda's sails. "You can't mean it. It isn't true. Can it be true—?" she muttered weakly. She was torn between anger and confusion. "He would not dare—my employee—daring to look at Elisabeth . . ."

"Go have a look at him now, in the drawing room. Stand where he can't see you." Pieter paused for effect, then added dryly, "Then decide on what to pack for Europe. I understand May is a good time to sail."

She hurried away. The next day Rollo Shipton was dismissed without notice, but with a frigid farewell. When he tried to protest, Hilda said a few earthy things to him that no society matron would have thought of; indeed, few knew such words. Red to the ears, he packed and fled from the mansion.

"To think I harbored such a creature!" Hilda remarked later to Pieter, virtuously.

"For five years," he reminded her.

"Will you come with us to Europe? You would enjoy it." She knew enough to switch the subject deftly.

"God, no. Europe holds no interest for me. My investments are here."

"What about Jacob?" She hesitated. "And the boys?"

"I told you, for them it's school and their tutors. And Jacob will go west this summer, as usual. I think I'm going to promote him to superintendent," Pieter reflected. "He's a good hard worker. He's tough, and the men respect him."

124

The girls were wild with delight at the prospect of going to Europe. They packed and repacked a dozen times, until they were reminded that they would be shopping for new, fashionable gowns in Paris, and needed to take little, only two or three trunks apiece.

When they had departed in early May, Pieter breathed a sigh of relief. At last, he would have some quiet. Only the big mansion was *too* quiet. He found he had become accustomed to the light chatter, to the laughter of his daughters, to the coming and going of the guests whom he despised, even to his wife's nagging. It was horribly quiet. He roamed from one room to the other, like a great, shaggy dog left alone in the kennels.

Wealth had not brought him happiness. He felt more alone than he'd ever felt in his life. He welcomed Jacob heartily when the young man came home from college. But Jacob stayed only a few days, and was quickly off to the West.

Pieter was alone again until Lodewick, Hans, and Blaine came home with their tutors. Their insane giggling drove him crazy, and their mischief made his housekeeper give notice twice a week. But, for all that, they livened up the place. Hans was fifteen, and Pieter decided it was time to start training him at the office. Fourteen-year-old Lodewick whined until he was allowed to come also, which left eight-year-old Blaine furious and upset. But, on the whole, they were good lads, bright and intelligent, and Pieter was glad for their company.

Hilda, far away in her Paris suite, was less contented. She sat in the chair near the window, and gazed out at the glittering lights and the iridescent blue of the early evening. Paris. They had "done" London, met some royalty, though not the Queen. Victoria was, according to reports, particular about whom she met, and not overly fond of the newly rich Americans who swarmed through London society during the summer.

From here they would go to Italy. The governesses had said they positively must "do" Italy, for it was the cradle of civilization. Hilda reacted favorably to that. Her cradles were all empty, she thought wistfully. All her babies were growing up, and had little need for her now.

Her feet ached from shopping, from walking the hard pavements, and from standing for long hours on the fitting dais of this or that famous designer. One of them, the celebrated Mr. Worth, had been haughty and downright rude to her, although it was said he was rude to everyone. She supposed she must consider it a triumph that he had consented to dress her and her daughters. He did not accept everyone.

Hilda looked down unhappily at her dress. It was a brown-and-cream silk taffeta, cut indecently low to show her round breasts, with lace about her neck, and down to her waist. She found it hard to sit in it, for it had a dozen petticoats, and the skirts stood out so far she had to sit carefully in a chair, or sprawl on a sofa, in order to give them room. It was a fashionable dress, but she felt like a stuffed stocking. The stays at her waist were pulled so tightly she could scarcely breathe. And when she looked in a mirror, she thought she resembled a Christmas pudding.

Elisabeth, on the other hand, was gayer than ever. She whirled about in her green-and-silver silk gown, her cheeks bright with excitement and rouge. She spoke now to her mother, but Hilda just stared at her daughter blankly. "Whatever did you say?"

"Oh, Mama, I'm speaking French!" Elisabeth said impatiently. "Don't you remember anything about our lessons?"

"Don't be impertinent!" Hilda said sharply.

Elisabeth's mouth tightened, and she turned away, muttering something. Katrinka gave her mother an anxious look. She was lovely in a full dress of red-and-blue plaid. Queen Victoria had made the Scottish plaids fashionable, even in Paris. The Empress Eugénie of France had made the full skirts the height of fashion. Sighing, Hilda thought again of her stiff petticoats. How she wished she had stayed in America, where she could at least be comfortable in her gowns!

Young Frieda was placid as usual. Pieter always said she had inherited the disposition of his own mother, who had been calm through storms and turmoil. She had submitted to having her hair done in plaits, and had turned and sat down when ordered to do so by the dressmakers. "What a lovely child," everyone had said, and Frieda had smiled serenely. Just now, her nose was buried in one of Katrinka's books, though it was probably too sophisticated for her, but at least she was quiet and good.

"We are ready to go, Mama," Katrinka said, finally, when Elisabeth remained sulking in her chair.

Hilda sighed audibly. She wondered what her beautiful, intelligent, bright daughters would say if she told them she wanted to go home. She didn't want to go out tonight. They were going to an opera, and she hated operas. The silly, shrill singing rang in her ears and made her head ache. Ballet offended her, since it showed the girls' ankles. And the Frenchmen would ogle her daughters all through the long opera, or try to flirt with them during the long intermissions. If only Pieter had come with them—or Rollo. She regretted having dismissed Rollo; she missed his whispered instructions and his constant attention.

She forced herself up from the chair and they went out, sweeping the streets with their beautiful silk dresses, the governesses following demurely in their black and white and gray silks.

That night, the performance itself was best enjoyed by those three young women who had been hired to stuff learning and grace into the heads of the three newly rich young Van Rhyne girls. Certainly Hilda did not enjoy it; Elisabeth sulked because a young man of her fancy did not appear; Katrinka thought the whole story of the opera was stupid and silly; and Frieda could not partake of any refreshments because they were alcoholic.

But they had been seen, and the next day they were

in the gazettes, two lines in all: "The beauteous young demoiselles Van Rhyne were at the opera last night, so gracious, so queenly. . . ." The governesses read the item aloud and happily translated it for Hilda.

Elisabeth cheered up, because five young men sent bouquets to her, bright nosegays of lilacs, roses, and camellias. Katrinka was happy because she and Frieda had discovered a wonderful bookstore, and their favorite governess had promised to take them there and let them buy as many books as they wished. Pieter had said to let them buy what they wanted, and, thought the young lady, what better to buy than books?

Hilda remained homesick. And bored. And nervous about the future. What was Pieter doing? She knew damned well what he was doing. He was sitting over in the apartment of that—that strumpet!—enjoying her company, and not sparing one thought for his miserable wife, who had borne him seven fine children!

She sat in a cafe with her three chattering daughters, and was unusually silent. From a distance, she had seen a tall, alert-faced man with sandy hair, and he had reminded her suddenly, achingly, of her father who had died several years before.

She missed her father so much. He had been kind, good, and devoted to her. If only she had not married Pieter, she could have kept house for her father. . . .

And painfully the memories continued to force themselves upon her. The way she had been loyal to her father, only to earn the hatred, yes, the hatred, of her own husband! Pieter had been so coldly angry when he had discovered that the deeds were missing—and she had only wanted to help her father, who had always been so loving to her.

"Mama! I said, do you want some tea?" Elisabeth asked, laying her hand impatiently on Hilda's arm. The bright blue, flashing eyes reminded Hilda suddenly of Pieter.

She gazed back, in a daze. "Yes, no," she said. The governess quietly signaled for tea to be brought. Madame was not herself, she thought.

128

Hilda was searching her memories, slowly, painfully, trying to bring herself to face the truth. If she had had the courage to be loyal to her husband instead of to her father, she would not be in this plight, she realized. All those years, Pieter had held it against her. She had reported to her father, and he had thanked her, beamed at her. But it had been wrong. She had listened as one of the governesses had read the Bible to Frieda, as she did every night. "Forsaking all others . . ." Alas, she had thought. It was even in the Bible, wasn't it? Leaving father and mother, cleaving only to one's husband . . .

She had not done that, she realized, there in that strange cafe with the lace tablecloths, the elaborate golden lamps, the deferential waiters bringing tea in silver pots. She felt outside herself, looking in, seeing, with fright and detachment, the truth of herself, of her father, and of her husband. She had betrayed Pieter, just as he had said. And eventually he had turned to another woman.

It was her fault, all her fault. She had betrayed her husband, of whom she had been so proud. Painfully, she recalled other times.

When Pieter had come to call upon the five sisters, bearing five bouquets of flowers. And five boxes of chocolates, with a red ribbon about her box. She recalled the proud, strange feeling when Pieter had come and asked for her—for Hilda! The maid had come to her and said, as if unable to believe it, "He's here again, miss, and he wants you, just you!"

They had gone walking down by the wharfs, just the two of them. Drawing a deep breath, Hilda could recall the smells of the wharf—the salty odor of the ships and their tar, the smell of freshly baked bread, of spices and flowers, of tobacco and tea. Tea . . .

"Your tea, Mama!" said Elisabeth, pouring.

Hilda put a hand to her head. It was whirling. She wanted to cry, but a lady did not show her emotions in public. Pieter had put that sparkling ring on her finger, had begged her to marry him. "You're the girl for me,

Hilda," he had said. "I don't want a giggling girl, I want an intelligent girl who will work with me—"

She had tried. She had tried, but she had failed, because of her father—her father coming, with tears in his eyes, begging her to help him find the money to recoup the loss of his ship. Even now, she would do the same, she would give him the money. She could not turn him away, her poor, proud papa, so desperate—

"Mama, you're crying!" Frieda whispered. Kindly Frieda anxiously reached over to pat her mother's arm.

"I have something—in my eye," Hilda lied, and sat up straight, carefully wiping the eye that had betrayed her with a single tear. She smiled bravely, and accepted the plate of cakes Elisabeth had moved in front of her. She chose two of them, though she knew she could not eat them.

Silently, she sipped her tea and thought gravely about her future. She had money, she had wealth, she had a mansion, she had wardrobes of fine clothes. But she did not have Pieter, not ever, in spite of the seven children she had borne him. And she no longer had them, either, she realized sadly. Her daughters looked at her critically whenever she said something awkward, or stammered in public. Her sons had grown away from her long ago. What was left?

Nothing, nothing was left. She was a husk of a body, sitting in a smart, gilt, uncomfortable chair in a Paris tea shop, with her graying hair piled high and bound with combs of jet and pearls. Her daughters wore silk and lace, and sparkled with beauty. But they despised her, as did her husband.

Why, why, why had she not had the courage, years ago, to be loyal to Pieter? She had had everything. And she had flung it all away.

Chapter 9

One glorious day in late June, Pieter decided to go down to the docks. His foremen usually met the boats to choose the best, the strongest-looking immigrants from Ireland, to work on the railroads. As the lines stretched westward, ever westward, with the rails stretching out onto the open plains, across the scorching deserts, ever onward toward the mountains, good railroad workers were more and more in demand.

The day was so balmy that Pieter drove down in his open carriage. The sky was as blue as Sunny's eyes, he thought, as the wheels jogged along the rough dirt road leading to the wharf. Later, he would often reflect on this fateful summer day. If he had not gone down to the docks . . . if he had not met that particular boat.

But he did go down. He often went down, for he liked the fanfare of the ships coming in, the excitement of the sailors swarming over the docks, and the startled looks of expectation, bewilderment, or wonder lighting the faces of the immigrants as they first laid eyes on the Promised Land. As always, customs officials met the boats and interviewed the immigrants, asking about their job prospects and their health, poking them and inspecting their teeth, then finally writing down their names, often twisting the old Irish, Germanic, French, and Jewish names into common American surnames.

Mr. Van Rhyne was recognized, and everyone made way for him respectfully. One of his foremen rushed over to him. "Nice day, Mr. Bates," Pieter greeted the foreman, nodding graciously over his pipe at the man.

"Oh, yes, sir. Indeed it is, sir!" Mr. Bates spouted anxiously, as though wishing to give Pieter the credit for it.

"Get on with your work," Pieter said abruptly. He got a little weary of the bowing and scraping. So few now spoke to him man-to-man. They thought of his money, and it made all the difference. Money was power, money was respect, money was what made these lackeys doff their hats to a man who was but flesh and bone decaying to the grave.

So why the gloom? It was a bright, cheerful day. Men and women who'd come to meet the ship were reunited with relatives not seen for years, and they wept openly on each other's shoulders. Irishmen in green vests stood with cigars in hand, watching sharply for Irish of the old country, in case they needed help. These Irish were a close-knit bunch, Pieter mused. He had seen their huddled-together shanties, where in a single room, a dozen or more might sleep until more space could be obtained. The famines had driven more and more of them to seek refuge in America, and had bound them more closely together than ever, as only adversity could.

Their broad backs and willingness to work hard had given them the jobs that native-born Americans had come to despise. They dug foundations for the new office buildings and mansions of Manhattan. They learned to handle dangerous explosives, and with it they broke ground for canals and railroad beds. They swung picks and shovels, exerting their brawn and muscle until they died early, or became crippled and went home to sit in chairs all day, their faces vacant.

He saw the two children coming along the docks. One was a tall, skinny boy with a gaunt face, carrying a pathetically small bundle wrapped in a tablecloth of red check. The girl tagging behind him was smaller and shorter, her cheeks thin, her eyes hungry and pathetic. But her head was held high, her blue-black hair had been brushed smooth and glossy, and her eyes—as she raised her head, Pieter saw her eyes. Turquoise-blue was the color of her eyes, bright as the June sky.

He watched them idly as they went up to Mr. Bates, who looked the boy up and down, then shook his head and turned away. Some came to the new country too

132

weak to work, and Mr. Bates wanted *men* for the railroad, not boys.

The boy dared to reach out, his eyes flashing. He touched Mr. Bates on the arm, and made him turn about to face him. Pieter moved closer, and heard the exchange of words between them.

"I was promised a job, when I come here! The papers said there was work. You got to give me work!"

The girl moved closer, protectively, her face troubled. Pieter came nearer to them, fascinated somehow by the belligerence of the scrawny lad.

"Go find someone else, then," Mr. Bates shot back curtly. "I need strong men, not boys!"

"I was promised a job," the lad repeated stubbornly. He had a dangerous gleam in his eyes. "By God, you'll give me a job, or I'll break your head in!"

Mr. Bates went red with fury, and lifted a hand in a threatening gesture.

The girl behind the boy spoke up with spirit.

"Now, Rowan, mind your tongue, will ye? That's no way to speak to the kind gentleman, who can tell us where to find work, if we but ask nicely! Tell him you're sorry for your thoughtless words, and we'll—"

"Be quiet, Molly! I'll speak how I wish!" the boy flared, with his skinny fists held up before himself menacingly. "We come all the way from Ireland to work. Work was *promised*, and before God and the Virgin Mary—"

"So you'll curse and damn yourself forever, will ye!" the girl said furiously. She caught at his arm and shook it firmly. "Rowan O'Neill, I'm telling ye to come away with me this minute, while I tell you to mind yer manners and be proper!"

Pieter, highly amused by this tiny child interfering in the matter between the two men, came forward as Bates was about to hit at the boy.

"All right, now, what is the matter?" Pieter bellowed.

They all whirled to look at him. The girl, for all her brave words, looked frightened. Her mouth quivered. She was so thin, so scrawny, that he figured they had

133

had little to eat on the ship, and maybe for long before that also.

"It's no matter, Mr. Van Rhyne, sir," said Mr. Bates. "Nothing I can't handle!"

The boy took off his cap, and holding it in his rough, red hands, gazed anxiously at the fine gentleman with the big blond beard and the gold watch chain across his fine, fat stomach.

"Sir, I wants a job. I'll work hard, I promise ye. Everyone back in Ireland said I'd have no trouble getting a job, for I'm that hard a worker, you wouldn't believe it! Ask anyone on the ship; they'll tell ye I worked my passage, and didn't shirk. Ask me sister Molly here. She'll tell ye, when Pa died I did the farm work until the landlord, he raised the rents so much we had to leave. After Ma died—"

"They all have a hard-luck story, Mr. Van Rhyne," Mr. Bates said scornfully. "Pay no attention to him. If he bothers me, I'll have him thrown off the docks."

"Thrown off, is it!" blazed Rowan O'Neill, turning on him. "Watch and see who gets hisself thrown off! Watch and see who gets thrown into the muddy waters!"

"Mr. Bates," Pieter said, his powerful voice overcoming all of them. "You go on about your work. I'll take care of this lad. Now, be off, sir, and do your work and hire the men I told you to!"

Under his flashing eye, Mr. Bates bowed and went off, highly humiliated. He was in a foul temper the rest of the day, snapping at his fellow workers, growling at the poor, frightened immigrants who didn't meet his standards.

The lad was shaking—with hunger? Fury? Pieter gave the boy and girl a curt nod. "You'll come with me right now," he said. "This is enough of a scene."

They followed him meekly, Molly whispering to her brother and pulling on his sleeve as he walked along sulkily. "Come along with ye, maybe he'll have a job for us, if you'll mind your quick tongue!"

Pieter suppressed a grin, and helped her up into the

carriage. He sat facing them, studying them. Both had on the same blue-black clothing, thin and worn by years of wear. The girl shivered in the cool breeze, and Pieter leaned forward to put a rug over her lap.

"And how old would you be, lass?" he asked, gently.

She gave him a wide-eyed stare, a mix of curiosity and suspicion. "I'd be twelve years old, and my brother Rowan, sir, he be sixteen. Ye'll find he's a grand worker, sir, and me as well. I can work like two of my size and more!"

"And what can you *do*, Molly O'Neill?" he asked gravely.

She sat up straight, clasping her red hands over the small bundle of goods on her lap. "Sir, I can sew and spin, keep house, cook, anything you like! You'll see, I'm a willing worker, I am, and took care of my pa until he died."

Pieter nodded gravely, suppressing a smile, then suddenly felt not at all humorous. These two pathetic mites had bravely ventured to the new country by themselves, cut off from their family. And back in the old country, they'd worked the land, striving to maintain themselves, after their father had died.

He thought of Frieda, just Molly's age, and shuddered. Imagine little Frieda trying to cope with a farm, a dying father, and a vicious landlord who snarled and raised the rent to get her off the land. He had heard similar stories by the score. They had not surprised him, and before this, they had not much touched him.

The Irish were better off away from Ireland, Pieter thought; it was owned by the bullying English, and they seemed to take pride in making the Irish bend the knee to them, and work for a pittance land their ancestors had once owned and worked.

"Your name, miss?"

"Mary Cecilia O'Neill, sir, called Molly by most," she said shyly. "And this is my brother, Mr. Rowan O'Neill." She indicated the sullen youth beside her. He had brightened somewhat since they had left the vicinity of the wharf, but still eyed Pieter suspiciously.

When the carriage arrived at the Van Rhyne mansion, both of them forgot their fears, and simply stared in awe. Never had they seen anything so grand. Pieter led them from the stables, through the kitchen door, and past the puzzled faces of the cook and the maids.

"We'll get some food into you, first," Pieter said brusquely. He told the cook to fix some ham and eggs, toast, coffee, and milk. Her mouth set tightly, she did what he asked, giving the children a disapproving look as they sat down timidly at the kitchen table.

"That's right," Molly said brightly. "We'll break bread together, and be friends, before we discuss business." She sounded so grown-up and mature that Pieter had to grin. Rowan growled, and Molly kicked at him under the table.

Pieter sat down with them at the kitchen table, to the stunned surprise of the maids, one of whom dashed off to giggle in the pantry. He ignored her. He wanted Molly and her brother to feel welcome. He had taken an unusual liking to them both, these two children who were worn to the bone, but gallant for all that.

They ate hungrily, but neatly, he was glad to see. Molly crossed herself and muttered a prayer before digging in. They would have need of her religion here in this land, Pieter thought.

Rowan kept giving him suspicious looks. Pieter had already breakfasted, but he ate some bread and drank coffee with them. When they had cleaned their plates, he led them into his study. They gazed about in awe, and Molly tried to step around the Persian carpets instead of on them.

He sat them down in chairs, then took the swivel chair at his huge mahogany desk. "Well, Rowan O'Neill, you first," he said gravely. "What can you work at?"

"Railroading," the boy answered promptly. His long, lean legs reached to the floor, but Molly's blue-stockinged legs dangled, not reaching it. Her feet were small and neat, her ankles well-turned. She kept darting anxious looks at her brother, as though ready to jump in and protect him if he should do something unwise.

"The work is hard and long. I have run a railroad for many years," Pieter said modestly. "I have worked at digging, and at blasting tunnels and cuts through the mountains. The work is long hours, six days a week, from dawn to dusk through the spring, summer, and autumn. Then you have a few months off in the winter, and we start again in the spring."

"And what is the pay, sir?" Rowan O'Neill asked.

"Your board, room, and a dollar a week."

"Done," Rowan said, and gave him a happy smile.

Pieter chuckled to himself at the lad's eagerness, but kept his face grave. These children were too quick to take offense. "Of course, after you do good work, you get a raise, sometimes up to four or five dollars a week," he added. Rowan beamed at him in incredulous wonder. "We'll be rich, Molly!" the boy said to his sister.

She gave him a frown. "You'll work hard and do him credit. Tell him, Rowan."

Pieter interrupted them. "And now you, Molly. What work would you like to do?"

She hesitated. "Oh, sir, could I be a maid? I do like them uniforms they do wear," she said, with a little worried frown between her fine, dark brows.

Pieter stroked his whiskers, in an effort to keep from smiling. "I think that would be a good idea. I have need of another maid in this house. Do you think you would like to live here, Molly?"

"Here—in this grand place, sir? Oh, ye must be joking, sir!" she gasped.

Rowan looked from one to the other. "And where would she sleep, eh?" he barked.

"With another maid, on the top floor," Pieter said blandly, guessing his thoughts. "We take good care of the maids here, never fear. New York can be a wicked city. She'll not go out alone, she'll go with one of the older maids, should she wish to shop or look about.

137

And we'll have her taught to dust and clean the way my wife likes it, and perhaps to serve at the table."

"Oh, that would be grand, sir," Molly sighed, her blue eyes shining. "Oh, this is really the Promised Land, sir!"

"And what will be her wages, sir?" Rowan asked, trying to sound grown-up.

"Fifty cents a week, like the other new ones, then up to a dollar after she learns her work. And she'll get board and room and clothes," Pieter added.

"Sounds good." Rowan turned to his sister. "And I'll come and call on you when I get home from the railroad, and make sure you're doing all right."

"Oh, Rowan!" Suddenly she looked weary and frightened. "We planned we would not separate! We was going to live together, and I'd take care of you!"

"That's hard to do in New York," Pieter said, with unusual gentleness. "How would this be? When Rowan comes home, he'll stay here, with us. There's plenty of room above the stables, where some of the coachmen live. So he can see you easily whenever he comes home, and you can each make sure you're both living well. How does that sound?"

His hard-working clerks would have been agape with stunned amazement to hear the tough magnate making plans for these two waifs. But Pieter was feeling fully alive for the first time in years. How wonderful to be able to do something good with his money and his power. It was worth it, to see the love between them, the devotion of Molly for her older brother, who represented all she had left in the world.

So it was set. Pieter sent for one of the older maids, to take Molly in hand, to see to her uniform and supervise her duties. He took Rowan with him to the offices, and then had one of his railroad foremen fit him out with boots, trousers, shirts, underclothing, stockings, and a jacket. They even gave him a heavy belt with a holster, and a big revolver. Rowan was proud of it, and quick to demonstrate his skill. Somewhere, he had learned to shoot, and he beamed with pride over his ability.

Rowan went out with the new team then, out to end-of-track. Big, scrawled letters soon arrived regularly for Molly. Their mother had taught them to read and write in English, and they had had some training in the hedge-row schools, for the Catholics could not go to the Protestant-run schools of Ireland.

Nearly a month later, Pieter went out to end-of-track, to pay one of his unexpected calls on the workers, and found Rowan a favorite of the team. The lad had grown bigger and huskier already, eating hugely, working hard. He had not oversold himself, thought Pieter, as he watched Rowan swing an axe. He was a willing worker, and now that he ate well and was happy about Molly, he had dropped his guard and was his normal happy self.

Pieter called him over, and the lad was obviously pleased to see him. Together, they went over the tracks, and Rowan beamed with pride. He was not afraid of this great man who had befriended him, and he wondered that the other men stammered and went white in his presence. Pieter Van Rhyne was his friend, his bene-factor, and he would have fought to the death for him. Since that was not possible, at least not now, he did the next best thing, which was to show him around.

Pieter found himself talking at length to the lad, somewhat to his own surprise. Rowan was quick and eager to learn, his blue eyes blazing with excitement at each new bit of knowledge. Pieter explained how the surveyors from the government would come out first, choose the best routes, and flag them with sticks and markers. The railroad men would then bid on the piece of track, laid out in eight- to eighty-mile sections. How high they bid depended on the difficulty of the road, and how much they thought could be accomplished in six to eight months.

Pieter liked Rowan so much that when he left the camp he took the young lad with him, on to where Jacob worked as superintendent of another camp. This camp was a more sophisticated one, with tents set up, for they were blasting a difficult path through the mountains, and spent weeks and even months at one site.

At first, Jacob eyed Rowan suspiciously. He seemed dubious about this lad who had wormed his way into his father's confidence. But soon, Rowan's warmth and eagerness won Jacob over as they had his father.

The three of them talked for a long time, stretched out on a blanket before a crackling fire. Jacob told them about some trouble he'd been having with a pack of gamblers who had persisted in setting up tents near the site. Naturally, the Irish workers wandered over there, nights and Sundays, to try their luck.

"They're taking all the boys' money!" Rowan cried. "That ain't fair! They've worked hard for their wages."

"What would you do about it?" Jacob, giving his father a quick wink, asked Rowan, to test him.

A slow smile spread over Rowan's young face. "Scare the pants off the slick-tongued, smooth-handed lot of 'em."

"How?" Jacob persisted. "I've tried to get them to leave. I have threatened, I have warned, I even got the law after them."

Pieter was listening with contented amusement to this exchange in the evening firelight. Stretched out on the blanket, his boots to the fire, he was happier than he had been in a long time. He keenly enjoyed watching his eldest son take charge.

"Let me have a try," Rowan urged, a devil of fun in his blue Irish eyes. He turned eagerly to Pieter. "Sir, let me have a try at it!"

Pieter smiled. "Go ahead."

Rowan jumped up and went over to one of the foremen, who shrugged and looked dubiously to Pieter. Then the foreman went into a tent, brought out a stick, and gave it to the boy.

Jacob and Pieter followed him to the gamblers' tent, a little way west on the plain. Inside the tent, the candles were lit, and in the warm evening, the glow reached half a mile. Three frock-coated men were shuffling

140

greasy packs of cards, as a handful of Irishmen watched intently for their luck to change.

Rowan came close, and observed them gravely, the mischief in him obvious only to Jacob and Pieter. "You are cheating the fellows," he said finally, in sober reproof, to the gambler dealing at one table. "I saw you palm your cards. That is very wrong. You ain't even giving them a fair chance at it."

Jacob and Pieter had lingered behind, and were watching from the dimness beyond the lighted tables. The open flap of the tent showed them the scowling faces of the gamblers, which reflected their contempt as they studied the boy who had challenged them. The hand of one of the gamblers went to an ivory-handled revolver. Rowan had his pistol in his belt, but he did not move to touch it. Instead he tightened his grip on the short, round stick in his hand.

"What are you going to do about it, you stupid ox?" one gambler growled. Pieter was reminded suddenly of that man in the frock coat who had called Paul names, and who had died so swiftly because of it, in the dust of the gold town.

"Break it up, and be on your way," Rowan said calmly. "You'll pack up and leave, or I'll send you away without your gear."

They sneered at him, and several men laughed. Then the Irishmen looked beyond Rowan to their boss, waiting quietly in the shadows, and they got up and moved out of the tent, and melted into the darkness beyond the candles' glow. They knew the boss, and they knew their own kind.

The gamblers were furious. "Go away, lad, and get your ma to wipe your nose for you!" one of them told Rowan angrily, then drew his pistol. "I don't care who you are, little whelp, but get you gone! We're having a good game here—"

"Oh, I don't doubt it," Rowan shot back, his hands on his hips, the stick gripped in one fist. "You're cheating and winning all the time. But Mr. Van Rhyne, he

141

wants you to go, so I'm sending you on your way. Right now." His tone was deliberate, cold, tough.

"How do you think you'll make me?" sneered the gamblers' boss. They had too good a racket going for them to leave now.

"With this." Rowan held up the stick.

The uncomprehending gamblers merely stared, then laughed. The one who had drawn his pistol aimed it at Rowan. "Go away, boy, before I get mad and shoot you!"

"If you do, you'll blow yourself up. This is a stick of dynamite, and I'm standing so close to you, you'll blow to kingdom come," Rowan intoned seriously.

"You ain't got dynamite."

"Yes, he has so!" yelled one of the Irishmen, and they began to run.

The gamblers hesitated. Then, two of them broke and ran to their horses, pausing only to scoop up the money from the tables. The boss hesitated further. His pistol wavered. "You ain't got no dynamite," he insisted.

Rowan put the dynamite to a candle, and the fuse began to burn. Then he flung the stick into the tent. He threw himself to the ground. Pieter found his son Jacob forcing him to the ground, growling, "That damn fool, that damn fool boy!"

The tent went up in a mighty roar of smoke and flame, then caught fire. The gambler was lifted off his feet, clear through the air, and slammed to the ground. From somewhere in the distance, horses could be heard, galloping away. The other gamblers had not even waited to find out what else Rowan might have in his bag of tricks.

Pieter was shaking with laughter, and Jacob howling above him, as the head gambler recovered enough to stumble away into the darkness.

Rowan came over to them, helped them up, and dusted Mr. Van Rhyne off reverently. "You ain't hurt, sir?" he asked anxiously.

"No, but God damn me if I ever take you up on any

142

such proposition again," the railroad magnate growled. He began to shake again, and a great guffaw burst from him. "Damn it all, if you ain't the gamest gamecock of them all!"

He and Jacob and Rowan laughed all the way back to camp. And they chuckled over it again as they went back to New York a few days later. Every time Pieter thought of that gambler and his shocked expression, he had to roar again. But Rowan, sobering, said, "Don't tell Molly, she'll only get upset. She don't understand how men are."

"Who's Molly?" Jacob asked.

"My sister, the prettiest, smartest girl in the world," Rowan said, his young chest thrust out. Jacob winked at Pieter.

Jacob teased Rowan, but the young Irishman took it, because Jacob was son to his idol. The two young men got along fine. All the way to New York, they talked, laughed, told stories. Rowan was very impressed that Jacob was going to college and "learning all that Greek and Latin stuff," as he said.

At home that autumn, Jacob was like an older brother to Rowan and Molly. He took to the young girl at once, teased her as he would one of his sisters, and tactfully saw to it that her duties were lightened so that she might be free to go out with her brother. And when Hilda and her daughters came home from Europe, and were outraged that Pieter had brought home two young shanty Irish, Jacob defended his father's action.

"Rowan is going to make a great railroad man," Jacob said firmly. "He's proving his worth. And Molly is a good soul."

"She sings about her work," Hilda said repressively. "And she tells jokes in the kitchens and makes the servants laugh, when they should be working."

"Laughter is what this grim house needs," Jacob said, infuriating his mother to such a degree that he had to leave the house and be gone for a time, she was screaming at him so.

He got his revenge by taking Rowan and Molly with

him down to the docks to watch the ships come in. One of his father's ships arrived, and they all watched the tea being unloaded, and the fine silks, and the porcelain. They toured the ship, for young Van Rhyne, Rowan noted enviously, could go where he pleased. The busy captain even took time out to show them around, and patted little Molly's head affectionately.

At home, Hilda complained to Pieter that Jacob was spoiling the young maid, and that Rowan had no place in their house. Pieter told her to keep her nose out of what did not concern her. They had a fine fight, and did not speak to each other for a week, which made Hilda doubly angry, for she had been dying to tell him about all she had bought in Europe, and about all the royalty she had met.

As the fall social season started, Hilda's mood brightened. At last, she would have the pleasure of taking out her grand Worth gowns, and planning a grand party. She would show Pieter how marvelous she looked! And she would wear her new diamonds and pearls, also, which she'd had set in Italy in some marvelous gold settings that hung heavily about her short throat. They would be the envy of all her friends!

Jacob and Pieter caught wind of the party, and cast each other knowing looks. "I wish I were going back to university before this," Jacob mourned. "Mother will throw me at the heads of all the prim, stupid young women who have money—or whose fathers have it."

"I'm not going," Pieter said firmly.

"Neither am I," Jacob said, and they cut the party, and took Rowan and Molly for a long drive along the docks in the new carriage, and up into the city, to see the gaslights at night. They did not return until two in the morning. Molly was enraptured, and even the stern scolding of one of the older maids did not diminish her excitement.

"You'll have the other girls jealous of you," Jane warned her, earnestly. "And you won't be able to work well with them. They think you spend too much time with the boss as it is."

144

Molly tossed her blue-black curls, and her eyes sparkled. "It was worth all the scoldings in the world. Oh, Jane, you should see New York City at night! It's so splendid, it's like paradise."

"More like hell with the demons in charge," Jane muttered darkly. "You don't know what goes on in the city, Molly girl!"

"Mr. Van Rhyne is the kindest man in the world!" Molly sighed. "What luck that Rowan and I met him on the wharf!"

"Luck or the devil," Jane said gloomily, eyeing her charge with reluctant admiration. The girl had seen so many hardships that death itself held no terrors for her. She merely set her lips, tossed her head, and did what she wished. For all her slim body, and her up bringing as a stern Catholic, she had a merry heart and a sweetness that Jane admired. And her will was iron. She would do what she would do, and take her punishment cheerfully, for it was all worth the birching, as she said.

And she was clever with her hands. The stern housekeeper had even set her to dusting the good porcelain vases, for she could be trusted not to tip one over. She was given the fine mending of the lace to do—the tablecloths, and even Hilda's berthas, because her sewing was so tiny and clever that one could not see where the torn place had been. Through all the hard work, she remained cheerful and good-hearted. When another maid was ill, she would do her work for her and somehow get through her own. She slept deeply at night, the sleep of the innocent. And somehow she bloomed, with the good food, with the knowledge that she was wanted here, and with the security of knowing that Mr. Van Rhyne was her friend, and that her brother was close by and well.

Chapter 10

Those years in the late 1850's were happy ones for Pieter. When he heard Molly singing as she dusted in the drawing room, he would open his door to listen better. Her voice sounded good to him—better than the shrill squalling of his daughters during their music lessons. Molly had a pretty voice, and she sang the old Irish airs in a quiet, sincere manner that he liked.

Jacob was still at the university, but he would come home on the holidays, and Pieter was always glad to see him. He was growing closer to his eldest son, and to his younger boys, Hans and Lodewick. All were taking hold, keen about the railroad business, and seemed to enjoy being with their father and learning from him.

Rowan thrived on the railroad life. He grew bigger, sturdier, and more confident. Here in America he was somebody—a friend of the Big Boss, and a comrade of the boss's son. And because he was quick to fight for his rights, he earned the respect of his fellow Irishmen, who walked about him cautiously, out in the tough railroad camps.

One summer day, Pieter sent for Molly O'Neill. "Tell Molly to come to my study," he told one of the older maids. "I have a letter from her brother."

He used any excuse to have the girl come and talk to him. His own daughters had nothing but clothes and beaux in their heads, he thought. And when Hilda came to talk to him, she was shrill with complaints. In the club, he talked warily to other businessmen; in his office, his clerks were too afraid to talk frankly.

Molly came in with eagerness and a smile, prancing on her long, coltish legs. Warmth and laughter lit her creamy-white face with a faint pink glow. Her blue eyes, sparkling, looked straight at him. Her hair was brushed firmly, so the waves shone to her shoulders.

Pieter always thought her delicate beauty an odd contrast to the drab maid's uniform she wore. The Van Rhyne maids wore plain black uniforms with white collars and cuffs. Molly took it cheerfully, though. "It's all right," she once told Pieter. "I'm in mourning for my folks. I don't mind the black."

"There now, sir, you did send for me?" The lilt in her voice never failed to charm him. He turned from his desk with a smile.

"Close the door, Molly. We'll read Rowan's letter together."

The door shut with a bang, and she clapped her hand to her mouth. "Oh, sir, excuse the noise!"

Hilda scolded her regularly for the noise she made, for the singing that echoed through the marble halls, and for her cheerfulness, which Hilda somehow misconstrued as an affront. Maids were not supposed to be cheerful, Hilda had often rebuked her sternly. Elisabeth, as well, would frequently turn up her nose at Molly, but she did not hesitate to send for her when she wanted her hair done up right, or when she needed a dress sewn tighter at the waist.

"That's all right," Pieter said. "Sit you down, and read to me." He held out the long, scrawled letter to her, remembering the days when he could not read at all, and Hilda had read him the gazettes.

She took the letter eagerly, and pulled a chair up to his desk. Gracefully, she sat down, studied the envelope, and smiled. "Oh, he's out in Missouri, Mr. Van Rhyne!"

"Yes, I wrote to him, and told him to report to Jacob. I thought they would work well together, especially since one of Jacob's foremen walked out on him during some squabble over the line," Pieter said. He enjoyed moving people about like chessmen. "Jacob seldom writes, so I get news of him from Rowan."

"There, now, what a clever man you are." Molly beamed with satisfaction. She opened the sheets and began eagerly, "Dear Mr. Van Rhyne. Well, I am with Jacob, as you said, and what a time we are a-having together, to be sure, as you will see. I arrived here last Sunday, having come on a horse which I managed to acquire from an Injun fellow. We was having a slight difference of opinion, you see, regarding a waterhole, and somehow my pistol, it went off, and that mean fellow fell down dead. So I took his horse, after burying him with respect and committing his soul to his Maker. I do figure we had the same Maker, though he be a heathen, poor soul."

"Good heavens," Molly exclaimed. "He shot an Injun!"

"So it seems," Pieter said, lighting his pipe to conceal his grin. Roman was a real character of a man! Only seventeen or eighteen, and able to handle himself like a man of far greater years.

She read on, with vivid expression, inserting her comments now and again. "Jacob and me, we figured on marking out a new line, for that government surveyor who—meaning no disrespect to our government—must have had an idiot for a father and a mule for a mother. He went clean through a mountain, in his wisdom, with his fool plans—instead of going through a little hill and around a pool, which could have supplied the line with water for the engines. So we changed them, and that fool engineer, he come hot-footing it back to us and hollered that we was defying the government. All I know is, if he is the government, we are in a very sad way, and so I told him to his red face. No jackass could have drawn the plans worse, I told him, and so Jacob said."

Molly paused again to shake her head. "I do think, Mr. Van Rhyne, I best write to him and tell him to mind his manners," she said seriously. "You don't go telling no government feller he is a jackass."

Pieter smoothed his beard with satisfaction. "A man after my own heart. But I wrote to Jacob and told him to keep Rowan away from government men, and to take care of his hide, and he will. Go on, Molly."

"You're a good friend to us, Mr. Van Rhyne," she said, sincerely. "I'd hate like crazy to have Rowan get into trouble after all the work you gone to over us, to get us good jobs and all. He's got a quick temper, but he has a good soul, I'm sure of it."

She went on with the letter, not noticing the happy smile on Pieter's face. He enjoyed these two children as much as, or more than, his own.

When she had finished the letter, they talked for a time. She would talk to him frankly, as to a father, he realized.

"Mrs. Van Rhyne said as how you would speak to me about something, sir, and what was that?" she asked, brushing back her curls.

He was a little uncomfortable. "Well, Molly, you know how you served us at dinner last night? And I winked at you when that tarnation-fool man made those dumb remarks? And you winked back at me?"

"Yes, sir. Wasn't he an idiot, though?" She chuckled. "Him trying to tell you how to mind your own railroad!"

"Well, you see, that's the trouble. I tried to tell Hilda it was my fault that you winked at me, that I had winked first, but she got mad. I have to admit, it doesn't look good to have the maid winking at me, and some folks noticed. After this, if I should forget myself and wink at you, Molly, you'd best not wink back."

She considered this seriously, then nodded. "No doubt you'll be right, as always, Mr. Van Rhyne," she said cheerfully. "I'll keep me face straight as a judge, I will, and do my chuckling later."

"That's a good girl," he said. "Now, I have a letter from my son Hans at school. Would you be good enough to read it slowly to me?"

He could read it for himself, but with some difficulty, for the boy's handwriting was like a hen's scratchings in the dust, and anyway, he loved listening to Molly's melodious voice. She read it to him, then discussed it with him in a lively fashion, and finally left a good hour later, to face the housekeeper's grim disapproval.

"Molly, where *have* you been? Mrs. Van Rhyne is asking about the lace on her dress, and you gone all this time!"

"Sure, and the boss sent for me to read him a couple of letters, ma'am," Molly said with a smile. "That good a soul that he is, and his consideration for my brother—my, how lucky we are to work for such a fine gentleman as he is!"

One of the maids snickered. The housekeeper sighed and flung up her hands, as she often did with Molly about. "Do go and sew the lace before I lose my patience!"

Molly was up until midnight, sewing, mending, adding pretty silk rosebuds to a blue, flounced dress for Miss Katrinka, but it had been worth it all, as she philosophized to Jane when she finally joined her in the room they shared.

"And isn't this a dream of a dress?" She held it up in front of herself before the small mirror above their washstand. She stood on her tiptoes to see the blue silk against her chin. "Oh, my, to be a-learning to dance so fancy, and stand up in the drawing room when the gentlemen come! And the girl a-whining to be back with her books!"

From her narrow bed, Jane smiled at her warmly. "Molly, you're pretty enough to be down there in the drawing room with them. But don't hurt your heart with dreams of what can't be."

"Oh, land, as though I would!" But when Molly had finished sewing the dainty red rosebuds on the blue silk, she folded the dress carefully, wondering just how she would feel if it were hers, with some beau coming to fetch her and take her out dancing! My, how happy she would be! She slept, and dreamed she was out dancing in a blue silk gown, and somehow the man who held her had the smile and the face of Jacob. She wondered at herself when she woke up. Why, whatever had she been thinking! She was no more than a sister to Jacob, and that was that! And with her usual will, she banished such thoughts from her mind.

Rowan and Jacob returned home in the autumn. Jacob had now finished college, and spent much of his time in his father's office, learning the bookkeeping and business end of railroading. One evening, he and Rowan came in the front door, laughing and joking. They had met at Pieter's office, and Jacob had offered the lad a ride home in his carriage.

They came in through the front hall, practically running into Hilda, who was carrying a fresh vase of flowers. Straightening, she stared sharply at Rowan.

"Why are you coming in the front way, young man?" she said angrily. "Your place is at the back. Use the kitchen entrance! And if you want to see your sister, the maids won't be finished until ten o'clock tonight!"

Rowan backed hastily away, flushing red. "Sorry, ma'am, didn't mean to offend. I'll come later—"

Jacob caught his arm, held him, and turned to his mother. "Rowan came in with me, Mother, and I don't use the back unless I'm coming from the stables with my boots dirty," he said, his eyes blazing. "Father wants to talk with Rowan in the study before dinner. So if you don't mind, we'll go to the study, and not disturb you!" And he tugged Rowan with him toward the study. Hilda glared after them bitterly. Those Irish upstarts were turning her son against her!

Her temper was not improved when she overheard Rowan say, "Now Jacob, lad, that's no way to address your respected mother! She's the only mother you got, and you should be grateful to her, she what gave you birth—"

"Damn it all, father asked you here," Jacob stormed, "and you'll come in the front door!"

"What's all the fuss?" Pieter stood at his study door.

"Mother said Rowan had to come in the back door!" Jacob said, between tight lips.

"Huh. My foremen all come in the front," Pieter said. "I'll just have to make Rowan a foreman right away, instead of waiting until next summer!"

Jacob's temper dissolved in laughter. He clapped Rowan on the back and pushed the dazed young man into the study. "There, there you are, Rowan, me lad," he mimicked. "Kicked you upstairs into the bossing, did Papa!"

"But sure, he didn't mean it," Rowan protested, flushed and miserable, glancing about the fine study, with its Persian rugs and its mahogany furniture, like a frightened animal. "Sure, I best go away and see ye at yer office, Mr. Van Rhyne, sir!"

"And have ye tell me," Pieter mimicked, getting into the game, "that I don't know me own mind, and can't appoint me own foremen when I choose?" And he laughed with Jacob, pushed Rowan into a chair, and poured him a mild, well-watered drink.

They had a good talk, then, with Rowan relaxed and more at ease after a few drinks. He began to tell them stories, with his usual Irish relish for detail and exaggeration.

"Sure, and the fellow told me, he says, that we'll be going nowhere with our rails, and he'll be from one end of the country to the other in another year. And I says to him, I says, when the rails cross the country, me lad, my boss, the finest railroad man in the United States of Americky, will be at end-of-track, making sure the rails get put right into place and the last spikes laid down just right, I says! For sure, there won't be no railroad from here to there without Mr. Van Rhyne, I tells him!"

Pieter laughed, and so did Jacob, who then urged Rowan to tell his father about the bear he had captured and taught to wrestle. Pieter listened, and roared with good humor at the wild stories of the bets the two lads had laid on their bear, of the men who had tried to wrestle the bear, and of how it had ended when the bear had met a she-bear and they had gone off to get married by the priest, as Rowan put it.

Wiping the tears of laughter from his eyes, Pieter urged Rowan on and on, until Hilda's dinner party that night was quite forgotten, and she was in another rage at him.

Rowan went back to see his sister, then, and sat in

the kitchen in equal familiarity, telling his stories to an enraptured audience. Even the sour cook had no bad words for him, and put her favorite pudding before him and urged him to tell them more. He sat there like a king at court, grinning from one maid to another, and told them of hunting great stags with antlers as wide as the room, and of losing them in mountains with snow on them in July! They scoffed at him, eyes wide and wondering. Snow in July! Who ever heard of it? But he swore on his honor it was so.

Jacob came back to find them at midnight, and laughed to see them sitting there, listening and drinking tea and urging Rowan on.

"There, now, you'll not be believing this Irish fellow," he mocked, as they jumped up when he came in. "Sit down, Rowan, and tell about the time you fought the German fellow from the West Coast, who tried to bribe some of our men away from us."

Rowan shrugged. "Oh, that, it was just a fight," he said. "Not interesting. Now, the time we was up in the mountains, and knelt down by that mountain stream, and put our hands in the water, and caught fish with our fingers—that was something!"

"You never caught fish with your fingers, Rowan," Molly said, aware that Jacob was looking at her as he leaned against the wall. His gaze made her self-conscious, and she smoothed her hair. "Don't be telling bigger stories than you can help!"

"It's true, isn't it, Jacob?" Rowan said, turning to appeal to him. "We caught big salmon, longer than that meat platter there, and slit them, and cooked them in the fire for breakfast, all a dozen fellows could eat. Sweet as honey, they was, and that tender. And all for picking them out of the stream by their tails!"

"You had best all be going off to bed, or work will come too soon in the morning," the cook said, softening her tone because the young master was also there. She shooed them off, and Rowan departed to his bed over the stables.

Molly O'Neill had a great time that winter. Ice froze

the ponds, and Jacob taught both her and Rowan how to ice-skate. Jacob was always coming around, toward late afternoon, and giving her a wink to come and join them. She would slip away from her duties, though Jane warned her that Hilda, if she found out, would scold her furiously.

She could not resist slipping out with Rowan and Jacob. And if Rowan was off about his own concerns, seeing a young girl in the city, then she would go off alone with Jacob. He was such great fun, like a big brother to her, and good and kind, just like his father.

They would go off ice-skating, with him sporting a handsome brown jacket and fine brown boots, and the finest ice skates money could buy. And he saw to it that she had a beautiful red plaid jacket over her black uniform—to hide it—and nice black boots, and good ice skates. They would hold hands and laugh like children as they skimmed over the ice from one end of the pond to the other, sometimes racing each other, until their cheeks burned like poppies in the wintry sunlight.

The cook would scold her, and the housekeeper would shake her head at her. But Molly would not give up these outings. Mr. Van Rhyne would have no objection, she felt sure. And she feared the displeasure of no one else.

Pieter gave Jacob a carriage of his own for Christmas that year, a fine black carriage with gold trim, and two black, shiny, sturdy horses to pull it. Jacob went wild with delight. He tried to get his mother and sisters to come out with him, but it was too cold, they said, maybe another time.

So he went looking for Molly, and found her polishing the silver in the back pantry, singing one of her Irish airs in a soft, lilting voice.

He put his head cautiously around the door. No one else was in sight. "Molly! Hist!"

"Oh, Jacob!" She looked up and smiled her lovely, radiant smile at him. "You give me such a fine present, I love it, and I got it on, here." She put her hand to her breast. A golden locket lay against her heart.

154

"I hoped you would like it," he said, his look lingering on her pink cheeks, her starry eyes. "Come on out now, get your coat and hat!"

She jumped up, then shot a dubious look back at the silver teapot she held in her hand.

"Leave it!" he said. "Someone else can do that stupid stuff! Come out with me!"

"Where?" she asked, but she laughed, and did not wait for an answer. She ran up the four flights of stairs to her attic room, pulled on her red plaid jacket, her red tam, and her boots, and danced down the stairs again. He caught her hand and pulled her out the back door to the stables.

A groom was holding the stamping horses, their breath blowing white plumes in the frosty air. Someone had cleared the snow from the stable yard. Jacob lifted Molly into the open seat, holding her up with his big hands about her trim waist. She squealed, "Oh, Jacob, it's a fine carriage! Isn't it beautiful?" She patted the leather seat, then looked about critically, rapturously. The groom gave her a curious look as Jacob got up beside her and took the reins.

"Do you like it?" Jacob asked her, then clucked at the horses, and they trotted down the drive and out into the street. "Isn't it fine? Papa took me with him to pick it out."

"Oh, it's the finest carriage I ever seen! It's even finer than your papa's," she said reverently. "All this black and gold, why, it's like the Pope's, I'll be bound!"

Jacob laughed. His mellow laughter indicated that he was happy with the world. He snuggled down under the rug with her, and whistled to the horses. They clop-clopped down the street, and people stared enviously at the two young people in the handsome carriage.

"I'll pretend I'm a grand lady," Molly said, and tilted her lovely round chin to the world, her nose in the air. With a merry giggle, she spoiled her mocking impersonation of a stuffy society matron. "Oh, isn't the air grand and crisp, like Christmas ought to be? Look at the icicles on the roof, shining like jewels in the sunshine! Look at the blue of the sky, like heaven ought to be! How smooth the ride is, and the leather smells so grand!" She sniffed luxuriously.

"We'll run around the park. It'll be beautiful today," he promised. And so it was, with other fine carriages pacing sedately along the park drives. Young ladies with fur muffs to their faces sat grandly beside their beaux, in carriages of red and cream, or gold and blue, or silvery colors.

Molly drew deep breaths of the sharp, clear air. It was like wine, and as intoxicating as the Christmas brandy they had had at dinner last night in the staff dining room, the butler presiding with great dignity, just like Mr. Van Rhyne, and with the housekeeper in the privileged seat at the table's other end. And the presents! She had remembered everyone, with presents carefully chosen and wrapped. And many had given presents to her. She'd received a little sewing kit from the housekeeper, with cunning little scissors in it, and a silver spoon from the butler, with a wink, and a word: "It'll be for your hope chest, Miss Molly!"

Jane had given her a new pair of mittens of bright red-and-white wool, and these kept her fingers warm right now. The other maids had exchanged gifts with her, little tokens: an artificial flower, some sweet-smelling cologne, a pretty clip for her hair.

Mr. Van Rhyne had called her into his study that morning and given her a huge box of writing paper, envelopes, a couple of pens, and a bottle of ink—to write more letters with, he had said, smiling. It was pale blue, and the finest writing paper Molly had ever seen.

Rowan had told her a couple of weeks earlier that he wanted to give her a new dress, a fine silk dress, and they had gone together down to the docks, to a little shop, and chosen the material. A dressmaker was making the dress even now, and Molly would finish it with a lace collar and cuffs. It was emerald green, like the soft turf of Ireland, which she would never see again.

The best, most unexpected gift of all had been the brown leather box handed to her by Jacob, which he had had to slip into her pocket when she protested. "I want you to have it, Molly," he had said with quiet intensity. And he had left before she could say more.

She had opened it when she was alone and found a gold locket, and inside the locket was a little painting of his father. It looked like Jacob, too, when she studied it closely through tears of happiness. One day Jacob would look just like that, with a fine blond beard, and shining blue eyes, and a grand look to him, she knew.

"You're very quiet," he said now.

She took a deep breath, and touched her chest. "I was a-thinking about your present, Jacob. If anyone had asked me what I wanted most in the world, and I'd known about this locket, I would have said this."

He smiled, pleased. "Even though you almost refused to take it?" He was looking straight ahead to the drive.

"You know why," she said shyly. "Your ma is mad with me whenever you speak to me. She would hate this."

"Never mind my mother," he said shortly. "I'll make friends where I wish. My father thinks you are wonderful, and so do I."

It crowned her day, and she sat there beside him in a fresh glow of happiness. He thought she was wonderful! Would he be amazed to know that she worshipped him? He was so like his father, all good and kind and fine. A gentleman, a real gentleman. And he thought she was wonderful! She would never forget his saying that.

They drove in silence, and in peace, once around the park, then twice around, and again. He pulled up the horses at the ice-skating pond to let them breathe, and they shook their glorious manes, pricking up their ears to the sounds of laughter and joy. He reached for Molly's hand in the red-and-white mitten, and held it. His hand was big and warm and sturdy, and he needed no glove to keep it warm.

She finally stirred. "I best get back," she murmured.

"The silver will wait," he said.

"Anyway, I have to help serve tonight. There'll be grand folks coming."

He drew a sigh. He was wishing she was coming as a guest, instead of as the under serving maid, to help with the sauces. But wishes were not horses, and no one could ride behind them or on them. He lifted the reins, chirruped to the horses, and headed them toward home.

Of course, when she arrived, the housekeeper gave her a scolding. "And there is Miss Elisabeth asking where you are, and furious that you have not done her hair," she concluded, with a long, thoughtful look at the glowing Molly. "You should know better than to traipse off with the young master, no matter what he says. His mother will be furious."

"I'll run right up and help Miss Elisabeth," Molly said, ignoring, with her usual optimism, the parts she did not want to hear. She raced up to her room, flung off her coat and hat and boots, tied on her slippers, and smoothed her hair. Then, properly attired once more, she went down to the second floor.

She tapped at Elisabeth's door. Another maid opened it, and gave Molly a frown and a warning shake of her head.

"There you are, finally, Molly!" said Elisabeth's furious voice. "I'll be late to dinner! What kept you? Never mind, I have finished with my hair, I shan't need you!"

Molly looked at her critically. "If you would let me just fix those curls at your throat, Miss Elisabeth, so they lay right—"

Elisabeth endured her in frigid silence, gave herself a satisfied look, and turned to go. "And next time, be there when I ring for you!" she snapped, and swept from the room.

After the door had closed, the other maid sighed. "And never a word of thanks! Ah, well, the poor dear, with her mother the way she is, and her expected to marry money . . ."

Molly sighed in agreement. She flew down the back stairs, to help with the serving of the dinner. Then, remembering to be demure and silent and helpful, she did not look at Jacob, even when she felt him looking at her. A little warm glow was still burning in her heart. He had wanted her to ride out with him. He had taken her hand in his and told her she was wonderful.

It was past ten o'clock before the help could eat their hasty dinner. The maids were starvingly hungry, and so weary they could scarcely eat at all. They picked at the remains of the cold salmon and the lukewarm beef, then nodded over the pudding, which was all that was left of the fine dessert trolley.

When Molly staggered upstairs to fall into her narrow bed, it was long past midnight.

Jane was turning and tossing from weariness. Older than Molly, she seemed to have aged in the past couple of years. Lines had formed around her eyes, and she was already turning gray at the temples. It was a hard life, thought Molly, as she eased her aching body onto the hard horsehair mattress.

What would happen to her? Would she go on being a maid all her days? At home in Ireland, in her innocence, she had pictured herself and Rowan working for a few years, living together. Then they would buy a farm and begin again on their own. A farm? She had to laugh wistfully at that now. There were no farms within miles of them. And they had no money to buy one. Farms cost dearly here, as they did in Ireland—that had not changed. Only they *did* have food, shelter and clothing, and some protection.

But what of the future? Rowan might marry one day, and she might live with him and his wife, and help with the babies when they came. For herself, she could not look ahead. She had met no man she wanted to marry—except one, whom she could not.

Jacob, like his sisters and his brothers, must marry for money and to unite business interests. This Molly knew, for in serving the coffee, waiting on tables, standing silently, and sewing on a dress for Mrs. Van Rhyne, she had caught the gossip with her keen ears. One girl and another was discussed for Jacob—one was not

159

wealthy enough, another had a disagreeable family, another was common. Common? So was she, Molly had thought. Yet Jacob liked her, and had sought her out.

Her fingers sought the golden chain and she pressed the locket to her breast.

No, he was not like a big brother. She did not feel toward Rowan as she felt toward Jacob. Jacob was a star shining brightly in her sky, glorious, yet so very far away. No, having tears in her eyes would do no good. He enjoyed her talk, he laughed with her, he teased her. But one day he would marry, and she would not see him except in the drawing room with his wife and his children. A son, he would have a son—

She turned and pressed her face into the pillow, weeping the first tears she had cried that day.

Chapter 11

"Hist! Molly!" It was the old familiar whisper, and with a quick smile for Jacob, Molly turned from arranging the dessert tray. He came into the room, fine and splendid in a new blue silk suit, his blond hair brushed until it shone, his blue eyes sharp and keen, his shoulders broad and grand. She reached up, brushed a speck from his velvet collar, and beamed up at him.

"How grand you look, to be sure, Jacob! It's a fine party tonight, isn't it?" She kept her tone cheerful, though her heart ached. She was sixteen, and it seemed she had loved Jacob forever. The house had been so empty when he had gone west with the rails in the spring. And she had sprung back to life when he had returned in the late autumn.

Now it was winter, and his mother was after him to marry before he returned again to end-of-track. One girl after another was paraded before him, each richer than the one before, but none of them quite right.

"I wish you were coming with us, Molly," he said. He caught her hands as she fussed at the lapels of his coat. "Why don't you come out with me after the party?"

"I can't. It'll be midnight, and I have to be up at six. And besides, you know how your mother feels."

"You're more beautiful than any of those stupid girls!" he muttered, his face flushing. He bent and gave her a quick kiss. He had kissed her before, but this winter, sometimes his hand went about her waist, or his mouth was warm and lingering on her cheek.

"Thank you, Jacob," she said, drawing back with reserve. "Now, you best be off to the drawing room."

He left reluctantly, and with wistful eyes, she watched him go. Everyone said she was beautiful. Rowan was proud of her and bragged to his friends that he had the prettiest sister in America. Pieter called her a young beauty, and privately worried about her, because sometimes he noticed the footmen leering at her as she walked naively past. Once, he spoke to her about it.

"Now, don't you be worrying about that, Mr. Van Rhyne," she had reassured him cheerfully. "They won't mess with me. I told them my brother is the best and dirtiest fighter in the world, and he'd be after them in a minute, if they dast bother me!"

But she was beautiful, and Pieter did worry.

The party did not end until well after midnight. Molly started wearily up the back stairs, after washing the last of the wine and brandy glasses. They had to be done carefully, so Mrs. Van Rhyne trusted none but Molly's delicate hands. That meant she was always the last finished at night.

She passed the darkened hallway at the back of the huge mansion, then gasped with fright as a big hand grabbed at her. She was quick to slap out, and her hand contacted a lean, hard face.

"Ouch! Molly, give off!" a familiar voice said, with a laugh in it.

161

"Now, Jacob, what will you be after doing?" she gasped. "Land, me heart is in me throat!"

"And me heart is in your hands, Molly," he mimicked, and caught her by the waist. "Come on to my room. I have some wine for you, and I saved you a cake."

He pulled her with him imperiously, and she did not protest. "For goodness' sake," she said when they were in his bedroom, with the door shut. "Are you gone mad? What if someone sees us?"

"They won't. They've all gone to bed." He laughed. He had discarded his jacket and put on a robe of rich red brocade, and she thought he looked as handsome as a king. His blue eyes flashed, and his blond hair shimmered in the candlelight. He had set out a feast on his desk, with napkins and glasses, wine bottles, and a plate of cakes.

Molly looked hungrily at the food. "I'll just stay a couple of minutes, then," she said, compromising with her conscience.

He seated her in his big easy chair, gave her a cake, and set a glass in her hand. He lifted his glass to her, his eyes shining, then he sat down on the edge of his wide bed.

She ate two cakes, and drank some of the red wine. Soon her head began to spin from a combination of tiredness and the wine. She shook her head when he would have refilled her glass.

"No, no more, Jacob. I must go to bed."

She rose to go past him, but he quickly set down the bottle, and held her by the waist. "I won't let you go," he said, his face laughing and mischievous.

She struggled, but he held her against his hard body, and she felt something warm leap and spin inside her. Finally, she rested against him, and his strong arms tightened about her thin body. He bent his head and kissed her passionately on the mouth, and she tasted wine as he slid his tongue between her lips. She started to shake.

One of his hands slid up over her back, down to her

rounded hips, and up again. He held her head up so he could kiss her throat and her chin, and again, her lips. His kisses were hard and cruel and hurting, for he wanted her wildly. She felt like she should fight him, but, oh, God, she thought, a girl would have to be a saint to fight him, and she was no saint.

He pushed her down on the bed, and stood over her. His robe sash had opened, and the robe was parted. He wore little beneath it. He lay down beside her. One arm held her tight, while the other went up under her black dress, and he was touching her so she nearly went crazy with it. "Jacob," she moaned against his mouth. "Don't do this."

"Molly, I love you so, I love you," he whispered against her mouth, and crushed her lips madly. His free hand was up under her clothes, baring her body to him. And his bed was big and soft and inviting, not like her hard mattress.

Her arms went up around him, and he felt her yielding to him. He settled on her then, and began to caress her silently. His hands and fingers went all over her, opening her dress, as he pressed his lips to her throat, then down to her small, rounded breasts.

When he entered her, she was startled, and tried to cry out. But he was beyond hearing. His masculine desires overwhelmed him as well as her, and he pressed home and had her. She wept then, and he kissed the tears away, and kissed her young breasts, and went to sleep against her.

She left him in the early morning. Jane heard her tiptoe in, silently, but pretended to be asleep.

It was the first of many such times. Jacob, having had her, could not keep away from her. He had tasted the sweet fruit of her innocence. He adored her. He vowed he loved her madly. And she loved him, with all her awakening passions and the fiery needs of her Irish heart.

She was beautiful, he told her, as she lay in bed with him, and he stroked her long, curly blue-black hair. He would leave a candle lit beside the bed, so he could see her naked in his arms. Then he'd kiss her all over her white body, and praise her soft breasts with the pink nipples. He said words that made her blush, but it was all part of the wild ecstasy of their lovemaking.

In a big mansion like that, with many people about, it was impossible to keep a secret forever. Hans whispered to a footman, who told a maid, and soon it came to Hilda's ears.

One afternoon she called Molly to her, in her private sitting room. "I won't ask you if it's true," she said, flashing her most outraged expression. "You might be tempted to lie to me. I'll just say that Jacob is a strong young man, and you might be overcome with him. But he'll marry well, you know that."

Molly, her face white, twisted her hands in her apron, and said nothing.

Hilda stared at her with contempt. "I told Mr. Van Rhyne that you and your brother were just shanty Irish, but he would have you in our house. Well, you asked for what you got, but don't think he'll marry you, no matter if you have a child or not. Are you increasing?" she shot at Molly.

Molly stiffened, but managed to shake her head.

"That's good. Keep it that way. We don't want to have to send you away. At least you keep Jacob from the whorehouses," Hilda said, and turning from her with disdain, motioned with her hand for Molly to leave.

Molly felt sick as she climbed up the stairs to her bedroom, Hilda's cruel words echoing in her ears. Could they be true? Was Jacob—using her? He had been so ardent last night. He had even sworn his love to her. Now, doubt stirred in her. He loved her, perhaps—but could he marry her? She thought of his parents' grand plans for him, which called for him to marry into some fine family and help the Van Rhynes to rise higher in the social life of the country. Why, the son of Pieter Van Rhyne might even be President some day!

She could not discuss the matter with Jacob, for early that morning he had departed for a short business trip with his father. When he returned, and wanted her ardently, she tried to refuse him, but he looked so hurt and puzzled that she came to his bedroom—just to talk, she said.

"Talk! Molly, girl, I've thought of nobody but you for a week now, and you want to talk!"

"Your mother knows about us," she said flatly. A shadow went across his face.

"Did she threaten to make you leave? If she does, I'll get a place for you, an apartment, where I can come and see you."

He did not speak of marriage, she was quick to note. She stared down sadly at his wide bed, the bed where she had known the terrors and joys of being with the man she adored. She swallowed.

"Molly, girl, come along, don't talk tonight! We'll talk tomorrow." His hands were on her, his strong hands, pulling the dress over her head, drawing her down onto the bed. He removed his robe, and flung himself on her hungrily. He was nothing if not a big young man full of hearty appetites.

Suddenly the door swung open. In his haste to have her, Jacob had forgotten to lock it. Molly sat up, frozen, to see Mr. Pieter Van Rhyne come in and shut the door after him. He stared at her, then at the clothes strewn about the floor, then at Jacob, his eldest son.

"So it is true. I thought Hilda was lying—but it's true. My son, how could you do this to Molly, who was under my trust?"

He spoke in a low, quiet voice. He did not seem angry, but rather sad and hurt and upset. Seeing him so hurt was like a knife thrust into Molly's heart. "Oh, Mr. Van Rhyne, it was my fault." She began to blame herself, even as she scurried from the bed and grabbed her dress.

"No, I wanted her." Jacob was pale under his tan, but he kept his blond head erect. "I love her, Father."

"Molly's going to her room," Pieter said carefully. "You'll come to my study tomorrow, young lady, and

165

we'll talk. Jacob, you'll dress and come down now, at once."

He kept his eyes averted from Molly as she pulled on the dress and fastened it with shaking fingers. He held the door open for her, and then followed her out, waiting there as she made her way to her room.

When he heard her door shut, he walked slowly down the stairs to his study. Drawing the heavy curtains, he stood gazing out the window until he heard the sound of Jacob's footsteps approaching.

He turned his head when Jacob came in, then motioned for his son to close the door and take a seat near the fire. Jacob did so, nervously. He had never experienced the full force of his father's anger, as had Hilda and some of his men. Would he beat him? He deserved it, he thought, but Molly was worth it—pretty, gentle Molly, with her shining hair draped across his pillow.

"Have you thought ahead?" Pieter asked abruptly.

"Ahead?" Jacob stared at him.

"Yes. Do you plan to marry Molly O'Neill?"

"Marry her?" Jacob asked, amazed. "But how can I? She isn't in our class. Mother would be furious. And besides—" He fell silent, flustered by the quiet contempt in Pieter's look.

"Was she innocent when you took her, Jacob?" Pieter asked.

This was worse than if he had raved and stormed. Jacob, flushing and uncomfortable, tried to speak quietly and honestly. "Yes, she was, Father."

"And you planned to make her your whore? The girl I brought to the house as a child, the girl I protected and swore to help? Did she struggle, or was she willing, when first you took her?"

Jacob held his head down. "She struggled," he said, in a tone so low it was barely audible.

"So you raped her," Pieter stated. "And I, thinking I was a father to her. And you, my son, raped her. And made her something to be mocked at in my own home!"

Jacob shifted. The fire was warm, but he was hotter.

"I suppose Rowan will be furious with me," he said.

"Furious? I think he would kill you, if he learned of it," Pieter said coldly. "That lad worships his sister. No, she must leave the house for a better job, with some woman who will protect her from—such as my son! I'll see about it tomorrow."

"No! Father, let her stay. I cannot endure it—not to see her again."

"But you would not think of marrying her," Pieter countered. "No, I don't believe so. You have great ambitions, like your mother."

Pieter's dry, dispassionate tone riled Jacob. He jumped up. "I am not like my mother! I am like you! You married well, you told me yourself, in order to give yourself a leg up."

He stared accusingly at his father. The older man seemed to shrink within himself, and to grow withered in his face. The wrinkles about his jaw and cheeks stood out in the firelight.

"I'm sorry, Father."

"God," Pieter whispered. "My sins come down on my head. Go to bed, Jacob. Tomorrow, you will start early for Virginia. I am sending you down there for two months or three, to learn how to handle the new explosives of the Vallette Company."

"Vallette?" Jacob asked blankly. All he knew of them was the insignia of their company on the boxes of cartridges and explosives he had used for years.

"Yes. Brett Vallette is a fine man. Hard and tough, but a fine man for all that. He is from a long line of explosives makers. His grandfather came from France, and had learned under some French chemist." Pieter waved his hand vaguely. "You'll learn of them down there. I'll give you the directions in the morning. Go to bed, Jacob. I'll tell one of the footmen to pack for you. Your carriage will be ready at ten o'clock."

Jacob began to protest. "But I want to speak to Molly, and help decide where she will go. Father, I cannot leave now."

Provoked, Pieter did raise his voice then. "You'll go

where I tell you, or leave this house and my company! Will you defy me, then? And you will not speak to Molly again in this house! If she is wise, and I think she is, she will not receive you again!"

Molly had gone up to her bedroom, crushed, humiliated, and beginning to see the seriousness of what she had gotten herself into. She could not stay, but where would she go? And Rowan would kill her if he learned of it!

Jane was still awake. She was sitting up in bed, sewing a nightdress. She gave Molly an odd look.

"How long is this going to go on, Molly girl?" she asked gently.

Molly shook her head, her eyes blinded with tears. "No more," she whispered. "Mr. Van Rhyne, he come in and saw us. He was that upset, I am fair sick with it."

She sank down onto the hard bed, and buried her face in her hands. Jane's face twisted. She sat up, swung her legs out of bed, and patted Molly's shoulders.

When the girl had calmed down, Jane said, "I've been thinking, Molly. I'm getting older and tired. And you never see anybody of your own sort. Young men you could marry, I mean. Let's leave here."

Molly stared at her in surprise, then wiped her eyes carefully with her apron and stared again. "You want to go? But where would we go? Who would hire us?"

"Well, I have a cousin, whose husband has an aunt," Jane said. "She runs her own dressmaking establishment. She has a big house, and rents out the flats above the shop. She is always looking out for girls who can sew. They learn the work, then marry and leave her, she says. We could go and see her on Sunday."

Molly thought about it. "Sewing? Dresses and hats and all?"

"Yes. She has a good list of customers, some fine ladies. We would sew on silk and taffetas, and lace, and all that. And she pays well, Molly, she's no pinch-purse. Five dollars a week to start! When I heard about it, I almost left here right away. But I, well, I was worried about you."

"Oh, Jane, you're a good soul, you are!" Molly got up and began to undress slowly. She washed all over, and shivering in the night air, put on her long nightdress and slid into bed, under the blankets. "We'll think about it?"

Perhaps tomorrow, Mr. Van Rhyne would not be so hard on her. Perhaps, with a scolding, he would let her stay. Her spirits began to rise again.

She waited all morning for the summons to his study. There was a hustle and bustle in the house, but she was up in the sewing room, mending lace for Elisabeth and Katrinka, and did not hear the gossip.

Finally, at eleven o'clock, a maid came for her. "The master will see you in his study, Molly," she said, with a curious look.

Molly jumped up eagerly. She smoothed her dress, ran her hands over her hair, and fairly raced down the long flight of stairs. Mr. Van Rhyne was sitting at his desk, waiting for her.

"Come in, Molly, and shut the door." He had a closed look on his face, aloof, and he did not smile a welcome. She missed that fatherly look of his.

She sat down timidly in the chair he indicated. He glanced at her, then down to his desk again, and shuffled the papers about.

"Molly, let me apologize most sincerely for my son's behavior toward you. When I brought you here, I hoped to protect you as your own father would have done. I am sorry, more than I can tell, that my own son was the one to betray you."

She went red, then the blood seemed to leave her head. She locked her fingers together tightly. "It wasn't all his fault, sir," she managed to whisper.

The sad look intensified. He suddenly looked his years and more. "Well. Um. That's all past, I think. Molly, you must leave. I thought to find you some other position in a household. Jacob has left."

It struck her to the heart. "Left?" she asked blankly. "Has he gone back to the railroad in the wintertime?"

"No. I sent him away for two or three months. You

169

will not be bothered by him again, Molly. Have you thought of some place where you would like to obtain a position? Mrs. Green was saying the other day that you had nice manners for a maid."

There was a roaring in her ears. Jacob had left, and never said goodbye. She was not to see him again! And she was being calmly handed over to someone like— like Mrs. Green, who was elderly, with three chins, and bossy, and particular. She would not like singing in the house, or put up with someone running out to go ice-skating with Jacob. But Jacob was no longer here.

She fought to regain control, to listen to what Mr. Van Rhyne was saying to her. She managed to surface after a time, and said, "Sir, Jane and me. That is, she knows a lady who runs a shop. She makes dresses, and she might give me a job. I mean, I might go on with her."

His face lightened; he looked relieved. The facial wrinkles disappeared as he held his head up and gazed straight at her.

"And you would like that, Molly?"

"Yes, sir, I think so. I like to sew."

"Yes, yes, you're a neat sewer, even Hilda says so. Well, take today off, and go and see the lady."

With the courage born of despair, she said, "Jane should go with me. It's her relations, you see."

"Very well, take Jane with you. Go on now, and see about it. Say you can start right away."

He couldn't wait to be rid of her! She stood up, and swallowed back some tears. He was bending over his papers. She started to the door.

"Molly?" he called after her.

"Sir?"

"I'm sorrier than I can say, that it was my own son!" he burst out. "You'll not think too badly of us—of me?"

"Oh, no. No, sir, you've been the kindest person I ever met in my whole life. I'm sorry I disappointed you."

She raced out, the tears streaming down her cheeks.

She ran to the kitchen, regardless of who might be watching, and sought out Jane.

"He says, the master says," she said feverishly, "we can go to her today, and see about the position—you know—" She was intensely conscious of the cook and a footman staring at her. Jane nodded, and got up from where she had been polishing silver.

They got their coats and hats. Molly scrubbed her cheeks until they were pink, instead of white, and washed away the tears. In the back hall, Mr. Van Rhyne met them.

"I told the coachman to drive you wherever you want to go, Jane," he said. "And don't come back until it's all settled. Take your time."

"Yes, sir. Thank you, sir," Jane said, taking Molly's arm protectively, like a mother or an elder sister. "It's good of you to let us go out today."

"The sooner set, the better," he said sorrowfully, and walked heavily back to his study. He went out to the office later, and gave all his clerks and managers such a hell of a time that they sweated and tiptoed around him.

Mrs. Hadley turned out to be a bright bird of a woman, graying of hair, with alert black eyes and a head cocked to one side like a robin searching for early worms. She knew her business, though. Her sense of style was shrewd and far-seeing, and she had more customers than she could supply. She hired Jane and Molly on the spot, for she knew Jane, and Jane vouched for Molly's sewing. She showed them upstairs to the third-floor flat, which they would share with two other girls.

As gloomy as she was, Molly could not help but be pleased. The rooms were tall and airy, with big windows in each. There was a sitting room for the four girls, so they could entertain fellows of an evening. There was a fine large kitchen, with its own stove and ice box, and a table for eating. Behind those rooms were two good-sized bedrooms with two beds in each room, rocking chairs padded with bright chintz, a large wardrobe for their clothes, and even a mirrored dresser. Mrs. Hadley treated her girls well.

"The hours will be nine to seven through the week, and Saturday you'll quit at two," Mrs. Hadley said, with a bright smile. "Sundays you always have off. But you'll mind the rules. No girl alone with a fellow; another girl must always stay to chaperon her. No staying out until after nine, no gadding about. My girls shall not get themselves a reputation! You'll fix your own breakfast and evening meal, and I'll furnish a lunch on the premises. Five dollars a week to start, and a raise after a year, if you do well."

"Just think," Molly said later, marveling. "A flat of our own. Can you cook?"

"Some. I learned early," Jane answered, with a pleased look. "I'll teach you. When you get married, you'll need to know how to cook. My sister says that if you feed a man well, you don't need to worry that he'll stray."

"I don't think I'll ever get married," Molly said sadly.

"Sure, you will," Jane said with assurance, patting her hand. "Warmhearted as you are, and loving babies like you do. You'll marry, watch and see. A girl as bright and pretty and home-loving—why, some man will come along and just sweep you off your feet!"

"For my cooking," Molly said, deep in gloom.

"Not yet. You don't know how!" Jane teased her. Molly managed to laugh, even though it was only a shadow of her merry laugh, but still she laughed, and she had thought she would never smile again.

They packed and moved out of the mansion on Sunday. Hilda was furious at losing Jane and another maid, though she was not sorry the other maid was Molly, who'd been a thorn in her side, as she had told Elisabeth. They had said nothing of the reason to the children; there was no need to spread gossip about their elder brother. But the children knew, as children always do.

Molly and Jane were moved to the rooms over the shop, and settled in with the other two girls, both young and spirited. The work began on Monday morning. At first, Molly enjoyed seeing the grand ladies sweeping in, and helping fit and measure and sew for them. But the days were long. She could not sing or prance about, or set her own pace as she dusted precious porcelain, or steal into Mr. Van Rhyne's study for a good heart-to-heart chat.

Her eyes ached at night from the fine sewing, and her slim fingers were pricked by the needles and pins. All the girls had to put cream on their hands at night, to keep from marring the soft silks and fine laces, or causing tears in the fine threads. There was a dull pain between Molly's shoulder blades from stooping over the sewing, and sometimes at night her head throbbed fiercely.

And her heart ached. She thought about Jacob, as she tried to get comfortable on the narrow bed and get some sleep against the coming morning. The other girls would giggle over their boyfriends, and sometimes Molly would sit demurely in the corner, embroidering or making a collar, while a girl spooned with her beau. To watch them hold hands, and sometimes exchange a blushing kiss—it made her hurt all over.

It hurt her, too, that Jacob never wrote her a word. Surely, he knew where she was! Rowan came up sometimes, to look about in amazement. "You are cozy here," he would say. "And all these pretty girls! I'll come more often!" He had accepted her explanation for leaving the Van Rhyne household—here the pay was better, she had told him, truthfully, and she was more on her own.

Nevertheless, he confessed his surprise. "I'm amazed you left the Van Rhynes'," he said to Molly, soon after she had moved out. "I thought you would stay all your life. They're fine folks, and they treated you grand! Just like a member of the family."

She managed a smile, but anger shook her. No, not a member of the family. A maid, of shanty Irish stock, and not one to whom Jacob should pay court! She had made up her mind that it was his parents who had separated them, and not Jacob himself. Had it been up to him, she felt sure he would have married her, for Jacob

173

loved her, and had said so every time they had been together. His voice had said it, almost in poetry, chanting verse to her smooth body, to the curve of her throat, to her small round breasts.

Yes, he had loved her dearly, she told herself. It was comforting. His parents had separated them, and it wasn't his fault. Oh, Jacob, when would he come back and see her? When he returned to New York? She lived with hope for a time, but the months went on, and still he did not write, or come.

He must marry well, she told herself, weary of heart and mind. He must marry well, into more money. Wasn't it money that made America go round, as Rowan often teased her. Hadn't she changed jobs to make more money? If he only knew—but she must not tell him; she would be too ashamed.

She had not even been able to go to confession. She could not tell that hawk-nosed Father O'Reilly about Jacob. She could not tell him what she had done. So she stayed away from church, and on Sundays she walked down to the park, and she and Jane looked at the pond and the ducks, and the folks strolling, hand in hand, and she had never felt so alone and frightened, not even on the boat from Ireland.

It was a lonely, bitter time, as she wrestled with her love and conscience. Jane could not help her. She was just there at her side, older, graying, and wordless, in sympathy, helping with the cooking and the cleaning and the sewing.

Molly missed the big mansion, even in her own flat with the three other girls. She missed Jacob's whisper, "Hist! Molly!" and his bright-eyed mischief as they stole off for a ride in the carriage, or a spin around the pond on ice skates. He did love her, he must. One day he would come back to her!

Months passed, and still Jacob did not come. He became a mirage, a dream, a dream of a prince, in a fine red robe, teaching her desire and passion and the fulfillment of love. In her dreams, he always went down on his knee, vowed to love her forever, and begged her to marry him.

She would awake, and find it only a dream. In New York City, a man married upward, not downward to the Irish maid.

PART II

1860–1870

Chapter 12

The hot summer nights in the flat were long, and often sweltering and oppressive, for it got extremely warm there. Many evenings, after dinner, Jane and Molly would walk out and stroll about the neighborhood, trying to cool themselves in the evening breeze, but they had always to return early to the flat, to try to get some sleep. Many nights the heat was so intense that they would toss and turn and find sleep difficult. In the morning, still tired and overheated, they would set off for work, and struggle through the day.

One of the girls married and left, and another girl came to work and live with them. When she moved in, she brought her sturdy brother to help move her suitcases and boxes, and he brought a friend to help him.

That was Evan McKenna. He walked into the flat, his arms full up to his chin with the girl's boxes that were topped with a hat with a feather. Molly giggled to see this nice, brown face with the helpless brown eyes, and she flew to rescue him from the tickling hat.

"Thank you, me dear," he gasped, and set the boxes down on a table, and gave her a long look. He had a brogue that could only be Irish, and his snub nose and peat-brown hair could only be from the Irish in him, she thought afterward.

"Me name is Evan McKenna, and what would your beautiful name be, me dear?" he asked.

She giggled again, her spirits rising after a long, dull time. "Me name would be Mary Cecilia O'Neill, but folks call me Molly," she told him shyly.

"Molly O'Neill," he repeated, and made a nice bow to her. "Pleased to meet you. And where would I be carrying these many boxes?"

She showed him into the other bedroom, and he took the boxes in and set them down neatly and tidily. He straightened up and gave a critical look about.

"The mirror is crooked, I see. If you would but find a hammer for me, I'd be setting it straight," he said. She found him a hammer and he set to work, not only straightening the mirror, but putting a few nails in the kitchen table so it did not wobble any more. Then, by giving it a little sanding, he fixed the cupboard door that always stuck.

"He's a handy fellow," Jane said approvingly. "And he's got his eye on you, Molly."

Molly blushed vividly. "Oh, that's fool talk," she said sharply. "He likes Susie best."

"Not the way I see it," Jane said.

He came up after work on Tuesday, to fix something for Susie. But, as Jane had predicted, it was Molly he asked to walk out with him the following Sunday. She gave him a dubious look. It was only the second time she had seen him.

"Won't you be going out with Susie?" she asked bluntly.

He shook his head, his peat-brown eyes serious. "No, she has a fellow, you know. And besides, I'm not courting her, I'm courting you, Molly," he said.

She felt helpless. Roman was farther west than ever, and his letters were few and far between. In his last letter, he had told her that Jacob had returned to New York, but not for long. He had been sent right out to end-of-track by his father.

"And we won't be working together this year," he wrote. "He's sent Jacob one way and me another. Damned if I know why!"

Molly knew why. She sighed, and put the letter, and some of her dreams away. But still she hoped that at the end of the summer, Jacob would come back, and maybe come to see her, after having had time to think matters over.

Jane urged her to go out with Evan. "He's a fine man, and a rising politician, they do say," she said, sewing on the collar of a dress. She made neat little stitches with her clever fingers. "He's a solid man, and going up in the world. And he likes you, I saw that at once."

"He's a lot older than me," Molly said slowly.

"Only ten years. He's twenty-six," Jane said, so promptly that Molly knew Jane had been making inquiries.

She finally said yes to Evan, and they began to walk out on Sundays. He proposed the second Sunday. They were walking down to the park, and he had caught her hand in his. She was wearing her new blue-and-red plaid dress with the little crinoline under it, making it stand out like that of the ladies in high society. Her bonnet was of blue silk, ornamented with a red rose on the top, and tied with silk ribbons under her round chin.

"Molly, I knew my own mind the minute I saw you," Evan McKenna said seriously, swinging her hand lightly. "I know I'm older than you, but you have a mature mind, and nobody to look after you but a brother who is gone more than he's here."

"I can look after myself," she said bravely, ignoring the little feeling of panic when she thought of being alone in the world. Now that Mr. Van Rhyne's protection had been withdrawn, she felt like a newborn babe thrust into a cold world.

"Why should you, when I can look after you, and long to do that very thing, Molly girl?" he said in his slow, calm voice. He had a nice rich Irish voice—the kind that could move crowds, she thought. He would make a good politician, for he could talk easily and calmly, or let his voice rise to emotional heights when necessary.

He was not tall, just medium height. He was heavyset already, with big red hands that held hers warmly. He had worked as a laborer for six years after coming from Ireland with his family at the age of fourteen. They were settled now, and his older sisters married. From laboring, he had turned to office work, and worked six days a week as a clerk in a railroad office.

He was smart. He had studied his sums at night, and

practiced reading and writing on his own, with some help from one of his older sisters.

Molly liked his brown hair, that reminded her of the soil of dear Ireland. And his smoky brown eyes, and the slow way he would smile, starting in his eyes, and going down his cheeks in creases, to his mouth, which broke at last into a broad grin. He was kind and comforting, and older, like a brother, yet not a brother. He was smart and shrewd, and he knew things about getting around, and how to get things done, and who to see about matters such as getting coal and food to the poor. And he cared about that, he cared very much.

At last Molly spoke. "You cannot be serious, Evan," she said, as firmly as she could. "We have scarcely met."

"I know what I want when I see it," he said, calmly, and let loose her hand to take out his pipe and fill it. Her hand felt lost without his clasping it. She watched him lean on the bridge railing, light his pipe, and get it going, before they turned to stroll on. "But I'll say no more for a time. I just wanted to get me bid in first."

"I'm no railroad contract!" she said tartly, and he laughed, his slow, rich, rolling laugh, and finally, she laughed with him.

They went over to the park, and she felt a pang at the memories of Jacob. But Evan liked to look at the ducks, and when a child rolled a ball near his feet he picked it up and rolled it back, with a kind look. She saw how he would be with children: thoughtful and kind and careful.

They stepped out almost every Sunday, when the weather was good, and on the rainy days he came up to her flat. He would bring a small tool chest, and go about the room, nailing up a shutter, putting up a picture, or giving some chair a new coat of paint, working slowly, thoroughly, his pipe between his teeth. The other girls teased her about her beau, who was so handy to have around.

"He's showing you what a good husband he will be," said Susie, a little jealous because her own beau was clumsy, and liked to give other girls the eye when they walked out. "But you watch out. What they do when they're courting and what they do when they're married, that's two different matters!"

Jane gave the girl a cross look. She was rooting for Evan, and she promoted him to Molly every chance she got. "Some as don't have what others have," she said sharply, "like to put down what others have, thinking to get the leavings."

Susie went an angry red, and shot out, "As though I'd have any leavings," and she tossed her pretty blond curls, and quickly became absorbed in looking over the designs for the new hats.

Autumn came, and Rowan returned home, feisty and laughing. He had had a great time, the work had gone well, and Mr. Van Rhyne had surprised him with a visit and a promotion. "He's made me a superintendent, Molly girl, though he did say I'd have to show more responsibility, and not be so quick to fight!" He roared with laughter.

"I hope you listened to him," Molly said anxiously.

"Sure, sure," said Rowan. "You know what? Some men think we're going to have a war! My men from Georgia say that if the North doesn't let up on telling them what to do , the South'll leave the Union."

"They'd never do that!" Molly said, shocked. Evan McKenna was brooding thoughtfully over his pipe, and Rowan was giving him looks, like a critical papa. "That's just talk in the papers, 'cause they don't have a crime to write up, that's what Jane says."

Evan said, "I don't know, Molly. The talk is getting serious. Some of the Southern states had their own Democratic convention in Baltimore, and have a candidate for President of their own. They want slavery permitted in the new states and territories, like Missouri."

"That's not worth fighting over," Molly said sharply. "Didn't we have enough of warring and fighting in Ireland? I thought in America we'd have peace and prosperity."

She looked from Rowan to Evan. Both seemed uncomfortable, shuffling their boots and looking grave. She hated the talk; she always flipped over the gazette pages quickly when she spotted articles about slavery and abolition, free territories, and the rights of states to decide for themselves. She did not think anybody should be a slave, but everyone had to work for a living, didn't they? The blacks in the South were treated well, people said, and as long as they had food and clothing, they should not come North and take jobs and bread from the mouths of hard-working Irish. She wished they would stay in the South where they belonged, and not bother others.

But Rowan was speaking, more seriously than his wont: "I've seen with my own eyes how some blacks are treated, Molly. They beat them with whips for nothing at all, and hang them from trees. It's a horror, it is, and no self-respecting man would put up with it. Slavery is a blight on this free country. We may have to go to war to convince the South they shouldn't go on like this."

"It's newspaper scare-talk," she said fearfully. "Isn't it?"

Evan shook his head. "No, it ain't scare talk," he said heavily. "I fear it is true. Oh, some stories are exaggerated, but some stuff, yes, it's true. I know that, for I've seen—" He stopped abruptly. "Let us change the topic. Rowan is just home, and probably wants a good visit with you. I'll be leaving, Molly. Shall I be seeing you next Sunday as usual?"

He got up to leave. Rowan's eyes sharpened. He rose, also. "Have you been seeing Molly regular?" he asked, almost casually.

"Regular," nodded Evan, meeting his eyes levelly.

"I reckon we'd better get acquainted. Why don't you stay for supper? All right, Molly?"

"Ah—yes, all right," said Molly. "I've got plenty of potatoes and bread and meat." She escaped to the kitchen to start supper, her brain whirring around.

In a few moments, Rowan followed her, and leaned against the kitchen wall. His tanned face was grave, his blue eyes sharp. "How much does that man mean to you, Molly?"

She said, not looking up from the meat she was basting, "He has asked me to marry him. I haven't said yes."

"I'll look into him," Rowan said worriedly. "He seems a decent man. But he's years older than you. You're only sixteen."

"Almost seventeen," said Molly. She finally looked at him. "And I'll make up my own mind, Rowan!"

"Sure you will, sure you will. But I'll look into him just the same."

"Has—has Jacob come home yet, do you think?" She tried to make the question sound casual, but it had pounded at her heart since Rowan had walked in the door.

"He's expected next week," said Rowan. "About this McKenna—folks say he's a politician?"

"That's right."

"He could do us some good, getting Irish people jobs in construction, and all."

She tightened her lips, and went back to basting the meat. Evan and Rowan did most of the talking during dinner. Jane and Molly were quiet, listening. The talk was of war, construction, ward politics, free soil, and the Pony Express, and how far the railroads had gone.

"It'll be years before we get to the West Coast," said Rowan gloomily. "You wouldn't believe the troubles. I've been in the Rocky Mountains; they're covered with snow all year long, would ye believe it? How can we blast through rock covered with ice and snow? Mr. Van Rhyne says it has to be done, so I guess we'll do it."

Molly was thinking about Jacob.

He came the following week, arriving one Friday night after work. He had just returned, he said, his face glowing with health. He was big and brawny and blond, his hands and arms burned teak-brown, his face bronzed, his hair almost platinum-colored from the sun. Molly feasted her eyes on him. Jane greeted him, and retired reluctantly to her room.

"I had to come up to see you, Molly," he said

quietly, when they sat side by side on the sofa. The other girls had gone out, and he was relieved to be alone with her.

"I thought you might write a letter," she said quietly, with no trace of emotion. "I would have written a letter to you, maybe two."

"I'm no good at writing letters," he said. "Molly—can't you leave this place? I'll get a room for you; you don't need to work. Look at your hands . . ." And he took one of them in his own.

She withdrew it slowly, sadly. "A place of my own, and you coming up to see me, Jacob? Is that what you want?"

"Yes, Molly," he said eagerly. "I'll see that you never have to work again. I'll take care of you . . ."

She shook her head, wanting to weep. He had never mentioned marriage, and now she knew he never would. "I like my work," she said bravely. "I like to feel independent. These days, a woman can work and not depend on a man at all, you know. I earn five dollars a week, and have the flat rent-free."

"But Molly, I want to take care of you, pay your way—"

"I'm not for sale," she said, her voice rising.

"Now, Molly, I never meant that. I only meant—"

Molly stood up, her dreams in tatters about her ankles, but her dignity intact. "I guess I know what you mean, Jacob Van Rhyne, and I'm ashamed of you. I may be only shanty Irish, but I've got me pride, and I don't need anybody to pay anything for me. I'll be saying goodbye to you now." And she stuck out her hand. Her head was high, her round chin stubborn.

He got up also, and shook her hand. Then, looking like a lost child, he turned and left, his boots pounding heavily on the stairs. Molly burst into tears and ran into the bedroom to weep into her pillow. Jane did not come to comfort her, but when Molly emerged later, she had tea ready, and encouraged the girl to sip it slowly.

Molly's tears had given way to anger. "Imagine!" she told Jane. "He wanted to buy me—not marry, but buy!

186

I never did think Jacob would do that," said Molly, sniffling into the teacup. "I thought he loved me!"

"Maybe he does, but his love doesn't include marriage," sighed Jane. "He means you no good. You'd best stay away from him, and keep him away from you. A girl has to protect herself."

Evan McKenna came on Sunday, as usual. He nailed together a load of cherrywood boards he had brought, making a bookcase for Molly and Jane. Molly set a vase on top of it, and thought it every bit as fine as those in the Van Rhyne mansion. But it was their very own. Molly's face glowed as she thanked Evan.

"No problem," he said, smiling at her. "Would you like to walk out for a time? I thought we'd eat at Mrs. O'Malley's boardinghouse. She's expecting us, and has a chicken on."

Molly tied on her blue silk bonnet and went with him. She was treated like a grand lady at Mrs. O'Malley's, where Evan roomed. There were curious looks as well, and from the way the other boarders acted toward Evan, it was clear that they expected great things of him. They called him "Mr. McKenna," and asked favors of him: to see about a job for a nephew; to find some more coal to help an old man through the winter.

He agreed, and wrote down the names carefully in a little black notebook. From the pleased expressions on their faces, it was obvious that they thought the deeds were as good as done. Molly watched him curiously, seeing this side of him, the solid, dependable man who could get action for his people.

She walked out with him later to the park, and suddenly realized that she hadn't thought of Jacob all evening.

"Are people always asking you for things, Evan?" she inquired, her hand tucked securely in his hard arm. She could feel the muscular strength of it, and it was reassuring.

"Only when they have need," he said absently. "Look how pretty the sky is today, Molly girl. As bright a blue as the sky over Ireland. And the grass as green as

187

home. Lord, do you ever think of home, now, or has this become home to you?"

She nodded. "It's home to me. When I think of Ireland, I sometimes think of the good parts, like the sun shining and the fields turning under the plow. But more often, I remember Ma dying, and the children dying from hunger, and crying, all that crying. Seems like when the sky wasn't crying, we were. And Pa dying—that was the last of it. The landlord came with his face all red and mad, and told Rowan to get out, and that was the end. He'd pay our way to the States to get us out from under him, he says. That's how I remember Ireland to this day."

"It wasn't so bad for us," Evan said. "We saw it wasn't going to get better, and Ma was sick, so we bought passage, sold everything but the family silver, and went on our way. Ever since, I've never looked back. Pa has a job, my sisters have married well, and the only problem is Ma nagging me to marry some fine Irish girl."

"Is that why you asked me?" she snapped, quick as a wink, and he laughed—his rolling, rich laughter that made people turn and smile at them, not knowing what the joke was, but sharing the warmth of his laughter.

"Now, Molly girl, you know better than that," he teased. "I took one look at your pretty blue eyes and your black hair, and went tumbling into love with you, head over heels, without being able to help meself. Never did a man fall so fast as I did, looking at ye over the stupid feather on that hat!"

She had to laugh also, thinking of those smoky peat-brown eyes gazing so intently at her. He squeezed her arm.

"What about it, Molly? Will you be thinking of marrying me? I had a long talk with your brother Rowan this week, and he's satisfied with my intentions and my prospects. He's your only relative, isn't he?"

"You talked to Rowan?" she gasped.

"Of course," he said simply. "I've been waiting for

188

him to come home, so I could ask him—you being under age, of course."

"But you asked me months ago!"

"I had to get me bid in," he said. She turned to remind him once again that she was not a load of lumber or rails, but a slow smile started in his eyes, spread to his brown cheeks, and down to his wide, generous mouth, and she laughed with him.

"Oh, Evan, you're too good for me," she said impulsively.

"How do you mean?" he asked, and she realized he had sensed that something troubled her.

"I'll tell you sometime—maybe," she said.

He said no more, but apparently her answer didn't satisfy him, for the following Sunday he took her right to the park, and started talking to her.

"Father O'Reilly says as how you haven't been to Mass these many months, Molly," he said.

"No, Evan, and I haven't been to confession," she said defiantly.

"Because of some man?" he guessed.

And she found herself telling him about Jacob, without naming him. She had been with a man, and wasn't sorry, she said, only the man didn't want to marry her, so she wasn't seeing him any longer.

She couldn't tell what Evan was thinking, for his eyes were shaded by his peaked cap. She fussed with the ribbons of her bonnet, and her voice became shaky.

"So you wouldn't want to be marrying me, Evan. I'm not a good girl—not any more."

He sat in silence after she had finished. She felt herself growing cold. He finally spoke.

"Do you still love him?" he asked, finally.

She shook her head. "He doesn't respect me," she managed to say. She was surprised at herself, wanting respect as well as love.

"You're warmhearted, Molly, and alone in the world save for a brother who had to go off about his work. It's not surprising that a man might lead you into mischief,"

189

Evan said simply. "If it's all over, then I'm satisfied. Could you ever love me, do you think?"

"But—but you wouldn't want—" Surprised, she turned to gaze up at him. His eyes were steady. He was hurt, but his gaze was soft and kind.

She almost cried when she saw how hurt he was. "Oh, Evan, I didn't mean to tell you all that . . ." She put her hand on his.

"I love you, Molly, and I always will," he said. "If you'll marry me, I'll try my best to make you happy. What do you say, Molly? Will you be engaged to me?"

She thought about it, and decided that being engaged to this kind man would not be a bad idea. He put his arms clumsily about her, and pulled her to himself. His mouth was cool in the autumn air, but grew warmer as he kissed her. "Oh, you're so sweet," he whispered against her mouth.

His arms drew her closer. He was sturdy and protective; she could lean on him and not fret, she thought. "I'd like to be engaged to you, Evan," she said, as he kissed her cheek and pressed his roughened cheek against hers.

"That's fine," he said. "We can be married in November."

She gasped with shock. "But I didn't say—not so soon—maybe sometime in the spring—"

"Molly, I want to marry you, and you've promised me. Why wait?" he asked simply.

And because he was strong, sure of himself, protective, and kind, and because with him she could forget Jacob, she gave her consent. Jane was delighted, and so was Rowan. He had worried more and more about his sister, as she had grown up and become so pretty.

Molly met Evan's folks the following Sunday, and felt like a part of his family at once. His mother was gray-haired and gentle, and loved to hold her grandchildren, rocking them to sleep in her arms. His father was like Evan, slow and drawling and sure, with a pipe in his hands, and a quiet smile at the babbling of the women, as he called it.

The marriage was arranged for mid-November. Molly went to confession and the priest scolded her for nonattendance at Mass, and she had to say so lengthy a penance that she thought she wouldn't have time to get ready for her wedding. But in a way characteristic of good Irish priests, he had been kind and understanding for all that.

The marriage was in the Irish church, and they invited Evan's family, the girls in the flat, Mrs. Hadley, and some neighbors. Molly was stunned when she and Rowan arrived at the church in their hired carriage. Carriages lined the streets, and people were jammed into the church, right to the doors. "Did we invite so many?" she gasped fearfully.

"Reckon they just came," beamed Rowan. He looked proudly at her. "You never looked so pretty, Molly."

She wore a cream-colored lace-and-silk dress over a funnel-shaped crinoline. Her bodice was ornamented with ruching of deeper brown. Her hair was brushed back into a chignon enclosed in a hair net, and Jane had sewn cream butterflies into the net. Her cloak was of light alpaca, and Jane held it for her at the church door, after she entered.

She walked on the aisle. The organ was playing Irish airs, and it was so pretty that it almost made her cry. Evan looked fine in his brown silk suit and white, ruffled shirt. He looked nervous, but composed as well, the way a nervous bridegroom should look, proud and happy. He held Molly's hand tightly during the Mass, and they took communion together.

It was as they got up to be blessed, and she turned around, that she saw Jacob. He was sitting in one of the front pews on the bride's side, and he had a dark look about him. Next to him was his father, Mr. Van Rhyne, looking handsomer than ever, with his large blond beard and his graying hair, his handsome blue silk suit with a gold chain looped across his broad stomach, and a high silk hat in his hand. They were the only ones in that pew.

Mr. Van Rhyne caught her gaze and smiled at her so

kindly that she almost cried again. She dared not look again at Jacob.

The great man and his son came to the reception in the church hall, afterward. Everyone was staring at them and whispering. They shook Evan's hand and congratulated him, and gave Molly their best wishes.

"I'm so glad you came, Mr. Van Rhyne," Molly said bravely, looking up into the hard, aging face of the railroad magnate. "It wouldn't have seemed right without you. You met us at the boat, and were so good to us always."

Pieter bent and kissed her cheek. "I wish you every happiness, Molly, now and always. If you ever need help, come to me; I want you to. But with Mr. McKenna as your husband, you won't need much help, for I hear he's a rising young man," he said, with a trace of irony.

Yes, Pieter had heard much about this young Irishman. The laborers loved him and looked up to him, and they might, Pieter thought worriedly, be easily led by him, when the time came.

Molly smiled, flushed and bright-eyed, her blue eyes shining with happiness. "That's what I hear, Mr. Van Rhyne," she said, thinking of the union talk she had heard recently.

Jacob shook Molly's hand, bowed his head, and kissed her cheek. "Wish you every happiness," he muttered, his eyes sad. "Katrinka helped me pick out a present. Hope you like it. She sent her love to you."

"Tell her I thank her heartily," said Molly, moved by that. "She's a good, fine girl." She did not ask about the others, and he did not speak of them.

Later, when they opened their presents, she was stunned at the grandness of what the Van Rhynes had given them. Mr. Van Rhyne had sent a complete set of dinner porcelain—twelve of everything. It was creamy-white, from China, with blue borders and a blue "M" in the center of each plate, cup, and saucer. It was almost as grand as the gold set the Van Rhynes had at the mansion, which Molly had washed so carefully after every dinner party.

And Jacob and Katrinka had sent a silver set: a dozen forks, knives, and spoons, along with a silver platter and a silver bowl for fruit or flowers. Evan whistled when he saw all that, but he said nothing unkind; he had no reason to question the folks who had been so kind to his Molly.

Everyone else had been equally generous; Evan had bought her a house, and his family had given them a set of furniture for the living room and the bedroom. Jane had given her lace tablecloths she had worked herself, night after night, after sewing all day for others, and the girls in the flat had given her napkins to match.

Others had given sheets, pillows, towels, pots and pans, so much she could not count it all. Everyone had been very kind, but, Molly thought, with her newly acquired shrewdness, they all had had their motives. They had given to Evan McKenna, who could and would help them with their problems. They were gifts from the Irish, to one of their own countrymen who was going up in the world. It was something to mull over in quiet times.

Chapter 13

When Evan did not come to bed by ten o'clock, Molly would begin to fret and fuss. Why did her husband have to work so hard? He always got up before daylight, even in the winter, worked his twelve hours, then came home and worked on his papers and notes for the greater part of the evening. She knew his work was important, with so many of his people counting on him, but she feared for his health.

She went to the sitting room and peered inside. Evan

193

was sitting at his desk, papers strewn before him, his pipe clenched in his teeth, though it was unlit. His brown hair was mussed and standing up on his head, as though he had been running his fingers through it.

"Evan?" She came into the room with her slippered feet soundless on the red Turkish rug that was her pride and joy. Evan had brought it home at Christmas, and she had helped lay it that very Christmas Eve. She had laughed and cried at the thought of having a fine Turkish rug in her very own house, and Evan had reveled quietly in her pleasure. "Why must you work so late, my dear?" she asked him.

"Eh? Is it so late, then?" he said absently.

"I heard the clock chiming ten."

"I haven't finished these bits of paper yet, Molly," he said, indicating the notebooks and pages before him. She looked worriedly down at him. He did look so gray and weary, and him but twenty-six!

"It won't do any good if you kill yourself over them people," she said tartly, to cover her worrying. "Sure, who would they go to if anything happens to you? Let Father O'Reilly help them, or the aldermen."

He leaned back with a sigh. "The aldermen can't help. Father O'Reilly is doing all he can. But when a man is hurt on the railroad, nobody helps him, Molly. Nobody. He lies there crippled on his mat, and worries he'll be thrown out of his house because he can't pay the rent. And there won't be enough food because his wife has no money to pay the grocer. No, it isn't right, it hasn't ever been right, for a good, husky man to be thrown away like an old shoe because he gets crippled doing his work like an honest man."

Molly perched on the edge of the sofa and studied him soberly. He talked more and more about these things. The workers had rights to higher pay and safer working conditions, and when they were hurt and could not work, the boss ought to provide for them. Mr. Van Rhyne didn't have to pay a cent to a man who got hurt. He just told the manager to put him off the payroll, and that was that.

"But what can you do about it, Evan?" she asked reasonably. "You can't pay for them all out of your own pocket, though goodness knows we'll help and do whatever we can. They are our own people, the Irish, and we have to stick together. But what can we do beyond bringing in food, and getting them a room in a relative's house?"

"The unions could do more," he said, leaning back to look at her in the light of the oil lamp. The flickering light brought out the lines in his face. He was young, she thought, yet he had lines in his face like Mr. Van Rhyne's. "If there were a union, the union could get together and make the railroad provide care for a man when he's injured. And food for the wives and children when he can't work. And if he dies, the union could get money for his family—something to live on until the children grew old enough to work."

"Why, Evan, who ever heard of such a thing? No one will pay a man and his family if he don't work. You have to work to live!" she said, deeply shocked and worried.

"Why shouldn't a company pay, if by their carelessness they injure or kill a man?" he demanded, as though he had been thinking long and deeply about this. "If someone sets off a charge too soon, and it kills a man, is it the fault of the man, being in the way? What about his wife, whom he loves and cherishes? What about his children? Should they starve and go cold in the snows, because someone got careless?"

"Friends and neighbors will always step in and help," Molly said firmly, shoving away the memory of men lying crippled and helpless on mattresses, their eyes weary and ashamed because they could not support their own families. Of men who died on the tracks they were trying to build. Of women old before their day, huddled in black shawls, rummaging in the garbage for scraps to feed their small children. "And the church helps, Father O'Reilly is always collecting for someone," she added.

"It should not depend on the charity of everyone,

Molly," said Evan. "It isn't like the old country, where neighbors would come and help plow the fields until a man is on his feet again, or his sons are old enough to do the chores. This is the big city, and there are no other jobs, there are no fields to plough, no cows to milk, no wood to chop. If you try to chop down a tree in the park, a policeman comes along and claps you in jail! No, Molly, this is a different society, and there has to be a different answer to its problems. For the railroad men, there has to be a union. That's the only solution. I've been thinking a long time, and so have others, that we must have a union, even if we go to jail for trying to form one."

"Oh, Evan, you must not talk like that! If you went to jail, what would become of me?" she cried in alarm. "I can still sew, but would anybody take me in? Evan, do stay out of trouble, do, say you will!"

He sighed, and his gaze softened as he looked at her sweet face. He got up, went over to her, and pulled her up into his arms.

"There, now, I'm scaring you with my talk," he said. "I was but thinking aloud, Molly girl. It's not your concern, and you aren't to worry your pretty head about it, understand? You leave it to us men, and we'll work it out."

His hand stroked her hair, and he drew her closer. She put her head on his shoulder, and pressed her face against his strong brown neck. He was so strong and sturdy, and so careful of her. She loved him so much. If anything happened to Evan, she would just go out of her mind, she thought.

His fingers stroked her neck, under her hair. "Oh, Molly, how did I get so lucky as to find you, and make you my wife?" he whispered. His hands were moving over her back, down to her hips, and he pulled her tightly against his hard thighs. "Let's go to bed," he said urgently.

That was what she had wanted, and she did not conceal her satisfaction as he blew out the lamp, and they made their way in the dimness back to the bedroom.

She took off her robe and slid into bed between the coarse cotton sheets, drawing up the blanket. It was a cold night in January.

Evan undressed quickly, put on his long nightshirt, and washed at the basin on the washstand. He was shivering as he slid into bed and reached for her.

She snuggled close to him, and his hands began to arouse her to sexual excitement.

She was so at ease with Evan, ever since their first week together. He was so natural, so kind and loving. With Jacob she had felt the first high thrills of ecstasy, and a little awe, for he was the master's son. With Evan, she felt more of an equality. He understood her; they had been brought up under the same conditions, they knew each other's backgrounds, and sometimes they thought the same thoughts without speaking.

She hoped they would start a baby soon. She wanted to have his child. He would be good with sons and daughters, and they would fulfill him, satisfy something deep inside him, and forge a link with the future.

His lips moved over her throat, parting the nightdress, and he kissed her breasts. His fingers were gentle on her silky flesh, pausing at the pink nipples, teasing them, then cupping the breasts so he could kiss them all over. His open mouth held the nipple, his tongue flicked at it, and she felt the mounting thrills inside herself. She held his head to her breast. One day, their son would drink from her breasts. She wanted that; she wanted his child passionately.

He sighed with desire, and moved to brush her nightdress up from her knees to her thighs. His hand touched the soft, moist flesh between her thighs, his fingers prodding softly. Somehow, from the first, he had known how to move her, how to stir her. He would kiss her, move his fingers, pause to kiss her again, and all the time his fingers were cleverly playing on her until she was aflame with love and passion.

He felt her readiness, and moved above her. He supported himself on his knees and elbows and bent over her, kissing her with more wildness. He kept control for a long time; he was a controlled man. She felt his hardness pressing on her, and she put her hands to the backs of his thighs, and pulled. She wanted him so.

"Now, Molly girl," he teased, laughing a little against her throat.

"Oh, come on, Evan, you know I want—" She writhed and twisted under him, her fingers playing on his spine to make him move faster.

"What, my honey-girl?"

"You know."

"Say it."

"Oh, you're a hard man, you are," she mourned.

His chuckle brushed against her breasts, and sent a shiver of delight down her body from head to heels. "Say it. Come on, now."

"Oh, I want you, I want you—"

"How bad?"

"So much, so very much—"

"Then, here, for a good girl," he whispered, and thrust home, and she wanted to shoot up to the sky in pleasure, it was so dizzyingly sweet and joyful, the way he held her, and moved, and pleased her and himself.

He fell asleep immediately afterward, he was so very tired. She lay awake for awhile, listening for the next chiming of the clock on the steeple down the street. She stroked his hair absently, as his head lay on her breasts, and his arm across her. This was safety, this was security, and more, this was love. Her man, hers, all her own, loving her as she loved him, in their very own house.

Yet his talk had disturbed her more than a little, and she could not put it from her mind. She brooded about it, half-awake, half-dreaming. Did Evan take things too seriously, worrying about other folks' troubles? Or was it true, what he said? Should folks in need be helped by their companies? Somehow, when Evan explained it, the idea did seem to make sense.

Then she thought of hard, tough Mr. Van Rhyne, and the way he got mad when folks tried to make him do something he didn't want to do. No, Mr. Van Rhyne wouldn't have a union in his railroad, she was sure of that. He helped who he would, and the others could go hang, the way he said it. It's a tough world, and everyone for himself; she had heard Jacob quote him on that. He had admired Rowan and Molly because they were spirited, independent, and hard workers. But what if Rowan had been injured, and crippled, and unable to work? What then?

It wasn't until midnight that Molly McKenna drifted off to sleep, a worried frown across her pretty brow. Her husband, the hope of the Irish workers, slept peacefully in her arms.

Rowan came over on Sunday after Mass. It was winter, and he was restless for the spring to come, when he could return to the railroad. He missed that wild, free life. He came over to see Molly and Evan every couple of Sundays. The others he spent with a girl, never the same girl more than two or three times, he said, with his wicked laugh, and the twinkle in his blue eyes. He wasn't to be tied down, not yet. But he took a keen interest in Molly's home, and enjoyed sampling her cooking.

Today he was upset about something. Molly noticed it the minute he came in, but she did not press him. During dinner, he ate in a quiet mood, quite unlike himself. He was usually high in the air, feisty and laughing.

After dinner, Molly was doing the dishes in the kitchen when she heard her brother's voice raised.

"And I hear that you're going to be precinct captain!"

Evan's voice was also raised. "Yes, I am, and a good thing, too. There's much work to be done."

"You may not last long in the railroad office, should you be dabbling too much in politics!" Rowan's angry voice replied. Molly wiped her hands, leaving the dishes, and walked back into the sitting room, her troubled gaze going from one man to the other.

"Did they send the message with you, like an errand

199

boy?" said Evan sharply. He had never spoken to Molly's brother like this before, and Molly gasped.

"Now, you boys, don't you be fussing with each other, and just after Mass, too," she said firmly, her heart quailing at the way they glared at each other.

They might as well not even have heard her.

"I can run my own errands," said Rowan furiously, red patches appearing on his tanned cheeks. "I just heard as how Mr. Van Rhyne was not pleased when he heard that you was behind some of the unionizing. In fact, he said, if you wasn't Molly's husband, you would ha' been turned off last December when you gave that speech in the gathering. Next thing, you'll be thinking of striking!"

"I might, should Mr. Van Rhyne not be reasonable about letting us organize. It's for the good of his own men, and he's always being praised by you for being so good," Evan said with a sneer.

"You'd best stick to your clerking, and let the unions alone!" Rowan shouted, striding about on the red Turkish carpet as if it were a railroad yard. He began to shake his fist at Evan. "You let well enough alone! Give the widows their coal, if you like, and see that the children get their food. But when you mess with the railroad, you've got a big fight on your hands, and one you can't help but lose!"

"Did Mr. Van Rhyne send you here to tell me that?" asked Evan, so mad he was purple under his tan. "You can tell him to take his fat ass where he can——"

Molly cried out at him. "Don't speak against Mr. Van Rhyne!" she cried. "He was good to us at the docks——"

"Yes, when his own foreman would have turned you back, for not being husky enough to work! And *then* where would you have been? Going to Father O'Reilly for charity, and finding work in the laundries!" said Evan, tight-lipped, to Rowan.

"Never! I got the job because I'm a good hard worker——"

"What about the ones who got crippled and can't

200

work? What about the men who are dead, and their widows weeping, and no one to give them anything but a kind, sweet word?" yelled Evan.

"They got to take their chances, like everyone else! It's a tough world, and those who can't be tough, well, they get lost in the—"

"Now, Rowan!" Molly said, troubled, her hands tight in her wet apron.

"You talk like that because you're young and strong," said Evan. "But watch. If you get crippled up, don't go to Mr. Van Rhyne for help! He has no use for cripples and men who can't go out and do his dirty work for him!"

Crack! Rowan's fist landed on Evan's chin, and Evan fell back against the wall. He was up in an instant, fighting mad, and he came at Rowan, taller and bigger than he, like a cock after an eagle.

"You stop this! You stop this right away!" screamed Molly, but knew better than to come between the two men and their flying fists. Rowan hit Evan another good one in the chest, and staggered him. Evan came back gamely, swung a hard right to Rowan's jaw, and Rowan blinked in surprise as he fell back against the sofa.

They came together again, tangled into a clinch. They were pounding at each other, and knocking the chairs over. Molly grabbed for the desk lamp and put it safely on the mantel. She surveyed them grimly from the side of the room, her fists on her hips, and thought they were like two street kids, kicking and hitting at each other.

Finally Evan lay back, panting, his hands raised. "All—right—no more—" he said.

Rowan raised his leg to kick him, and Molly said, "You kick him, Rowan O'Neill, and you'll never see the inside of my house again!"

Rowan's leg lowered to the Turkish carpet. The red slowly faded from his cheeks. He sat down in a straight-backed chair, panting for breath. Evan caught his own breath, then finally sat up.

"Well!" said Molly, outraged. "I do hope you have both gotten that wickedness out of your systems! I sincerely trust you feel better, having bruised and battered the only two men in my life I do love! I never in my life saw anything wickeder than you two, fighting each other over something so ridiculous!"

Evan looked sheepish, rubbing his jaw. A bruise had come up on his cheek. Rowan was scowling, rubbing his chest where Evan had managed to strike so hard. They glared at each other.

"And you two in Mass this morning, as though butter wouldn't melt in your mouth," Molly said severely, so angry she could hardly form the words. "And not two hours after taking communion, you're after each other like sworn enemies! It's enough to make the angels weep, it is, that such wickedness is here on earth!"

"Now, Molly," Evan said.

"Molly, you stay out of what doesn't concern you!" Rowan said at the same moment.

"Not concern me, is it? Not concern me? When it's my husband and my brother beating each other to a bloody pulp, and all for words passed in polite conversation? Now, you'll shake hands and say you're sorry, and mean it, or I'm getting truly angry with ye both! And I'm telling Father O'Reilly about it, no matter what! It's prayers you'll both be saying, on your knees for the next three months, if you don't shake hands now!"

Rowan gulped, then grinned. He stuck out his hand, and Evan got up and clasped it.

"That's much better," Molly said. "Now if I can trust you to sit down together and be decent, I'll be finishing my dishes. However, if I must remain and sit between you to keep you apart, just say the word!"

She went back to the kitchen, and heard the rumble of voices through a troubled haze. They had been so angry that they had come to blows, her dearly beloved husband and brother. Oh, that such things could happen! Did it portend something ominous in the outside world? Those damned unions, she thought fiercely. Yet

202

the thought of crippled Mr. Dugan in the next block, and the poor widow Annie Murphy and her two small ones, the woman not three years older than Molly and all alone in the world . . . their images rose up to haunt her.

"What would I do if Evan got himself injured or killed?" she thought, and shuddered. "Today, I could manage. I'd get meself a job again, sewing, or as a maid to someone. But if I had two or three little ones to feed, and was in poor health—oh, God, what is right and what is wrong?"

She brought coffee back to the sitting room with her, and made them change the topic to politics and the coming war. Rowan was sure it would come, and so was Evan. It seemed remote and distant to Molly, and something safer to talk about than ward politics and railroad unions.

That spring, both Jacob and Rowan went out to end-of-track, this time to work together again. "The boy is a good lad," Pieter told Jacob "but he's not ready for command yet. You keep him under your wing for a time, Jacob. He needs to learn how to control himself, so that one day he can control others."

"You're right about that," Jacob said, grinning as he remembered some incidents even his father had not heard about. "I'll look after him."

"Your mother wishes you would announce your engagement before you go," Pieter said casually.

Jacob laughed shortly. "To what girl? Has Mother picked her out for me? No, thanks, not me. I like my freedom."

"Katrinka will be marrying her man when you get back," said Pieter. "Seems odd, to think the third child will be marrying first."

"Elisabeth's nose is out of joint." Jacob grinned. "Hasn't she hooked her millionaire yet? I thought he was eager to get hold of her dowry."

"Now, Jacob, don't talk so." Pieter studied his eldest son with a troubled look. "I'm eager to have grandchildren, and you're the one who'll be inheriting the railroad, probably. You and your sons, you'll have to take care of it all. You ought to be thinking about marriage."

Jacob shrugged. "You'll have brats aplenty when Katrinka marries her Howard. They are crazy about each other." There was a cynical twist to his mouth that belied the sadness of his eyes.

Pieter sighed. "He hasn't much money, but he's a good lad, of good blood, and that Massachusetts family of his gave him a good education." Hilda was against the marriage, but Katrinka had held surprisingly firm. Sometimes she could be as stubborn as either of her parents, and she had loved Howard for two years now. Hilda had thrown many a young heir at her, and Katrinka had turned up her nose in distaste. She admired learning, and Howard was a lawyer, very earnest and bookish. Pieter didn't have much in common with him, but Howard pleased Katrinka greatly. And somehow, when the girl came to him and put her arms about his neck, and pleaded, "Please, Papa, make Mama see how I love him," Pieter was not able to say no.

Jacob was bending over a railroad map, pointing to a place on one of the charts. He seemed to have forgotten marriage already.

"I think we should try for these lines, Father. If we take over the lines from here to here, we would have control of most of the state."

Pieter nodded, and put his attention to it. The lad was sharp, and getting sharper all the time. They had added to the railroad lines, and Jacob, acting as his troubleshooter, would go from one end-of-track to another, speeding up the work, ordering the supplies so they would arrive when needed, bawling out the workers when they were too slow. Jacob was more capable than most men, thought Pieter proudly, though he was only in his twenties.

Jacob left sooner than Rowan, traveled by himself for a couple of months, then hooked up with the lad out in the West. He placed Rowan in charge of one of the teams linking up a section of thirteen miles, across a mean stretch. It looked even enough, but it was all shifting sand across the desert. Some of the engineers' pegs had blown away, and had to be resurveyed. And the water holes were so scarce that water was as precious as gold.

Jacob ordered eight men to go searching for water, and to bring it back in kegs. He hated to use manpower like that, but they had to have water for themselves, the horses, and the hard-working mules.

When the team of eight men came back one day, six were in the saddles of their horses, and the other two lay in the wagons, dead.

"Who did this?" Jacob barked furiously, his mouth a straight, hard line.

"Some fellows with guns. They said we had to pay for the water, since they owned it," one of the hard-faced railroad men replied. His gaze shifted uneasily before Jacob's hard blue stare. "Couldn't help it, boss—they shot Fred and Al, and had the drop on us."

"You came back without water," Jacob stated. The man nodded.

Jacob turned and surveyed his men. "I'll take twenty of you," he said flatly.

Rowan came along too, his eyes blazing with excitement. They rode to the water hole, having divided their forces into three groups, with Jacob leading one, Rowan and another man the other two. They found the desperadoes laughing and talking around their campfire. As Jacob rode up with his outfit, they drew their guns in readiness.

"You shot two of my men and refused us water," Jacob said.

"You an easterner?" The man spat between the legs of Jacob's horse. "You got no rights out here. It's our land."

"Your land? You never owned anything but your shirt and your gun," said Jacob. "You're the bastard son of a whore and a mule, and I'm taking that water!" He fired his pistol, knocking the gun from the leader's hand, and the others drew in defense.

Jacob tossed his gun aside. "Is there a man here,

205

brave enough to fight with his fists?" In a flash, he was off his horse and in the midst of them, his eyes half shut with the sheer pleasure of fighting. No thinking, no brooding, just a good, wild fight and winner take all.

Rowan's group had pulled up, and was watching from behind some rocks. He signaled his men, and they rode in with a wild Irish yell, right into the midst of the fighting men, scattering the campfire with their horses' flying hoofs. He saw Jacob fighting two men at once, banging their heads together, and laughing and yelling with sheer glee. Then he, too, was off his horse, his fists flying in every direction.

He fought his way to Jacob. There were more men than before, and it was about twenty to eighteen. A real gang of owl hoots, he figured, for they were tough, dirty-looking, unshaven, and mean. He knocked one out, and headed straight for Jacob. Jacob was toe-to-toe with one man, and knocking him for fair. Rowan saw another man sneaking up behind Jacob, a Bowie knife in his hand.

Rowan caught the man with his hand upraised, about to plunge the knife into Jacob's back. "Got ye!" he yelled, and they fought for the knife. They rolled back and forth across the dying coals of the campfire, and Rowan vaguely felt the heat of the coals through his jacket. Finally, he managed to twist the man around. The outlaw lost his balance and fell on the point of his own knife.

When it was over, five of the outlaws were dead, and the others had made off on their horses, riding wildly across the desert. Jacob lit a new fire, and counted their losses. Two men dead, eight badly wounded. They buried the dead, filled the butts with water, and went back to camp.

Jacob decided to remain at that camp for awhile. He thought the outlaws might come back, and one night they did, riding through the camp at three in the morning, flinging torches at the tents, shooting at anyone who might try to come out. He and Rowan were ready for them, and managed to shoot three from their saddles, leaving several others clinging to the pommels as they rode off.

They were all glad to see the end of that stretch of track. Jacob wired home, "Track finished," and the crew went to celebrate at a crude frontier town that had sprung up about twenty miles away, at another end-of-track. They drank whiskey, and joked and laughed until the wee hours of the morning. They were alive, and in that time and place, it was something to celebrate.

Chapter 14

At home, all the Northern states had been shocked and wildly excited when the news came from Fort Sumter that the forces of the Confederacy, under General Beauregard, had demanded the surrender of the fort from the loyal Major Anderson, who had refused. The Civil War had begun.

New York seethed with excitement. The Irish came to join up, answering the call from a man they all respected and honored, an Irishman who had fought in Ireland for liberty, been exiled to Tasmania, then had escaped and come to the States. Thomas F. Meagher, called "Meagher of the Sword," had rallied them to fight for the flag and the nation that had given Irishmen shelter when their own land had rejected them.

The ads read:

Young Irishmen, to Arms!

To Arms, Young Irishmen!

Irish Zouaves

One hundred young Irishmen, healthy, intelligent and active, wanted at once to form a Company under command of

To be attached to the 69th Regiment, N.Y.S.M.
No applicant under eighteen or above thirty-five
will be enrolled in the Company. Application to be
made at 36 Beekman Street, every day, between
the hours of 10 A.M. and 5 P.M.

Molly McKenna was expecting her first child. She
shuddered when she saw the ads, and she wept when
Evan thought he should go. She cried and begged until,
reluctantly, he saw that his first duty was to her. She
was glad that Rowan O'Neill was far enough away not
to become involved.

In late May of 1861, Meagher's Irish Zouaves left to
join the 69th Regiment, down in Washington, D.C.

In July, they saw their first action at Bull Run, and a
bloody one it was. Not only was the battle devastating
to morale, but it left many of the Irish Brigade wounded
or dead. The words that brought news of the Confederate victory gave praise to "the Fighting Irish," and the
Irish relatives of New York, Pennsylvania, Ohio, and
many other states wept, and took pride in their sons and
husbands.

Even the rebels praised the Irish. One newspaper
said, "The Irish fought like heroes." Another said, "No
Southerner but feels that the Sixty-ninth maintained the
old reputation of Irish valor."

The "fighting Irish" returned to New York, to a
hero's welcome. Many signed up again at once, full of
battle fever. The war might be over in a year or so, but
they wanted to be in it. With fear in her heart, Molly
watched the parades and listened to the excitement.

Rowan came home early from the railroad that year.
He had heard the news, brought by letters and the newspapers, and he had come home to enlist. In vain Molly
protested, wept, begged.

"Let others fight," she pleaded with him.

"Now, Molly, this flag has sheltered us in this new
land," he said, pointing to the flag in the park. "Would

you have me be disloyal to it? And to the country that gave us hope, when we was all but ground down into the dust of the old country? No, no, I'll fight for the federal republic that gave me freedom when I had none, work to do, and life and hope."

"No, it's the fighting and the rough life you want," she blurted out. "You have ever wanted to fight, Rowan O'Neill, and you know it. Fighting is your life. Why can't you settle down and have a son, and behave yourself? Four years older than me, and no serious girl yet."

"Not till the war is over," Rowan said.

They drilled, marched, and had parades, and Rowan was off with the new Irish Brigade before Molly had her son. The boy was born in November, 1861, and Evan named him for his grandfather and for Rowan, "Vincent Rowan McKenna."

Three days after his godson was born, there came a letter from Rowan, who was with the Army of the Potomac. He wrote, "We got all the Irish from the Eastern coast, canal diggers, track layers, railroad men and gentlemen, lawyers, cabmen, porters, and drivers. We got bartenders and waiters, and fine gentlemen in silk shirts. And we got *me*!"

Molly held her new young son to her breast and worried about his godfather. In the midst of her pride, she felt deep fear. Rowan was always so reckless and so wild. She wanted to write to Meagher of the Sword and beg him to look after her brother, and make sure he didn't dash into trouble.

"Now, Molly, you cannot do that," Evan said, torn between amusement and concern. "A woman doesn't write to the colonel and ask him to look after her boy!"

Rowan did write home, telling of the laughing in the lines, and of the pranks they played and the fun they had. He did not write of the thick Virginia mud, in which someone sank a flagpole for ten feet without touching bottom, where a team of horses would sink, and have to be rescued. He said nothing of the wounded and the dead, of his fear that their beloved general whom they trusted, General George McClellan, might be replaced by some stupid ox.

He told instead of the food that McClellan got for them, even the strange vegetable twist. "You put it into hot water in your mess tin, and you got a vegetable soup, fine as in New York," he wrote. "It has potatoes, onions, carrots, and all in it. Tastes good on a cold day."

Molly would answer his letters, asking him worriedly if he was warm enough in his house. "House, is it?" Rowan wrote back. "I have the finest tent in the land, room enough for half my body!" And he told about his buddies, and about how they had sneaked out one night and stolen a chicken to add to the pot.

Then, in April and May, she did not hear from him for a long time. The seige of Yorktown had begun. Then came the Seven Days of daily battle: Gaines Mill, Peach Orchard, Savage Station, White Oak Swamp, Glendale, Malvern Hill. Slowly, McClellan's army retreated to a safer position along the James River.

Washington seethed. Armchair generals were sure that Little Mac could have swarmed forward and captured Richmond. Gossip said he lived in a great white house, and fancied himself a new George Washington. The rumor was untrue, but scandal fed on it, and the gallant McClellan was replaced by a general from the West, Major General John Pope. The Brigade had seven hundred casualties, killed, wounded, and missing, about twenty percent of their strength. And they had had to leave their wounded behind, to be sent to Libby Prison.

"Now, will they see the foolishness of war?" stormed Molly. "All them killed and hurt and prisoners, and for what? Call them home, that's what I say. If the South wants to leave the Union, let them, I say."

Evan had about given up explaining the war to her. Women rarely understood the need for war, and the Irish women were torn between pride in their men and horror at the devastation of the Irish Brigade's ranks.

Then came the Second Battle of Bull Run, in which the Union forces suffered a terrible defeat. The Irish

Brigade was not much involved in that one, for which Molly sent up thanks, and lit four candles on the altar of her favorite saint, St. Patrick.

"Bring him home safe," she prayed daily, in the flickering lights. "Oh, St. Patrick, you know how stupid wars are, and what suffering they bring! This is a green and pleasant land, and Rowan was happy in his work. Oh, tell the Virgin Mary what suffering there is, and intercede for us at the Blessed Throne of God, and tell Him, oh, pray God, to make the war to cease. Wars is ever foolish things, and should never happen at all, to be sure!"

But the war went on. Pope and McDowell were relieved, and McClellan was put back in command of the Army of the Potomac. Little Mac set out in search of Lee, and found him at Sharpsburg on Antietam Creek in western Maryland. On September 17, 1862, they fought a fourteen-hour battle, some of the bloodiest fighting of the war. Both Union and Confederate troops were clever now, seasoned by a year of fighting. Their officers knew what they were about. And the stakes were high—control of Maryland and Pennsylvania, where Lee could cut the Pennsylvania Railroad in two, as he had already broken the Baltimore & Ohio. The way to Philadelphia, Baltimore, and Washington would then be left wide open for the rebel forces.

The Irish Brigade went in together, the three New York regiments with their green Irish flag, and the 29th Massachusetts, under General Meagher. They forded the Antietam River in water up to their hips. On the opposite bank, the men emptied their shoes and wrung out their socks, looked to their cartridges and their rifles, and wiped them off. Then they moved out to high ground, and a view of the battle.

The Brigade had as its objective a sunken road, no more than a farm lane, in which the Confederates were entrenched, sending out a terrible fire at the whole field before them.

Rowan looked, and swallowed the excitement in his throat. He let out a wild Irish yell, and grinned at his

211

buddy beside him. "Looks like they're ready for us," he said.

They charged, and a line went down, then another. With a wild yell, Rowan leaped up and ran forward. "Follow me, boys," he called. "Follow the green flag, and we'll wipe them out! Follow me, boys—"

A rifle bullet pierced his chest, and he fell, without a sound, onto the ground. Father Corby bent over him a few minutes later, and shook his head.

A week later, Molly went out for the post, as she did every day. "Strange," she said, turning over the letter the postman had handed her. "Now why would a captain be writing to me?"

She went back into the house and opened the letter. Her face went white at the first line, and she sank to the floor in a dead faint.

Her neighbor found Molly in the sitting room, out cold on the floor, with the baby crawling around her and whimpering.

The woman called for Evan, and he came home at once. Lifting Molly carefully to her feet, he carried her off to bed, where she lay for two days, stricken and silent.

When she was herself again, she read and reread the letter, until Evan had finally to frame it, so blurry had the ink become from her tears. It read:

My dear Mrs. McKenna,

It grieves me deeply to inform you of the death of your gallant brother, Private Rowan O'Neill, of the 69th. It was my honor to command him, and he was a grand fighter, to be sure. It happened on the seventeenth day of September, 1862, in a battle over the Antietam River. Your brother called out to his friends around him, "Follow me, boys, follow the green flag." I know this, for I was nearby.

He was a magnificent soldier and a fine Irishman, a credit to his old country and to his new

212

country. He will be a sad loss, for he would have had strong sons and daughters to give to our grand country.

My sympathy is with you in your grief, and with us, for his loss is grief to us as well. How often he cheered us with his high spirits. He was never cross, no matter how difficult the situation. I will ever remember his good nature, his high spirits, his courage, his honor. . . .

Jacob heard about Rowan's death, and it struck him hard. He went over to the McKenna house that night in his carriage. It was an early-October evening, with a chilling rain in the air.

He had been past the house several times, driving in his fine carriage, eyeing with curiosity the house in which Molly lived. It was a one-story frame house, painted white, with vines growing over the porch railing, and a brave show of red and white flowers in the small yard. He did not like to think of Molly there with Evan McKenna, but it was right, and he hoped she was happy.

He hitched the horse to a hitching post outside, and went up on the porch. He had heard the sound of music—a fiddle and some laughter—and had thought they came from elsewhere on the street. But sure enough, as someone opened the door, the blast of music was louder.

He stared at the bright, pink-cheeked girl who opened the door to him. "Is this the home of Evan McKenna?" he began, and Molly came up behind the girl.

"Why, it's Jacob Van Rhyne!" she cried in surprise. "Come ye in, Jacob, come in. Ye'll have heard about Rowan, then?"

Someone burst out laughing, and a group of men were laughing with him. The fiddle stopped for a minute. Jacob stared down at Molly. Her eyes were reddened with tears, but her smile was bright.

"I heard that he—but it must be a mistake," said Jacob, glancing uneasily about the crowded hall and sitting room. "I thought—but I am relieved that he is not—"

"Rowan is dead and in heaven," said Molly, her voice quivering. "He went down at Antietam, beside some godforsaken river, and who cares about the river now? We're having a wake for him, come ye in, Jacob."

Her hand on his arm urged him inside, and the rosy-cheeked girl closed the door after him. Molly led him into the sitting room, where a short, sturdy man rose up to greet him. Jacob shook hands soberly with Evan McKenna.

"Good of ye to come," said Evan. "Ye'll have a drink? The priest will be coming presently to lead us in prayers. For now, we're remembering Rowan and all the good times, and singing the songs we all like."

An Irish wake. In later years, Jacob would close his eyes and remember the scraping of the fiddle, the singing of the lusty, mellow Irish voices, the chatter, the smell of flowers in the warm, crowded house, and Molly's face—red-eyed, with tears coming down and rolling into her open, laughing mouth. Laughter and tears, singing and memories, prayers and warmth.

He sat down with them and listened. Most of the men were those who had worked with Rowan on the railroad, and he began to recognize them behind their Sunday best clothing of bottle-green, brown, and black. The women were dressed in their best cotton dresses or even silk gowns, with black shawls about their heads and shoulders. Molly wore a blue sprigged cotton dress, with a black shawl about her shoulders.

The baby awoke, and she brought him in from the bedroom and held him on her hip. He wore a red and blue dress, and his sturdy feet were bare, digging into her side as he held onto her, big-eyed and wondering at the company. Jacob put his hand on the baby's head, silky soft, with black, curly hair.

"A fine lad," he said awkwardly. Molly beamed down fondly at the baby.

"Yes. Vincent Rowan McKenna's his name, and he'll

214

be a big, strong man like his daddy and his uncle." She jiggled him on her hip, soothing him. "Now, there, don't be a-puckering up your lip like that." She laughed down at the infant until he cooed back at her.

The priest came and led them in prayers, then joined them in a stiff drink of whiskey, sitting among them like the friend he was. The memories flowed. One man told about working with Rowan on the railroad, and it brought back fine memories to Jacob, until his eyes stung with tears he would not shed. He thought himself of the laughing boy, flinging that stick of dynamite into the gamblers' tent, and he told about it, to their appreciative laughter.

"There, now, if that wasn't Rowan to the life," said one of the men. Molly had listened hungrily, as though storing all they said in her heart.

They talked, laughed, then sang to the plaintive wail of the fiddle. The old songs of the old country, Irish airs, the new, militant songs of the war, and songs of the railroad camps. The priest sang with them in a deep bass voice, thumping out the rhythm on the table beside him, his hawk's nose fierce, his smile gentle, as little Vincent crawled over to him and staggered upright, clinging to his knee.

"He's just starting to walk, and so soon," Molly said proudly to Jacob, as they watched the child. "Only eleven months, and trying to walk already."

"You're right to be proud of him. Such a sturdy lad," said Jacob quietly, thinking that the boy might have been his, if he had been willing to marry Molly.

They began to talk about how it had been, coming over on the ship. Molly told about how Rowan had worked their passage, and how lonely they had been on the dock, "until Mr. Van Rhyne come along in his fine suit and gold watch chain, and gathered us up and put us in his carriage. He took us home and give us jobs, that was how it was with us." And she flashed Jacob a wistful look.

Others told of their experiences, and how they had met Rowan, and he had helped them get a job with the railroad, or brought food when someone was sick, or fought alongside them. Little memories and big ones, all gathered around the green memory of the lad they had loved.

Jacob noticed that Evan McKenna, in the midst of all this, spoke little, but when he did, the others listened respectfully. He wrote things down in a little black note-book. Someone whispered to him that they needed coal against the winter. Someone told him of a crippled brother coming up from the battlefield. All this he wrote down, carefully.

This was the man his father grumbled about, even cursed about, when alone with Jacob? "If that Evan McKenna wasn't married to our Molly, I'd turn him loose and let him starve!" Pieter Van Rhyne had once said to him, fiercely. "Damn it, that man makes me furious! Does he think I can take care of everyone who ever worked for me? Damn it, people have to look after themselves!"

Jacob studied the lined face of the man, who was about his age, but looked years older, as he bent to hear the whisper of an aged woman in a black shawl. He noted the sympathy, the compassion, with which McKenna listened. He noted, too, everyone's respect for Evan McKenna, and he knew now why his father feared the man. These people looked up to him as though he were a god. Surely, they would listen to him, they would follow him, and they would fight for him. The Irish were fighters, that he knew. Just how far, Jacob wondered, would they go for Evan McKenna?

The priest stood up, went over to Molly, blessed her, and said, "Molly McKenna, you'll be coming to Mass on Sunday. I'll have a fine grand Mass for your Rowan, and he'll be singing with the angels that day."

"God bless ye, Father," she responded, and went with him to the door. His hand patted briefly the head of her son, and his keen old eyes were gentle on Molly as he smiled and departed.

Jacob took the opportunity to leave, also. He suspected that the wake would go on all night.

216

He went to the door that Molly was just closing. "I'll be leaving too, Molly. I wanted to pay my respects, and Father's as well. He wanted to get out of bed and come, but we would not let him. He's had a bad spell of the fever."

"There, now, I hadn't heard of it. Give him my best regards, and tell him to take some lemonade with a drop of whiskey in it—"

He had to laugh at her concern. "Now, Molly, you know he'll be taking whiskey, with no drop of lemonade in it. He's fevered, but he would have come. He respected and liked Rowan O'Neill, and it grieved him to hear of his death."

"Give him my regards, Jacob. And best wishes to ye both, and all your house."

"And my respects to your house," Jacob found himself saying to Molly, and to Evan, standing behind her. He went out, and shut the door. He felt cold in the open air, away from the warmth of the crowded Irish house. He shivered as he untied his patient horses and got into the closed carriage, draping the reins through the window before him.

The footman met him at the side door of the mansion. "Mr. Van Rhyne will have you come to his bedroom, Mr. Jacob. He wanted to see you as soon as you came back," he said respectfully.

"Yes, right. I'll go up."

The footman still stood in his path. "Could I ask, sir? We was wondering, how is Miss Molly taking it, about Rowan?"

Jacob sighed. "She's weeping and laughing about it, like the Irish do. They're having a wake tonight." He paused for a moment. "Her lad is the image of herself and Rowan. Tell cook. She was fond of Molly."

"Yes, sir. Thank you, sir!"

Jacob went upstairs, and down the back hall to his father's room. He reflected that his father and mother had not shared a bedroom for many a year. If he married, was that the condition he would find himself in, after some years of marriage? Not wanting to be near

217

one's wife, the mother of one's children? He could not believe that Molly and her Evan, their hands clasped tightly, and the baby on her hip, would put up with that for one moment.

He knocked quietly, and went into the big, shadowed bedroom. The only light glowed from the fireplace, for the lamps had been blown out. He hesitated near the bed.

"I'm awake, Jacob! Sit down and tell me about it."

Jacob came closer, and put his hand on his father's forehead. Lying in bed, the huge railroad magnate did not seem so formidable, and his jowled face was lined with pain. His hot forehead moved irritably under Jacob's hand. "I'm all right. How is Molly taking it? What took you so long?"

"They were having an Irish wake, laughing and singing, and praying with the priest there. I stayed for a time, to pay my respects."

"Tell me about it." There was a hunger in the big man's voice. Jacob found himself telling his father all about it: the baby on Molly's hip, the priest having them kneel while he prayed for Rowan's soul, the fiddling, the singing of Irish songs, and the talking of old times.

"Molly was ever a good girl," sighed Pieter, as Jacob's voice died down.

"Yes, a fine girl."

"Married a strong man," he growled. "Too strong. I may have to fight him one day. Do you realize that? We may have to fight him, over that damned unionizing. Foolish notion, but once the Irish get an idea in their heads, it takes a blast of powder to get it out." He sounded grumpy, but proud.

"We might have to give in to them one day," said Jacob, leaning back in the hard chair beside his father's bed.

"Give in? Never. A Dutchman is every bit as stubborn as an Irishman any day."

"You don't have to convince me of that, Father," Jacob said ironically. He was rewarded with a faint chuckle.

"So, Molly has a fine son," said his father, after a little silence. Jacob had thought he was asleep.

"Yes, a fine son."

"You should marry and have sons, Jacob. What about marrying soon? It would please me, and your mother, also."

"Which girl?" Jacob asked dryly. But he had been thinking of a beautiful girl he had met recently at a charity benefit. Antonia Townsend was the daughter of a diplomat, with smooth manners and a haughty disposition. But there was a twinkle in those beautiful, large violet eyes, and she was as slim as a butterfly, graceful and blond and long-legged. He had held her close in a waltz, and she had made his heart thump.

"Anyone you fancy," Pieter said impatiently. "Just pick out a good one, close your eyes, and jump in! You're getting afraid of marriage, Jacob, and that's the truth."

"Now, don't try to dare me into matrimony," Jacob said with a laugh. "You know I won't fall for that. Mother irritates me, pushing girls at me every time I turn around."

"I won't do that. But I'd like to see my grandsons soon, Jacob."

"You will. Katrinka is increasing and her child should be born any time, as you well know."

"Katrinka and Howard! Their son will be born in a lawbook if they aren't careful!" But his voice was drowsy. Jacob stopped talking, and presently his father fell into a deep sleep.

The young man tiptoed out softly, and shut the door after himself, nodding to the valet in the outer room. "He's asleep. I think he'll sleep for a while. Has the doctor been?"

"Two hours ago, but the master refused the sleeping draught," the valet said with resignation.

Jacob grinned, and went down the long back hall to his own bedroom. He pulled on his white linen night-

219

shirt, flung himself into bed, and tried to sleep. But somehow he found himself thinking of Molly, with the baby's tiny feet digging for foothold into her side, with her blue eyes glowing as he had made love to her, her soft, pink, shining body in his hands, under his own adoring body.

He turned over restlessly. He had no right to think of Molly in that way anymore. She was the wife of another man. But the warmth of that crowded Irish house, the emotion and laughter and tears, had gotten to him, and he found sleep difficult that night.

Chapter 15

The wedding of Jacob Van Rhyne and Antonia Townsend was a grand event of the year 1863. It even managed to crowd some of the war news off the front pages of the New York newspapers.

The bride wore a cream lace gown, imported from Brussels. It was tunic-style, with a tight bodice buttoned to the fitted waist. The overskirt of cream lace fell over a full, crinolined underskirt of white silk caught up with small blue ribbons. Her hair of blond silk, as the fashion editors gushed, was partially concealed by a mantilla of white lace that hung to her waist.

The reception catered to more than five hundred guests. Champagne flowed, and the tables groaned under the weight of turkeys, hams, and bowls of exotic fruits. There were such delicacies as shrimp in aspic, snails in their shells, and French bonbons. The wedding cake was eight tiers tall, and required a sword to cut it. The presents brought to the reception filled three long tables, and were guarded by giant Irishmen with pistols.

Jacob and his bride went home to a mansion, hastily built in eight months, near Jacob's former home on

Fifth Avenue. It had Corinthian pillars of white marble, lacy wrought-iron fences, and was filled with precious Persian rugs, ivories from India, Ming vases from China —many of them relics of Antonia's father's tours of service abroad.

Jacob had courted Antonia for a long, cautious time. He found that underneath her sophistication, she was spirited and lively. She was beautiful; tall and slim and blond, with a haughty chin that he loved to pull down with his teasing. Her violet eyes could be cool and distant, or warm and passionate. She was the only daughter of a diplomat, from a long line of Boston diplomats and ambassadors. She had lived more in Europe than in America, and Hilda was both awed and delighted at the thought of her new daughter-in-law.

Jacob and Antonia arrived at their new mansion and sat down to a late supper of champagne and sandwiches. The anxious butler and servants hovered about curiously. They thought it strange that their new mistress was bright with high spirits, not pale with exhaustion, after the church wedding and the long reception. Her eyes fresh and gleaming, she sat in her new drawing room, and looked about her with satisfaction.

"It turned out well," she said proudly.

Jacob looked at his bride. It had been a long day, and he was impatient to take her to bed. She had been coy during their courtship, allowing him only a few brief kisses on her lips or hand, never more than a quick, chaste embrace. Was she cold, or did that haughty visage hide a passionate spirit? Tonight he would find out.

"Toni," he began. "I think we—"

"Oh, please, no more nicknames! I'm no child now, I'm a married woman. Please call me Antonia from now on!"

Jacob's mouth tightened. Giving orders already, on their wedding night? Or testing him?

"Well, Toni, let's go to bed. I'm tired," he said, and left the room abruptly. She raised her delicate eyebrows and hesitated, her foot tapping. Then she followed him meekly up the stairs to their master suite at the front of the house.

Jacob had ordered a huge bedroom for himself and his wife, and another bedroom at the back of the mansion, like his father's, where he might work until late at night on his papers. Antonia's mother had not said a word, although she had supervised much of the planning. Evidently Antonia's father had had such an arrangement with her.

Tonight Jacob went right to the master bedroom, with Antonia trailing behind him. He slung off his long frock coat, dismissed his valet curtly, and shut the door in the maid's face.

"Really, Jacob, I need her aid in getting undressed," said Antonia frostily.

"Why? Can't you fasten and unfasten your own buttons?"

When Jacob's voice was like that, Antonia eyed him cautiously. She shrugged, removed the mantilla from her hair, and began to unfasten the buttons down the length of the lace gown. It took her forever. He was undressed and in his linen nightshirt long before she was down to her second petticoats.

He lay down in the great bed, under the huge canopy of blue silk, and watched his wife curiously. She was beautiful, no doubt about it, willowy and graceful, her white hands moving like lilies, as one beau had written in a poem to her. Jacob's mouth curled downward. Would the beautiful and wealthy Antonia Townsend have married the rough, tough, rather crude son of Pieter Van Rhyne, if he had not the wealth of the formidable railroad millionaire behind him? He knew she would not.

But he forgot all that when she donned the white silk-and-lace nightdress, and came to bed, her blond hair falling down about her, shining, to her waist. She blew out the lamps, and slid into bed beside him.

He moved at once to take hold of her.

"I thought you were tired," said the demure voice.

"Toni, damn it—"

She laughed, and he bent over and kissed her wildly on her pink lips and her white throat, sliding the night-dress down so he could kiss the shoulders that sloped so gracefully to her long, white arms. She sighed, and put her arms about him shyly.

He moved more slowly then. She must be a virgin, to be so slow and unsure of herself. He made love to her tenderly, skillfully, moving his hands over her rounded body, down the long, graceful thighs. She met his kisses with her own, her arms tightened about his body, and she quivered when his hand moved between her legs.

"Oh, Jacob, that hurts," she moaned against his mouth.

"I'll go more slowly," he panted, trying to draw back. His passion was increasing by the moment. He took a deep breath, and fought for control. He wanted to make this first time for her not too painful, not too bad. She was narrow in the hips, and he knew she might have a rough time of it.

He came to her again, after more kisses and caresses, and found her more willing. Her body moved under his, slowly, and he held himself carefully on her, not press-ing down too tightly, as he longed to do, to crush her beneath him, to take her mercilessly, out of hunger and need.

Instead, he remembered that she was young and scared, for all her sophistication. She had moved in smart circles, and knew the talk of the times, but in her own life she had been discreet. Her mother had seen to that.

"Oh, Jacob—" Her tone had changed, and was yearning, breathless. He pressed his mouth softly to her throat, to the rapid pulse that beat there. He loved her, he thought, she was so soft and desirable, so quick to fire up, to sparkle. "Jacob—oh, my dear—"

He pressed home, and felt her gasp and stiffen. He held firmly, and she began to relax as he soothed her. She had been a virgin, and he was curiously pleased and relieved at that.

The next nights were more enjoyable, as Antonia

learned the delights of sex, and Jacob became more sure of her. They lay abed in the mornings, and Jacob was often late to work.

They had no honeymoon. Antonia wanted to go away on a journey, even to Europe. But Jacob flatly refused. "Father is ill, he needs me on the railroad and in the office," he said.

"But I want to have you to myself," she pouted.

"You do, my love—every night," he countered, laughing, giving her a long, slow look as she sat on the dressing table bench. She brushed her hair every night, one hundred strokes, or the maid did it for her, and the shining tresses gleamed and glistened down her silk-clad back.

"But darling, why can't we go away for a few weeks, even to Vermont, to the mountains? We could get a cabin. A friend of mine has a cottage of about two dozen rooms—"

Jacob laughed. "A cottage of two dozen rooms!" he echoed, thinking of the farmhouse of his uncle Lars. "How plush!"

"Not at all. We would only need a cook, two or three maids, your valet, a footman, a couple of grooms for the carriages—"

Jacob burst into roaring laughter and rolled over and over on the wide bed. Antonia was furious. "You're laughing at me!" she stormed, and came over to pummel him. He defended himself easily, laughing and laughing, as she tried to hit him on his head and chest. Finally he pulled her down on top of him, and kissed her into silence.

Jacob had always worked hard. He could not imagine taking a long, leisurely journey, with no object in mind. Antonia, on the other hand, was angry that she could not boast to her girl friends and relations that Jacob had taken her on a tour of Europe, or at least to the mountains or the sea. She kept after him about it.

Exasperated, he walked out of the house one evening. He was tired from work, and he hated her nagging at him. He had said no, and thought that ought to be enough.

He went over to see his father. He found Pieter in his study at the back of his mansion, engrossed in charts and maps. Pieter gave him a keen look when Jacob walked in.

"Well, lad, how goes it?" he said.

"Fine, fine, fine. What are you doing, Father?"

"Looking over the maps. Our railroad is going well, now, all the way to St. Louis, and hauling freight every day. No need to supervise," Pieter said. "Do you ever think of expanding the railroad lines? Shall we start a line in the Southwest?"

They bent over the charts, and talked for more than two hours. There were problems. The Indians were attacking the lines, tearing up the rails, even trying to lasso the locomotives, though they killed themselves trying. The talk was that a line would be built west from St. Louis, to meet a line coming from Sacramento, California. Should they try to get in on it, or not?

They discussed the pros and cons. Pieter and Jacob usually thought alike these days, for they had worked together for years.

"The bankers are not putting their money into the lines," Pieter said thoughtfully. "They are a cautious lot, yet their judgment can be sound. This is a very daring experiment. What if we can't get across those deserts and mountains? We'd lose a packet. The bankers know it, and the great houses won't put a cent into the lines."

"The bankers weren't even around when you started building, Father," Jacob said dryly. "I think the industrial men have to go ahead when their judgment is that the venture is sound, and will work, despite difficulties. The banker boys will jump on the bandwagon when we get finished, as usual."

"Um," said Pieter, shuffling the papers. "I hear talk that some of the men are planning to form a corporation and shut us out, keeping it all to themselves."

225

"Then it *must* be a good thing," grinned Jacob. "We could bid on a part of the line."

"It might not work that way. It may be a giant corporation building the line from the East, and another from the West, or maybe the whole line will be owned by one monopoly. Our lines are going well. We've managed to sell or trade so we now have one single line to ourselves. If we join in the corporation, we might have to take partners with us to finance the new parts."

Jacob agreed to give the matter more thought, and finally went home, at midnight, to find Antonia stewing.

"We had guests for dinner, as you seem to have forgotten, Jacob!" she shouted at him as soon as he had set foot in the formal drawing room. She looked splendid in an ice-blue satin gown, with sapphires at her throat and ears. But she screamed like a fishwife on the wharf. "How could you humiliate me so? Lord Bottomly was here, and he asked after you. I had to tell him you were ill!"

"Why didn't you tell him the truth, that I had forgotten your little dinner party?" drawled Jacob, dangerously quiet.

Antonia picked up her coffee cup, fortunately empty, and flung it at his head. He ducked, and the cup shattered against the cream-colored wall.

"You bastard! You left me on purpose, to humiliate me! You think nothing of society, of the need to be a perfect hostess, of all the work and planning that goes into such an important dinner! Do you realize that this might have been in the society columns tomorrow? Now, we'll be in the gossip columns instead. They'll write all about the party put on by Mrs. Jacob Van Rhyne, which her husband didn't bother to attend, and does he have a woman on the side, and all that!" she yelled.

Jacob regarded her through narrowed eyelids. This was a side of her he had not seen before: this nasty temper, this uncontrolled display of bitchiness. It reminded him unpleasantly of his mother.

"Where did you get those sapphires?" he demanded, going up to her, and flicking his finger at her necklace.

She paled for a moment, then her haughty chin went up. "I went to the stores, where you are too busy to accompany me, and bought something that would flatter my gown," she said defiantly, her violet eyes glittering.

"Did you expect me to pay for them?" he asked quietly.

"You wouldn't dare make me take them back!"

"Don't ever dare me," he said. Deliberately, he unfastened the necklace and weighed it in his hand. "What store?"

"Oh, Jacob, you wouldn't! Please, I told Mama you bought them for me as a wedding gift."

"The house was your gift, as you well know," he said harshly.

"That was for both of us, not me!" she pouted.

He hooked a finger into one earring and yanked it off, then did the same to the other. She watched, her lips compressed, her violet eyes beginning to sparkle again with rage.

"I'll take these back tomorrow," he said very quietly.

"Jacob, you will not!"

"I will. If you had asked me to buy you these, I might have done so. But going behind my back, and buying such things—you'll never do it again, do you hear me?"

She burst into tears, and weeping loudly, raced up the stairs to their bedroom. Perhaps she hoped he would follow and, in bed, give in to her demands.

But Jacob did not go to the master bedroom that night. Slowly and heavily, he walked up the stairs, along the long hallway lined with precious tapestries from monasteries in Europe, and went to his own smaller bedroom at the back of the house.

Jacob undressed and went to bed. The sapphires lay on the table beside him. In the morning he called for Antonia's maid, and demanded of her which store had provided the necklace. Then, grimly, he took them

227

back, and told the store that his wife had no further credit there. He knew they tittered behind their hands after he left, but he was too furious to care.

Antonia walked softly around him for a few days, but her mother was less tactful. She came to dinner one evening, and tried to reproach Jacob afterward.

"I did not think you would be mean to her," said Mrs. Everett Townsend, thin, brittle, graying, and suave. She had handled diplomatic chores with her husband for years. She did not plan to lose this social battle. "You love her. Don't you want her to be happy?"

"Not to the extent of breaking me financially," Jacob said, in his most dangerous drawl. "I expect, if I go broke, she'll be quick to leave me. Then I wouldn't have a gorgeous wife at all, would I, Mrs. Townsend?"

She flinched, just a little movement of her chin, but he caught it. "You surely do not expect to 'go broke,' as you so crudely put it, Jacob, my dear boy?"

"I am not a *dear boy*. I am a man, who has been in business for many a year," he told her rudely. "And if my wife thinks she can go in and buy thousands of dollars worth of baubles without consulting me, she is sadly mistaken. She'll stay within her allowance, or be cut off completely. You can tell her that for me."

He stood up, dismissing her from his study. Her ears red, she returned to her daughter, to report the mission a failure. Antonia pouted and sulked, meaning to refuse Jacob her bed, but he did not seek it. Instead, he slept in his back bedroom until spring came, and he was able to go out to the railroads.

He found consolation in the work there. They had decided, he and Pieter, to bid on a portion of the road, and work on it with their own equipment and men. The hard work of laying rails across deserts and plains, in the blazing sunlight, with Indians a constant menace, kept Jacob busy and alert. He hardened, toughened to his old self again. In the meantime, back at home, Pieter was having his own troubles. Hilda was anxious for Elisabeth to marry, and marry well. But her eldest

228

daughter's bitter temper had driven off more than a dozen suitors, and Hilda was furious and concerned.

"Look at your sister Katrinka," Hilda said unwisely. "She has a baby, her son Philip, already. She is as happy as a bird in its nest! You need to marry before you sour completely. Marriage is the only life for a woman, or the joy sours in her, and she finds life stale and tasteless."

"Katrinka, Katrinka! She can do no wrong, because she married a student lawyer and has a son! Is that all there is in life, to marry some stupid fool less intelligent than oneself, and have babies, and hurt one's body, and smell the nappies all day?" Elisabeth sneered defensively.

"I'll speak to your father. Maybe he knows someone else to introduce to you," Hilda said, ever hopeful. "As it is, Frieda will be marrying before you!"

That stung, for Frieda was seven years younger, but of a sweet, gentle disposition, more like Katrinka and her grandmother than like Hilda or Pieter or Elisabeth.

Pieter flatly refused to have anything to do with the matter. "She's a bad-tempered girl, she is. I wouldn't have anyone but an enemy married to her," he flared. Already he had begun to worry about Jacob and Antonia. He had approved that match, and it had been a mistake. The girl was a nagging female like Hilda. No wonder Jacob had hurried West.

Hilda cried and wept until Pieter could stand it no longer. One day, he packed his things and moved out. He was in his fifties; he supposed he should not act like a lad half his age, but he had had enough. He had bought a fine apartment building near to Sunny Malone. Now he moved out, taking with him his valet and his footman, two grooms, and his favorite carriages. He stabled the horses and carriages behind the building, and took over two of the apartments, on the first and second floors.

New York seethed delightedly with the scandal. Mr. Pieter Van Rhyne had left his wife! Elisabeth was so overcome with humiliation that when an elderly widower in his late forties, with grown children and a handsome house, and one hundred thousand dollars a year, proposed to her, she accepted at once. She was married and out of the house before Jacob had even returned from the West.

Pieter went over to see Sunny Malone. "I suppose I was at fault, Sunny," he said gloomily, in the sitting room of her bright apartment. He stretched out his aging legs on her plush hassock, and sighed with relief. "She would never have married that elderly idiot if I had been home."

"Now, Pieter, you can't blame yourself," she said briskly. "Elisabeth had some fine suitors; I read about them in the newspapers. But she has soured, and maybe this marriage will be good for her. He seemed devoted to her, from what you said."

"Old enough to be her father," Pieter sighed. "Doting on her, fondling her. He couldn't keep his hands off her at the reception. Graying and stooped, and one of his sons her age! It's sickening!"

Paul knocked lightly on the outer door, and let himself in. He had his own apartment now, and carried his black doctor's bag with him. He had matured, and was bigger and huskier than he had looked like he would be, when he was a young lad. His blue eyes smiled affectionately at Pieter, and he came over and kissed his father on the cheek.

"How are you, Papa?"

"Good, fairly good, Paul, how are you?"

The young doctor's keen gaze took in the graying cheeks, the sagging jowls, the thick limbs up on the hassock. "Have you had a checkup recently? Did you get over the pneumonia last winter with no chest pains?"

"Don't, not now," Sunny urged quietly.

Pieter mock-scowled at him. "Don't play the doctor with me, young man! I came here to forget my troubles."

Paul laughed and went out to the kitchen, to bring back a tray of tea and a bottle of wine. He served them with his usual deftness, and sat back to savor the wine himself.

"How are Jacob and Antonia getting along now?" Paul asked.

Sunny gave an obvious sigh and Pieter shook his head. "I was telling your mother, they get along like cats and dogs. Jacob has not even written, and doesn't know he's to have a child in November. If he doesn't come back, I may have to go out West myself and drag him back by the collar. Antonia's so upset that her mother wonders if she'll bring the baby to term."

There was silence in the apartment. "I miss Rowan O'Neill," Paul said abruptly, into the silence. "The good, hearty, laughing lad. Dead in the mud down there, and for what? All that fighting spirit, and dead of a bullet. It sickens me, it does."

How is Molly taking it?"

Pieter shrugged. "She misses him. She had a picture of him made by an artist, and has it hung like a shrine in her living room. But that wee son of hers takes up her time and energy, and Evan takes her out every Sunday to the park. He's a good man, with crazy ideas in his head. Wants to look after every poor, crippled sod in the country, and have me pay for it."

Paul and Sunny exchanged a quick look. "I've been working with Evan McKenna," said Paul presently. "I look over his charity cases and prescribe for them. I help get them medicines. Most of them are undernourished, and the women have too many children. When their men are hurt and killed, they have nothing to fall back on. We might *have* to have unions one day, to help pay for the widows and orphans, just like after a war."

"Unions!" snorted Pieter, sitting up straight. "Don't say that word to me, young man!"

"They will come, Papa, for they are needed to help correct the injustices of our society," Paul said, with his own sweet stubbornness.

Sunny hastily changed the subject, and quieted Pieter down. But he brooded over his son's words for many a week, and many a month.

231

Jacob returned from the West. He was stunned and shocked to find Antonia seven months pregnant. She was sullen with him, hating him for abandoning her at that time.

"But I didn't know about it," he tried to say.

"You didn't stay to find out," she said, sticking out her lower lip in an unpleasant imitation of her father, who made the same face when he was baffled.

He tried to pamper her. He stayed out of her path when she was cross, and he left her with her maid at night. But his temper was sorely tried, again and again, before she was finally put to bed in November, and bore him a son.

At first, Jacob did not want to see the child. He had to muster up all his courage to walk the stairs to the nursery where his tiny son lay sleeping. He opened the door slowly, looked around at the pale blue room, and then at the crib, draped with silk and lace. He walked over and gazed down into the red crumpled, sleeping face, and felt a surge of almost terrifyingly deep emotion. His son!

Antonia wanted the boy named for her father. But by this time, Jacob disliked her father so much that he refused to name his son for that man. They compromised on her grandfather Errol, and on Jacob's uncle Lars, whom even Antonia could not dislike. Errol Lars was baptized in late November of 1864.

Jacob stayed home much of that winter. He would sneak up to the nursery when he was sure Antonia was away from home—which she was, much of the time. She adored the social round, and had missed it when she was with child. Jacob refused to be drawn into it. He thought it an atrocious waste of time, sitting around long dining tables with cads, flirts, European princes, and nobility from China, as Jacob told her in a rash moment.

He would say he had some business to attend to, then steal back home when he was sure that the carriages carrying Antonia and her mother had departed. Then he would go up to the nursery, sit down in a rocking chair, and hold his son, wondering at the bright blue eyes and firm chin. He became adept at giving Errol his bottle. When he was finished, Errol would give him a milky, sleepy grin, and Jacob's heart would turn over in his chest. His son. His son! Errol soon came to know his father, and would crow in his crib and hold up his little arms for him when Jacob stepped inside the door.

When the lad was a bit older, Jacob bundled him up and took him out to visit Sunny Malone. Antonia knew nothing of these visits, for if she had, she would have been horrified. But Jacob had long ago come to think of Sunny as his mother, and of Paul as a brother. Sunny adored little Errol. She held him and rocked him, holding him to her breast, smiling down at him. Then Paul came in, and they had a good visit, as in the old days.

"What will you do this spring, Jacob?" Paul asked, setting down his black bag near his chair, on one wintry day. "Go out West again?"

"Probably," Jacob said reluctantly, looking at Errol cooing in Sunny's arms. "Hate to leave the little fellow, but he is too little to take along!"

"Take along!" echoed Sunny. "I should say so. You wouldn't do such a fool thing, Jacob."

"He is teasing you, Mother," smiled Paul.

"Maybe now. But one day he'll come with me, on the rails. He's going to be smart and learn from the ground up, the way I did with Father. He's going to be with me, and work with me, and learn the business and inherit it all," Jacob said proudly. "You ought to get married, Paul, and have a son. It's worth it, the fighting and all."

His face had shadowed when he said this, and Sunny shook her head sadly. She would not say one word against Antonia, but she devoured the newspapers and read between the lines. That girl wanted social success, and would sacrifice everything for it, even her husband. Jacob deserved better than that, she thought, looking at him as he bent over his small son, holding out his hand so the baby could catch hold of one of his fingers in his little fist.

Jacob took the baby from her, wrapped the blankets

233

about him, and went down to the waiting carriage. "That's the way it's going to be, my boy," he said, softly, into the baby's ear. "That's the way of it. You and me against the world. We can lick them all!"

On the way home, he stopped by his father's quarters. Often, Jacob would find the old man with Sunny Malone, but today, she had told him, he was working at home, on some important business.

"What have you got there?" Pieter exclaimed, opening the door with a beaming grin. Jacob leaned over and put the boy in his arms. "Well, now, if that lad isn't the image of you when you were a baby, Jacob!"

"Is he now?" Jacob asked with interest. He watched the great railroad man rock and sing the child to sleep, then place him gently in the tiny crib he kept for his grandson.

"What's this important business you're about?" Jacob asked, when they were settled comfortably in the drawing room, drinks in hand. "Thinking more about the lines to the Pacific?"

"Thinking about financing them with other folks' money," said Pieter. "How would you like to go to England with me?" he asked suddenly.

"England?" Jacob laughed, then realized his father was serious. "What's in England?"

"Bankers and money, and investments to make, while we're at war," Pieter said.

"The English invested heavily in the South, and have only notes for it," said Jacob. "Now with the South losing the war, the English won't be in a mood to invest more in America."

"Ah." Pieter waved his finger in the air. "That's the point. They are taking a licking in the bonds for the South. They'll never get their money back. But railroads are out West, and our own bankers are too cowardly to back them. What's to stop us from looking into the matter of *foreign* investments in the rails? It might give us a headstart on shares in the Pacific railroad."

"Go on," Jacob said thoughtfully. He was beginning to see the old man's point.

"I confess I don't like it that some of our stock is already in other hands. We had to sell some of it in order to finance the line to St. Louis. But if we can get money from England, we might use it to buy back *all* our own stock, and run things ourselves, the way we did before. Then, with the rest of the money, we can pledge our own stock, and still build the line in Maine that we talked about."

"You're a cunning old fox," Jacob said, with a grin, and poured them more drinks. "To England," he toasted. Privately, he was already thinking of Antonia. If she found out he was going to England without her, and on business, she'd rave and yell! It would be wise not to tell her until the deed was done.

Chapter 16

Jacob and Pieter left for England the first of March, 1865. Jacob wanted to be able to return in time to make a good start out West, in case they decided to bid on a portion of the intercontinental railroad.

Antonia found out, a few weeks before, that Jacob was going to England. She stormed into his study, where he pored over charts and papers.

"I found out you are going to England, Jacob," she cried out, standing with her hands on her slim hips, like a peasant wife—not at all like the aristocrat she was supposed to be. She glared at him. "I'm coming with you! I have longed to go again, and visit my many friends there."

"Who told you?" he asked abruptly, glancing up at her.

"Mother said she heard it from a gentleman of your father's acquaintance. The humiliation of it, to learn such news about one's own husband—"

"If you stayed home more, I might have told you," he said coldly. They had not slept together since Errol's birth. She made it clear that she was punishing him for deserting her during her pregnancy. Oddly, it mattered little to Jacob. He did not care to sleep with Antonia. He had lost all interest in her.

"I'll tell my maid to start packing at once. How long will we be gone?" she asked eagerly, her irritation with him overwhelmed by her desire to go to Europe.

"I'm going on business, and you are not invited," he said shortly, and looked down at his papers once more.

She drew a deep breath, and began shouting at him. "Jacob, you must take me with you! You must! I will not endure being ignored and set aside, like some poor, dumb wife—"

"I have work to do, Antonia. Please leave my study."

She refused. He got up, took her by the arm, and dragged her out of his study, locking the door against her. She became hysterical, and her maid had to put her to bed and send for the doctor.

She kept after him all the next week. Fortunately, the trip was near, and he kept out of her path as much as possible. Her mother tried to intervene, and received a few harsh words from Jacob for her trouble. She reported back to her husband, "Why, he is nothing but a boor of the worst sort! It was a mistake to allow Antonia to marry that—that Dutch peasant!"

"You wanted the marriage, for his money," her husband coolly replied. Out of diplomatic circles, he was not always discreet.

"You are crude," she told him frigidly, her eyes blazing. "I thought he would be good and kind to her."

"You told me he adored her so much he would pay anything for her foibles. And we wouldn't have such a drain on our own finances," said Mr. Townsend, adjusting his black tie to a nicety. "So he turned out *not* to be a drooling idiot who would let her run through all his money in a few years. I admire him for it."

They did not speak to each other, except for polite exchanges before company, for nearly a month.

Meanwhile, Jacob and Pieter were aboard a luxury liner to England. They wondered at the pleasures of first class. There were red plush carpets on the stairs, marble walls, paintings of nudes that were lighted and not hidden, as Pieter said. "Do you think this would go in polite company?" Pieter asked, standing before a scene of naked women lying on a grassy plot with dressed gentlemen lounging beside them, champagne glasses in hand. "I might get one for my drawing room, but what would folks say?"

"They'd say what they thought, you know that, Father!" Jacob laughed, giving one nude a second look. It reminded him of Molly O'Neill, all pink flesh and plumpness, with glossy dark hair and turquoise-blue eyes.

They discovered some gentlemen with interests similar to their own. Among them were several Britishers, returning to London. Before they docked, they arranged to stay at the home of one of them in London, while the gentleman, a duke, retired to his country home.

Jacob had also struck up an acquaintance with a burly, tweedy gentleman who strolled the decks at dawn, as Jacob did. They would see each other, nod, and stroll on their separate ways. Then, one day, they struck up a conversation, over a match for Jacob's pipe. They talked for a time, and the tweedy man deigned to speak of his interest in railroads.

Two mornings later, the tweedy man managed to convey the idea that he had built the railroad from Birmingham to London. After that, he and Jacob talked every morning. Jacob introduced him to Pieter, and by the end of the ocean voyage they had an invitation to tour his line.

Tweedy, as his friends called him, had not intended to remain in London, but he found he enjoyed the company of Jacob and his father. They had so much to talk about, the three of them. Tweedy introduced them not only to other railroad and steel and iron men, but also to some attractive women, or "bits of fluff," as he called them.

Jacob had a fine time, returning at three in the morning, more often than not.

Pieter said grumpily one morning, "You're not sticking to business, Jacob."

Jacob shrugged, and drank his tea with a grimace. English tea was bearable; their coffee was not. He rubbed his unshaven cheeks and yawned. "I haven't had a woman for a year, Father," he said. "Antonia's temper is too sharp for me."

"She's too much like Hilda," Pieter sighed. "Looked so different, but the same damned temper. Where do you find a sweet woman these days? What did Antonia say when you left?"

Jacob grinned. "I didn't wait to find out. I sneaked out before daylight."

"At least you have a fine son," Pieter said.

Jacob nodded, in silence. He did miss Errol. He wondered if the little fellow missed him, or if the nurse soothed him and gave him his bottle, and hugged him so that he didn't notice his father was gone.

Tweedy took them to the theater one night. Next to them, in an elaborate crimson box, sat a beautiful lady, her blond hair piled high atop her head. She was in her late thirties, Jacob judged, but well-preserved. She was well-built, with a large bust, large hips, and a tiny waist that a man's hands could have spanned. She wore diamonds in her hair and at her throat. And she gave Pieter an interested look.

Pieter sat up straighter. Out of the corner of his mouth, he muttered to Tweedy, "Is she giving me the eye, or don't the English ladies act the same as Americans?"

Tweedy noticed the direction of his gaze. "Oh, that one. She's Lady Philippa Rawlings," he said, as though that explained everything.

"And so?"

"Her husband always ran around. After she gave him three sons, and put them in school, she began doing the same. Sauce for the gander, what? He couldn't say much, having a mistress in London and one back home.

She's choosy, though. You are most fortunate, Mr. Van Rhyne. Yes, she *is* giving you the eye, as you say." He gave her a thoughtful look. "I expect, if you send her a bunch of flowers and a diamond bracelet, you could have her."

Pieter snorted. "Diamonds indeed!"

But he lay awake that night, thinking about the very beautiful Lady Rawlings. In the morning, he went to a nearby florist, and had a huge mass of early spring flowers and roses sent to her. Pieter was amazed to find that the florist knew her address at once.

That afternoon, he received a beautiful note from her, in a black copperplate hand: "Lady Philippa Rawlings acknowledges your kind gift with gratitude, and wishes you would come to tea on Thursday next."

"What the hell is Thursday next?" growled Pieter, rummaging around in the huge mahogany desk for a calendar. Jacob picked up the note and read it with interest and a grin.

"What are you up to, Father?" he mocked. "Did you send her diamonds?"

"Hell, no, I sent flowers. I don't pay in advance for anything!"

Jacob roared with laughter, and kidded him about it. But on Thursday, Pieter dressed carefully in his new gray silk suit, black spats, and flowered silk waistcoat, and took his beaver top hat in hand. His side whiskers had been beautifully brushed by his valet, and his blond-gray hair shone.

When Pieter came home, Jacob questioned him avidly.

"I drank gallons of tea, my boy, gallons of tea," groaned Pieter. "And I asked *her* to come to tea on Sunday. She said she would, cuss it. I wonder if the housekeeper could slip me some brandy in my tea-cup?"

"Were you among many suitors?" Jacob asked curiously.

"No. Nobody was there but a deaf old aunt of hers who went to sleep halfway through our talk."

"Is she willing?"

Pieter grimaced. "Damned if I know. The English are so cussed polite, I wonder if they really do anything in bed? We talked about America, and society—about which I know nothing. We talked about railroads, and she wanted to know if I'd ever shot any Indians. I said she'd have to talk to you about that, since you were the one who went out shooting Indians. So she wants to meet you, too."

"At tea—on Sunday?" grinned Jacob. "Do you mind if I cut you out, Father?"

Pieter looked so obviously disappointed that Jacob's heart was touched. He patted his father's shoulder. "Go on, Father, have your fun. I have a bit of fluff on the side myself."

"We've been in London too damn long! You're even starting to talk like these Britishers!"

On Sunday, Jacob accompanied his father, out of curiosity. He found Lady Philippa formidable at first, her wit sharp, her beauty rather overwhelming. It was hard to listen to her when one wanted to stare at the porcelain skin, the bright hazel eyes, the lovely slim waist, and the graceful, long, white hands sparkling with diamonds and sapphires.

"I understand you attended the ball of the Hartshares," she commented, turning to Jacob. "Were you amused?"

"Amused? Yes, ma'am—I mean, my lady," he said, his eyes twinkling as he remembered some of the more colorful incidents.

"Oh, they are great snobs," she remarked mildly, her eyes flashing like her diamonds. "They don't receive me any longer. When my husband was having an affair with Lady Hartshare, we were received everywhere. But now that he has left her for a Miss Plum in the music halls, we are cut dead." She said this with such mild indolence that Jacob could scarcely believe what she said.

He blinked. Pieter stared at her thoughtfully. "You mean," said Pieter, "that affairs among the—uh—nobility are okay, but not with theater folks?"

"Oh, right," she smiled at him with great charm. "Shall I pour some more brandy for you? Or would you rather have it in a brandy glass?" She indicated his teacup.

Pieter stared, and Jacob flung back his head and howled with laughter. The ice was broken, and from then on, Lady Philippa proved a most amusing, witty woman. Her mind was sharp, and her husky voice told the most amazing stories of London society, the icing on the top of which was kept unbroken and smooth, while all sorts of things went on beneath.

"Have you heard about Lord Brashore?" she asked. "Well, his sister, Lady Priscilla, was mad about this poet. She went and married him, can you imagine? She could have had an affair, and kept it quiet, and had his child and made her husband adopt it. But no, she ran off with this poet, and they live in a cottage in the country. All London was horrified. Her husband divorced her at once. He said she must be mad, and he would not have a mad wife. Actually, anyone married to him would have gone mad eventually, for he was an idiot who thought of nothing but horses. I declare, someone told me that he *slept* with his horses, and I believe it. It is the sort of thing he would do."

She said all this with a little wave of her fingers, a dainty sip from her teacup. Finding an interested, even fascinated new audience, she rambled on, telling of the foibles of the very wealthy and titled of British society.

"Her Majesty disapproves, of course, so no one speaks of it before her," she commented. "Everyone pretends to be polite and dainty and genteel, and even churchgoing. But all know, though it does not appear in the gazettes. It would distress Her Majesty."

Presently, she looked about her, and said apologetically, "I really must go and freshen up. May I use one of your bedrooms? I declare, my hair is all in wisps."

Jacob stood up at once to summon a maid, but Lady Philippa shook her head. "No, Mr. Van Rhyne. Won't *you* show me upstairs? I long to see those beautiful rooms you told me about." She held out her hand to

Pieter. He blushed like a schoolboy, leaped up, and went with her.

Jacob, chuckling to himself, sat down again, and tortured himself by wondering what was going on upstairs. She was certainly the loveliest, boldest, most daring female of his acquaintance, and a lady for all that.

About two hours later, Pieter came back downstairs. He entered the drawing room, still fastening his tie. His face was flushed, but he was smiling.

"She wants you to come up now, Jacob," he said.

Jacob, half asleep before the warm fire, started. He stared at his father, unbelieving.

"Come up, she said," Pieter repeated, grinning happily. "She is—a real female, my boy!"

Jacob was still shaking his head incredulously as he entered the guest bedroom. He found the Lady Philippa reclining on a dozen pillows, covered only by a silk sheet. Beneath it, her long, lithe body was stretching in satisfaction. Her blond hair was unbound, and streamed down over her shoulders and breasts.

She stretched her wide arms, yawning like a cat, and he half expected her to purr. "Your father is adorable, Jacob," she murmured, her long-lashed gaze following him as he entered and came over to the bed. "But I thought it best not to overtire him the first time."

Jacob studied the recumbent form snuggled in the pillows, the line of her thighs just revealed by the silk sheet. He drew a deep breath, and began to remove his jacket.

She watched his every move hungrily, and when he had stripped himself to the buff, she smiled up at him. "Handsome and sturdy. So strong," she murmured in satisfaction. "Come and make me happy, my dear!"

He lay down beside her, and found her as soft and silken as she looked. She was plump from good living, and he stroked the rounded forms of her shoulders, her breasts, and down to her thighs. She wriggled a little as he took his time, studying her, teasing her a little with his slowness.

"My dear man, I cannot stay all night," she said tartly.

"Why? Do you have a dinner engagement tonight, my lady?" he murmured against her arm. His lips nibbled over the arm, up to her shoulder, then down to the full breasts, and he took the nipple between his finger and thumb, and squeezed it hard. Her eyes closed. She gave a sigh, and snuggled closer to him.

He found that his father was right. Lady Philippa was, indeed, all female. She clasped him tightly as he moved over her, and straddled him with her strong thighs. He gazed down at her, at the beautiful face and form, and wondered that her husband had strayed. Who could be dissatisfied with this woman?

Her fingers played over his spine, sending shivers of delight all through him. He settled on her, and attacked in earnest. He found her ready, all feminine softness and eagerness. They rolled across the wide bed, and back again. When she was on top of him, she laughed down into his face, and deliberately rode up and down on him. He let her, then pulled her tightly to him, and ended the game as he wished.

But the delight brought desire for more. The bout was no sooner over than he wanted her again. He had not felt such desire for a woman since—he did not remember when. He let her rest on his arm, while she half-slept, her face nestled against his chest. Then his hand began to roam again over her long body, her rounded hips, stroking, teasing, testing, exploring.

She moved. "I must go home. I have a dinner tonight."

"Send your regrets," he murmured, and kissed her ear.

"I am the hostess!"

"You were at the bedside of a sick friend a very, very sick friend," he muttered against her white throat. He turned her on her back, and lay on her, his legs pinning her down.

"My dear Jacob, I cannot stay—"

"You cannot leave," he laughed down at her. "I have you fast. You know those bold Americans . . ."

Her eyes opened. "Did you ever really fight Indians?" she asked.

"Really."

"Tell me about it."

"*Now*?" he asked incredulously.

She nodded her blond head, and grinned at him like a mischievous imp.

He conceived an idea. "Well, there was this Indian girl in the camp, all alone. I went to her tent, and she was lying on her stomach—if you would turn over, I'll show you how she lay—"

Lady Philippa obediently turned over. "And then?"

"Then I attacked. Like this . . ."

She squealed. But though she fought him, she enjoyed it—and so did he, holding her up to him with strong arms, and pressing himself on her. They played for a long time, and it was late when she finally left the bed and reluctantly began to dress. He lay back, smiling drowsily at her, watching her as she put on her many undergarments, then pinned her hair back into place.

"You never did tell me about the Indian fight," she said, pinning her hat onto the neat strands of blond hair.

"Next time. You'll come again, won't you?"

She gave him a look over her shoulder. "I might."

Lady Philippa allowed the two Van Rhyne men to escort her to the theater, along with her deaf old aunt, who knew better than to notice anything untoward. She came frequently to their home for tea, attended balls with them, introduced them to polite society. Both of the men enjoyed her favors, and laughed themselves sick at her stories. However, the stories were true, as Tweedy confirmed.

They also managed to conduct their business. They found Tweedy and two other men to back them in railroad ventures in the States. They inspected the new steel rails that Tweedy had told them about. They looked closely at the new locomotives, the comfortable waiting stations for passengers, and the luxurious parlor cars for the wealthy.

Then Hans wrote to them. He was in charge of the office while his father and brother were away. He had sent them dry letters from time to time, from the office. Now, in his own handwriting, not the clerk's, he wrote, in heavy, black script:

Dear Father and Jacob,

I think you had best wind up your business in England and come home with haste. I think something Dirty is goin on, and father had best deal with it. The share holders is holding meetings, and I ain't invited and neither is Howard and he is lawyer as you said, Father. And Lodewick and me think something is rottin and you better Come home.

Can they vote against you when you ain't here?

They voted a stock dividend and it seems High and Too much to me and so thinks Lodewick.

Can you get a boat soon?

Your respectful son,

Hans

"He can't spell worth a damn," Jacob said critically.

"Neither can I," said Pieter. "But the lad has sense, and we're going home."

They sent a reluctant farewell to Lady Philippa, along with several dozen red roses. She was truly sad to see them go, as was Tweedy. He gave them a riotous farewell party, attended by many bits of fluff. Many bottles were killed.

They arrived home to find the nation in mourning for the dead Lincoln. The President of the United States had been shot at a theater in Washington and had died soon thereafter. But the remnants of the Confederate

245

army had surrendered during April and May, and the war was over.

They noted the black mourning streamers all over, and the black armbands on men.

"They hated him while he lived, and couldn't write mean enough things about him," Pieter said thoughtfully. "Lincoln couldn't do anything right in their eyes. And now he's dead, and they're weeping and screaming and crying. It's enough to make a body sick."

"I think they're beginning to realize what they lost," Jacob said somberly. "Do you think it'll mean another depression?"

"Maybe."

However, their energies were soon turned to their own affairs. Hans and Lodewick were right, and Howard, Katrinka's lawyer husband, came to advise them awkwardly but sincerely.

"I think they mean to water the stock, then sell it," he said. "They've driven up the price something terrible."

"We'll see about that," Pieter said grimly. He had enough money from England to buy them out, but not at inflated prices.

He tried his old trick of talking to a few newspaper friends on financial columns. Soon the stock began to drop. Rumor had it that the Van Rhyne line was about to go under. When the stock owners panicked and sold, the stock was bought up by Pieter's agents.

One man caught on, and tried to hold out. Jacob went to visit him in his office.

"I understand you don't want to sell out," he said pleasantly.

The man eyed him nervously. "I think Van Rhyne has a great future, and I believe in investing in the future," he said pompously.

"I hear you're investing also in the Erie line. That's competition, isn't it?"

The man drew in his lip. "That's my business. Where did you hear about that? It isn't true, anyway."

"Fine. I wouldn't want you to go in with our competition, and try to work out deals. Father wouldn't like it, not one bit, and neither would I. In fact, we're prepared to buy you out, for seventy-two per share."

"It's worth ninety-five now!" cried the man.

Jacob smiled coldly. "If you hold out, the shares are going to go down, because Father and I have been thinking of selling out and buying ourselves a new line. We may go West and get rid of all our Eastern stock."

The man went pale. "But it would be worthless—worthless—" he whispered.

"That's right. If you decide to sell today or tomorrow, send word. The next day will be too late." And Jacob left him.

That night, the man sent word that he would sell, and the Van Rhyne firm bought him out, and owned their line completely once again.

Pieter was quietly pleased. "I was wrong to bring anybody else into the firm," he confessed to Jacob, in the study of his elegant apartment. "Remember this lesson, Jacob. Don't sell stock in your company unless you're willing to let someone else hamstring you and tell you what to do."

"That's true of more than railroads, Father," Jacob said, his mouth turning downward.

"You and Antonia have not made up?"

"No more than you and Mother," Jacob said tautly.

Pieter grimaced. "Like father, like son. Well, well, we're old and set. Antonia and you could change. Don't hold her ways against her, Jacob. With a mother like that, what could she do? She's set on making a figure in society, and she's doing it. If that makes her happy—"

"She can have it," Jacob said shortly.

"At least Katrinka is happy."

"Yes. She is increasing again."

"Philip is a nice little boy. Visited them yesterday. Are you going to bring Errol over to see me?"

"Yes. He's teething now, and crying a lot. I'll bring him when he's better."

There was a little silence in the study. Jacob was looking at the fire, thinking about little Errol, who had

247

cried when he saw him. He had forgotten him already, his own father, in the two months he had been gone. But Jacob had been patient with him, and soon the baby was eager to see him again, and nestled contentedly in his arms whenever he came to the nursery. He had grown in those two months. He had bright blue eyes and an eager, intelligent look.

Antonia had been coldly haughty when Jacob had returned. "Well, don't expect me to fall into your arms," she had said, when he came up to the master bedroom. "I won't forget how you went off to England without me!"

"And I won't forget how you piled up bills for dresses while I was gone," he said, shoving the papers under her nose. "These are enough to last you a year, Antonia, and don't forget it. Not another bill of yours will I pay until next year!"

She had raged at him, and he had flung the bills at her and gone to his own bedroom. Damn it, no peace in the house, no peace anywhere, except in work.

Pieter broke the stillness. "Are you going soon?"

Jacob nodded. "Next week, unless you need me here."

"No. I'll miss you, but Hans is doing well. A bookkeeper's soul, but he's useful," his father said honestly. "Lodewick, he's a wild one, but no depth. I won't be able to depend on him. So take care of yourself and write to me, so I know where you are, should I need you."

"I'll do that, Father. I'll go see Sunny tomorrow, before I get ready to leave."

The older man's face softened. "She's a good woman," he said softly. "And Paul—I'm right proud of that boy, though some of his fool ideas irritate me to hell! Always playing doctor with me, he is!"

"You should let him give you a checkup. It'll be good practice for him," Jacob said, warding off his father's ire. "And besides, the way you romped in and out of beds in England, maybe you've done yourself some damage!" He roared with laughter at his father's expression.

Then Pieter began to laugh also. "We'll never meet a female like that lady," he said, shaking his head. "Wasn't she some woman?"

"That she was," Jacob confirmed. "You know, at the end I felt sorry for her. I think she would have made a fine, faithful wife and mother, if that bastard husband hadn't been stepping out on her all the time. She was just too proud to stand for it."

"And too smart," Pieter said. "It doesn't pay for women to be too smart, and start thinking all on their own. By wanting the vote and all, they'll make themselves a peck of trouble. Leave it to the men, and let the women stick to their homes and children, I say."

Chapter 17

The Van Rhlyne railroad had invested cautiously in a section of the transcontinental line. Jacob went to supervise the work personally. Too much money was going down the drain in payments of bribes, and in payments of higher prices on the wood and commissary and wages. By being at the site, he could keep the sky-high prices under control.

When they had completed one section of twelve miles, he bid on another, and they started work. It would all link up somewhere out in the plains—some said near Denver, some said farther north.

Jacob didn't care where. This operation would mean more money for the Van Rhyne line, that was all he knew. Every bit of their profit would go back into the line and to their English backers. And profits were there to be made, if a man was careful.

Jacob kept up the books himself, for he wanted no padding of the accounts. He would go hundreds of miles to the nearest banks, with two stout Irishmen, and carry back the payroll in bags.

They were hiring more and more men, but not many were Irish now. Some were Union soldiers who had come west for work as soon as the war was over. Confederate soldiers had come also, galvanized Yanks, they called them, prisoners who were out on the condition that they take jobs with the new railroads.

There was trouble enough to keep Jacob busy and happy. Because he had to keep a sharp eye out for outlaws and Indians, protect the payroll, settle quarrels among his men, oversee their work, and make sure that the supplies arrived on time as needed, he would sleep hard, wake up, and not think once about Antonia and his troubles back home.

He slept in a tent, with a rifle at his side. He had one of the new rifles that could shoot six times without reloading.

The work went fast that summer. There was a keen competitive spirit among the units of the various outfits bidding on sections of the line. As soon as a section was finished, Jacob would saddle up quickly, and get to the nearest town or end-of-track, where the heavyset men who managed Union Pacific and Central Pacific dealt out contracts, from the elaborate parlor cars in which they lived.

Jacob was returning from one such trip, ready to pay off his men and rehire them for the next contract he had wangled. He had had to bribe several flunkies to get in to see the bosses, but it had been worth it. They knew him now, and welcomed him.

August on the desert was an audible sizzle of heat waves, and dust blowing into one's eyes. Even the water one drank from a canteen had a gritty feel to it. He squinted against the sun and shoved the brim of his tan sombrero down over his eyes.

He was relaxed in the saddle, having learned to ride in a slouched position, against the back. He was grinning to himself, remembering how the bosses had welcomed him this time.

The first time, it had been, "Who are you? Can you run a gang? Did you say you were from New York City? What experience do you have?"

He had bluntly told them he had been railroading since he was a boy, with his father. The mention of Pieter's name had made them sit up, but they had still eyed carefully his smart suit and new boots.

After he had managed several jobs, brought the rails in on time or ahead of time, bargained coolly for more contracts, and figured his prices accurately, refusing to accept less, they were much more respectful.

This time it had been, "Come in, Mr. Van Rhyne! Glad to see you! Hear you got through five days ahead of schedule. Have you come to bid for more? The winter may close in early, but you'll get done in time, won't you?"

All the railroad men were anxious to get ahead of schedule. The government would pay according to miles completed. Besides, it was a matter of pride to get more miles of track laid than the Central Pacific line, who had hired Chinamen and brought them in from San Francisco to work. Rumor had it that those Chinese worked like demons, as long as they had their tea and rice provided by their own cooks regularly.

"Working faster than *us*," grumbled the Irishmen, veterans of railroad building, and the soldiers, hardened by years of fighting in mountains and swamps. "Small as they are, and no muscles. And thinking they can beat us!"

Every week, word clicked along the telegraph lines about how many miles of rail had been laid that week. The desert carried the word, and the plains, and the mountain air, so that everyone knew almost at once how much track had been laid.

The sun glowed straight into Jacob's eyes. He straightened and looked about. They were near the waterhole for which he had been aiming.

"We'll stay the night, boys," he said to the two burly

251

Irishmen who rode with him. "No sense traveling after dark, when the horses are tired."

His companions sighed with relief, and went on with more spirit to the water hole. They swung down from their horses, made them comfortable, gave them water, and then dipped their own tin cups and drank eagerly.

Then they lit a small fire and cooked some ham and beans. Jacob moved back from the firelight to sit against a rock and do some figuring. He scrawled some notes on the notepad he always carried in his pocket. They could complete one more stretch of rails, and then he was through for the winter. No scrabbling about in the snows for him; he had seen what that did to his men. No, he would lay them off for the winter, then start early again next year.

They had made a good profit this year, he and his father. They could pay off their British backers, and still have some left over to put into new locomotives. That might be a smart investment. He would have to talk to his father about it when he returned home. Home. For a moment he pictured Antonia, then shoved her image aside to think of Errol.

The galloping hoofbeats of a horse roused him, and he reached automatically for his rifle. A man rode into camp hurriedly, his hand upraised.

"A friend," he said, glancing about from under his black sombrero. "Indians are coming this way—about twenty of them."

He swung down, and Jacob was already on his feet. One of the Irishmen stamped out the fire, flinging the rest of the coffee on it. They made for the rocks at the back of the camp, where the horses were tethered. Jacob scooped up the money bags into a blanket, and slung the bundle onto his horse.

The stranger had come up behind them. "My horse is played out," he said, and Jacob caught the slow drawl of a Southerner. "You go ahead. I'll hold them off for a time."

Jacob's mouth tightened. The man didn't have a chance.

"We'll *all* stay, with the rocks at our backs," he said. "Tie the horses up good, and load up, fellow." He checked his rifle.

"You don't need to stay for me," the Southerner said, his voice proud.

"Hell, man, we're in this together," Jacob said curtly. "Get down, now. Got any cartridges?"

Silence. Then the man said, "No," in a slow drawl. "I ran out about two miles back."

Jacob took the pistol from his left holster and handed it over. Then he gave the man a box of cartridges. "There you are. I suppose you know how to use them."

"Reckon I do." The man wasted no more breath. He lay on his belly, like a professional. An ex-soldier, Jacob thought, confirming his earlier judgment of the man. He watched as the Southerner expertly loaded the pistol Jacob had handed him, then placed it aside and quickly loaded his own.

"You got one of them new Colts?" Jacob asked, in a whisper.

"Right you are."

At first, they heard nothing. But presently, against the dark skyline, Jacob saw shadows of darker hue. He watched and waited. The Indians bent to the dead fire, sniffed, and moved on.

The stranger touched Jacob's arm, and motioned off to the right. Then slowly, without making a sound he crawled over the rocks and twigs and gravel, in the direction he had indicated. Meanwhile, one of the Irishmen was crawling off to the left. Jacob remained in the center, poised, his eyes gleaming.

The Indians straightened up, conferring with gestures. Then they started toward the rocks.

Jacob let out a yell. From his right came a Confederate yell, like so many banshees, as one of the Irishmen said later. The Irish joined in, yelling and screaming, and firing their guns at the Indians. One Indian fell, and another, and the rest turned and ran for it, pursued by a fusillade of gunfire.

The ponies padded away on unshod hooves. Silence

fell again. The stranger went out quietly, and bent over the dead Indians. Jacob watched from a distance. Strange fellow, this Southerner, he thought. A tough one, but quiet, too, and somehow sad.

He went to join him where he stood.

"I'm thanking you, stranger," he said, his hand outstretched. "My name is Jacob Van Rhyne."

A brief grin parted the Southerner's lips in the pallid moonlight. "Leigh Sheldon," he said. "Reckon I'll be on my way."

"Stay the night, and go on with us. There's a tent city at end-of-track, and you'll be welcome."

Leigh Sheldon hesitated, then shrugged, as though he would just as soon be in one place as another. "Thanks. I will."

In the morning, Jacob was up early, for he had taken the first watch. As he walked past the sleeping men, he saw something that startled him. The stranger lay face-up on his blanket near the cold fire. His face was pallid, as though seen in moonlight, scarcely tanned at all, and his hands were long and white. A gambler? Maybe. Many a Confederate, and many a Union soldier also, had come west to make his fortune, and found that his only talent was with cards.

The man rolled over, coughing, and Jacob frowned. He pretended not to notice as the man sat up, still coughing, his hand at his throat in an attempt to stifle the sound. One of the Irishmen, who already had a fire going, took a cup of hot coffee to him. "I thank you, sir," the Southerner said.

"Welcome. Grub's ready when you are."

They ate, saddled up, and went on, keeping their eyes peeled for more Indians. They knew these tribes were clever and quick. They could come over a hillock, riding like demons, and strike and be gone before a body knew they were there.

But they had no more trouble that trip. Jacob was relieved when they arrived in the tent city, shortly before dusk.

Leigh Sheldon looked around curiously. There was a

mess tent, a blacksmith's tent, and several long tents to house the men on rainy nights. There was a railroad car with a load of iron rails, the remainder from this job. And there were long, shining rails stretching out into the desert to the east, stretching toward the sunrise. Before long they would stretch to the sunset as well.

The Southerner wore a black suit, neat in spite of the desert dust that had settled on it. His white, ruffled shirt looked immaculate. He had donned it that morning, after washing at the waterhole. When one looked at him in daylight, he looked ill, Jacob thought.

And he *was* ill. Ill unto death.

But the kind of illness Leigh Sheldon had lasted a long time. He could starve to death before he died of it. Jacob sat that night in his tent and thought about it.

The next morning, he rose as usual. He found Sheldon washing a shirt in a small basin the cook had lent him. His belt was off, and his double holsters lay on the ground nearby.

"Mind if I have a look at your Colt?" Jacob asked.

Leigh Sheldon hesitated, then nodded. Jacob picked it up respectfully, and examined it.

"Nice piece. I'll get myself one back in the city, when I get there," he said.

"You going back to New York soon?"

"Not for a couple of months. I've got another job to do, another fifteen miles of track." Jacob waved his hand vaguely toward the west. "Care to come along?"

"Laying track?" Leigh Sheldon's mouth curled down. "I wouldn't last a day," he said abruptly. "Time was, I could do work. Now I just have my gun."

"That would be useful to me," said Jacob. "There'll be lots more Indians as we go west. How would you like to sign on as a guard?"

The man's dark eyes narrowed, and he looked hard at Jacob. "I don't need your pity," he said abruptly.

"I offered you a job. I'm a businessman, not a charity worker," said Jacob harshly. "You know how to use that gun. I can use you and your—talent."

The man frowned. Something was still eating at him.

255

"I'll think about it," he said. He finished washing his shirt, and hung it out to dry on a tent pole.

He stayed around the camp, watching the work curiously: the first team marking the way, laying the first ties; then the team who bedded the intervening ties; then the trackmen, carrying the heavy iron rails, dropping them precisely into place on the ties; then the head spikers, driving six spikes to hold each rail to the ties; then the screwers, who finished spiking the rails and bolted the joins; then the track liners, wielding crowbars to set the track into perfect line.

Beside them along the track, paced the water carriers. The men would drink briefly from a cup, then go back to work. It was hot, hellish work in the blazing, deadly sun of the desert, but the work must go on from dawn to dusk. They had a job to do, and the faster they did it, the more pay they got, and the sooner they would go on to the next section of track.

The next day, Leigh Sheldon went out with several men in the food detail. They returned with rabbits and a buffalo. Leigh had sighted a herd, and had gone after it. It had taken four of them to cut up the buffalo and bring back the pieces. The crew was jubilant. A meal free of dried beef! They had buffalo soup and meat for supper that night.

During dinner, Jacob went to Leigh, who was sitting off by himself as usual. "Now, will you be persuaded that we need you?" he asked.

Leigh stared down at his empty plate. "That's not the reason I hesitate," he said, so quietly that his voice did not carry more than a couple of feet on the dry air.

Jacob dropped down beside him, his coffee cup wrapped in his big palm. "So?"

"I'm a gunfighter," said Sheldon. He looked off in the distance. "I left the war a broken man, in health and spirit. I went home. My plantation was ashes—my family . . ."

"Your family?" Jacob prodded.

"Dead. My wife had been raped and murdered by Yankee soldiers," said the monotonous voice, as though detached from the spare, thin body. "My baby son had his head smashed in by a rifle butt. Niggers stole back to bury them both. They told me. I left, and came West. Nothing back home for me."

Jacob bent over his coffee cup. There had come to him a vivid picture of his baby Errol with his head smashed in. He swallowed his nausea. "War is hell. I'm sorry," he said. "Got a son myself. Are you wanted?"

"Yes," Sheldon said. "My only talent is this." He patted his gun. "I hired on in a couple of places, got myself a reputation, and moved on. Men will try for me. I can't keep them from trying. So I kill—and move on." His tone was that of a man three times his age: weary, resigned, ready to die.

"We can still use you on the railroad," Jacob said, forcing himself to sound practical, when he wanted to cry for this man who had probably never wept for himself. "You can forage for fresh meat for us, and keep an eye out for the Indians. The job will last three months, or maybe less."

Leigh shrugged, picked up his coffee mug, and drained it. "All right," he said indifferently.

He stayed on with them, hunting relentlessly, and they had more fresh meat than they had ever had. When Indians came around and saw him, they speedily moved on. He was too ominous, that black-clad figure, standing with his legs apart, with his rifle trained steadily on them, his eyes shadowed by the wide brim of his black hat. Most of the railroad hands avoided him, too. He was too strange for them.

But Jacob was drawn to the man. He would come around evenings, and they would talk, or be silent. Leigh knew the West fairly well by then. He told Jacob about the land to the southwest. "It's some desert, some mountain, but not like this. Dry and quiet, with the smell of pine and cedar. There's a big canyon there, with colors like rainbows in it, as the sun shifts over the rocks. There's a river down at the bottom of it that looks like a little creek, but the Indians say it is a raging river, with many rapids. Strange country—I like it."

The job was finished when the first cold winds blew from the mountains, and the night air was cold enough to frost their breath. The last spikes were driven in, and they finished that fifteen miles with a sense of relief. Jacob paid off his men, and they went their ways.

"Come East with me," said Jacob to Leigh. "Come back to New York, and you'll have a job with the company."

"With this?" Leigh half-smiled, his hand on his Colt. "No, I'll go west and south, I think. Down to the canyon lands and the solitude and the winds blowing dry, and the pine trees. I like it there."

"Oh, come on. You can come back west with me next summer."

Leigh shook his head. "You know," he said quietly, "when I came to your camp with word of Indians, and I heard your voice—your Yankee-flat voice—I about turned tail and went away again. I didn't care if you lived or died."

"I figured that," Jacob said, prodding the small fire before them. "I don't care how you feel about me. But you've got to take care of that chest, you know."

The Southerner's thin mouth went down at the corners. He started to say something, then stopped. "I can't go back to any Yankee land," said Leigh. "Thank you anyway. Jacob, you've been a friend, and I'm grateful. But I'll go my own way."

Jacob could not change Leigh's mind. He paid the man, and watched him leave, and was sure he would never see him again, and it made him sad and angry. A war and a hatred had lain between them, and they had never quite broken that barrier.

Jacob went back East himself and arrived home in November. Errol had his first birthday, and cried at the strange sun-darkened man who said he was his papa. Jacob gritted his teeth, and started in all over again to get acquainted with his son. Leigh had said, leaving, "Take care of that son of yours, Jacob."

On his second night home, Jacob went to Sunny Malone's cheery apartment and was greeted with hugs by

Sunny, Paul, and his father. Paul listened carefully as Jacob told them about Leigh Sheldon. "I begged him to come to New York with me. I'm afraid he will die out there," Jacob said sadly.

"Staying out there may have been the best thing he could do, Jacob," Paul said, his head leaning back against the soft chair. "His chest sounds bad. He might have had to go right to the hospital when he came to New York. Out in the open air, in the dry desert, in the mountains, he'll have a chance."

"What kind of a chance? To die among the buzzards? He was a decent man, given half a chance."

"That may be his chance. In medical school, one of our British professors talked about the care of consumptives. He believed the dry mountain air helped them, and might even cure them. It eased their chests, anyway, that air. He probably did the best thing in the world to keep himself alive."

"You really think so?"

"Really," Paul said, and changed the subject.

They listened to his stories of the West, of the Indians, of the rail lines laid, of the workers from North and South, carrying on a silent feud at night, but working side by side during the day. Pieter listened hungrily. Now an old man, he would no longer be able to go out West. His face sagged with tired lines, Jacob noticed, and he was much heavier. His legs often got too tired to walk, and he would take the carriage much of the time.

Jacob went home that night feeling thoughtful and weary, yet relaxed. That was from being with friends, he thought. He let himself in, and the butler hastened to hold the door, giving Jacob a reproachful look for not allowing him time to jump into position.

" 'Evening. Who's around?" Jacob asked.

"Er—Mrs. Van Rhyne is waiting up to see you in her sitting room." The butler took Jacob's coat and hat, bowed him into the sitting room, and shut the door gently after him.

Antonia was waiting there alone—unusually alone, he thought. She wore a gown of lilac silk trimmed with

259

cream lace, sashed with cream silk, with a bouquet of violets at her waist. She turned her head when he entered, and looked up at him wistfully.

"Jacob," she said, smiling, and held out her hand to him. He took her hand awkwardly, squeezed it, and set it down carefully. "I thought I would have to make an appointment to see you," she said. Her pink mouth pouted a little. He eyed her warily. Did she want jewelry, more gowns, or what, this time?

"What's the trouble, Antonia?" he asked abruptly, and sat down gingerly on the edge of a stuffed chair opposite her chaise longue.

"Trouble? I saw you only briefly last night with Errol, and you've been away for almost six months!" said Antonia. "My dear, this isn't what I thought our marriage would be."

A new approach for her, he thought, half closing his eyes.

"Now, don't! Please don't, Jacob. Don't close me out!" She sat up passionately, her violet eyes flashing. "I know it's partly my fault—oh, all right, it's very much my fault! I was carried away by my wish to make an impression in New York society. I was young and giddy and foolish. Are you going to hold it against me all my life? Jacob, I've missed you so terribly! And you treat me as though I'm a stupid, foolish—"

She stopped, raising her handkerchief to her eyes. In spite of himself, he wavered. She was a damned attractive woman. But tears alienated him completely. He watched her in silence.

"You—you pay more attention to Errol than to me," she said, biting her lips to control her voice. She twisted her handkerchief in her hands until it tore. "Jacob, I can't bear it that we're strangers!"

"What do you want from me?" he asked.

"To be your wife! To let me love you as I did when we married—" Her cheeks were turning crimson. She dared a look at him, then down again at the floor. "Oh, Jacob, I've been such a damned fool! I do love you, but

260

I think—I think you've stopped loving me . . . if you ever did . . ."

He thought of Lady Philippa Rawlings, her pride and her passion, her husband and his damned foolish ways. Antonia could be another such lady, he thought, and it made him wince.

"You want to give our marriage another chance?" he asked slowly.

She nodded. "I love you so much . . ." she whispered. "My pride—I could have killed you for neglecting me—but it was my fault, I now realize. You hated the crowd I went around with, and I can see now how frivolous they are, how stupid. I am sick of them, Jacob. Do you believe me?"

"I don't know," Jacob said.

She bit her lips. "I can't blame you. But will you give me another chance to prove it?"

He hesitated. She flared, rising to her feet angrily, "All right. Make me beg, Jacob! You're a cruel bastard, but I love you. I can't bear for another man to touch me. You've spoiled me for other men. I can't stand nights without you in my bed. I want you!" she cried, and stamped her foot.

Jacob stood up and stared down into her face. Then he reached out and hauled her to himself, up on her tiptoes in the silvery shoes, hard against his lean, muscular body. He kissed her as though he had been starved for her. His mouth crushed down on her pink lips, she opened her mouth to gasp, and he covered her open mouth so she could not breathe at all. She sagged in his arms.

He let her go a little, and her arms went up about his neck.

"Oh, Jacob—oh, Jacob—"

"Toni," he whispered against her silky white neck, where the lace fell back. He pushed the dress down and kissed her shoulder, her arm, and cupped her breast in his hand through the silk and lace.

He pushed her back on the chaise longue and followed her down. She struggled weakly, though her arms were still about his neck.

"Jacob—the bed—in the bedroom—"

"The hell with that," he said, his cheek against her bared breast. He took the nipple in his mouth and bit. His hand went to her skirts. He pushed them up, and found her naked beneath the silk and lace.

She weakened and moved beneath him, as he rose above her. His lower body was soon stripped of the tight-fitting trousers, and he came to her, full of desire as when they were first married. And he found her truly needing and wanting him, as he wanted her.

They fought each other for satisfaction, savagely, sweetly, on the hard chaise longue. When it was over, she lay back and said, "You're a brute, Jacob Van Rhyne, but I need you. Oh, God, how I love you."

He looked down at her. Her silver satin shoes were tossed on the carpet ten feet away. Her robe was ripped from her shoulders, and he could see the glorious pink-and-white flesh of her beautiful shape from her head to her heels. He stroked her with his hand from her shoulders to her waist. Her hair was pulled from its neat chignon, and hung in blond disorder to her breasts. He picked up a lock of it and put it to his lips. She stroked his blond hair with her fingers, her violet eyes dreamy.

"Get up, woman," he said suddenly.

She opened her eyes wide. "Why?"

He smiled slowly. "So we can get dressed—"

"Oh, Jacob!"

"And go to bed again. Or do you want to parade through the hallway looking like that?"

"Oh, Jacob!" She began to laugh, like old times.

They got dressed and went up to the master bedroom, and went to bed. And it was as good as, or better than, before. They lay all that night and part of the next day in the big bed, and she locked the door against her maid. Jacob learned all over again how wild and passionate she could be, his Toni, the girl he had loved and married.

And it continued like that, for the rest of the winter.

It was the best winter of his life. Antonia had given up much of the social crowd, although she still went out at times. She coaxed him to go to the opera with her, and he endured it, and was even pleased, because she looked more stunningly gorgeous than anyone else there. She could lift her chin, turning her profile, and it was more hauntingly beautiful than any opera singer, society lady, or ingenue. She ornamented her clothes, not the other way around. She wore crimson, and Jacob thought no one could be more lovely—until she wore a gown of ice-blue satin with sapphires and diamonds—or a dress of cream lace with an undergown of ruby satin.

And the dream continued. Jacob would go to Errol's nursery to play with him, and Antonia would come in in her dressing gown, and smile at them. "Mama," Errol said, holding up his arms demandingly, and beaming at them both, his idols, his beautiful mama, and his big tanned papa who told such marvelous stories about Indians and bears.

"How is my baby darling?" Antonia cooed, and hugged him, and held him to her breast.

She was so lovely when she smiled and held the baby, thought Jacob, still searching for flaws.

He did not find one. Christmas came and went. He gave her splendid presents: a locket of gold and pearls; matching pearl earrings; a long rope of pearls, which was all the rage; a Chinese lacquer jewel box; a new dressing table of cedar and mahogany, with a triple tier of mirrors. She protested, her cheeks pink with excitement, "Darling, it's too much!"

"What shall I return?" he teased her, lying back on the bed, watching her in the mirrors as she fastened the long strand of pearls about her graceful throat. She laughed, and took it off, to lay it carefully in its soft box.

She came to bed, and lay down beside him, putting her head on his chest. "I have everything in the world I want, except one thing," she whispered.

Ah, now I shall know, Jacob thought. "What is that, darling?" His eyes were narrowed.

She leaned on her elbow, gazing down at him, the dimples showing in her cheeks. She had gained a little weight, attractively, on her rounded hips and about her waist.

"Another baby, darling," she said demurely, but her color was high.

He was relieved. There was no question, now, of her love for him. He reached for her, and kissed her softly. "That is not difficult."

She leaned down to hide her face on his chest. "You've started one already," she muttered.

He made her repeat it. She did, her violet eyes sparkling and eager now. "Are you happy?" she asked. "Are you happy, Jacob? I do want another baby, so very much."

He laughed a little, with sheer pleasure. "You don't mind? You really want one?"

"So much, so much."

They lay together in silence, in harmony. He could not believe his happiness. Another little fellow, or maybe a girl this time! And Antonia loving him, and wanting him in her bed. There was nothing greater in life than this.

Chapter 18

When spring came, and Jacob began to prepare to go to the West again, Antonia was upset. She did not scream or throw a tantrum. Instead, she became tense and overwrought, and looked at him with troubled, violet eyes.

"Jacob, I wish you would not go."

He looked at her tenderly. "I have to go, Antonia."

She clasped her slim hands together tightly. "I beg you not to go," she said in a low voice. "When you talk about the dangers, I get cold chills. What if an Indian kills you, or a bear, or an avalanche? Jacob, what would I do? I think I would die."

He hated to leave her. She was expecting the baby in early September. But he knew there was no choice, the business depended on him. He tried to reassure her. "Look, Toni, I can defend myself, and I have good men. I've been scratched a time or two, but I know enough to stay out of trouble. You don't have to worry."

"I will worry though," she said simply. "Until you return." Her face had paled to a pearly white, and her eyes looked haunted. "Oh, Jacob, I can't bear for you to leave me again for so many months."

She looked at him so pleadingly that he began to weaken. He sat before the fire and thought for a time, and she did not interrupt his thoughts. He was intensely conscious of her sitting there, her chin proud, but her shoulders drooping. And she was so beautiful in the loose dressing gown, her pregnancy showing somewhat. She was a good mother, he thought. She was so proud of Errol, and would take more time with him now, dressing him up in his playsuits, taking him out in the carriage with her, showing him off proudly. And she would come up to the nursery to play with him, and hold him, and tell him stories.

"I'll tell you what," Jacob said reluctantly. "I'll go out, sign the contracts, and take a good man with me to carry on. I'll try him out. If he can be trusted, I'll come home as early as I can. How would that do?"

"Oh, Jacob—" Antonia said, her mouth quivering. She flung herself at him and hugged him. "Oh, Jacob, thank you, darling! You won't be sorry. I'll give you another grand boy this time."

"Actually, I was thinking about a girl, with your violet eyes," he said, laughing down at her. Then he kissed her passionately.

Jacob went west in early April, taking two good men with him. They heard that the Mormons were going to contract to deliver wood and other supplies to the railroads. So, his father had been right! There *was* some wheeling and dealing going on behind the scenes.

"I don't trust that Credit Mobilier lot," Pieter had said confidentially to Jacob. "I've been hearing rumors. Try to find out what is going on while you are out West. We may not want to continue."

"Not want to go on with the line?" Jacob was dumbfounded. "But Father, it's the road of the century! The whole way across the United States! The whole continent! I want to be in on it until the line is finished!"

Pieter scowled, then patted Jacob's shoulder. "You have done plenty, Jacob. Your mark is on a good part of the line. But it may be time to get out before scandal breaks. We can put our efforts into our own line. One of these days, I'll want you to take over management of the Van Rhyne lines. And maybe you could go to England and buy some pretty locomotives and parlor cars. I'd like a special parlor car of my own, all red plush," he said dreamily.

Jacob kept his ear to the ground on that trip. It was not difficult to learn things, if one knew whom to ask, and when to listen, and what to believe. He made friends with a smart young telegrapher, and managed to get some news illegally, in exchange for gifts of whiskey, a new Colt revolver, and regular supplies of buffalo tongue.

Eventually, Jacob decided his father was right. It was time to get out. As the road had increased in size and wealth, the turmoil and conflict between the big managers of the Union Pacific and the Central Pacific had become greater. There would be a big bust-up one day, and the Van Rhynes might as well not be a part of it.

He finished the second contract in August, paid off his men, and pulled out. His one regret was that he had not seen Leigh Sheldon, nor had he found anyone who had heard of him. He must have gone to the Southwest, as he had planned.

Jacob returned home in late August, to a happy Antonia. "I was determined not to have the baby until you came," she sighed.

"I'll bet he's going to be a big one," Jacob said, fascinated by her size.

"Or twins. Your mother says I may have twins!" She patted her stomach proudly. "Oh, I can scarcely move around. I have quit going out completely. It is too embarrassing. I have never read so many books in my life. Now, do sit down and tell me all about your summer!"

Their second son was born in late September, about ten days late, but he was such a big, husky fellow that the doctor was not surprised. "He got a good start in life," he said approvingly.

They named him Bernard, after a dear cousin of Antonia, and the boy thrived. Errol was fascinated by his baby brother, and was often at his crib, gravely offering a toy train or a stick of candy to the baby, who cooed and kicked up his heels.

"Doesn't he want my locomotive?" Errol asked Jacob wonderingly. "It's my nicest one!"

Jacob picked him up and hugged him. "You keep that one for yourself, Errol, my lad. He's too little for such things yet. By the time he's your age, I'll get him one of his own. But you're a good lad to think of it."

When Bernard was two months old, Jacob secretly wrapped him up one day, and put Errol in his thick coat, and took both of them out in the carriage. The coachman grinned to see him laden with two boys and a basket of goodies.

They went over the familiar streets to Molly's house. Jacob had not seen the McKennas since last winter, and they received him with a warm, hearty welcome. Evan came out to help him from the carriage, and lifted Errol high into the air.

"Now, here's a grand, fine lad!" he marveled. "Two years old, and as big as three! And the wee one! Molly will be glad to see all of ye!"

Molly was at the door, beaming. Huddled around her were her own children—four-year-old Vincent, two-year-old Muir, and little Molly, just one year old. Jacob grinned to see her wobbling around on her plump sturdy legs, gazing up at them gravely with Evan's large, brown, serious eyes.

"Oh Jacob, how good of you to come and bring the dear ones!" Molly said, taking little Bernard in her careful, plump arms. "Ah, what a fine one he is! We heard all about him. And little Errol, too! Such a good lad. She's a good mother, your Antonia. I can see it," Molly said approvingly. "Look how blooming her two sons are." She took off Bernard's outer wraps and admired his sturdy legs and body. He cooed and blew bubbles for her, enchanting them all, especially little Molly, who came to lean on her mother's knee and stare at the baby.

It was a few days before Thanksgiving, and Jacob had brought them a basket of turkey and apples and cranberries. "You'll take with you one of my plum cakes," she said, and went to wrap it up.

Errol, Vincent, and Muir were playing trains on the floor. Jacob sat back, watching them, and lit his pipe with satisfaction. This was a happy home, he thought. The fire sparkling, the red Turkish carpet on the floor, the rose-colored curtains drawn against the cold. He and Evan and Molly began talking about his adventures of the summer. He told them about the increasingly frantic Indian attacks.

"There, now, them savages ought to go farther west and leave us alone," said Molly, shaking her head.

"There's no place farther west for them to go to, Molly," Jacob said, sighing over his pipe. "You have to be a bit sorry for them, ferocious and savage as they are. They have no more land. They are to be set aside on reservations, unless they go north into Canada, where it is much colder, and there are fewer animals for them to hunt."

Evan frowned. "It is so serious, then? There is no land left in all that vast wilderness?"

"The rails have crossed much of the wilderness, and settlers are following. A tent city last year is a town of ten thousand this year," Jacob told them. "Towns sprout out of the forest and desert as if by magic. Settlers and immigrants are coming from the old countries, from Scandinavia, France, Germany, and from England and Ireland, even from Poland and Hungary and all those far-off places. I reckon they would all like to live here, what with their revolutions and such."

"Can't blame them. It's the best country in the world," said Molly, proudly tossing her head. She had become more plump, what with having the children and eating her own good cooking. Evan was as lean as ever, smoking his pipe comfortably, letting little Molly climb over his legs, leaning over to set up a locomotive or bit of track when the boys needed some help.

There was a knock at the door. Evan went to it, as Molly still held Bernard. "Ah, come ye in, Mrs. O'Callahan," they heard Evan saying cordially.

Molly had time to give Jacob a quick briefing. "A widow, she is, the poor dear."

Mrs. O'Callahan was plump and red-haired, with green eyes and a wistful look. "There, now, it's company ye have," she exclaimed, as she saw Jacob rising from his chair.

"Now, then, it's but an old friend, come with his boys to show them off to us. Come in, Deirdre O'Callahan, and be introduced. Jacob Van Rhyne, Mrs. O'Callahan, our neighbor these two years."

Jacob reached out his great paw, and gently shook the slim hand, noting its smallness and redness. How different it was from Antonia's delicate, white smooth ones.

The woman smiled and greeted him. She must have recognized his name, for she became reserved. Evan had to persuade her to take a chair.

"You'll be asking about the other job," said Evan.

"There, now, it can wait a bit," she said, sending Jacob a nervous glance. So they spoke no more of it. She admired the children. Muir came to her, to gaze up in fascination at the fine pile of red-gold hair on top of her head. She bent and picked him up, slowly, in order not to startle him, and held him on her lap.

"A fine lad he is," she murmured. Little Molly came

269

over, staggering on uncertain legs, to be drawn up also, until Mrs. O'Callahan had an armful of the two of them.

"Mr. Van Rhyne has just returned from working the railroads out West, and fine adventures he was telling us about," Molly said easily. She seemed to adjust readily to one person, then to another, with the graceful manners of one who enjoys people.

"There now, you'll be continuing your stories," encouraged the widow, looking over Muir's dark head at Jacob.

"Wild stories," he said with a grin. "They like to hear how many bears I have killed in the summer. But it was only two this summer, seeing that I returned early in the year."

They all had a laugh over it, and he went on to talk of the rails, and how hard his Irishmen worked, and how far along they were. Everyone in the country was aware of how the work went, for the newspapers reported it daily, and talked eagerly of the day when the rails would be joined at some point in the West, and a person could go from one end of the country to the other, all on rails, instead of in a bouncing stagecoach.

"And are the Indians still so dangerous?" Deirdre asked.

"That they are, and with reason," said Jacob. "They hate the idea of going onto reservations, and having to live with the government controlling them. But if the land is to be settled, one cannot expect folks to plow and tend cattle with Indians swooping down whenever they get angry. No, they'll have to be put onto reservations, and they don't like it, for they always lived free."

"It doesn't seem right somehow, but I suppose it has to be," the widow murmured. "We don't always like what happens to us, but the good Lord always has His reasons." She gave a wistful look to small Molly in her arms. Muir had wriggled down, to return to the fascinating game of building the railroad.

Jacob studied Mrs. O'Callahan. Her pink, blooming face, the haunted look of her green eyes. Finally he had to leave. The day was turning darker at the windows, and he had to get the baby home.

He beckoned Evan with him, and went to the kitchen to collect his coachman, who was warming himself at the stove.

"Do you have a job for her?" he muttered, as Evan picked up the plum cake Molly had wrapped for Jacob.

Evan shook his head. "She can sew, but so can all women. I'll have to look further. She's been scrubbing out office buildings these six months since her good husband was crushed to death in a construction job. I'll find her something, but it will take time."

"I hear that ladies like their dresses handsewn. Could she manage a shop, if I should set one up?"

Evan gave him a long, keen look, and was slow in answering. "I reckon it could be done. She has sense and manages her money well, what little she has. What was you thinking about?"

Jacob improvised rapidly. "Well, I have an office building with the third and fourth floors vacant, and some display space on the first floor. You'll come tomorrow with me, and we'll have a look. There may be some other ladies who could use the work, and Mrs. O'Callahan might manage it all. The females of New York City are always thinking about new dresses and bonnets."

"You're a good man, Jacob," Evan said gravely. "There are three women besides Mrs. O'Callahan that I can name at once, who could use the work and welcome. Are you serious about it?"

"Dead serious. It would be another venture. A man has to branch out, you know."

"I'll be meeting you wherever you say," Evan said.

Jacob named the building and the street, and they decided on ten o'clock in the morning. He came back into the warm room, gathered up his two sons, and said his farewells.

"You'll bring the lads again, will ye, when ye can?" begged Molly. "It's good to see the children a-playing

271

together, and to hear all your good stories, just like old times, only with Rowan missing from us."

He patted her cheek. "He's gone but not forgotten, Molly. He was a fine, brave man, and he'll live in our memories forever."

"You're good to say so. God bless you one and all, and have a good Thanksgiving." Tears brimmed in her eyes, but she smiled and waved at them as he departed, with Bernard carefully nestled in his father's arms, and Errol holding onto his hand.

Errol returned the wave, and said to Jacob, "I like them, Father. When can we go again?"

"Soon, soon," promised Jacob, thinking of the brave smile of Mrs. O'Callahan, and her pretty, sad, green eyes.

He managed to keep his promise. From then on he went often to see Molly and Evan and their children, taking Errol with him. He and Evan would sit and talk politics, railroads, unions, and wages, while the children tumbled around their feet, making railroad lines and bridges.

Antonia was happier than ever and so was Jacob. They slept together in the master bedroom most of the time. She still went out, but less often. She took some interest in his business, but he could tell when she got bored, for a blank look would come into her eyes. Still, they had come to a new, deeper understanding of one another, and their marriage was much improved. And he adored his two sons.

The following summer, Jacob did not go west. He missed it badly, for he loved that outdoor life, the knife-edge of danger, the comradeship of husky, outdoor men, the challenge of building the rails faster and better than any man around. But he and Pieter were now concentrating their energies on improving the Van Rhyne line. They had paid back their British backers, and were looking around for new worlds to conquer.

Pieter bought a sailing ship, and stocked her for a trip to China. The China trade was going well. There was much risk in it, but his captain was a good one, who knew his ship. He brought back the goods, and in good time, and Pieter made a fine profit. Encouraged, he bought three more ships, and sent them out.

Jacob was more interested in real estate. He quietly began to buy up more and more land in New York and New Jersey. It was exciting to be free of debt, to have money to gamble on new investments, but Jacob missed the railroads and their excitement.

In June, 1868, Antonia had a baby daughter, a darling beauty with blond, curly hair and her mother's violet eyes. Regina, as they named her, was the pet of every visitor, to say nothing of her parents. Jacob was tickled when he heard that Molly McKenna had had a baby girl that month also, whom she named Jessie. "The image of her dear father," as Molly said proudly.

The following spring, Jacob became restless. The newspapers were full of stories about the transcontinental railroad, due to be completed in April or early May of 1869. He longed to be there, and was overjoyed when he received an invitation to the ceremonies. He took a train and was there by mid-April, watching the final work with nostalgia. He saw the burly men driving themselves forward, the rails clanging down, the shovels flashing in the bright sunshine, the superb coordination, as the men worked together on the final stretch of track.

The top railroad magnates began to arrive, to hold court in their parlor cars, to open their bars, to drink toasts to themselves and their accomplishments, while the Chinese and Irish and Yankees and Southern laborers toiled away quietly over the graves of their fellow workers who had died.

Jacob was out early every morning, watching, longing to get a hand in. But the work was practically done. Just the last few miles remained. There were false alarms. Rumors flew. Dates were set and discarded. The men were sure it would be done on May 8th. But on that date there were still ten more miles to go.

Then came May 10. At Promontory Point, the Casement brothers were hosting for the Union Pacific. Excursionists arrived, eager to be in on the finish, the linking of the rails from East and West. Two trains came in, one from the East, one from the West, and the noses of the engines almost touched.

There were shouts and cheers. At the driving of the Golden Spike, Jacob watched with amused, detached curiosity as the big shots, with their plump bellies, attempted to swing the heavy sledges. Suddenly a quiet voice behind him said, "Jacob, is that you?"

He swung around, and stared at the tall figure dressed in black. The man tipped back his sombrero to reveal a tanned face, well filled out, with steady eyes, the lips in a half-smile. It took Jacob a minute to recognize the man. His hand shot out and gripped the hard hand that met his.

"Leigh Sheldon! I can't believe it!"

Leigh nodded to the scene before them. "We'll watch it, then go and talk, eh?"

He was poised and hard and seemed well, Jacob thought. The two men stood side by side and watched the final ceremonies. There were long prayers, led by Reverend John Todd of Pittsfield, Massachusetts, then one led by the "railroad bishop," John Sharp of the Mormons. Leland Stanford gave a five-minute speech. The spikes were dropped in, and the sledge hammers were handled by the railroad magnates, grunting and sweating in their fine suits. While they swung uneasily at the spikes, the telegrapher got impatient and tapped out the three dots that set off the national celebration across the country.

"That's it, I reckon," said Jacob. "The rails across the land. It's done."

Leigh had his hand on Jacob's shoulder. The two men watched silently for another minute or two, then turned away.

They strode toward Jacob's tent on the edge of town. Jacob had opened a bottle of whiskey, poured them each a cup, and they sat down on the rough blanket. Then, grinning a little, they raised the cups in a toast.

"To the railroad," said Leigh. "May it bring peace

and prosperity to this torn land of ours." A shadow crossed his bronzed face briefly. They drank.

"It's good to see you, damn good," said Jacob.

"I couldn't stay away. I figured you might come here, and I wanted to say thanks."

Jacob poured them each another drink. "What happened to you?"

"I went down to the canyon lands," Leigh said, crossing his legs easily. He seemed harder, yet more relaxed, surer of himself. "I found a small patch of land and bought it, from a rancher giving up and going to California. The following summer, I supplied the railroads with beef from April to November, and raised enough money to go back with a half a dozen horses and some cattle. I'm a rancher now."

"And you're well. You haven't coughed once. What the hell—was the mountain air that good?"

"Well, I guess so. You set me to thinking. You knew I was a Confederate, yet you took me in and treated me like a friend. I took the chip off my shoulder, and dug into work. I hadn't wanted to live, that was the trouble, and I felt so damned bad at times. Then I found—well, there are several ranchers in the valley. One of them had a daughter, pretty and sweet and capable, a fine woman. I didn't think she'd take a second look at me— old, and a wreck, and finished. But she did, and persuaded me to keep on trying. Well, we married, and I have a son." His smile was infinitely sweet, and Jacob thought the light in his eyes had changed his appearance even more than his newly tanned and sturdy body.

"That's good. That's good! Oh—I have a second son, and the prettiest daughter you ever saw! Regina is her name." Jacob grinned, and kept on grinning and drinking. He felt so happy, so peaceful.

"Fine, fine," Leigh said. "We named our son Jacob. Figured you wouldn't mind. You were a friend, when I had given up thinking of friends. I wanted to remind myself always, when a man thinks he is down, it isn't the end. You just have to pick up and start in again."

Jacob was deeply touched, struck with the pleasure

and the honor. Leigh went on talking. The man who had been closed for so long, now opened himself up freely, as if in genuine relief. He talked of his ranch, his small house, the vegetable patch. He told Jacob how they hunted through the winters, he and his wife's brother, and sold the furs in the spring. Then, through the summers, they ranched together, and ran the place.

"Some outlaws about," he drawled. "Bothering the ranchers some. A couple of fellows and I gave them a good scare, killed off three of them, and the rest took off like they were burnt. Folks were grateful. The banker even opened up, and told me he would loan me any amount I wanted to buy the ranch and stay. So I did, and soon paid him off. Now they have us over to dinner. Imagine, me—a gunfighter—and the banker. But we don't talk about that over coffee," he said, and quietly chuckled.

Leigh had been examining Jacob's features. "You look happier, too," he said.

"Yep. The wife and I got together again. She has settled down some," Jacob said with satisfaction. "I reckon she was just young and flighty."

"It happens that way. I'm glad. You going back East?"

"Right. Taking a train in two days. Father is going into shipping; he's sent three ships to China. You should see our house, crammed with Chinese rugs, ivories, and porcelains." Jacob grimaced. "Father always lets Antonia have the best of the lot, and she sure takes plenty. But she has good taste, and it looks great in the house."

"Imagine. China. It's just a blot on the map in school," said Leigh. "Did you ever think of going to China?"

"Never did."

"Me neither. I hear the Chinese worked well on the railroads."

"*Too* well. Lots of folks don't want them around, now that the work is about over. They want to send them back to China. They're getting all the menial jobs, and working cheaper."

"That's a problem."

They had a long talk, then went out to dinner at a nearby restaurant. They talked into the night. Leigh brought over his bedroll, and they slept outside Jacob's tent. All the next day, they strolled around, eyeing the tents and the tracks, and the fine parlor cars. Occasionally they were called in for drinks by railroad men who remembered Jacob. They looked curiously at the quiet-faced man with him.

One man took Jacob aside and asked, "Who's your friend? He looks like a gunfighter, with his hand near that holster of his, and that deadly look to him."

Jacob smiled casually. "Him? Oh, he's a rancher. Supplied meat to the railroads. He can use the gun."

Before they parted, Jacob gave Leigh a souvenir, a Chinese lacquer box he had meant to give as a gift to a railroad magnate of his acquaintance. He thought he would rather have Leigh put it in his rough ranch house. Leigh gave Jacob a gift too—a Colt.

"You said you wanted one. And this is a good one. I filed it down myself, so the sights are good."

Jacob was touched. "Come East when you can, Leigh, come and visit us."

"And you come West. You'll find me north of Spanish Pass, and a bit west."

Both men knew there was little chance of their ever meeting again. They clasped hands, and parted.

Jacob boarded the train for home. All through the long trip he thought about the years he had spent railroading—those years that were finished for him now. The railroads spanned the continent. The years of frantic building were over. What was there left for him to do? He would settle into a desk job, he supposed, unhappily. He was only thirty-three, yet suddenly he felt old.

He got into a poker game that night to help forget his sad thoughts of the old days. It was the first of many.

He won some and lost some, but had broken even by the time he reached New York City.

When he got off the train and stood on the platform in New York City, it was with a sense of finality. The old days were gone forever. He was an older man, with a wife and three children. He had roistered, fought, built, managed some of the toughest men in the world, and matured in the process. And he had made some fine friends. He thought of Leigh Sheldon, striding to his magnificent black stallion, setting his black sombrero on his head, lifting his hand in farewell. Their paths had parted, and they might never meet again.

But he would never forget Leigh Sheldon. And he would never forget Rowan O'Neill, nor the Irishmen who had died at his side, some even in his arms. Nor would he forget the tough, laughing, bragging, drinking, working, hustling bronzed men he had lived among, and fought beside. He would never forget the friends he had made, the men he had bested, the railroad magnates whose grudging admiration he had won. No, he would never forget any of them.

The end of an era was at hand, as he well knew, and he was startled to feel sad as he strode to a waiting carriage.

Chapter 19

Antonia was restless. She had had three children, and was proud of their intelligence and good looks. She had exercised and dieted until she had regained her slim waist and fine figure. Jacob was pleased with her. But something was missing. She began to look about for new fields of conquest.

Her mother encouraged her. Her daughter was the most beautiful and brilliant girl in the world. She was wealthy, and her husband indulged her. Why should she not be a leader in society? Why not go to England and conquer royalty? Who was more suited to wear Worth gowns, to be received by the French emperor and empress, to travel triumphantly throughout the world of fashion?

The only trouble was that Jacob was not willing to accompany her. When Antonia sweetly asked him to, he had growled, "I have work to do! Do you think I can just traipse over to Europe whenever I want? And fritter away six months? The railroad would fall apart!"

They quarreled briefly. Then she kissed him and apologized sweetly. She was learning how to act toward him. But Jacob saw through her. He wanted to believe in her; he wanted to think her good and motherly and wifely. But he knew Antonia had other aspirations, and that her mother encouraged them.

A week later, she approached him again. "If you cannot tear yourself away, Jacob, do you mind if I go with Betty and Tom French? You like them, you said so."

They were a sensible couple, with too much money, and with too much idle time on their hands, and not enough to do with it. Childless themselves, and adoring Antonia's three children, they came over often.

Antonia was persistent, and finally Jacob agreed, and Antonia took off with her mother and the Frenches. They were to be gone for three months. Antonia had tried for six months, but Jacob would not hear of it.

He began to see their pictures in the New York gazettes. "Mrs. Jacob Van Rhyne and her mother, Mrs. Everett Townsend, at a ball for charity. Mrs. Van Rhyne wears a gown of ivory satin, with diamonds and emeralds in a parure of striking design."

Another time, he read: "Mrs. Jacob Van Rhyne was splendid in a violet satin dress and polonaise edged with ruching of purple. Her jewels were amethysts of a deep purple hue, set in gold by Messrs. Tiffany and Co., New York." And on another occasion: "Mrs. Van Rhyne was seen at the country home of the Duke of M—— in

279

a country toilette of light gray silk, with a simple diamond brooch and matching earrings."

Jacob read, and shook his head. When had she purchased all these things? Sometimes he simply signed bills and his clerk paid them. Antonia! What a wily woman she was!

He was working hard these days, sometimes spending weeks in the northern part of New York State, where there were difficulties with worn-out track. They finally decided to replace the iron rails with steel, and he traveled to Pittsburgh to arrange for their manufacture. When he returned, the children swarmed over him.

They had spotted him coming back in his carriage, and were dancing all over the upper hallway. Errol was now more than five years old, Bernard three and a half, Regina a little more than a year. He delighted in their glee. Scooping Regina up into his arms, he held her high in the air, as each boy clung to a leg.

"I'm dusty and dirty, and you should not," he half-scolded, hugging them, beaming down at them. "Regina, my pet, how very pretty you are! Have you been Papa's good girl?"

She nodded and put her face against his bronzed neck, her body smelling of baby powder and soap fragrance. He carried her back into the nursery, and sat down in his own big chair there.

"Papa, what did you do?" demanded Errol. "Did you fight Indians this time? And bears?"

"Not in New York State, my boy." He ruffled the blond hair, so like his own. What a tall, sturdy lad, he thought proudly.

"What did you bring me, Papa?" asked Bernard, and was frowned at by his nanny.

"A suitcase full of things, which you shall have tomorrow," promised Jacob. "What have my darlings been doing?"

They all talked at once, clamoring for his attention. Too excited to eat, they climbed over him, tugged at his arm to show him some drawing and Errol's first attempt at sums.

He saw them bathed and into bed, then went down to his own supper at the long drawing table, which seemed so silent, so empty, so large and lonely. Hastily he ate the delicious food the cook had prepared for him, then went to bed early. Damn it, he missed Antonia. The master bedroom was full of her clothes, her favorite violet scents, her very presence. He moved to his own bedroom at the back of the house.

The next morning he read letters. Some were from Antonia, telling of her pleasure abroad: how many dukes and duchesses she had met, how many men had begged for the honor of a dance with her, how many country houses had been opened to her.

"We may go on to Italy in the spring, dear Jacob," she wrote. "You will not really mind, will you? Could you not come over and join us in Venice? It would be like a honeymoon!"

So she was paving the way for more months abroad. He sighed, and went off to find some solace in his work. But it was no use. He could not keep his mind on it.

He came home early, played with the children, and showed them the toys and scraps of railroad tickets he had brought them. The boys loved to play "train," and were delighted to have "real tickets." They took turns being engineer and conductor, while Regina obediently sat in whatever "parlor car" they set her in, smiling like an angel.

They had their supper, and Jacob faced another long evening alone. He thought about visiting his father, then remembered he was having dinner with some railroad friends.

He thought of Evan and Molly, called for his carriage, and went off to see them. They welcomed him joyfully. Their children were in bed, but Vincent got up and came out in his pajamas to see "Mr. Jacob," as he called him. The boy was eight years old, but taller and straighter and more serious than his years.

He listened in silence as Jacob told of his trip upstate, of the decision to change to steel rails, of a bridge that had collapsed, carrying sixty-eight persons to their deaths in the icy waters below. The lad's vivid blue eyes reminded Jacob of Rowan's and Molly's. He had her hair as well, blue-black and springy and curly on his young head. He sat on a stool at his father's feet, and leaned sleepily back against Evan. But the blue gaze never left Jacob's face. It was as though the boy memorized all he said.

Jacob noted a pile of newspaper clippings carefully set in a small box on the desk where Evan worked. He stood up to get an ashtray for his pipe, leaned over the desk, and saw his wife's smiling face as she held the lead of two fine greyhounds.

He picked up the clippings and glanced through them. "Quite a pile," he said, and laid them down, reaching for the ashtray.

"We've been collecting them," Molly said, half-guiltily. "My, she is beautiful."

"Yes, she is," Jacob said, his face expressionless. Evan changed the subject.

They talked about the unions, Evan's new work as a precinct captain, and the unemployment lines that had sprung up since the war.

"Mrs. O'Callahan's shop is going well," Evan said. "She is grateful to you for backing her, and she has given jobs to eight women now. And your loaning her your head clerk to teach her bookkeeping—she can't get over that. It was fine of you to help her out."

"She shows a good profit, and has paid me back," Jacob said shortly, uncomfortable. He had had his own motives in helping the widow, and he was a bit ashamed of them. She was a fine figure of a woman, and he had been attracted to her. Since she had set up the shop, they had had several meetings, all formal and business-like. She had promised him earnestly to pay him from her profits, and he had felt mean.

"You'll have some good Irish beer," Molly said tactfully, and bustled out to the kitchen to get it. She brought back a tray of three chilled mugs, and they drank to the railroads.

He stayed until ten. Then, aware of their weariness,

he took his leave. Evan had to rise early in the morning, for he still worked for the Van Rhyne bookkeeping department, in addition to his union activities and ward duties. And Jacob could sleep as late as he chose, for he was the boss.

He went back often that winter. Sometimes he took Pieter with him, and they talked railroads, but not unions, for that made Pieter flamingly angry. The McKennas were more formal when Pieter came, for the old man was a wealthy tycoon now, with his own parlor car, and his name in the financial news. "Mr. Pieter Van Rhyne of the Van Rhyne lines says that . . . " His words were listened to as gospel, for he was a shrewd, canny man, as the journalists said.

Sometimes Jacob went over to visit Sunny Malone, or accompanied Paul, now a doctor with a thriving practice, on his rounds. Paul had patients who were very wealthy, and those who could hardly afford to pay him for his services.

"The rich ones pay for the poor," Jacob said shrewdly, one day, as they rode along in Paul's sober black carriage.

"Yes, that they do," said Paul calmly, with a little, sweet smile. "I would be a poor doctor to turn down their appeals. So I just charge them according to their ability to pay."

Jacob frowned. "That's socialism."

"It is also the teaching of Jesus Christ," Paul said, managing the reins lightly on the icy streets.

Jacob was silent, thinking it over. There must be a flaw in Paul's logic somewhere, but he could not find it.

One day he received a letter from Antonia, who was now in Venice. "I knew you would not mind; I did get so cold up north!" she wrote, and he could almost hear her plaintive, wistful, sweet voice. "So we came south to get warm. Venice is adorable. You would love it! The Italians all sing to us in their beautiful boats, and we are invited to dine with a marquis tonight! There is a masked ball this Saturday. I shall go as a shepherdess,

283

with a crook over my arm, and only my pearls. Why do you not join us in Rome? You would like Rome."

Jacob set his mouth. She had been gone for four months now, and showed no signs of returning. He had to admit the children did not miss her. They had a devoted Irish nanny who adored and scolded them alternately, and they obeyed her, which was more than they did Antonia.

It was spring. He strolled in the park one Sunday, and remembered ice skating there with Molly, so long ago. He clasped his hands behind his back and walked along, not noticing the curious glances at his full blond beard, his fine clothes, his erect posture, his bronzed face, so unlike the wan, pallid faces on the city bankers and clerks.

Among the passersby, he caught a green eye that seemed to know him. He bowed, and she curtseyed, and then he recognized her.

"Good day to ye, Mr. Van Rhyne," she said.

"And a good day to you, Mrs. O'Callahan," he said, smiling. On impulse, he turned to walk beside her for a few moments. "You are looking blooming today."

"Oh, thank ye, sir! Fine I am, and the day so beautiful and all. One would not think it so early in April, with all the chill in the air. I note the wee flowers are springing out, the little primroses and the spring beauties."

He had not seen them. He paused to admire them now as she pointed them out with her white-gloved finger.

"I hope all goes well in the shop?" he inquired, reluctant to leave her. She was the first person he had spoken to all day, except for the servants in his house.

"Very well, sir. I am grateful to ye for setting up the shop, and so say we all. Ye must stop by one day and see the books. You would admire them, I feel sure! I have trained a new woman on the books, to give me more time for the fine sewing. We sold thirty-two bonnets last week!"

"Splendid, splendid! And Sunday is your day off."

284

He felt foolish, spinning out the conversation like this, but her green eyes were bright and sparkling, and she had lost the wistful look. Her plump figure was encased in a dress of green alpaca, and over it she wore a paletot of black velvet with a white velvet border. It was very smart, and he thought she must have made it herself. A little black velvet hat sat perched atop her red-gold hair.

"I hope the children are all fine?" she asked.

"Fine and healthy." He smiled. "They are off to a party this afternoon. The boys are reluctantly wearing fine suits, and Regina is all dressed up, in a violet silk dress the color of her pretty eyes."

"There, now, what a lucky man you are, to have such children," she said.

"You did not have children?" he said gently.

She shook her head, and the long lashes came down over her green eyes for a moment. "The Lord did not see fit," she said simply.

He strolled on with her, and they spoke of the white swans on the lake, the blueness of the sky, and the news in the papers of trouble in France. A cloud came over the sun, and the day turned abruptly cold, with a keen wind whipping across the waters, rippling the lake.

"A cup of tea would taste fine today," she said as they reached the end of the park drive, where his carriage was waiting for him. She smiled and held out her hand, to shake his offered one.

"Would you brew a cup of tea for me?" he asked suddenly.

The green eyes looked startled. She gazed up at him, then flushed a little. "Oh, sir, I'd be pleased to do that. You'll come up to my wee place?"

"I'd be happy to come." He assisted her into the carriage, and gave the coachman directions. They trotted along the April-gray streets to Jacob's office building, where her apartments were on the third floor.

As they went in, he said to the coachman, "There's a pub on the corner. Go refresh yourself. I'll come and find you later."

"Yes, sir," said the coachman, and put his fingers to his cap and drove off.

Jacob tucked his hand under Mrs. O'Callahan's arm and led her inside. They walked up the two flights of stairs, and she unlocked the door to her "wee place." It was a pleasant series of rooms, with a southern exposure, and she had a few plants on a stand near the sitting room windows.

The floor above was where the women sewed. He had seen it on an inspection trip with the local firemen. He owned the entire building, and the others on this block, although he did not advertise the fact. But this was the first time he had been inside her apartment since she had moved in.

On the dining room table sat several unfinished bonnets, with veiling, netting, flowers, and such strewn about. She sighed over them. "There, now, and I meant to have all cleared up. You'll forgive the disorder, sir?"

"You planned to work on the bonnets on Sunday?" he asked.

She giggled unexpectedly. "You sound like our priest," she said, a flush rising into her pink-and-white cheeks. "There, now, just a wee bit of sewing to finish them off against tomorrow. The ladies are that impatient."

"They can wait," Jacob said, frowning. "You're not to work seven days a week. You are doing well financially, are you not?"

"Well enough, well enough," she said evasively, and went to put on a kettle for tea. He followed her to the kitchen, and leaned against the wall, watching her with pleasure. For a plump woman, she moved deftly, and her ankles were slim below the green alpaca dress.

"Do you give much to charity?" he asked mildly.

She gave him a sidelong glance. "Well, sir, having been helped meself, it would be wrong not to help others, would it not, sir?"

"Not to the extent that you make yourself poor, and deprive yourself," he said. "Next time, ask *me,* and I'll

286

help them. And give yourself a day of rest once a week!"

He had caught a glimpse of the cupboard shelves as she had opened the doors to take down the canister of tea and two cups and saucers. There was very little on those shelves, just some jars of homemade preserves and a few cans of beans and other vegetables.

She prepared the tea and brought in a plate of bread slices, a big jar of jam, and a small one of butter. He ate hungrily. It all tasted good, especially in her company. He liked the way she listened to him, with a waiting look in her eyes. And she giggled like a girl when he amused her with his stories.

"There, now, you would not fool me, would you? Sure, and you would not have wrestled a bear with your arms, sir?"

"You would, if you had decided to have the bear for dinner, instead of letting the bear have you for dinner!" he declared soberly, and she burst into a fit of giggling.

"I declare, Molly McKenna did say as how you could spin out the tales like a true Irishman," she said, then blushed. "There, now, I'd be insulting you, maybe?"

"By calling me an Irishman? Never."

He lingered. He did not want to leave this cozy apartment, with the green, flower-printed cushions on the wide sofa, the big, comfortable chairs, the plants in the window, the sunshine drifting through the white lace curtains. And he did not want to leave the warmth of her lilting Irish voice, so like Molly's, and the flash of her green eyes, and the bursts of giggles, like a young girl's.

He finally rose, very reluctantly. His house would be dark and empty, but for the servants. Pieter would be over at Sunny's, as he was most Sundays.

He started slowly for the door. "I don't like to go," he said, his mouth turning down. "This has been the most pleasant afternoon I've had in quite a long time."

She blushed with pleasure. "There, now, thank ye, and do come again soon," she said politely.

He had his hand on the doorknob. He turned around

and looked at her, and caught her wistful look. "Do you want me to leave?" he asked bluntly.

Her color was high, but she met his gaze bravely. "No, I don't," she said in a low voice.

He came back to her slowly, letting her have a chance to draw back. He put his hands on her shoulders, and they were soft and warm and womanly. He pulled her into his arms and she rested against him. Oh, God, she was so soft and fragrant, and sweet and willing—

He pushed back the red-gold hair, his hand on the back of her neck, and gazed longingly into the green eyes. "Oh, Deirdre . . . " he groaned, and it was the prettiest name in the world.

He looked at her full mouth, the full, sensuous lower lip, the quivering upper lip, and he put his mouth onto hers slowly, luxuriously, exulting in her shivering as she pressed herself closer to him. His lips came down harder, and he felt her resistance give way, her own lips answering his.

They stood like that for a long time, his arms wrapped around her warm softness, her arms about his neck. He kissed her cheeks, flushed and warm. He kissed the soft creases of her throat. He rocked her back and forth, to feel her against his hard thighs and chest, holding her closer to press her into his very bones. She seemed to melt against him, as though he pressed down into a fragrant pillow that would not let go of him.

Then, kissing was not enough. He led her, his arm still about her waist, to her bedroom, and tenderly undressed her. She lay on the bed, her body open to him, and he feasted his eyes on the plump, delicious curves, the white flesh, the roundness and the softness of her. He ripped off his own clothes, and joined her there on the bed.

Her arms came up around him hungrily. She whispered, "I have not wanted anyone—until I saw you. Oh, Jacob, I do love you . . . I do love you . . . "

Her confession almost stopped him. He had not thought about love. He had wanted and needed her sexually, not loved. But he could not stop now; his desires were raging in him.

He pressed his tough body against hers eagerly. She welcomed him, opening her thighs, and he slid between them easily, no fighting there, no resistance. Nothing but welcome, a warm, luscious, hungry welcome. He moved into her, and lost himself there, and it was feast after famine, to move in her and with her, and feel her passionate response.

She was crooning to him, her hands caressing his back, neck, and head. "Oh, me love, oh, me love, come to me, ye are so delightsome to me . . . "

The green eyes were half closed by her long red-gold lashes. Her hair was loose on her pillows, and he reached to pull out the rest of the combs and let it fall about her shoulders in silky waves. He buried his face in the hair, moving on her slowly, drawing the moment out, enjoying, delighting . . .

Then the desire rose up so strongly, he wanted so much, that he became fierce in it, but still she yielded, crooning to him, stroking him, so that he burst out with desire, and finished to his own satisfaction.

He half-lay on her, his legs across hers, his arm pressed to her breast, recovering. Her hands still stroked him, her mouth half-smiled, in that satisfied look of a tender, loving woman. When he had caught his breath, he moved his hand, cupped a rich, full breast, and played with the rose-colored nipple. His lean hips moved closer to hers, and he felt a new desire rise up in him.

Her hand reached down naturally, and stroked him. He caught his breath in pleasure, and watched as she prepared him. She smiled shyly, and pressed her face to his chest, and her hand and fingers went on stroking him.

He moved over on her, and had her once again, and this time she cried out, gripping him with aching fingers, and her hips rose up off the bed, to meet his.

He slept in her arms, and awakened much later. He cursed himself, not for himself, but for her. He dressed and went out to the pub, where the coachman tried to look bland and unknowing.

Jacob went back to Deirdre again and again, and always she welcomed him eagerly, with delight. He found laughter and forgetfulness with her. She could soothe him and comfort him when he was sick at heart.

How strange it was, he thought sometimes. He had married in his social range, dutifully, as his father had done, choosing with his mind instead of his heart. He had found the result cold and bitter. Antonia wandered where she would, having done her duty and provided him with heirs. Now, subtly, she was telling him that she wanted her own pleasure elsewhere.

He wondered sometimes what would have happened if he had dared to marry Molly. Would she have become accepted, in time, by society? Or would society have laughed at her behind her back, and broken her sturdy, Irish, loving heart? No, Molly was better off with Evan McKenna and her Irish brood. She cared for them, and they, in turn, kept the tilt to her chin and the happiness in her blue eyes.

She and her Evan would never be rich; they would never have mansions and servants and fine clothes. But what did it matter, after all? The making of money was an end in itself, and not a means to the end of a happy fruitful life.

When war began to rage over the continent of Europe, Antonia returned. But by now, they were almost strangers. She would go out nightly, until three or four in the morning, seeking the pleasures of New York society.

He went to bed at ten, rose at dawn, worked twelve hours as his men did, and on Sundays, he often went quietly to Deirdre. There, in her arms, he could find peace and comfort. He was anxious to protect her reputation, so there were no meetings in public places. He took her nowhere. But he did give her money, and a few jewels to keep against need. She protested even at those small gifts, but it made him feel better, for he felt that he had cheated her, though she never complained.

She cooked simple suppers for him, even porridge on a cold winter's night, with molasses on it. And he ate with more gusto than at one of his wife's banquets. He ate ham and green beans, and homemade cakes, with far greater pleasure than shrimp and oysters, petit fours and frozen gelatines.

And he could talk to Deirdre of the railroads, of his problems with the ward politicians, of the unions, and of the trouble in the mines he owned. She did not always understand, but she would listen and soothe his troubled spirit. And always, there was her wide bed, where, after the loving and the passion, he could find rest and peace. In her arms, he found tender love and devotion, gentleness and adoration, and an unquestioning submission to his every desire.

PART III

1888–1898

Chapter 20

Errol Van Rhyne rolled over in his wide bed, yawned, and finally opened his eyes. By the sunshine gleaming in through the space between the two loosely drawn, brown velvet drapes, he knew the hour was late. He was usually up at dawn, but last night he had arrived at midnight on the train from the West. His very bones still felt the rocking and creaking of the Pullman car.

He got up and went to shower and shave. His valet heard the sounds, and by the time Errol returned to his room, his morning clothes had been laid out neatly on the couch: a steel-gray, single-breasted morning coat with a narrow collar, a waistcoat to match, and narrow-legged trousers. His bowler hat and walking stick were set out nearby.

"Fine to have you back, sir," the valet said in his low, calm voice.

"Thank you, Malcolm." It was good to be back, Errol thought, though he knew that here in the East, he would soon be restless again. The West was so different: the vast plains, the mountains, the cattle ranches, the wheat lying golden to the very horizon.

He dressed, brushed his hair back vigorously with two brushes, trying to slick back the blond curls that had been the bane of his teenage existence in the rigid boys' school he had attended with his brother Bernard.

"Did I hear Bernard coming in after me last night?" he asked the valet.

"Yes, sir," Malcolm replied, meeting his gaze for a fleeting, understanding moment, before moving to offer the snugly fitting jacket. He eased it onto Errol's broad shoulders. "My word, sir, every time you come back from the West, you seem bigger. I must see your tailor, sir."

Errol grinned. "You mean, *I* must see him about some new clothes, before mother catches sight of me."

Malcolm permitted himself a smile.

"Where *is* mother?" he asked.

"Sleeping late, sir. She is quite well, and enjoyed your letters. Your father, Mr. Jacob, did not go to the office. He is waiting to see you in his study."

"Right. I'll go down."

"Do you wish your breakfast in his study?"

"That will be fine." Errol shook his head at the offered cane, and went out quietly into the hallway. He and his brother had rooms of their own, in a wing away from the main house. Regina's apartments were on the other side. His sister was growing into a beauty, he thought fondly. He wondered if his mother had found a suitable match for her yet. Poor Regina. He knew his mother was aiming high.

Errol stayed out of his mother's way as much as possible. *He* was not going to get married until he was good and ready, and that might be years yet. He had seen too many bad marriages, for him to want to rush into one of his own.

He had learned years ago, so long ago that he did not recall when he had not known, that his father quietly kept a mistress. Bernard had been outraged when he had learned of it in his teens, but Errol had persuaded him to keep his mouth shut. "Mother goes her way, and has her fun. Why not Father?" Errol said reasonably. But it did not endear the state of matrimony to him.

He tapped at the study door, and Jacob called out, "Come in!"

The blue eyes, so like his, gazed up at him eagerly as he entered. Jacob got up from the huge mahogany desk, and came over to his son. They shook hands formally, their large hands clasping tightly.

Jacob smiled at the boy, and drew a deep breath. "You were gone so long, I thought you had forgotten you had a home here!"

"Could I forget?" Errol said mildly. He sat down in the easy chair opposite the desk. Jacob patted his shoulder, his only gesture of affection now. In the old days, Errol could remember how his father had taken him in his arms, picked him up to hold him high over his head, then brought him back down and hugged him to his chest.

Regina got everything her heart desired, from clothes to jewels to a coming-out party at eighteen. Bernard, too, was pampered and spoiled. But Errol got dusting-outs, harassment, harshness. And he understood. Jacob depended on him, for he was training his eldest son to follow in his footsteps. Errol was the one who would inherit the railroads, and manage them, and he was aware of that, without a word being spoken.

Regina was a girl. Bernard was spoiled, weak, and mischievous. But Errol had always been dependable, smart, and coolly in command of himself. His teachers had nothing but praise for him. He had graduated from engineering courses in university, and now spent all his summers out on the railroads. Like his father, he loved the railroads, and his greatest joy was going out West and working on them.

The valet tapped, and came in quietly with a large, silver tray. He set the plate of ham and eggs before Errol, poured coffee for them both, then departed, as quietly as he had come.

"Well?" Jacob demanded.

Errol leaned back, wiping his mouth. "Rate wars," he said succinctly, "just as you surmised. The superintendents are starting in again, cutting the wheat harvest. I learned that when I got there. Now they are making promises to the farmers on the next crops."

"Damnation," Jacob muttered. "This peace agreement won't last any longer than the others. What took you so long? When you didn't get home for Christmas, Antonia raised hell!"

"I was learning some more facts," Errol said with his accustomed calmness, unusual in a young man of twenty-three. "I went down to visit with Leigh Sheldon.

297

He's fine, and sends his regards. His boys are growing up quickly. One of them is as fast with a gun as Leigh was, and they worry about him. He's a wild one."

Jacob shook his head, his blue eyes cloudy with reminiscence. "And he *was* fast. He was mighty fast. Never saw another one so quick and accurate," he said.

"He told me some gossip. I went to check on it. It was true. The Southern Pacific is going ahead, building more rails, even though they have overbuilt through that area."

"More roads? Damnation!" Jacob exploded again, his fist pounding in irritation on the desk. "They'll cripple us all with their competition! It's downright idiotic, it's the action of a jackass—"

"When other roads are moving into your territory, it's the only way to strike back," Errol said thoughtfully. He finished the ham and eggs, ate the thick bread heartily, then pushed aside his plate to drink down the coffee. Usually he ate only to stock his tough, muscular body, scarcely noticing the food. But this morning, after months of outdoor living and outdoor cooking, the perfectly prepared breakfast tasted delicious.

"There has to be some other answer, or we'll all go bankrupt," Jacob muttered. "Morgan's banking house has tried to mediate again, but how long will the agreements last, with everyone going behind each other's backs to cut rates again?"

"It killed Grandfather," Errol said quietly. "Don't let it kill you, Dad."

The gazes of the two men, so much alike, met with understanding. They both were thinking of old Pieter. He'd had a stroke in the terrible winter of 1883, during the rate wars, the fierce jungle warfare of the railroad barons. He had died in Sunny's arms, as he would have wished, with Paul attending him. It had caused a scandal at the time, and Antonia had been very upset. Jacob had shrugged. If his mother had died before Pieter, he thought Pieter would have married Sunny. Pieter hadn't believed in divorce, but he had thought more of Sunny than of any other woman in the world.

"I don't know the answer yet, but, Errol—keep this under your bowler—I may get out of the West."

"I was thinking about that, Dad," Errol responded. "We have plenty to do here: consolidate, tighten up, get rid of our rails out West, sell out to Central Pacific—"

"Damn you, boy, are you telling *me* what to do?"

Errol grinned. "Just reading your mind, Father," he said with respectful laughter.

Jacob shook his head, finished his black coffee, and got out his pipe. They both lit up, and smoked in silence for a time. Then Errol went on with his report, telling his father in detail about what he had seen, what men he had contacted, and about the rate wars spreading through the Southwest into the Missouri River area.

Jacob listened, taking mental notes. His decision was being made for him; they must get out before they went to the wall. It would cripple them to try to compete with the cutthroat tactics the other railroads were employing. Only the strongest would win, and even they might lose in the long run, with no profits to show after carrying freight for rates far under cost.

They finished reviewing the situation, and Errol stretched and started to get up. Jacob motioned him to sit down again.

"There's something else, boy," he said, his face settling into heavy, worried lines. "You'll soon hear, so I want you to hear from me first."

Errol waited.

"It's Bernie," Jacob said slowly. "He is playing around with some actress named Daisy Bloom. Isn't that a godawful name? She's older than he is, acts in melodramas, and sings some. I went to see her. If I were twenty years younger I might have fallen for her myself, since she's so pretty and cute and always laughing. Damn it, he gives her diamonds, and his mother is having fits."

"He'll be sowing his wild oats," Errol said, frowning a little.

"That's not all. You know how he and your Uncle Lodewick's boy Clinton were always daring each other on, all through their teens? Well, Clinton got onto this girl first, and he's jealous as hell. They had a knock-down-drag-out fight about it right in public, at the theater one night. The girl loved it. It got in all the papers and gave her publicity, damn her eyes!"

"Young puppies," Errol said, although Bernard was only two years younger than he.

"His valet tipped me off. Bernard has started carrying a revolver, because Clinton is. Errol, I'm worried. Can you talk to your brother? He might listen to you."

"You don't believe he—? Well he might, damn it," said Errol, finally moved to anger. "Yes, I'll talk to him, and make him give me the gun. He is in New York City, not the Wild West, damn it. If I don't take it away from him, the police will."

"Well, you talk to him. He won't listen to his mother, and he just sulks when I bawl him out. We spoiled him, between us; he was ever a handsome lad," Jacob sighed. "His mother was always showing him off at parties from the time he was three. How did you get out of all that, Errol? I always wondered."

A cynical curl flicked at the corner of Errol's mouth. "After a few such parties, with ladies patting me with their hands and making me recite poems, the whole business made me so sick, I got so I could sniff a party coming. When I got dressed up, I would sneak out into the garden and fall into the pond right at the last minute, too late to change and go with mother. You know how she hates to wait when the carriage comes. Or I would roll over in the mud, or go out to the stables and get into muck. How she hated it!"

Jacob shook his head reproachfully. "I knew you were doing something, Errol, but you—damn it, you were only a small lad! And so Bernard went to the party, and Regina, but you were sent to bed!"

"Sent to my rooms, with Nanny hovering over me with hot cocoa to ward off a chill, or one of the kitchen boys sneaking up the back stairs with fried chicken and cakes, they were that sorry for me!" Errol laughed, a gay, rollicking laugh that made his father join in. "Oh, Dad, if you only knew . . ."

"You never pulled those tricks on me," Jacob said. "You came right with me to the office, where I put you on a stool and made you do sums the way the clerks did."

"Oh, I liked that. They talked to me about the accounts and the railroads, and sometimes I could come into your office when you talked to the men who came in from the West. I loved that, and all their stories. I decided right then and there, I was going to be a railroad man."

They laughed over that, and then Jacob spoke of Christmas. "You missed a real big fight, Errol. I came back to the study and hid out, I was that cowardly. Your aunt Elisabeth has never forgiven Father for his will, and she lets us know it. Hans is bitter over his small amount of shares, after giving his life to the accounts. Lodewick—well, he hates my guts, and he enjoys it that Clinton is giving Bernard hell. Even Blaine was cold for a time, until I got it through his thick head what Father was about."

"If old Pieter had left his shares evenly divided among all of you, the company would have been split up. This way, you manage it, and keep the company together," Errol said, nodding. "But I can see their point. And of course, they bitterly resent Sunny Malone and Paul."

"Yeah." Jacob was silent, remembering how the room had seemed to explode when the will was read. All of them, so proper in black, dabbing at their eyes with lace-trimmed handkerchiefs, until the lawyers began reading the parts about the stocks and the money.

Pieter had left ninety percent of everything he had to Jacob. Flat, clear. Everything. Hilda had gotten her house, and enough to live on. Sunny Malone had gotten her apartment and the office building it was in, which would easily bring in enough money to make her comfortable for the rest of her life.

Paul had received $250,000 outright, the same

amount as each of Pieter's children, and that had outraged them further. Father's bastard, to get the same as
them! Of course, Hans had his wages from the office;
he was chief clerk there now. And Lodewick and Blaine
had their income from stocks in coal mines and shipping that Pieter had bought them. But the railroads had
all gone to Jacob. Elisabeth was especially bitter. Her
millionaire husband had been jabbing at her spitefully
ever since the will. Not that $250,000 was bad; only she
had expected a fair slice of Pieter's estate, well in excess
of twenty-five million dollars. Instead, it had all gone to
Jacob! And they could not forgive him.

They still came around. They would not cut dead a
brother who was a multimillionaire, and whose exper-
tise kept their money coming in regularly. But they got
their jabs in.

"The reason I brought it up now," Jacob said quietly,
"is that I'm making the same kind of will. Everything to
you, Errol. You might as well know, it isn't a kindness.
It's what old Pieter did for me. I'm leaving you the railroads and the shipping and the mines, just as he did.
And it'll be a burden on your shoulders, and a bitter-
ness to your mother and brother and sister. And you'll
damn it as an albatross, as I do. And you'll grit your
teeth, and go ahead and handle it all, and keep your
feelings to yourself, because you know your duty and
you'll always do it. Not like them; they'd throw it over a
windmill and grouse because there isn't more. But you'll
take care of it all, and keep it together for all of them."

Errol sat there, staring at his father, feeling overwhelmed and jubilant and scared to death all at the
same time. Suddenly, what he had vaguely felt all along,
that he would some day manage the business, had become a reality. And the way his father had flung it at
him, coldly and clearly, without any warning, had taken
his breath away.

Jacob puffed on his pipe, then laid it down. "Think
about it, son. Think about it, and keep it to yourself,
like it was sacred truth revealed," he said wryly. "I had
to do that myself for ten years, before Father died. But I

was prepared. I braced myself and took their reproaches and tears, and held out—because it's necessary. Someone has to be boss, and sit on top of the peak, and see the whole view clear and bright, and make the decisions, and hang on when the going is tough. I am that person now, and you will be one day."

"But you aren't—you aren't going—" Errol's voice seemed strangled in his throat.

"Going to pop off soon? Hope not! I'm fifty-two, and in good condition; Paul just checked me over last week. He says that if I learn to keep my temper and not worry so much, I'll last as long as Dad, if not longer." He grinned wryly again. "Can't promise a thing! If those newspaper fellows get my goat, I'll let them have both barrels. And when I read about the rate wars, I get sick. And Antonia—" He stopped abruptly, and scowled. "Well, that's private," he said gruffly.

They talked longer, considering plans for the future, and Errol felt already like more of an equal. He showed his father his proposed maps for more lines, to parallel some of the present ones, then branch off into little-touched lands in the far Southwest, to pick up more of the beef-cattle business.

They were both startled at a tap on the door. Antonia walked in, smiling at them both.

"My darling boy, you have come home!" she cried dramatically. Errol had risen, and she flung her arms carefully around him, in order not to muss her dress. He kissed her painted cheek dutifully, then held her back.

"You look splendid, Mother," he said. She wore her favorite purple, in the new bustle-style gown, with a close-fitting jacket bodice, edged in a deep frill about her handsome throat. The skirt was frilled in narrow pleats. Diamonds flashed at her throat, on her ears, and about her wrists.

"You looked terribly tanned and rough," she complained. "And you were gone five months! Really, Errol, you might have considered us!"

"He did," Jacob growled. "He was on company business, so you might be able to buy your dresses and furs!"

"Now, Jacob, don't fuss!" she said sweetly. "Darling Errol, I'm giving a dinner tonight; you must come! Nobody believes I have such a handsome elder son, and I have a girl I want you to meet."

Errol looked at his father over his mother's carefully set blond curls. Jacob was making a ferocious grimace. Errol touched his mother's perfect curls, and she squealed. He dropped his hand hastily.

"I'll try to make it, Mother. But I have a lot of work to catch up on."

She sighed. "You sound just like Jacob. But do, do try to come, darling. You are twenty-four, and not married yet!"

He smiled. "Not twenty-four until November, Mother. Only twenty-three, so I may stay single for a while yet."

"It would not hurt you to be polite to some young ladies," she said firmly. "You will forget your manners in that wild West! Do say you will come."

"I will try to come."

"And dress up, please! I cannot forget how you were always so dirty and muddy when I wanted to take you to a party, when you were a boy. I quite gave up on you."

"It was a pity," Errol said solemnly. Jacob made a choking sound in the background. "However, I now wash behind my ears, if my valet makes me."

Jacob gave up, and guffawed. Antonia gave both of them suspicious looks, and began to retreat. When the men ganged up on her, she knew enough to quit.

"Do try, darling. And there is a tea this afternoon. Dear Regina will pour. She is so graceful! I have great plans for your sister, Errol." And she vanished, with a little wave of her white hand.

Jacob was still chuckling, wiping tears of mirth from his eyes. Errol patted his shoulder, then said, "I'll be off to work, Father. Can I get you anything?"

"Wait five minutes, and I'll go with you. With a gaggle of chattering women coming in to tea, I want to get away."

Errol called for his carriage, his valet brought down his bowler hat and cane, and Jacob soon appeared. They took off with the furtive manner of two criminals escaping the scene of a crime.

At the office, all was work. Errol disappeared into his own office to put his sketches into more permanent form on maps. Jacob was roaring around about some profit figures he wanted, and Hans scurried about to urge the clerks to hurry. Things were back to normal.

Hans brought the morning papers in to Errol. "Jacob wants you to have a look at these, my boy," he said, with a worried look.

Errol took them, and his mouth tightened grimly. He read the entire account, the banner headlines, the captions under the pictures, and then the text. Bernard and Clinton had had a fight last night over the actress Daisy Bloom. A picture showed Daisy, her eyes sparkling delightedly, and the two men squared off with fists in the best John L. Sullivan manner. A crowd in the background seemed to cheer them on, rather than attempting to part them. But the expression on the faces of his brother and his cousin worried Errol. They both looked angry and determined, even vicious.

"Your mother will hate this," Hans said hopefully, peering slyly at Errol. "And her with a grand party tonight!"

"I'd best get home, then. Is father ready to leave?"

"He left half an hour ago. I'm to give you a ride in my carriage," Hans said.

Jacob was not at home when Errol arrived at five o'clock. Errol guessed that he had gone for the attention and loving he did not get from Antonia. He could not blame him.

Errol's valet had laid his evening clothes out: his black tie and tails, his white ruffled shirt, and an assortment of studs. He showered and dressed, then sat down in his shirt sleeves to go over some more papers. At seven o'clock promptly, he made his way downstairs.

The guests were assembling in the huge dining room. Errol went in quietly, to the head of the table. He found a man there, with his hand on the back of the carved chair.

Cecil Meryon was not Errol's favorite person. Tall, gangling, with an Adam's apple bobbing up and down, he was too good at dancing to please Errol, too good at flattering the ladies. He was Antonia's "social advisor," and Errol loathed the sight of him.

"My place, I believe," said Errol, as Mr. Meryon was about to seat himself at the head of the table.

Meryon started, and turned about as though he had seen a ghost.

"Why, Mr. Errol, my word! I was *so* surprised. No one thought you would appear tonight!" He recovered from his surprise gracefully, and proffered a lean, narrow hand—like a cold fish, Errol thought.

Antonia was watching them from the opposite end of the table, her thin mouth compressed. Mr. Meryon gracefully walked to a place farther down, and the footmen hastily moved the plates to give him room between a gentleman and a lady.

Errol sat down and turned with a smile to his right, introducing himself to the dowager there, then to the left, to a graceful girl with bright, curious brown eyes. He smiled at them both, making himself behave pleasantly to them, but seething inside. So, when his father was not there, Antonia let that—that worm sit at the head! Instead of asking one of the older masculine guests to do the honors, she had that cringing excuse of a man, that hand-washing fashion plate—

"My, you are so brown! Have you been to the Mediterranean?" the girl on his left drawled.

"No, out West, overseeing our railroad lines," Errol said pleasantly.

She gave a shudder of fear and pleasure. "So dangerous! So terrible!" she murmured. "Weren't you frightened?"

"No," he said. "I have often been out West. Tell me, I believe your mother is in the Opera Society?"

That occupied them through the soup. Then Errol turned to the matron on his other side, and discussed the latest fashions.

His first duties done, he leaned back during a change of courses and surveyed the long table. Bernard was not there. He recognized scarcely half of the guests. A lovely girl halfway down caught his eye. She was blond, stately, with violet eyes. She smiled at him, and he caught his breath. Regina! He had not even recognized his own sister! She was dressed in such a mature manner, in green striped silk, with emeralds and diamonds at her throat and in her ears. Yet, for all her finery, there was a sad look to her mouth. He must talk to her soon.

Oysters were followed by slices of beef in some strange wine sauce. It spoiled the flavor of the beef, he thought, remembering the bawling cattle he had often helped load onto boxcars when they were short of hands. These society people would shudder fastidiously if they knew what had been done to get the cattle, raised out on the open range, herded into town to cattle cars, then to the slaughterhouses of Chicago. They wouldn't much like to visit the slaughterhouses. The thought made him smile so broadly that the girl on his left thought she was really making a good impression on the hard-boiled Mr. Errol Van Rhyne. She cheered up, and tried harder.

The dinner comprised ten courses, each with its wine. Errol was glad when the three long hours were over. He stood as the ladies left the room, led by Antonia. He gave Regina a secret wave and a wink, then strode over to where Cecil Meryon was standing.

"I must return to my work, Mr. Meryon," he said coldly. "If you will see to the port and brandy, sir?"

"Of course, of course!"

He was glad to get away. He escaped to his rooms, where he kept his own study. He took off his coat, gave it to his valet, and sat down at the desk. Before midnight he had completed the sketches of the new parlor car he was designing. He enjoyed that kind of work. It provided a rest from the tough financial haggling of the rate wars, the endless fighting of the bankers, and the railroad rivalries.

He indicated brown velvet for the plush seats, scratched in some window designs, and sat back to contemplate it. It looked luxurious, but this was an age of luxury. People would no longer put up with the crude conditions that had prevailed for so many years on the railroads. They wanted comfortable rides, air brakes, fewer stops on a long run, and no switching from one train to another in the middle of the night. The Van Rhyne line had added some sleeping cars, and they were a great success, especially on the line from New York to Chicago.

He finally got up, yawning, and went to the sitting room. He found Malcolm sitting on a chair near the door, his head down on his chest, sleeping. He roused him gently.

"I told you to go on to bed! I can get myself to bed, you know!"

"Yes, sir. I just thought I'd give you a hand." Malcolm had jumped up guiltily, and now bustled about to help Errol out of his trousers and fancy shirt.

"What do you think I do when I go out West? Hire an outlaw with two guns at his hips to help me undress at night?"

Malcolm chuckled, then put his hand on his mouth. "Dear me, sir, I'm sure I don't expect—"

"After this, you hear me and go to bed when I tell you."

"Yes, sir."

But both knew he would not. Malcolm knew his duties. He had been strictly trained by his uncle, the butler.

Errol slid into bed, but could not sleep. From the distance came the sound of a violin and a piano. The party went on. He grimaced. No wonder Jacob escaped as often as he could. They would go on half the night, drinking brandy and champagne, smoking cigars, and gossip-

308

ing about everyone who was not present. He could do without that.

He thought of his father, and of the will he had made, and a chill went down his spine. He hoped fervently that nothing would happen to Jacob for years and years. He was not ready for the kind of cold, dreadful responsibility that Jacob had.

Chapter 21

Regina Van Rhyne sat demurely in the rose chintz armchair and lifted the heavy cup to her lips. "Yes, Aunt Molly," she said, and smiled.

Molly McKenna was chattering on about her children, her husband, and her neighbors, her kindly blue eyes taking in every detail of Regina's smart dress. The dress was of violet and white silk with stripes going down the thick bustle to the frilled hem, and Regina wore a matching little violet silk bonnet, set back on her blond curls. She was a picture of fashion that Molly was delighted to see.

"To think you're all grown up now," Molly exclaimed. "I well remember how you would come here with Jacob—I mean, Mr. Van Rhyne—and sit on my knee or down on the floor with Jessie, playing with dolls."

Vincent strolled back from the window, and sat down neatly on the straight-backed chair opposite Regina. "She gave up dolls some time ago, I think," he murmured.

Molly gave them both a keen look. "Well, I'll just go along to the kitchen, and see about starting the supper. You'll stay, Regina?"

"I cannot. I must return by six-thirty, thank you,

309

Aunt Molly." Molly nodded and departed briskly, leaving them alone.

"You look beautiful, my dear," Vincent said, after a pause. "But unhappy. Is your mother pushing you again?"

Regina nodded. "That—that British lord is coming," she said, her mouth set tight. "She thinks it would be grand if we got married. And I haven't even met him! He has a castle in some remote part of England, and a town house in London, and a seat in Parliament, which he rarely attends."

Vincent nodded sympathetically. "But she is all for the gesture. She wants you to marry higher than any other girl in New York City, eh?"

Regina bit her lips. "Oh, Vincent, I tried to tell her that I love you and want to marry you. She was furious. Can you not speak to Father?"

"I want you to be sure in your own mind, my darling," he said. He got up and went over to her, for she was trembling. He drew her up into his arms and held her carefully against himself. She was tall, but not nearly so tall as he. He was so grand and sturdy, so big and dependable, so calm in any crisis. And he was a fine newspaperman; even Jacob said that, although he growled at the young man's columns about the labor problems.

"I *am* sure," Regina whispered.

"You are but eighteen, dear, and scarcely that." His hand stroked her soft blond hair, pushing off her bonnet, which fell to the carpet.

His hand went to her cheek and caressed it, then his fingers tilted her chin upward. They looked at each other until she felt she was drowning in the deep, clear blue of his eyes. His head bent toward hers, and his mouth covered hers, slowly, surely.

She closed her eyes, and the world went away. There was only Vincent, Vincent Rowan McKenna, her darling big man, her steady support, the only sure thing in her world. The man she had loved since she was a little girl, a blushing teenager, a frightened, quiet young woman, hiding behind the mask of coolness she had early on learned to adopt. "The beautiful Miss Regina Van Rhyne," the gossip columns said, underneath her picture at an opera or a dance. "The lovely, cool beauty"—"the wealthy Miss Van Rhyne"—yet few knew her. She had become so adept at acting a part, that only Vincent McKenna knew the real Regina, soft, quiet, loving.

She didn't want to marry a duke. She wanted to marry Vincent, and have a lovely little home, and his babies, and the joy of knowing she would never be frightened again. He would look after her; he would protect her from all the horrors of the world, the terrors of the future her mother had planned for her.

Her arms tightened around his neck, and she rejoiced in the strength of his shoulders. His hard hands pressed on her back, drawing her closer to him. Their lips clung together hotly, and as he pressed harder, her lips opened against the insistence of his.

He drew back a little. "I love you, my darling," he whispered, his voice shaking.

"And I love you. So much, so very much," she said.

"Then why are you afraid?"

Regina shuddered. "She wants me to marry so grandly," she muttered. "She is so willful—even Father says so—she gets whatever she wants. I am afraid, afraid . . ."

"He might be fine, this duke—he might be splendid. You might fall in love with him."

She shook her head fiercely. "No, no, no. I love *you*, I love *you*, and how could I love anyone else but you?"

"I am so much older—"

"I don't care!"

"And your money—"

"I'll give it all away. I don't manage it anyway. I have to ask for an allowance. Mother is afraid to trust me with money; she's afraid I'll run away!"

"And would you?"

"I'd run right to you!"

Their lips met again, passionately, and her head was

whirling. She felt safe only with him, yet they could meet only for minutes, or perhaps an hour, in a dim restaurant somewhere, with him scribbling nonsense in a notebook to make it look as though he were interviewing her for a story.

"Will you talk to Father?" she asked, when she had gotten her breath back after their embrace.

"I tried to," he said ruefully. "I've gone to his office five times. He only sends word that he won't talk to reporters! I'll get in sometime, my darling, but what can I say? 'I earn fifty dollars a week, and I want to marry your daughter.' He would laugh in my face!"

"You're a splendid reporter! And you have had two raises in six years," she pleaded anxiously. "I would live with you anywhere, in a flat, in a cottage . . ."

"Without fine clothes for the opera? Without trips to Europe? Without jewels on your birthdays? With your pretty hands turning red with house work, the scrubbing and the washing up, and babies?"

She trembled. "I would love to have your babies," she whispered daringly.

His arms almost crushed her before he remembered to be tender. His hands stroked her back and shoulders. "I love you," he said. "But we have to wait. When I get another raise, and you are sure in your mind, and a bit older . . ."

"I'm afraid she'll marry me off before I can get my breath—"

Molly came into the room, her kindly face anxious. "Jessie and her beau are coming up the walk," she said bluntly. "Regina, you'd best go home before your mother worries."

Molly darted forward to pick up the violet bonnet.

"Here's your wee hat, me dear," she said, and Regina fastened it again onto her blond curls. "You're white, me dear. Won't you have a cup of something?"

Regina shook her head numbly. Jessie was coming in the door, laughing, her brown eyes bright, followed by her beau. On seeing Regina, she stopped short.

"Oh, I saw the carriage," she said, her gaze going

312

from the guest to her eldest brother, then to her mother. "Miss Regina Van Rhyne, Mr. Padraic Cassidy," she said proudly, slipping her hand into the arm of the tall, bronzed young man beside her.

Regina managed to smile, shake the hand which was held out to her, and say, "Good to see you, Jessie. I must be on my way. Thank you, Aunt Molly, for all the—the conversation."

"You're welcome, and anytime, my dear," Molly said, and saw her to the door. Vincent walked her to the carriage and helped her in, but could only squeeze her hand briefly.

Then she was alone. The carriage rolled up one street and down another, but Regina was not aware. She thought only of Vincent—darling, strong Vincent, and something at the pit of her stomach made her fear she might never see him again.

They arrived at the mansion and she managed to slip inside, and up to her rooms unnoticed. Her mother was engaged with guests, her maid told her. She changed her dress to a less comfortable one, and was down in time for dinner. Errol was not there. He often managed to avoid occasions like this. And Bernard was in trouble, the maid had whispered. Something about some girl. Regina thought her mother's face looked anxious under the polite, smiling, charming mask.

The evening dragged on, but it was finally over. Antonia beckoned her daughter to come to her room with her. In the master bedroom, which showed no signs of any male occupancy, Antonia let her maid take down her beautiful blond curls, and brush them soothingly. Over the collar of her fine cream lace negligee, she said to her daughter, who was standing nervously at the window, "Well, Regina, I suppose you have seen the newspapers?"

"No, Mama, I went visiting today, to Letty's."

It was not a lie. She had hastily visited her friend Letty, who had a new son, then gone directly to Molly's.

"Well, your brother Bernard is in another scrape, and

313

over an actress! I could scream! The scandal could not have come at a worse time, with the Duke of Kildare coming next week!"

Regina held tightly to the curtain. "Next—week?"

"Yes. I'm sure you will like him. But about Bernard! I shall speak sternly to him. I want no more such disgraceful episodes while royalty is here! I will not have it! He is to give up that—that female! I know he wants to have his fun, but he is too brazen about it. Let him sow his wild oats in private, if he must! Why must he get into the papers?" she ended plaintively.

Regina did not attempt to answer that. Her mother resented answers anyway. She could outtalk anyone, even their father, which was why, Regina thought, her father often escaped to his study or his office.

"Everything must go smoothly! It must! I will not be a laughingstock. Everyone knows how I have dreamed of entertaining royalty. Madge has not done so, nor Lillian. I shall be the first, the very first. A duke. A royal duke," she whispered, her violet eyes gazing critically at herself in the mirror. "His Grace. I have been practicing the curtsey. Oh, not so deep as they do it in England, for we are, after all, Americans. But I shall curtsey, so he will know I have manners! A duke. His Grace, the Duke of Kildare. Imagine. A guest in our home. Of course, we shall go to Whitecrest for the season. He will adore Newport, I shall see to that. He loves to ride, so we shall have the horses sent up there. I am buying more horses; your father shall not prevent that! It is important. He must be seated properly!"

Regina clung to the lace curtains until the edging cut into her delicate palms. It was absurd; it could not be happening. The most important thing in her mother's world was that a duke should be seated properly!

Antonia yawned, and patted her mouth with a sleepy palm. "There, now, you must not keep me up talking, Regina," she said. "Do go to bed and get your beauty sleep. I'll talk to you tomorrow about new clothes. Yes, you must have something new and quite fashionable, something in blue. I hear that the duke likes blue. Yes, you shall wear blue, and look feminine and sweet and capable of having royal dukes for sons."

"Mother!" Regina gasped.

"Oh, don't be coy, don't be *coy*," Antonia said impatiently. "You have said often enough that you want children! Why not royal dukes! You will be a duchess, when I have done with you! And why not? We have more money than anyone in England! We have manners! You have been educated at the finest school in America. He will find you charming, I am determined of that! And don't be coy about it, Regina. You can blush and all that in public, but for God's sake don't be coy with your mother! We can be frank with each other!"

"I want to marry Vincent McKenna!" Regina cried, clinging to the tall bedpost as her mother climbed into bed, wearing a pretty lilac cap with a strap to keep her chin firm.

"Don't start that tonight!" Antonia's eyes closed in sheer aggravation. "I will not hear of it! You'll marry the man I choose for you, and that's that! Now go on to bed. Go!"

Regina went to bed, and wept herself to sleep. By morning she was convinced that nobody loved her, not even Vincent, and she moped about the house until her mother caught her up sharply.

"I won't have such a long face about," said Antonia. "We are going out to order some new gowns for you. And while we are at it, I might as well order some for myself."

To Antonia, shopping was a cure for-just about any illness, real or imagined. She adored buying, and she bought as though everything might be snatched away from her at any moment.

Alastair Henry Carstairs, His Grace, the Duke of Kildare, arrived the following Wednesday on a ship from England. He was tall, thin, and lanky, with stringy blond hair, and a long nose that seemed to point downward at everything American. He was about thirty, and he stuttered. His gray eyes seemed blank at times, as though his mind were far away.

He was more polite to men than to women, and managed to keep up an intelligent conversation with Jacob and Errol about railroads, so they rather liked him. With women, he was much more brief. "Don't know much about fashions," he said to Antonia.

It was a point against him, but she did not take offense. After all, how *does* one take offense at a real duke, as Antonia later said to Regina.

They went to Whitecrest, at Newport. It was a thirty-room cottage, set on a high cliff that jutted out daringly over the ocean. Antonia was proud of the way it looked. She had hired the best architects and interior decorators, and a staff of eighteen gardeners.

Carstairs looked around him. "Do you like it?" Antonia asked eagerly.

"Not much like Kildare," he said. "Modern, this."

She led him through the vast cedar-paneled hallways to the summer drawing room, which overlooked the gardens and the terraces. He glanced briefly and incuriously at the great glass-enclosed bookcases that held curios the architect had chosen: ivories, porcelains from the Orient, and a set of British china figurines.

In the summer drawing room, he seated himself in the best chair, quite naturally, as his right. He stretched out his long legs and watched Regina sit down gracefully in a little silk-covered straight chair of the Queen Anne period. He regarded her every so often, looking her up and down—as though she might be a horse he was considering buying, she thought resentfully. She hoped she did not please him.

"The Castle Kildare," said the Duke of Kildare, in his clipped, nasal voice, scarcely opening his mouth, "was built about six hundred years ago. Of course, it was completely renovated recently, about 1820."

Antonia drank it all in greedily, thinking to repeat this to her nearest and dearest rivals. "Of course," she breathed. "We have seen pictures of it in magazines. So splendid! And the view!"

"We hunt," he drawled, as though that explained the view. "About a thousand acres of woodland."

He had inherited it all when he was sixteen, after the death of his father. His mother lived in London, in a town house. She did not care for the country, he stated. He had no brothers or sisters.

Antonia kept trying to exchange happy looks with Regina. Regina steadily avoided that exchange. He must marry and have heirs, she thought angrily, but why couldn't he pick on someone else? Some British girl, who would be happy to fall over in curtseys to him and his lordly title.

"Regina," drawled Alastair Carstairs, "would enjoy the gardens there. Roses. Just like her. A white rose today, eh?"

Antonia took a deep breath. He had complimented her daughter! Matters were progressing. Jacob came in from the carriage house. He sat down with them, and they talked railroads. Antonia was annoyed, for she wanted to hear more about Kildare and its possessions. But that could wait. The duke would remain with them for several weeks. He had practically promised, and Lillian was especially green with envy. Antonia had captured the social lion of the season.

A real duke. Antonia sat still as a mouse and let the men talk, while her thoughts roved happily. Regina, her dear daughter, a duchess. Of a real dukedom. In a real castle. She pictured herself, at a ball, telling her friends, "My daughter the Duchess of Kildare, wrote to me only last week, and said—"

While they talked railroads, she planned a party for the weekend. It would be something really grand! About one hundred guests, with Japanese lanterns in the gardens, a twenty-piece orchestra in the ballroom, flowers in every vase, and catered by Delmonico. It could not fail to be the talk of the season.

Regina would, of course, wear her new dog collar of pearls, and the cream lace over violet silk. But what should she, herself, wear? She must not outshine her

317

daughter, yet there were her diamonds, the new gown of pale gold brocade . . .

The railroad conversation had reached a lull, and Antonia could not resist breaking in and telling them about the party. Jacob privately counted up what it was going to cost him. But the duke seemed impressed and Antonia congratulated herself on having scored another point.

Urgent business called Jacob back to New York before the weekend. Errol sent his regrets that he could not come up. Bernard was there, sullen and furious that he had to appear, and leave Clinton a clear field with Daisy Bloom.

Regina went riding with the duke in the mornings. She wore an adorable outfit of green linen, with a hat like those Antonia had seen in pictures of English ladies. The duke really looked at her those mornings, and seemed to approve.

"You look quite English this morning," he said, each day when she arrived at the stables.

It got to be a private joke. Only she could not share it with anyone. "You look quite English this morning," said the duke.

"Thank you, Your Grace," she would reply. And they would go riding.

He rode in a jerky, upright position, and was constantly critical of Regina's seat. Errol had taught Regina to go with the horse, to sway with its movements. The duke showed her how to ride in the English fashion. It was the only correct way to ride, he told her haughtily.

So she wrote to Errol, joking a little: "I am being retaught to ride, my dear brother. Kildare thinks the English way is the only right way. Mother is even beginning to talk like the English, with her mouth shut. Father may find it an improvement."

The weekend was a vast success. More than one hundred guests appeared, and the ball went on until early morning. The duke wore a uniform of scarlet in which he looked immensely handsome, and Antonia and others were very impressed by his medals and

318

crested ring and studs. "Mostly inherited," he said of the medals. He did not seem a fighter, Regina thought, but kept that thought to herself.

The duke led Regina out in the first dance, and hovered about her much of the evening. Instantly, gossip linked their names together. Antonia's daughter was the object of much attention, but she kept her chin up, and her manner cool.

The duke danced correctly, holding her about a foot from his chest. She was relieved. She hated to be held close by any man except Vincent. She wondered what it would be like to dance with Vincent. Her eyes turned dreamy and she thought of him, so far away.

Photographers appeared, asking them to pose for pictures, and they held the poses until Regina's mouth ached from smiling. But Antonia was thrilled. She knew they would appear in the Sunday newspapers, and she had a man make a special trip to New York just to bring back a load of them.

Regina was thrilled to see the newspapers. She went through them thoroughly, skipping over the society pages. Finally she found what she was looking for—a byline of Vincent's. He had written an article about a possible railroad strike. She read it eagerly. It was so intelligent and well-reasoned. It was just like him.

"Well, I am glad you are taking some interest in your photos," said her mother, finding her with the newspaper in her lap. Regina smiled, flipping back to the society pages.

"You look stunning in this one, Mother. It is particularly good of you."

"Yes, I do take a good picture. Good bones, Regina. Never forget that you have good bones, and always use your gowns and jewels to show them off to advantage."

On Sunday evening, Jacob had gone to see Deirdre. She was sewing on a bonnet when he arrived, but she set it aside, gave him a hug and a kiss, and said, "There, now, it's good to see you. You'll have some beer with me?"

"That sounds good." He followed her out to her little kitchen, and stood there while she poured beer into chilled mugs. They carried them back to the sitting room, and he settled into his favorite big chair, and she into her rocker.

"Did you see the morning papers?" he asked.

She nodded. "My, but Regina is growing into a beautiful young lady."

"Too many parties going on," he rumbled.

"I saw Mr. McKenna's article in the paper. Is there going to be a railroad strike?" she asked.

He scowled. "I like his father, but that lad is going to be the death of me! Too smart for his britches!"

She let him go on, smiling and encouraging him, and letting him blow off steam as he pleased. He talked about the possible strike, how unreasonable the men were, how tough the unions were getting, how he would like to bang their heads together, and how he couldn't have a profit on his lines with the wages and pensions they were asking.

Then she got him on the subject of some new electric engines, and he glowed. He went to the desk for some paper, and drew her a picture of how one would work. She held it upside down; he righted it, and explained it in detail, and she listened and exclaimed at the right moments.

"And how is the dress salon going on?" he asked presently.

"Fine, Jacob, fine. I want to show you the books one day soon, for we are making a profit, and I was thinking maybe I ought to invest in some better fabrics . . ."

He listened thoughtfully, and finally said, "I can get you some China silks when my next ship comes in, Deirdre. How would that be? You can have them at cost, and advertise for them. The ladies are all mad for the China silks."

She beamed. "Oh, Jacob, that would be wonderful! But I'll pay you the usual price, it wouldn't be right, otherwise."

"Nonsense. You can have them at the price I say.

320

And when you go to invest, let me know. I can get you some municipal bonds at a good rate, and they are safe right now."

He liked to organize her life as well as his own, and it was satisfying, the way she turned to him for advice. He liked to feel needed and listened to and cared for, with his slippers on his feet, and a fresh mug of beer in his hand.

Presently they went to bed. He lay with his arm across her rounded form, caressing her lightly. "I like a bit of a cuddle," she murmured against his bare chest.

He laughed. "Is that all?"

She pounded his arm gently with her fist. "Now, Jacob, you know what I mean."

"We're getting older, Deirdre. Sometimes I wonder what's wrong with me, that I need you so much, and more all the time," he said.

"Now, that ain't wrong, Jacob. It's human nature, to want to love and give to people. A body can't be cold and alone, a body has to be needed and to have someone to give to." She stroked his graying beard with her loving hand, and her red-gold hair flamed against the pillow in the dim light from the lamp.

He drew her against him, enjoying the feel of her softness against his muscular legs and chest. He tickled her playfully, all down the soft length of her, until she squealed and giggled with delight.

"Jacob, stop!"

"Like this better?" He pressed a kiss into the crease at the base of her throat.

She moaned softly.

He smiled down at her. She could make him forget the whole cruel world outside, and all the problems of it. She held out her arms, and he moved on top of her, and pressed into her, and lost himself in the sweetness of her embrace.

In New York, Evan McKenna was making his own way slowly through the Sunday papers on Monday evening.

He paused at the full-page spread of the party at White-crest.

"Look at this, Molly. Our little Regina is having a ball up there at Newport."

"I saw it, Evan," she said, coming to sit down in her favorite rocker. Her face was troubled. "Is that the duke they are all talking about? You know, I don't trust the English."

"Now, Molly, this is America."

"Yes, but he ain't American. Is he good enough for our Regina? Such a sweet, gentle, loving girl under that cool manner of hers."

Evan lowered the paper, keeping his gaze fixed on a picture of Regina, cool and aristocratic in bearing, next to the duke, who was gazing down at her.

"Her mother will plan that marriage, that's for sure," Evan said. "Well, better than her brother Bernard, chasing after that actress."

"Jacob should take a hand in their upbringing," Molly said, rocking back and forth, as she did when she was upset. "He should put his foot down, and handle them the way he did Errol."

"Too late for that, honey." Evan sighed. "They're all grown up now. Is there any more in the paper about that actress?"

"In today's paper, yes. She and Lodewick's boy, Clinton, are staying out on the town, gallivanting till dawn. I think Bernard is in the pictures from up at Whitecrest."

A knock at the door startled them both. Evan went to answer it and Molly heard him say, "Come in, now, Mr. Oakley, come in. You're out and about late to-night."

"Hope I'm not disturbing you, Mr. McKenna. Thanks, I'll come in a bit, if it isn't disturbing you and the missus."

Molly was up, yanking off her apron, smoothing her graying hair. She was all smiles as Mr. Oakley walked into their parlor.

"'Evening, Mr. Oakley! Nice night, isn't it?" She

eyed him nervously. These uptown politicians scared her half to death. She had become accustomed to the downtown ones who usually came to see Evan. But now he was a ward politician himself, and she had to expect this.

She shook hands with the man, excused herself and went off to the kitchen. In an hour she would bring coffee. It was always coffee for the uptowners, beer for the downtowners.

Jessie came in the back door with Padraic Cassidy. "I saw the carriage, Mama. It's grand. Who came to call?"

"Mr. Oakley, so don't go in. How are you this night, Paddy?"

"Well, Mrs. McKenna. Very well, thank ye." They sat down to gossip at the kitchen table. Molly noted that Jessie kept looking at Paddy, and he at her, so protectively and nicely, and she nodded to herself. He was a good lad.

If only Regina could find herself such a nice beau! Molly thought naturally of her son Vincent. She was not unaware of his attraction to Regina, or of hers to him, although she had pretended not to notice. Ah, yes, but that match would never be. For a wistful moment, she remembered an afternoon in the park, long, long ago, when she, too, had thought such dreams were possible.

Chapter 22

The party had lingered on at Newport. It was unusual for Mrs. Antonia Van Rhyne to stay anywhere but New York City for very long. She adored shopping and being seen in the best restaurants. Regina grew increasingly uneasy.

Alastair Henry Carstairs showed no signs of wanting to go anywhere else. He enjoyed their horses, and he complimented Antonia on them. Antonia, who rode only behind horses, with a competent groom or two in attendance, nodded and spoke knowledgeably about getting the right bloodlines.

"Important. Very important," Carstairs said, looking very serious. Horses were the only things he seemed to consider with any seriousness.

"You can't be too careful about bloodlines," Antonia said, looking hopefully at Regina.

"Right. R-right," Carstairs said, catching her meaning. "Horses. And people." And he said not another word through dinner, but stared absently off into space. Only the three of them were present, for Bernard had returned to New York, pleading business. Antonia was privately convinced he had gone back to see what Clinton was up to with his actress.

Carstairs came to Antonia the next day in her morning room. He asked politely if he might speak with her. She smiled, and pushed away the tray of coffee on which she had been breakfasting. She had been eating too much lately, anyway, with all their entertaining. If she was not careful she would gain weight, and none of her elegant dresses would fit.

"Please come in, Your Grace," she said, rising.

He accepted the invitation, bowed, and seated himself in the straight-backed chair opposite her desk. Antonia sat down carefully, her bustle in the way. She disliked bustles; they had not been in style when she was a girl. Crinolines and a full, round hoop seemed more suitable, somehow. Bustles were awkward, with their weight at the back. But one had to admit they showed off a woman's lines in the front.

He stared into space. She drew a deep breath, controlling her temper. Thank God, she did not have to live with him. He was silent for hours at a time—worse than Jacob. At least Jacob would react, and yell at her, before stamping off to his study.

Her patience was rewarded.

"I've come to talk to you about your—your daughter, Regina."

324

She swallowed her eagerness. "Oh, yes, Your Grace?" She did adore saying "Your Grace"; it was so elegant.

"She's a fine girl, with nice bloodlines."

Antonia felt faintly appalled, then remembered it was she who had initiated a similar discussion. "Thank you, Your Grace," she said quickly.

A faint trace of color came into his long, melancholy face. "I wish to speak to your husband, Mr. Van Rhyne, about her."

"Oh? But he—my husband—is in New York." Inwardly, she cursed. If she had brought the duke to scratch, Jacob ought at least to be here to manage the rest of it. "I'll write to him, and have him come up here," she said firmly.

The duke leaned back in his chair, his fine, long hands on the arm rests. The crest of his ring glowed in the firelight. "I am considering making an offer for Regina," he said. "She is a fine figure of a woman. Good bloodlines."

If he said it once more, she would scream. She managed to smile instead. Errol and Bernard could manage their own weddings. If she got Regina safely married, she would quit this business, she vowed fervently. It was more than her delicate nerves could bear.

"She is a fine girl," Antonia managed to say. "She has been educated in the best schools, and of course she had a governess in the tender years. And traveled in Europe with me," she added.

"Yes. Yes. Her French is good. Can't speak it myself. If someone can't speak English," the duke said, "he usually isn't worth talking to, anyhow."

Antonia thought of insolent Frenchmen at hotels and restaurants, and teasing Italians, and staring Greeks. "You are so right, Your Grace!" she agreed fervently. "There isn't anything like English, is there?"

"Quite so. Q-quite so." He stared again into space.

She reached frantically for another topic of conversation. "Ah—would you like to take Regina through the gardens this morning, and, ah, discuss it with her?"

"You would consider this?" he asked, bringing his vague, gray eyes back to focus.

"Of course," she said coyly. "I would trust her anywhere with you—Your Grace."

"If only I might speak with her, and learn her feelings on the matter."

Antonia thought quickly. "Ah—why don't you just stroll with her—and tell her about Kildare? I'm sure she would enjoy that."

He bowed, and left her. Antonia fell back, limp with relief. Then she picked up a pen and scratched a hasty note to Jacob. He must, must, must come at once! Before the duke changed his mind, or met another girl who was warmer and more amiable toward him. And she would speak to Regina about minding her manners. If that stubborn daughter of hers cooled him off, she would spank her!

A maid directed the Duke of Kildare to the sunny morning room at the back of the mansion, where he found Regina sewing a bit of embroidery. A cushion cover, he thought—quite proper. She sewed neatly and beautifully, and she looked like an angel, with her blond head bent over the work, her white dress tied with blue ribbons at the waist and throat.

"Your mother permits me to walk in the gardens with you, Miss Regina," he said, bowing formally to her.

"Ah—of course, sir." She rose, and went before him out into the formal gardens. They strolled among the roses, passing the gardeners who were busily clipping and trimming the hedges.

"Fine r-roses," he managed to say, after ten minutes.

"They are lovely, are they not?" she asked, with cool composure.

Her head was erect, and she showed not a trace of emotion. He admired that.

"We have roses—many r-roses—at Kildare," he said.

"How splendid."

"Fancy of mine," he said.

"I am so glad."

"Like to walk among them after riding in the m-mornings."

"That must be jolly," she said mock-seriously. She turned her head away so he would not see her biting her lip: Vincent would roar with laughter if she could but imitate the duke's stiff, stuffy manner.

The duke brightened up a little. "Very j-jolly," he said. "Splendidly j-jolly. Mornings, I mean."

"I am sure of it."

"You would like it."

She swallowed. "I am very fond of my own homes," she said frostily.

"Of c-course you are. A home g-girl, your mother said."

She saw that she had not gotten through to him. "I like America, and my homes," she said, with emphasis.

"Of c-course you do. Home g-girl. Sensible. Keen on sewing, are you?"

"I like to do embroidery," she said.

"My mother used to do embroidery. Nothing much else at Kildare to do." He frowned. "That was what she used to say. Went off to London after Father passed on. Wanted some lights, she said. Never embroiders anymore. Pity. She did all the chairs in the five drawing rooms at Kildare. There were two more rooms to do, but she didn't stay."

Regina felt a little hysterical, but she took a firm grip on herself. "I can see how she felt," she managed to say, with only a faint quiver in her voice.

"Do you really? Never understood females much. Went off to school when I was eight; had a tutor before that," he said. "Know much about English schools?"

She told him she did not. He spoke at length about English schools, and their advantages, and the splendid, "jolly" times he had had in school until his father passed on, and his mother gave up embroidery and moved to London.

That lasted until they returned to the mansion. Regina saw her mother's face as she peered hopefully from

327

the morning room, only to withdraw hastily as they approached.

"What did he say?" her mother demanded of her later, in the doorway of Regina's bedroom. Regina had gone up to change for luncheon. They changed four times a day in the country, and she wearied of it.

"He talked about the British school system, and its advantages over the American," Regina said dryly.

Antonia's face fell ludicrously. "But he wants to marry you, Regina! I know he is leading up to it."

Regina stiffened, and pushed away the pink dress her maid had laid out for her. "What did you say, Mother?" she demanded, her back very straight, her violet eyes blazing.

"He wants to marry you. He has asked to speak to Jacob. I have sent for your father," Antonia said triumphantly.

Regina wet her dry lips. All this was suddenly very unfunny. "You sent for Father? Oh, Mother, but I don't want to marry him. Oh, do let us return to New York and talk sensibly about this!" she begged.

"I am very sensible. I am always sensible," Antonia said coldly. "And Regina, you will not spoil my plans with your little tempers! The duke will do very well for you. He is intelligent and well-bred; he owns four homes in England—"

"I don't want to live in England!"

"How do you know that? You have never lived in England."

"I don't love him!"

"Now, Regina, don't be irrelevant!" Antonia said. "I mean to make a grand marriage for you! Your father is wealthy, and I am fashionable. We can make the best marriage for you that a girl could ever have or want! You are going to be so happy! Oh, how I envy you this opportunity!"

Antonia was so swept away, so carried off by her plans, so completely dazzled, that she did not see the white, desperate look on her daughter's face, or the tears that had begun to form in her eyes.

Two days later, Antonia received a letter from Jacob. He was very busy with his work. She must return to New York if she wished to speak with him. She was furious. How could she explain this to His Grace?

But to her surprise, the Duke of Kildare took it very well. "He is a busy man," he said, drawling with his mouth closed, in a way Regina no longer thought amusing. "We shall go to him, eh? And you said you wished to introduce me to some of your friends, eh?"

Antonia nodded enthusiastically; but privately, she was worried. Lillian, her dearest friend, had a daughter just one year older than Regina, a fast girl with red hair and a flirtatious manner. If she captured the duke, Antonia would be humiliated for life! She would never forgive Jacob for throwing away this chance!

But she could do nothing else. They must return to New York and persuade Jacob at once to agree to the wedding.

The duke had something else on his mind, Antonia felt. He mumbled something about dowries, asking Antonia whether she understood the dowry system, and if Regina was wealthy in her own right. Antonia got the point at last.

The duke would want a financial settlement on Regina. It was all right with her. He needed some money—to help him repair Kildare, as he said. She knew enough about society in Europe to know this was the tradition there. A dowry was sent along with the girl, to help in her new home. What if the duke *was* a bit low in the pocket? So much the easier to get him as a match for Regina! Lillian did not have nearly as much money as the Van Rhynes did. Lillian could never match the money Jacob could put on Regina.

They prepared at once for their removal to New York City. Antonia sent the trunks on ahead, then took the train down with Regina. The duke came by carriage. He preferred carriages, he said, no offense to Mr. Van Rhyne and his railroad. He just liked horses. It would take him several days, but he would see something of the countryside. Fine countryside, he said—It almost reminded him of England. This was intended as a great compliment.

Once she had arrived in New York, Antonia sent for her social advisor, Cecil Meryon. She had wanted him to come to Newport with them, but he had discreetly declined. One look at the Duke of Kildare, and a few minutes' conversation with him, had confirmed Meryon's suspicions. A few words in the wrong direction, and all would go wrong.

And Cecil Meryon did not like Regina. It would serve her right to have this marriage, he thought spitefully. She was a stubborn, stuck-up little piece, who sided with her brother Errol. This was what Antonia wanted, and she should have it, but he would stay well clear of the whole business until the plans were sealed.

"Consult with your husband," Meryon urged her. "Butter him up a bit, but not too much—you know how suspicious he is. Tell him Regina is young and shy, and not sure of her mind. Tell him what a splendid marriage it will be. Let them settle the price between them."

Antonia heeded his advice. She went to Jacob in his study, and told him excitedly that the Duke of Kildare wanted to marry their daughter.

"Marriage? Regina? She's only a child," Jacob barked, looking up from his papers with a frown.

"She has had her coming-out," Antonia said, her violet eyes sparkling. "And I could tell what a hit she made with the duke. She is shy and quiet, demure and dignified. He told me she would make a splendid, very mannerly duchess."

"What's the problem, then?" asked Jacob, impatiently. He was having his own difficulties. He had just learned about the new breakdown in negotiations to stop the rate wars. It could bankrupt him in the West if this kept up much longer. He could not endure the thought of the freight going through, over his lines, *below* cost. It appalled his thrifty soul.

"The money, Jacob. The dowry."

"Dowry? What the hell is that?"

"He needs money to repair Castle Kildare, and all

330

that," Antonia said vaguely. "You know I don't understand money matters, Jacob. I'm leaving it all to you, to talk to His Grace and settle it all. I think he will want a large settlement for Regina."

"I not only give him my daughter, I get him out of debt too?" Jacob barked, with a scowl.

"In Europe, it's the custom. And of course, that is the reason he came to America looking for a bride. The Europeans have bankrupted themselves," Antonia said, waving her hands in a helplessly feminine manner that had deceived her father for years. "You know how little business sense they have. That's why His Grace has to marry an American."

Jacob scowled. So that was why Carstairs had come here. To get his money! And his daughter, too. His beautiful, gentle Regina. Well, he *had* the money, that was a fact, and he supposed his daughter could do worse than marry this titled fellow.

"Well, send him in to me. I can give him two hours today," Jacob said with resignation.

"I should warn you—he said three million dollars, Jacob," Antonia murmured, looking at him wistfully.

Jacob shot up from his chair. "Three—million—dollars? The gall of him, the crass gall of the bastard—"

"He isn't a bastard, Jacob; he is the son of a long line of English royalty!"

She calmed Jacob down somewhat, then sent in the Duke of Kildare. Antonia left, and the two men sat there for a moment, eyeing each other.

Finally Jacob's gruff voice broke the silence. "I understand you want to marry my daughter Regina."

"She is the loveliest, most serene person I have ever met," the Duke of Kildare said thoughtfully. He was more at ease with Jacob than with Antonia. He leaned back in his chair. "Sh-she is a fine female. Doesn't chatter me to death."

"No, you can say that about Regina. She knows when to keep her mouth shut." Jacob eyed the duke with approval. "How does she feel about you?"

"Oh, she likes me immensely, we have much in common," Kildare said confidently. "We went riding every morning at Whitecrest. And we walked among the roses, and talked about gardens. I can picture her at Kildare— a queenly figure."

He didn't talk much like a man madly in love, but the British were reserved chaps, thought Jacob, remembering Tweedy and his ways. Very reserved. And the fellow was right about Regina. There *was* something queenly about her: the tilt of her chin, her composure, her gentle manner.

"Ah—is Kildare mortgaged?"

"Good heavens, no!" said the Duke of Kildare, visibly shocked. "Never! I never go to money lenders. Never. No, it merely needs extensive repairs. More then eight hundred years old, you see."

"Oh, yes, I can see that. Drains and all, I expect."

"That's right." The duke's face lit up. They talked for awhile about drains and plumbing, pipes and poor lighting, the necessity of replacing some woodwork and some shabby rugs.

Then Jacob got cautiously down to business, and so did the duke. They understood each other, the language of finance. They settled on the three million dollars, to be deposited in pounds sterling in the duke's London accounts. Jacob would have his British advisors make the necessary arrangments.

"Have you proposed to my daughter?" Jacob finally asked.

"Oh, no, no, it wouldn't be proper! I have merely hinted about it to her, and she seems amenable. I had to speak to you first—her father, and all that."

"I will speak with Regina myself," Jacob said. "And then we shall see." He sighed. He hoped Antonia had already spoken to the girl, and that she was agreeable. Regina could be pretty damned independent.

"Of course! Then may I come tomorrow, to propose formally? I shall wish her to wear the Kildare emeralds—an engagement ring and a bracelet, handed down from four generations."

"Fine, fine. We'll speak of that later."

After Kildare had left the house, Jacob sent for Regina. She came, her eyes reddened with tears. Shutting the door behind her, she flung her slight body at Jacob. "Oh, Papa, you have not consented, have you?"

"Now, now, no tantrums, Regina! We will talk sensibly!"

He sat her down in a chair, and eyed her keenly. She was like her mother to look at, although he had a feeling that she had more of his own nature in her.

"He came to see me about marrying you, and we agreed on a marriage settlement. He wants to come and propose to you tomorrow."

Her face went white. Her violet eyes looked dazed. She put her hand up to her long, slim throat. "No, no, no," she whispered. "Oh, Father, no. I don't love him."

"Love? Love can be nonsense," Jacob said, brusquely. "I'd prefer for you to make a sensible marriage. He seems fond of you. He talked of you quite nicely."

Regina straightened her shoulders. Her father hated tantrums. He had had more than enough of them from Antonia. She tried to keep her voice from quivering.

"Mother will not listen to me, she just talks on and on. But Father, I don't want to marry him, I don't like him. I love Vincent."

"Vincent who?"

"Vincent McKenna," she said proudly, her head up, her face brightening. "Vincent Rowan McKenna. We love each other."

He stared at her. "That young pup! That newspaper journalist? Why, he couldn't keep you in shoes!"

"I don't care. I have enough shoes. I just want to live with him, and have his children, and love him. He loves me. He has told me so."

Jacob sat back and thought, and oddly, he thought of Molly O'Neill, and years ago, when he had loved her wildly—but had not wanted to marry her. If Regina had been a boy, he would have advised an affair. But Regina was a girl, and that was different.

"You would soon tire of love in a cottage," he said

dryly. "You dress well, you have jewels, you go to the opera. How long would you last, married to a newspaperman who makes less than I pay one of my clerks?"

"I love him," she said stubbornly.

"You are young, Regina. You may change your mind by next week."

"I have loved Vincent all my life," she said quietly, her hands clenched together in her lap. Jacob looked down at them. They were slim, delicate hands, soft and dainty and white. He thought of Molly's rough, red hands, the lines and wrinkles on her face, the gray in her hair.

"My dear, it would not work," he said gently. "Forget him. The duke seems a nice fellow—"

"I don't even *like* him, Father. He is boring, cold, and cares only for horses."

"He seems to think you like him!"

"Because I was polite to him? I have manners, Father! But if I had thought this would be the result of my politeness, I would have kicked his shins!" Her eyes blazed with fury, and he laughed.

"Well, well, let it go for a time. Nobody is in a hurry, Regina. You may change your mind. I like Vincent. Maybe I could take him into the firm and give him a kick upwards. How about that?"

"Oh, Father!" She jumped up and clasped her slim arms about his neck, her face radiant. "Oh, Father—I do love you!"

Later that day, Jacob approached Antonia. She was furious, and went raving off into one of her tantrums. "Marry that—that *journalist*? The son of a *maid* here? Are you mad, completely mad? She could marry a duke, and you calmly turn about and say she might marry Vincent McKenna! An Irishman! A poor, shabby Irishman! You are mad!"

Jacob retreated. "Well, settle it among yourselves," he said. "I have business to do. Besides, what is the hurry? She is only eighteen!" And he went out to his office. He had more important matters on his mind.

Cecil Meryon soothed Antonia. "Come now, there is

no harm done. Warn His Grace that the girl is timid. Have him bring flowers to her, give her jewels. Gradually she will get used to the idea. And we'll have the wedding in the autumn." He rubbed his long hands together gleefully. "It will be the event of the season—no, the decade! I promise you! We'll go ahead quietly with the plans, and Regina will fall in with them, I am sure of it!"

Fortunately, he thought to himself, there was little chance of interference. Errol was out West with his work, Jacob was absorbed in the rate wars, and Bernard was busy with his actress. Regina could be fooled; she was but a child. Antonia would do whatever he told her. And he, Cecil Meryon, would pull the coup of the decade! The wedding of Regina Van Rhyne to the Duke of Kildare!

Chapter 23

Bernard Van Rhyne looked suspiciously around the gaudy apartment of Daisy Bloom. Did he smell cigar smoke? Had Daisy been entertaining another man before he came up? He sniffed. Wasn't that some other man's cologne he smelled?

Daisy swept into the room from her bedroom, looking radiant and feminine in her blue-striped silk gown, the bustle enormous over her slim hips. Her black curls danced about her neck, and smaller curls wavered over her broad forehead.

"Darling Bernard, you came," she drawled, and came over to kiss him delicately on his cheek. "I thought you had forgotten me."

He scowled. His father had kept him busy for a week, day and night, and Bernard thought it was deliberate.

"I have been working, but I managed to get away from a dinner party tonight," he said.

She cocked her head to one side and looked at him coyly. "And did you bring me a pretty little present?" she asked, pressing a fingertip to the dimple in her cheek. "Did-ums get me a wee little present, honey?"

He brought his hand from behind his back, and handed her the dozen red roses he was holding. She stared at them, and began to laugh, but there was anger in her laughter. "You are joking, aren't you, Bernie? You promised to give me a *real* present tonight!"

He was flushed with embarrassment and fury. "I couldn't," he said bluntly. "Father has cut off my accounts. I tried to buy some diamond earrings, and the store refused me credit."

"Don't you even have your own money?" she scoffed. "And you said you were a millionaire!"

"I said that Father is, and I would be some day," he corrected her. He felt like kicking the furniture. "Father keeps us all on a tight rein. I tried to get some of Mother's diamonds. She has loads, but she got furious with me when I told her what I wanted them for."

The green eyes of the actress were blazing. "You *told* her? You little fool!"

Bernard turned his back on her, and went over to the curtains at the window. He stood there, his back very straight, his head high. He had never felt so humiliated in his life.

"Your cousin said he would bring me a diamond bracelet tomorrow," Daisy drawled behind him. She sat down in a plump armchair, and put her feet up on a hassock of pink fluff. She studied the broad back critically. "Clinton is much more generous—or perhaps his father is better off!"

"My father has much more money than—" Bernard stopped abruptly, biting his lips. The thought of Clinton had made him feel so rash and angry that he had almost told the truth. Clinton did have more money to spend, but not from his father. His mother had some money of her own, and she indulged her son's every whim. Lodewick would be mad as hell if he knew about the gems Clinton gave away to women like Daisy Bloom.

Daisy got up and went over to him, and put her arms about him, pressing her breasts against his rigid back, and running her hands coyly over his stomach. He shivered with intense desire, and closed his arms over hers.

"I like you so much better," she whispered to his back. "I like my sugar daddy so *much* better . . . you do make love so sweetly, honey. But you know a girl has to make her living! I thought you wanted me to quit the theater."

"I do, I do," he muttered, although he had to admit he enjoyed seeing her up on the stage, kicking up her pink-stockinged legs, and laughing and singing in her lusty fashion. He could not picture her away from the stage; it was her life, her setting. And the flamboyant, outrageous outfits she wore looked right only onstage: the white feather boas, the swansdown-trimmed robes of red satin, the pert, feather-trimmed hats.

"Well? I can't if you don't marry me."

He swallowed. He had almost proposed to her one night when he had been drunk. The next day, he had vowed to avoid her. But something kept drawing him back. He knew he could not marry Daisy. She would never be acceptable to his mother. And his father—! Jacob would say she was vulgar and cheap, any man's toy. And, thought Bernard, he would be right. Yet, try as he would, he couldn't stay away from her; she was like a drink he had to have.

"Come to bed," she whispered, her hands caressing him indulgently. "We'll forget all this. You can talk to your father, tell him you are serious about me . . ."

Bernard did not answer. He could picture his father's amazement and wrath if his son should indicate any serious intention of marrying this actress. He would kick him out, clear to the West Coast, and beat him to boot! Jacob had been angry enough that Bernard wanted to give her jewels.

"Jewels, to that female?" Jacob had flared. "Are you mad? Give her glass—she won't even know the difference! You don't give women like that anything but a ten-dollar bill!"

"She would know glass, Father," Bernard had protested. "She takes everything to a jeweler she knows and has it appraised."

At Jacob's glare, Bernard had shrunk back, and finally slunk away, his shoulders down.

He tried to put the scene from his mind. He was with her now, and her lips were pressed to his neck, and he wanted her. A mad desire rose up in his loins. He turned around, grabbed her, and bent her back over his arm. She made a sound in her throat. "Oh, Bernie," she moaned, sinking against him.

He carried her to the bedroom. He would have ripped off her dress, but she protested, and made him undress her slowly, with due regard for her new gown. He took off the blue-striped silk, the chemises, the lace-trimmed pantaloons, and finally saw her lovely pink body, rather plump and rounded.

She took off his clothes for him. It was an art, the way she did it, easing off his jacket, unbuttoning his trousers. Her hands slid coyly over his limbs, arousing him, tempting him.

He laid her down on the bed, her wide, heart-shaped bed, with the white silk coverlet and the red cupids embroidered on the canopy above it. She had turned down all but one lamp, and it blazed, so they could see themselves in the mirror cunningly placed in the canopy. He turned over and stared up at himself for a moment.

"You're sweet," she breathed, and her hand roamed over his naked torso, and the curly hair of his chest. "You're the handsomest man I know."

He turned over, to avoid looking at himself in that damned mirror. He bent over, and knew she watched, over his shoulders, with intense delight, as he kissed and fondled her. This aroused her, she said, to watch them making love.

He suspended himself over her, and pressed himself to her lush, round body. She shivered, then closed her eyes tightly, moaning as he pressed home. "Oh, you're

338

the best, honey, you're the best," she groaned, as he forced his way in. "Oh, honey . . . nobody makes love like you do . . ."

He grimaced, unseen by her, against her powdered shoulder. He hated to be reminded that he was one of many. It made him angry. If he could only afford to give her diamonds and pearls, she would belong to him alone. Then he would not have to lie awake nights, thinking of his Daisy in some other man's arms. He could afford to pay for her apartment, her gowns, her jewels, if she were his alone. . . .

He groaned his satisfaction, and fell back among the silken sheets. She cuddled up to him, and began running her hand over his chest and thigh. "Honey-ums," she murmured. "Tomorrow you'll bring me a pretty present, won't you? Something for your pretty dolly? Something nice and expensive, like the others do? Ummm?"

"I'll try," Bernard muttered, through a haze of sexual pleasure.

He had tried, but Jacob, furious, would not advance him a single penny, and his mother was too busy even to speak to him. She had her head in the clouds, anyway, Bernard thought, planning his sister's wedding to that stupid duke. Regina looked haggard these days, and had tried to speak with him, but he had his own problems, and had told her so.

That night, he went to see Daisy at her show; but she did not give him her customary quick wink at the close of her number. Instead, she turned her head away from him, and kicked her red slipper toward Clinton, who sat at the front table nearest the stage. Clinton's youthful face shone bright red. Bernard was furious. By God, the boy was only eighteen! He could not possibly have gotten his hands on so much money! Daisy must be playing them off against each other.

But she sat down at Clinton's table with him, gazed into his eyes, and laughed as the young man drank champagne from her red slipper. And there were roses on the table. She drew one slowly from the vase, put it to Clinton's lips, then tucked it into her ample bosom.

Daisy was perfectly aware that Bernard was glaring at her. With pretty deliberation, and a satisfied pout on her red mouth, she smoothed back the ruffled sleeve from her wrist, and let the diamond bracelet glitter in the light.

Bernard stared incredulously. Clinton could not have given her diamonds; they must be fake. But Clinton, grinning at his cousin triumphantly, raised the plump wrist to his lips and kissed the pulse above the diamond bracelet.

Bernard rose abruptly, kicked over his chair, and stormed out of the nightclub. Daisy's laugh rang out shrilly after him.

Bernard did not go home. He went to one bar after another, grim, furious, hating the world and everyone in it. He tried to drink enough to blot out the memory of that bracelet, and of Clinton sitting close to Daisy, his hand on her knee, his hand holding the wrist with his bracelet on it.

Damn them all!

Bernard drank and drank. His last memory was of being helped upstairs to a room, and of someone with an Irish brogue soothing him, saying, "There, now, son, you'll be just fine in the mornin', sure you will. Just lie ye down and get some sleep, that's all ye need."

He slept heavily, till past noon, and woke with the father and mother of all headaches. He groaned, tried to raise himself, and was violently sick all over someone's counterpane. He made it to the bathroom, and was wretchedly sick again.

He washed and dressed, putting on the clothes someone had removed from him. He got to the office about four in the afternoon. Jacob came out and scowled at him.

"Do you have the least idea what time it is?" his father barked.

"I don't know and damned if I care!" Bernard shouted at him. He sat down at his desk, his head in his hands. He felt sick all over again.

Jacob went away. Bernard sat there for two hours, then went to the apartment he kept for when he didn't want to go home. He slept a fitful sleep. But he turned up at the office on time the next morning.

"Good, you're sober this morning," Jacob said sarcastically. "Take your pistol, and go with the guard down to the bank. I'm sending in some stocks and cash."

Bernard nodded, his mind far away. He kept seeing Clinton and Daisy Bloom in the light of that golden lamp, her red dress shining, her green eyes gleaming at him over the diamond bracelet. A cold fury was rising higher and higher in him, more bitter than the gall of sickness.

He escorted the guard to the bank, then left him there. He went back to the Grand Union hotel. They had a good bar there, where he had credit. Maybe he would drink himself into another stupor.

It was just past noon when he strolled into the hotel, the pistol in his pocket. He started for the bar, but something drew his attention toward the stairs. He looked up. A grand red carpet covered the stairway from the upper rooms down into the lobby. At the top of the stairs, just turning the corner from the upper floor, was Clinton! Bernard thought he might be dreaming, but no! It was Clinton, all right, his red face shining boyishly, his hair slicked back from his forehead, one lock twisted into a love-curl.

Bernard watched, transfixed, as Clinton turned and held out his hand to assist the lady who was coming down behind him. Daisy! Her skirts swished about her long legs. Her head was held high in a lacy red hat whose brim sheltered her face. She held up her red-striped silk dress to show her scarlet slippers. One sleeve of her dress was deliberately pushed back to reveal the glittering diamond bracelet on her arm.

She saw Bernard, was shocked for a moment, then smiled down at him triumphantly. She held up the arm with the bracelet on it. He saw the red mouth he had kissed so passionately, he saw the diamonds, he saw

341

Clinton at the same time that his cousin saw him, and he saw the smirk on Clinton's lips.

His hand was in his pocket; he felt the cold solidity of the pistol. He did not think. Afterward, he swore he had not thought. A crimson fog was before his eyes. He drew out the loaded pistol, and in a wild rage aimed at Clinton, and shot.

Bernard was a good shot. His father had taught him, and Errol had polished his technique. You needed to be good when you went West, where your life depended on being able to shoot straight the first time, at a wild animal, a snake, an Indian, an outlaw. Bernard shot straight.

Clinton fell slowly down the stairs, tumbling like a rag doll over the red carpet and down the marble stairs to the lobby. He lay sprawled on the lobby floor, his legs still on the stairs above him, like a dummy with straw spilling out of him. Only it was not straw. There was a hole in his chest, and red blood streamed out of him, onto the crimson carpet.

Women fainted. Daisy, her eyes wide with horror, screamed and could not stop screaming. Bernard stood still, the pistol hanging from his hand, until someone reached him, and took it cautiously from him. A policeman appeared, then another one. They bent over Clinton, and shook their heads. Then they turned and stared at Bernard, who was looking down at his cousin.

Bernard was not thinking of Daisy Bloom just then. He was remembering the time he and Clinton had gone sledding in Central Park, on a cold, wintry day, and Clinton's face had turned red and shiny with pleasure. He had been laughing and yelling, and Bernard had felt the patronizing delight of being able to show his younger cousin how to run the sled properly.

"He's dead," someone said brusquely.

Dead. Dead. The word echoed in Bernard's ears, blotting out the hum of voices that rose up around him. "Who did it? This young man? Your name, please? Name? Name? That's young Van Rhyne, isn't it? My

God! Who's the woman! This way, young man. This way."

They took him off to jail, and sent for his father. Bernard sat in the small, dingy jail cell and stared at the bars. He had been in jail once, out West. It had been amusing, watching the sheriff stride about in his big sombrero. This was not amusing. He kept seeing Clinton lying dead. His cousin. Dead. Blood all around him. He shut his eyes, but the image would not go away.

Jacob had been summoned from work. At first, on hearing there were policemen to see him, he had refused to let them in. "Tell them we'll make a contribution in the usual way. I cannot be bothered." Finally, a clerk convinced him that it was serious.

When they told him, he did not utter a sound, but his big fists dug into the side of his desk until his knuckles turned white. Then he buried his face in his hands.

The policemen escorted him down to the jail, and took him to Bernard's cell. Jacob stood at the cell bars, and gazed down at his son.

"Why, Bernard? Why? Why?" he demanded, again and again.

"I don't know. I don't know," Bernard said in a dull monotone.

"I'll get a lawyer. I'll see what I can do," Jacob said, and turned away, rubbing his head. He went out to find Lodewick sitting on a bench in the outer room—Lodewick, his brother, sitting there, tears running down his cheeks, eyes staring off into space.

Jacob went to sit down beside him. "I'm damned sorry," he said.

Lodewick finally looked at him. "You have everything," he sobbed bitterly. "Father left you all the money and the stocks, and the power. I just had my son. And now you take away my son. You killed my son!"

Tears were flowing down his whiskery cheeks, and he smelled of liquor. Jacob clenched his teeth. "He didn't mean to. They were fighting over that damned actress. Damn her to hell," he added under his breath. He had

343

seen the woman giving an interview to avid reporters, and she was wearing black already. Enjoying it, Jacob thought savagely. Enjoying all the publicity. She didn't give a damn for the man who had died, or for the man who had killed him.

His mind worked busily. A good lawyer, and some money into the right palms— He had to get Bernard out of this, and quickly. The disgrace was horrible, the jail cell not fit for an animal. Antonia would be weeping and wailing. The newspapers would have a field day with this.

The Van Rhynes, fighting among themselves over an actress! Not even a good actress! A doxy with good legs and a bosom. She would have it fine, he thought bitterly. Her price would go up for a time. The woman over whom the two Van Rhyne boys had fought.

That evening it was on all the front pages. Jacob read several accounts grimly, and wished Errol were here to help out. He would know the right lawyers to get. Not Katrinka's husband, Howard. He must get someone from outside the family, someone high-toned, who would say the right words to the judges.

He had been temporarily out of his mind. He hadn't meant to do it, Jacob thought. Was that a defense? Goaded beyond control? No matter, it must not come to trial. He must get him out. He had to persuade Lodewick not to press charges. Money could do that; Lodewick was always needing money.

Jacob was late for a dinner meeting with the Morgan banking interests. The great J. P. Morgan met him at the door, and patted him on the shoulder.

"Come in, my boy, come in," the great man said, with unusual sympathy.

No one referred to the incident, but they had all read the newspapers. It was in their eyes.

"Shall we get down to business?" someone suggested. And they did, with curious, covert glances at Jacob.

They talked about the rate wars, and agreed that they must be solved in an amiable way. But Jacob barely listened. He was suffering inside for his son and his nephew. Clinton, dead. It could not be true, but it was. It seemed only yesterday that Jacob had taken the two boys out in his new carriage to give them a thrill.

"Don't you agree, Mr. Van Rhyne?" Mr. Morgan asked.

Jacob started. "I beg your pardon, would you repeat that?"

Mr. Morgan repeated it, and Jacob tried to concentrate on his words. He wanted to lie down and weep, but he had no time for that. Work must come first. He must attend to the business of the day, the great work of the railroads.

Chapter 24

At home that summer, Antonia had everything her own way. The Duke of Kildare came with them on a yachting trip. Regina remained cool and distant, in light muslin gowns that showed off her beautiful slim figure. New York City was too hot for the summer, and so were the scandalous headlines in the newspapers.

Jacob was frantically busy. The rate wars were the main object of his attentions, and he kept Errol out West to watch the competition closely. All of Jacob's spare time was spent poring over Bernard's case with lawyers, trying to get his son freed on a technicality.

"We cannot get him out while it is still in the newspapers," his shrewd lawyers advised him. "Wait until some other story pushes it off the front pages."

And wait he did. For weeks, months, Bernard remained in jail, growing a beard, acquiring lice, his face becoming gray and haggard. Jacob wept for his son in the silence of his own rooms. Antonia was so furious at Bernard that she did not even write her son a single note.

"I warned him!" she screamed at Jacob. "The disgrace of it! I told him that actress was no good! That she'd get him into trouble! Why don't you disown him?"

Jacob stared at her, then went back to his study and slammed the door. Sometimes he could not understand Antonia. Other times he understood her only too well.

As the summer sizzled on, Regina's anxiety grew. She tried again to talk to her father, but he waved her away impatiently. "Settle it with your mother. If you don't want to marry him, she won't insist," he said, very irritated.

"She *is* insisting, Papa. I don't want to marry him! I detest him. Oh, Papa, please listen to me. Please listen!"

He had no time for all this. Antonia had told him Regina was being coy, in keeping with her youth, of course. "But this is the perfect marriage for her. She will be a duchess! And the duke adores her. He has sworn that he adores her."

"How much?" Jacob asked, his voice dripping with sarcasm.

"Three million dollars. The price may go up," Antonia said anxiously, "if you can't get Bernard out of the newspapers! The duke hates scandal!"

Jacob paid the three million and the wedding arrangements went forward. Then he headed out West for a brief consultation with Errol. He found trouble on the rail lines. Not only were the freight wars driving the prices down, but thugs were beating up his passengers, and strongarming the farmers who had paid to send goods on his lines. He lingered there.

Back East, Antonia sent for dressmakers. It was a golden opportunity; Errol and Jacob were both gone. Errol wrote to Regina, but Antonia intercepted the letters. She showed them casually to Cecil Meryon.

"Errol is anxious about Regina; she must have gotten a letter through to him," Antonia said.

Cecil scanned the letter. Errol was most certainly anxious about his young sister. "Keep them waiting until I get home," Errol wrote. "I'll soon straighten it out, if Father won't listen."

Cecil tossed the letter into the fire, and watched it burn to an ash. "Anything more from that reporter, McKenna?" he asked.

Antonia showed him two letters from him that Regina had been intended to receive. Cecil opened them, scanned them, and flung them into the fire as well, his mouth curling with contempt.

"Much love—reassurance—hold out," he said, and laughed. "*Keep on,* as we are doing. She shall be a duchess in September!"

"I can't lock her up!" Antonia protested, "or she will scream and complain to her father."

"He isn't here. Lock her up," Cecil advised her.

Antonia looked doubtful, and put her finger to her lips. "Well, I *could* say she is ill . . . "

"She *is* ill. Mentally ill, for turning down a duke! Of course, you won't say that to His Grace." Cecil grinned, striding across the length of the room to stare happily out of the grand windows overlooking the autumn gardens. A few more weeks, just three weeks now, and all his grand plans would reach their culmination. He would be famous! It would be the wedding of the decade, and he would have managed it! His services would be in demand from one end of the country to the other!

Regina was locked in her rooms, and only allowed out with trusted servants and her mother. She went for stately carriage rides with the duke. No letters came from her room that were not scanned and burned by her mother. With no reassuring word from outside, the girl wilted. Everyone had forgotten her.

"Haven't there been any letters for me from Errol?" she begged. "Or anyone?"

Antonia said coldly, "Nothing but letters of congratulation on your wedding. I told you Errol was busy. I had a note from him last week. You saw it."

Regina bit her lips. "I thought to hear from Vincent McKenna." She glanced anxiously at her mother. "Oh,

Mother, you would not withhold letters from me, would you?"

Antonia was furious. "Thinking about that poor Irishman! When you are marrying a British duke in two weeks! Are you mad?"

"Mother, did he write to me?"

"Yes," said Antonia, rashly. "And I burned the letters! Such impudence, to write to an engaged girl, without her parents' consent! And him without a penny."

Regina's complexion was like a white pearl, with no hint of pink in it. Her waist was like a wand, she had eaten so little these weeks and months. "Mother, I want those letters," she said firmly, her violet eyes blazing. "I will hear from him! I have the right—"

Cecil had advised Antonia how to deal with this. "All right," said Antonia. "And I will go to my desk and write a letter also."

"What—what do you mean?"

Antonia went to her desk. "I have been composing a letter. Here, you may read it, it is not yet completed. It is up to you whether I shall finish it and send it."

She thrust the pages into Regina's hand. The girl started to read, then sank into the silk-covered chair and continued, her hands trembling as she read.

It was addressed to the managing editor of the *New York Times*.

Sir:

I think I should bring to your attention a matter of grave concern to Mr. Jacob Van Rhyne and myself. You have on your staff a young reporter named Vincent McKenna. He has taken it upon himself to write fervent love letters to our daughter Regina. The girl is young and easily swayed. She had known Mr. McKenna in years past; he is the son of a former maid in this household.

You should know that this young man is pestering our daughter with his attentions. I have tried to discourage him gently, but to no avail. Therefore I am writing to ask you to speak harshly with him, and to take whatever measure you must, to prevent him from bothering our daughter.

Our daughter Regina is shortly to be married to the Duke of Kildare. Any harassment along this line is difficult for one of her delicate temperament. . . .

"The letter is not yet finished," Antonia said, watching her daughter's face closely. "I have but to say that I advise him to send the man away, or fire him from his post—"

"You would not!"

"And that Mr. Jacob Van Rhyne is seriously upset at the unwanted attentions of such an upstart toward our daughter—"

"No, Mother, no!"

"And of course, that he is impertinent, untrustworthy—"

Regina sighed, and crumpled the letter in her fist. She threw the pages into the fire and watched them turn to ashes. "You have no mercy, have you? You want this marriage, not for me, but for yourself," Regina said weakly, as though all strength had drained from her.

"You will not be impertinent to me!" Antonia flashed. Her head was uplifted, a danger signal her husband knew well. "I will not have you speak to me in this manner!"

Regina stood up unsteadily. "Of course I do not wish Vincent to lose his position," she said wearily.

"I thought you would see reason. The duke comes tonight; I want you to show more warmth to him. And wear the blue gown! The new blue silk with the sapphires. He admires you in blue."

Regina left the room, her back erect. It was only in her bedroom that she collapsed across the silken bed and lay very still for a time, her head buried in her arms.

From then on, she was locked in her room during the night, with a guard posted at the door. The servants whispered, but only among themselves. Antonia paid them too well for them to be indiscreet. During the daytime, Regina went out only with the duke and her mother, in a closed carriage, a wide hat shading the pallor of her face.

The wedding took place in late September, as the gardens were turning to scarlet and gold. The newspapers called it the wedding of the century. Cecil was delighted, and bought copies of every journal that carried stories and pictures. He carefully clipped those that made reference to him—"The social advisor, Mr. Cecil Meryon . . . " If only they knew! He had arranged it all! And it was a triumph! He congratulated himself on a job well done.

Jacob had returned hastily with Errol, just in time to don wedding clothes. Bernard, too, was there, for the lawyers had finally been successful in getting him out of prison. He was brought home, deloused, shaved, and shoved into clothes a size too large for him. Jacob could have wept again, at his son's ghastly appearance, but his dismay over Bernard was nothing compared to the shock he had when he saw Regina. She was so white and thin, so listless. She looked years older than eighteen.

"What the hell has been going on here?" Jacob exploded, as Errol stood by, looking anxiously at his sister.

"Regina's wedding is an enormous affair, and we have been very busy arranging it this summer," Antonia said tartly. "If you had been here, you could have helped in the arrangements." Her violet eyes sparkled warningly at Regina.

Regina thought of Vincent—his job, his prospects, his vulnerable position—and managed to smile wanly. "It has been—a busy summer," she whispered.

"God keep me from marriage, if this is the way it affects one," Errol said, putting his arm comfortingly about his sister's shoulders. He was appalled at her thinness, her frailty. Still, she had not written to him in answer to his letters. She must have been busy and happy.

Why, then, he wondered, did her face look so solemn? She was young, Antonia had reminded them, and marriage was, after all, a serious business. He vowed to stay away from it himself for as long as possible.

He was troubled, too, about Bernard, and spent long hours with his brother. Bernard seemed relieved to talk about the incident. After so many months in jail, the shock had worn off, and had been replaced by feelings of guilt and remorse. "I didn't mean to kill him. I don't know what came over me," he said, over and over.

"Women are never worth it," Errol said fervently. "Just remember that, my lad! Women are never worth it! And when they are after your money, forget them!"

"How can I? I'm a Van Rhyne. They are *all* after the money," Bernard said wretchedly. "Am I to become a monk, because of the money? What woman would look at me without it?"

"That's a good question," Errol said, with a grimace. He had often wondered about that himself, and it had made him cynical early on.

"The Duke of Kildare is getting his share," said Bernard, with a twist of his mouth. "Did you hear that father is giving him three million with Regina?"

"Do you like him?"

"No. He's an idiot," Bernard said. "Thinks only about horses. I wonder if he thinks Regina is another horse?" He laughed feebly at his own joke, but Errol looked grave. He was thinking about his young, vulnerable sister, and the haunted look on her face.

He ought to have a good, long talk with Regina, but she was kept so busy with teas and morning gossip sessions, that he hardly saw her. There was no chance for intimate talk at the state dinners almost every evening, and she had fittings and sessions at the dressmakers, and people were constantly coming and going with gifts and letters and notes of congratulation.

The morning of the wedding was cool, cloudy, and rain threatened. Antonia went from one window to another, glaring anxiously at the sky, daring it not to shine bright and blue. Still the clouds hovered.

Regina, in her room, stared at the layers of clothing she was to don. "No," she said. "No, I cannot do it."

At first her maids thought to persuade her. Growing anxious as the hour grew late, they finally sent for her mother. Antonia swept in, locking the door after her.

"Now, what is this, wedding nerves?" Antonia demanded grimly. "I'll have you know, you won't be the first bride nor the last to feel this way."

One maid smiled sympathetically, until a glare from Antonia turned it into a nervous cough.

"You will get dressed at once," Antonia ordered her daughter.

"No, Mother; I cannot go through with it."

"You *will*! Get that clothing over here," Antonia demanded. The maid hastened to bring the exquisite lingerie, the white silk stockings, the white shoes. When Regina shook her head, Antonia came to her and dragged the silk robe roughly from her white body. Regina cried out, and shrank away from her.

"Go in the other room," Antonia ordered the maids, tightly. They scurried away.

Antonia put her face close to Regina's. "You will *not* disobey me!" she hissed furiously. "This is the chance of a lifetime. For you and for me! I will not have you make me a fool in the eyes of the world! To stand up the Duke of Kildare at the altar! To defy me before my friends! Regina, I will not have it."

"I cannot marry him. He is so cold, so callous. Oh, Mother, I pray you, do not force me into this."

"Do you want me to go through with my threat? I will, you know. You have but to say the word."

She paused, and Regina bent her proud head.

"I will write out a letter." Antonia moved to the neat rosewood desk, with its dainty pens and thick, creamy stationery. Deliberately, she selected a sheet, and sat down. "Dear sir—"

"No, Mother!"

"You do not defy me lightly," said Antonia, so angry she could scarcely speak. "I shall write at once to the editor. That McKenna person will not only lose his job,

I shall see to it that his father loses his position, and they shall go poor—go poor, I swear, Regina! You don't know the power of money, do you? You are so naive and stupid! Money *is* power. He will lose everything, and so will his parents! They will lose everything, I swear it!"

"No! No! Mother—"

"Are you going to dress?" She picked up the pen, wet it in the ink, and held it over the page.

"Yes—Mother—" Regina picked up the white silk stockings, almost ripping them as she pulled them onto her long, slim legs with shaking hands.

"Just remember, Regina, I can write that letter at any time. Any time at all. All it takes is a note, and my personal visit to the editor. I have met him; he will do what I say. If you show the least reluctance; if the duke withdraws; if you say no at the altar; by God, I will wreck McKenna!"

Regina was white to her very lips. Antonia called the maids. They came in hastily, and began to dress the pale bride. Antonia watched critically, with nervous looks at the clock. They would not be on time. They would be an hour late, maybe two. She sent Cecil Meryon to the church, to assure the duke and the minister that the shy girl had had an attack of nerves but would be there presently.

Regina would pay for this, Antonia vowed silently. She would pay and pay for the humiliation!

"Put rouge on her cheeks," she ordered curtly. "She need not be so white."

Rouge was applied, and a light dusting of rice powder. Then the satin dress was drawn carefully over her head, and over it, the tiers of Brussels lace. Next, came a dog collar of pearls, three tiers of pearls, which fit about her throat like a noose, thought the sad girl. A court train, covered with seed pearls and silver trim was drawn about her shoulders. Finally, the light tulle veil with a wreath of orange blossoms was set upon her head. The maids drew a deep breath of delight. What a beautiful bride!

Antonia smiled with satisfaction. There, that was done! Now they could get on to the church. She grabbed up the bouquet and placed it into her daughter's hands. Regina looked down at the cluster of creamy white orchids, scentless and cold. She stood there, holding them limply, their long, trailing leaves spilling down over her hands.

Antonia gave her daughter a last critical stare, then led her down to the carriage where Jacob was waiting. Contrary to custom, her mother was to ride with them in the carriage to the church. She would take no chance on leaving Regina alone with her father.

At the church entrance, a crowd of people had gathered. There were newspaper reporters, women, small children, shabby onlookers, fashionable women, the whole world. Several footmen forced a path through the crowd for the bride and her parents.

Someone cried out, "Good luck to ye, Miss Regina!" Regina, recognizing the Irish tone, lifted her head and smiled in the direction of the voice. A reporter took her picture. The flare of the flash powder was so bright that she was almost blinded, and her father helped her into the church.

"Are you all right, my dear?" Jacob asked, as Antonia went ahead to her pew.

She nodded, her head erect. She felt numb, cold, uncaring, and unbelieving. This nightmare could not be happening to her. They started up the aisle behind the beautiful bridesmaids, eight of them, who had stood waiting for two hours in their tight shoes, and were cross with her.

Regina Van Rhyne could afford to be coy; she had the catch of the season, the bridesmaids had muttered to each other, shifting from one hurting foot to the other. But what about them? They smoothed their white satin dresses, adjusted their white picture hats, fiddled nervously with the blue sashes, and hated her for several reasons.

Regina went up the aisle on the arm of her father. Blindly, she gazed straight ahead, and saw everything in

354

a blur of candles and faces. She did not even see the duke waiting for her, his long, horsey face annoyed. He could have killed her for this embarrassment. It would be in the gazettes in England, that he had been kept waiting at the altar for two hours.

She went through the service mechanically, faltering over her vows. The duke spoke up in his clipped, quick speech, and scarcely anyone could understand what either of them said. No matter; the pastor was making sure they were well and truly tied.

"I now pronounce you man and wife. . . ." She *did* hear that, and went ice-cold inside. The duke flipped back her veil nervously, and she had to reach up and help him. He touched her cheek with his lips, and he felt as cold as she did. She shivered.

They turned, and her father stepped forward and kissed her warmly, holding her closely for an instant, and gazing down into her wan face.

One hundred guests accompanied them back to the Van Rhyne mansion. They rode in a long line of fine carriages, with the horses tossing their heads, trying to dislodge the white ribbons that had been tossed coyly over their noses. Regina sat beside the duke, and could not bring a smile to her frigid face. Antonia glared at her, then turned to smile at the best man, The Most Honourable the Marquis of Huntford. She enjoyed saying "My dear Lord Huntford" to him, and pictured herself visiting her daughter in England, and speaking to all these grand people at dinner, at balls, and at the opera. She was quite carried away by the scenes in her mind.

Jacob was leaning back in the plush carriage, impatient to be about his business. Regina was safely married, though, by God, she *did* look pale. Should he speak to the duke about being kind and tender? Regina was such a gentle and timid soul. But no, there was no opportunity to do so. He glanced over at his daughter. She looked quite regal today, in the white gown with pearls, her head high under the crown of orange blossoms. Quite regal, he thought proudly.

When they arrived at the mansion, there was a wedding toast, and several speeches were made. The British ambassador made a beautiful speech, but Regina only half-heard it. The Duke of Kildare responded graciously, only stammering occasionally. The best man toasted the bridesmaids, who gazed longingly and calculatingly at him. Not as good as a duke, but a marquis was not to be sneezed at.

After the toast, Regina was escorted upstairs to change to her going-away outfit of blue satin trimmed with Brussels lace, and a wide picture hat of blue brocade and ribbons. When she came down, Jacob was waiting in the hallway for her. Antonia was still in the massive reception room.

Regina went to her father's arms. She clutched his shoulders with both thin, nervous hands. "Father," she whispered rapidly, "please, I beg of you, don't let Vincent McKenna lose his job!"

"What?" Jacob held his daughter off from him, wondering for a moment if she had lost her mind from the strain of all the ceremonies. "What are you talking about?"

"Vincent. Please, Papa, don't let him lose his job. I did everything Mama said, but you know how she hates."

"Has he been pestering you?" Jacob asked sharply.

Regina went so white he thought she would faint. "No, no, I didn't even get a letter, not a word! Oh, please, Papa, he has done nothing. I have not communicated with him, I promise you! Only do not let his job be taken from him, his reputation smeared. Don't let Mother do anything to harm Aunt Molly and Uncle Evan! Oh, God, here she comes! Oh, promise— promise me, Papa!"

She was so white he would have promised her the moon and a couple of stars thrown in. "I promise, darling. Take care, now, and be a good girl." He kissed her tenderly, and she managed a pallid smile for him. He felt her body stiffen as Antonia approached.

Guests were still milling about. Antonia forced a

smile, as she looked suspiciously from her husband to her daughter. "Whatever are you doing, lingering about the hallway? The carriage is ready to take you to the station."

"I'm ready, Mama." Regina glanced about automatically, taking leave of this great house, which had been her home since birth.

"You might thank me," Antonia said sharply, in a low tone, "for all the trouble I went to in order to make this a grand wedding for you and His Grace!"

Regina managed a smile, which did not reach her violet eyes. "I know you went to a great deal of trouble, Mother. We are—overwhelmed."

Antonia felt the sting of her irony. His Grace was approaching, however, looking his usual bored self.

"Take care of my daughter," Jacob said gravely to him.

"Of course, of c-course!"

His gaze was off in the distance, not on Regina. Jacob felt again the sharp intuition that something was wrong. Tenderly, he kissed his daughter's cheek, and saw her out to the carriage. The wind lifted the brim of her picture hat, and the crowd outside the gates *ooh*ed and *aah*ed. Then they were in the carriage. The coachman clucked to the horses, and the carriage sprang out of the gates into the cheering crowd, which barely parted to let them pass.

"Come back to the drawing room," Antonia ordered Jacob. "You have scarcely spoken to the guests."

"I thought it was *Regina*'s wedding," Jacob drawled. He returned reluctantly to the drawing room, still pondering his daughter's frantic appeal. He must look into this. Vincent's job? What had Antonia been up to?

But then he saw Bernard, leaning against a wall in the drawing room, looking haggard and grim. Errol was hovering near his brother, as though to support him. Jacob decided to leave early. The party was breaking up anyway, now that the bride and groom had departed. Some of the guests longed to dash home or to friends, to give a breathless account of the wedding. Jacob walked toward the door, motioning Errol and Bernard to follow him.

In Jacob's study, Errol helped Bernard into a chair, and put a glass of whiskey into his hand.

"Well, now, what's to be done?" Jacob asked rhetorically. "I think it's out West for you, Bernie," Jacob said, with a deep sigh. "I need a man out there—"

"Then send Errol!" Bernard snapped, flushing red.

"Nonsense. You're old enough to do this job," Jacob said, moving maps before him. "I want you to keep an eye on the Western, and see if they cut rates this winter. Keep your ear to the ground. Let me know at once if they start offering the farmers a lower price for moving the winter wheat. And any offers against next summer."

"I'm out on parole," Bernard said gloomily. "Will they let me get that far from jail?" He shuddered, and took a deep swallow of his drink. Jacob and Errol exchanged glances.

"I'll tell them I need you out there. You go out West and stay put. The talk will die down. The lawyers are on the job." They had better be, Jacob thought grimly; he was paying them enough. "By spring or next summer, it might be safe for you to come back."

"What about Uncle Lodewick?" Bernard set his glass down carefully, his hands shaking.

"He has accepted my offer—of money," Jacob said slowly. "He's up to his eyeballs in debt, including the bills for some diamond items Clinton charged to his account. If I were him, I'd snatch them off that actress and take them back to the jewelers. I advised him to do so, but she's a spirited cat." He was watching Bernard closely, but the lad did not even wince. Good. He must have gotten over her.

"All she wanted was gems," Bernard said wearily. "She doesn't even care who gives them to her."

"You've learned your first real lesson," Errol said ironically, patting his brother's shoulder. "That's all women like her really want. Remember that, and the passion will die down fast, believe me."

"Don't be so cynical to the lad, Errol," Jacob snapped.

Errol's eyebrows rose, but he slumped into a chair and kept his mouth shut. Jacob gave Bernard more instructions, then wrote them down for him, for he realized the boy was scarcely hearing him.

They got a seat for Bernard in a train going West, and preferential treatment—Bernard was still a Van Rhyne, after all. Errol and Jacob saw him off two days later, and exhaled a sigh of relief.

"That's done; he's gone. I'll go out later in the year to check on him, but I told him to write to me weekly," Jacob said, as they walked back to the waiting carriage.

"He seemed in a daze. Do you think I should have gone with him?" Errol asked, helping his father up into the carriage.

Jacob settled himself on the seat. Errol swung up after him. "No, he doesn't need a wet nurse," Jacob said. "He needs to grow up. And out West, he will."

Errol sighed. "I hope so."

They drove to the office in silence.

Chapter 25

A large suite had been prepared for the newlyweds at Whitecrest, in Newport. They arrived late at night, and Regina went to bed alone. The vast bed was cold and damp from the ocean air, and she shivered much of the night.

She woke up late the next morning. With enough blankets, she had finally gotten warm and slept. But she still shivered in nervous reaction.

"Himself has gone off riding," her maid volunteered cheerfully. "My, he does love horses."

"Yes, he certainly does," Regina said absently. "Did he say when he would return?"

"No, Miss Regina."

Regina had tea and toast, then went downstairs to consult with the housekeeper who had been sent up from New York to help out during the week. Together, they planned the meals for the week, then Regina went for a walk in the autumn gardens, her cloak over her shoulders.

The duke returned from his ride, lifted his riding crop to her from a distance, and entered the house. She continued to walk. Presently, properly attired in a morning suit of dull gray, he came down to join her in the garden.

He did not speak to her at first, but simply gazed off into the distance. She wondered what he thought about, and if their minds would ever be in tune.

"You must speak to your maid," he said abruptly, after ten minutes or so.

"Speak to her?"

"Yes. She must now call you 'Your Grace' or 'Madam.' And I am not to be addressed as 'sir.' I am 'Your Grace' to her. She has no knowledge of what is fitting, none at all."

Regina swallowed. "I will speak to her, sir—I mean, Your Grace."

"Don't be absurd, Regina," he said sharply. "You will address me in private as Alastair, or Carstairs. In public, of course, you will refer to me as His Grace. I am amazed at you. Your mother assured me you were conversant with protocol."

"It takes some time, ah, Carstairs," she said ironically.

"Never mind. As for your maid, that problem will soon be settled. In England, you shall have an English maid. I have sent word to Mother to hire someone appropriate for you, someone who can advise you discreetly. She will find someone, and have her ready when we arrive."

"But what about—"

Her maid had been with her for ten years, but Alastair dismissed her with a flick of his fingers. "She is not suitable for the post," he said, and that was that.

They walked until lunchtime. He had nothing else to say to her, but paced with his hands behind his back, his eyes on the distant view. She reflected uneasily that all this was going to be even more difficult than she had imagined.

She embroidered in the afternoon. She was glad she had thought to pack her embroidery. It gave her something to do, and it was one occupation of hers of which her new husband seemed to approve. He read the gazettes, frowning over them. They were not as intelligent as those in England, he commented. Now that her mother was not with them, he did not seem to feel the need to be polite about things American.

They dined in the small dining room, with Regina at his right hand. "At Kildare," the duke said, "we will always dine at opposite ends of the table. It is correct."

"Yes, Carstairs," she said. She was learning.

She retired early, weary of embroidery, and still suffering from the long strain of the wedding. Her maid was subdued. Regina guessed correctly that the girl had already been told about her dismissal.

"Do not worry about it; I shall recommend you highly," Regina whispered to her, feeling as heavy-hearted as the maid.

"Oh, Miss—I mean, Your Grace. I'm sorry I won't be with you. You'll need a friend, that far away and all."

Regina felt the same way. She said goodnight to the girl, and got into bed. She had no more than settled down under the covers, and was about to blow out the lamp, when the door to her husband's adjoining room opened. He came in, seeming taller than usual, dressed in a long, dark robe, his hair brushed straight back.

A wave of deep fear swept over her. She sat up and pushed the pillows behind her carefully. "Well, Carstairs?" she managed to ask lightly.

361

"You may call me by my first name in our bedroom," he said solemnly.

She wanted to laugh hysterically. Instead, she watched him as he took a chair near the bed and seated himself, hitching up his robe.

He gazed at her, or past her. She was never quite sure of the direction of the stare of his gray eyes. His long nose seemed more pointed than ever tonight.

"I wish to have a frank talk with you, Regina."

"Indeed?" It seemed rather late for that, she thought, her mind switching briefly to Vincent McKenna. As far as she knew, he had made no further effort to reach her by messenger or letter. He must have become discouraged, after not hearing from her this summer. She wondered if he had tried again to write, and if her mother had destroyed the letters. Thinking of her mother made her feel cold in the pit of her stomach. She would never forgive her—never.

"As you can imagine, I have heard the gossip in New York. I heard about your—shall I say—lover? McKenna."

She flinched as though struck. "He was not my lover . . ." she began, in a whisper, her hand to her heart.

"Oh, whatever." Alastair shrugged distastefully. "I don't know or care how far you went. Your mother insisted that you were a virgin. I hope so. One can't taint bloodlines, you know."

It was a nightmare. Regina stared at him, her violet eyes growing larger and larger. He sat there, stroking his long chin, his legs crossed in his striped silk pajamas. He stared beyond her as though he did not care to look at her.

"However that may be, I wish to inform you that you have not made all the sacrifices in this marriage." His voice was thin and controlled. "I, too, loved—and lost. I am—still am—in love with—someone else. This marriage is a suitable one. I hope to produce a son directly, an heir to Kildare. That is necessary, or I am the last of our line. I hope you will be amiable about this. It will

362

help matters if you are calm and understanding. I do not care for temper tantrums, fits of depression, nerves, and all that."

He said all this in a calm, understated manner, as though he were bored by the subject. She felt quite cold in the bed, her feet and hands icy.

"Why didn't you marry her?" she burst out. "Oh, why did you not marry her, and make her happy, and leave me to be happy with another? I cannot comprehend—"

"It was impossible. I had to marry money. And you are very presentable, Regina," he said critically, and now he stared at her, from the top of her head, down to her shoulders, above the silk sheets. Nervously she held the sheet up higher, as though his stare burned her. "Yes, you are quite presentable. With a schooling in manners and etiquette, you will do quite well in London. Any blunders will be explained, at first, by the fact that you are an American. But you must learn rapidly to meet my requirements. Your mother assured me you are intelligent, and will learn quickly. I wish to present you at court, as soon as you are schooled."

He spoke of her as though she were a horse, Regina thought, dazed and incredulous.

"And of course," he went on, "you will forget that newspaper fellow. Any attempt to carry on a correspondence with him, or even worse, to meet with him, will meet with my keenest displeasure. I will not tolerate an affair."

With that, he rose, slipped off his robe, and came to the bed. She was literally frozen in place, unable to move. He blew out the lamp and slid into bed beside her. Having said his piece, he was now prepared to make her his wife.

He turned to her. She felt the rigidity of his body, and realized that this was as distasteful to him as it was to her. She bit her lips, as his hands went over her mechanically, icily. God, she thought, oh, God.

He moved his hands under her nightdress, stroking her hips. "Slim as a boy," he muttered, and moved over

363

her. He took her quickly, making her bleed, tearing her flesh, and she bit her lips against tears. She felt the driving of his flesh in her, the moving of his body on hers, rhythmic and passionless. He completed the embrace quickly and callously, and finished in her.

He grunted, and moved off. "That's done," he muttered, and got up. She heard him moving about the room, swinging into his robe. The door opened, closed. He had left her.

Regina, frightened and in pain, crept to the bathroom and washed herself, wincing with pain. So this was marriage, she thought bitterly. Her mother had told her about what would happen, but she had never dreamed it would be so bad. Maybe the next time would be easier. But Alastair did not love her; he did not even like her! If only he had not needed the money! If only he could have married the girl of his choice!

She slept little that night. She started when he came into the bedroom the next morning, dressed for riding. "I am going out, Regina. Shall I wait for you? Pleasant morning," he said cheerfully.

She stared only at the riding crop, unable to look in his face. "I—I am sorry, I cannot, this morning," she stammered. "I—f-feel pain—I am sorry—"

He shrugged. "No matter. Lie in bed. I shall be home for luncheon." And he strode out jauntily, having done his duty.

He came to her several nights that week, did his duty, and left with evident relief. She was shocked, frightened, and chilled to the heart by his attitude. He wanted only an heir from her, and oh, yes, the three million—she must not forget that.

As she sat alone in the mornings, while he rode, she thought with hatred of her mother, who had pushed her into this. She could not forgive her. It had been done deliberately, so that Antonia would be the mother-in-law of an English nobleman. At this very moment she was, no doubt, planning to parade her daughter about when they returned to New York. Regina would not allow it. It was the one revenge she could make. She brought up the topic casually on one of the last afternoons of their honeymoon week.

"Alastair, when we return to New York—before the boat sails, might we stay at a hotel?"

"A hotel? Why? Your mother has invited us to remain with her." He lifted his teacup to his lips, then set it down again elegantly. His thin hands were always elegant, his wrists slight, but strong. He crossed his legs, clad in gray-and-white pinstripe.

"I have never stayed in a hotel. I should like the experience. And dining out in a restaurant. May we not do that? I have several new gowns I should like to show off." She forced herself to smile in his direction.

His eyelashes flickered. "Well—why not? It might be pleasant. Which one do you recommend?"

She named one on impulse, an elegant hotel, newly built, and far from her mother's residence. He nodded, and drawled that he would send a message ahead to make reservations for them. "The ship sails on Tuesday, so we shall have four days in New York."

"Splendid," Regina said, maintaining a steady smile. "I think there are several races on over the weekend, Alastair. You might enjoy them. Splendid horseflesh, Errol says. While you attend the races, I might gossip with some of my girlfriends. Do you think that would be a good plan?"

His eyes narrowed. He finally nodded. "Horses, eh? Yes, I would like that."

They left Whitecrest. The honeymoon had been a ritual they had been unable to avoid. But the duke was anxious to return to England. And Regina ached to get back to New York. There was one person in the whole world who could advise her, and she was determined to see her.

Antonia was stunned and hurt when she learned they were staying at a hotel. "But, my darling girl, I expected you yesterday!" she cried to Regina, in the hotel suite.

"Oh, we wished to stay in a hotel," Regina said calmly, setting the wide felt hat with the ostrich plume on her head, and cocking her head critically at her reflection. "Do you think this purple suits me, Mother?" She watched her mother's face in the mirror.

"It's too old for you," Antonia said sharply.

"Oh, really? But you chose it two weeks ago," Regina said, smiling secretly to herself. Her mother was cross, and it gave her childish pleasure to know why.

"Never mind, never mind. Where is—His Grace?"

"He went to the races with some friends. I thought you and I might lunch in the restaurant here; they permit women without escorts."

"Nonsense, let us dine up here, in your suite. I want to talk to you."

"And I want to dine in a restaurant, Mother," Regina said, lifting her chin. "I have made our reservations. Are you coming?" And she swept to the doorway, her gray skirts with the purple velvet trim showing only a glimpse of her gray suede boots.

Antonia followed her in bewilderment. Her daughter had changed. Why, she was already acting like a duchess! And only married for a week! Well, she was still her daughter, and Antonia would simply not stand for that kind of grand behavior.

But stand for it she did. As a duchess, Regina kept the conversation strictly to the topics she wished. Briskly, she ordered for them from the menu, ordered wine to go with each course, and kept her mother on the subjects of her bridesmaids, her girlfriends, what Aunt Elisabeth had said at the reception, what Aunt Katrinka was doing with her charities, and Aunt Frieda, who was teaching in college now.

"You must be sure to write to me of all your social activities in London," Antonia said desperately, toward the end of the meal.

"Oh, we shall not remain in London, Mother," Regina said, forcibly gay and brittle. "You know we go directly to Kildare. The drains have to be repaired before the winter, you know."

"Drains?" Antonia whispered, visions of presentations and coronets wilting.

"And the roof must be mended. Much work to be

done. And two rooms with chairs and sofas to be embroidered. Carstairs thinks I embroider well. I can take up where his mother left off, when she walked out on him," said Regina.

"Oh, hush, hush! Someone will hear you!"

"I am sure all of England, and any of America that cares to know, will know all about his mother leaving him," Regina said gaily. "It is common knowledge. I wonder if the castle is very drafty? I had better take some long red flannels, just in case."

"Regina," her mother groaned, glancing about in agony.

Regina kept the smile pinned on her face. Her mother would have lingered after the meal, but Regina got up to go.

"I have only a few hours to run about in the carriage and visit some of my friends. I might never see them again, you know. Carstairs does not care for America, and we might never return," Regina said deliberately.

Antonia went white. "You are teasing me! Tell me you are teasing! Of course you will visit often."

"Not at all. His Grace has said so to me. And besides, he gets dreadfully seasick. Now that he has me and all that money, why should he return?"

"Regina, I must protest your flippant attitude—"

"Don't worry, Mother. Carstairs is schooling me in my etiquette, and soon you shall not know me at all!" And Regina dismissed her mother, and went off in her own carriage, hired from the hotel.

In the carriage, alone, she sank back with relief, and put her handkerchief to her face. She had played her part well, and gotten even with her mother. The pressure was gone, but now the grief started. She was imprisoned for life, for Carstairs would not let her go. He had wanted that three million dollars enough to give up his own beloved. She still could not get over that. She wondered how he acted when he was with her. Did he treat *her* tenderly? Did he kiss her, embrace her joyfully? She shivered at the memory of the horrible nights

367

in his arms, those brief sexual struggles that were all she knew of marriage.

She wiped the sweat from her forehead, and straightened her hat. The carriage had stopped in front of Molly McKenna's house.

"Please walk the horses," she instructed the groom. "There is a tavern at the end of the street. Come back for me in two hours."

"Yes, Your Grace," the groom said.

Regina let him go on, then went up to the house and tapped at the door. Molly opened it, then opened her arms wide.

"Me darling girl," Molly said, and hugged her tightly. Regina pressed her face against the graying hair, and felt tears threatening to overcome her. In the warmth of this embrace was the motherly love she wanted so desperately.

"Oh, Aunt Molly—Aunt Molly—" Her voice caught on a sob.

"Come in, me dear, come in and warm yourself. Sure, it's a cold day for late September. Winter will be a-coming soon." Molly urged her into the warm, bright living room, to a seat near the fire.

She studied the pale face before her. "Is everyone at work, Aunt Molly?" Regina asked, stripping off her long, gray gloves and holding out her hands to the blaze.

"Sure, and where else would they be on a Friday?"

"And—Vincent?"

"At the newspapers, or goin' round to find news, as usual."

"Aunt Molly, I haven't much time. Mother stopped my letters to you, and to Vincent." Regina's pale face turned to her. "I want to—I need to—speak frankly to you." Regina continued in a low voice. "She forced me to marry Kildare. I detest him, and he feels the same way toward me. Father was too busy to listen to me."

"Lord, Lord, child, whatever are you saying?" Molly gazed at her in bewilderment.

"It's true. She stopped my letters. I told her I loved

368

Vincent and wanted to marry him. Father said all right, but Mother was furious, and forced me into marrying the duke. If I had known Kildare wanted only the money—well, that is past. We are married, and I must make the best of it. But I wanted to warn you."

"Warn me, me dear?" Molly wondered if the girl was feverish. She had known girls to get so excited over their weddings that they went a bit off their heads. But Regina seemed herself, albeit a bit thin and pale, hugging her knees as she sat on the low chair before the fire. She was a mere child, in spite of her smart gray gown and purple toque and the jewels on her slim fingers.

"Yes. Mother threatened to write to the *New York Times* and tell the editor that Vincent was pestering me. I told Father, but I don't think he understood what I meant. If—if Vincent is troubled in any way, or threatened, I want you to write to Father at once. Remind him that he made me a promise. Vincent should not suffer because of me." She was white, but determined, her violet eyes blazing fiercely. "I wed Kildare as I promised, but I fear Mother may try to strike at Vincent anyway. Remind Father that he promised me he would help Vincent in any way he could."

"Good land, child! Do you *mean* all this?" Molly asked sharply.

"Yes, I mean it, Aunt Molly," Regina answered. "He is threatened, and so are Uncle Evan and you. I think Mother has always resented your friendship with Father. I don't know what lies behind it, but she—she knew that father could come here anytime to relax, and that Errol and Bernie and I could always come over with him."

Molly's graying head drooped, and she rested it on her palm for a long moment. Finally she sighed deeply, and looked up.

"All right, me dear. I'll do what I can. If Vincent's job is threatened, I'll send word to Jacob, as you say. You're not to worry about it."

"Good." Regina drew a deep breath of relief, and looked about her. "How—how is Vincent?"

"Thin. He works too hard, has to run all about New York State, and New Jersey, too. But he likes his work."

"And Uncle Evan?"

"Same as ever. Deep into politics, with folks dropping in at all hours. T'other night a man knocked at the door at three in the morning, a-wanting Evan McKenna. I goes to the door and I says—"

Molly rattled on gaily, stringing out the story, for she saw the weary lines on the girl's face, the tense way she clenched her fingers together. She made Regina smile, even laugh a little, then she got up to fix some tea. A little desperately, she looked about for something to amuse her sad guest.

"There, now, here are some clippings of Vincent's articles about the railroads. I don't understand a word, but you might have a look at them," she said, and handed them to Regina before departing for the kitchen.

She came back, to find Regina poring over the articles. Her eyes seemed steadier and brighter, as she read. But when she finally put the clippings aside, the same sad, haunted look came over her face. She looked up at Molly and spoke frankly.

"Aunt Molly, I must tell you—I am so puzzled. When—when Alastair came to me in bed—it hurt so much." She explained, rather flushed, what had happened. Molly listened, hiding her mounting anger at the innocent girl's remarks.

"Will it always be like this, Aunt Molly?"

Molly talked to her, kindly and gently, explaining how Regina must help herself, with creams and ointments if necessary, to make it easier. "Evidently, he ain't used to delicate females," Molly said bluntly. "And you'll have to protect yourself. Once you start a child, have the doctor tell him not to share your bed. I mean it, Regina. It sounds as if he don't have no con-

370

sideration for you. But maybe it will work out, me dear, and he will come to love you—"

Regina was shaking her head. "He loves someone else, he told me."

"For God's sake, when?"

"The first night!" Regina managed a wry smile at Molly's shock.

Molly took the girl's white, delicate hand and pressed it firmly between her own rough ones. "Me darling, protect yourself. Write to me, once you're set, and I'll write to ye. Sure, he won't stop the letters of an old woman like me."

Regina went over and sat down at Molly's knee as she had as a child, and rested her head in Molly's lap. "Aunt Molly, how shall I endure it?" she asked in a muffled tone. "Among strangers, and alone? With a man who is cold and hateful and a snob? How will I stand it, all the years. We may never come home again."

Molly stroked her hair tenderly. "You'll endure, my dear, as others have before you. There is good, strong stuff in you. You're of strong stock, like your father and your father's father. You'll suffer, but you can make it less painful by relieving the suffering of others. Your suffering is of the heart and mind and soul. Others are starving, hungry, and cold, with needs so great that they will bless you for helping them. On his Lordship's great estate, there will be many who need your aid. If he's as cold as you say, he won't pay them no mind."

"But they are his tenants. Surely—"

"I remember well how it was in Ireland," Molly said, her lips tight, "with the English landlords collecting the rent from across the Irish Sea, and no one to care if we starved or emigrated. When Rowan and me left Ireland, there was no one to weep for us. If it hadn't been for your grandfather, we might not even have had jobs here in America. Someone *has* to care, Regina. You be that someone. *You* care. You care for them, and their love will reach out and flow about you, and help you heal."

"It seems such a hard life, Aunt Molly," the girl whispered. Her hands were still clasped in Molly's.

"I never seen a life that was easy, girl," Molly counseled her. "It's all hard, one way or another. Be grateful that you have food in your mouth, clothes on your back, and a roof over your head. Then look to others, to make sure of the same for them. Fill your days with good works, and your sleep will be peaceful."

"Will it? Will it be enough?"

"That, the child to come, and faith in God," Molly said gently. "The child may make a difference. You have a son for him, and he may soften to you, Regina. There is nothing like being a father to change a man. I will pray daily for you. I'll light candles, that your way will be made clear to you."

"Thank you, Aunt Molly. I'll try." Regina drew away and wiped her eyes carefully with her linen handkerchief. "Aunt Molly—money is a curse."

"Being without money is a far worse curse, believe me," Molly said, patting the girl's head kindly. "You see to it that the folks that need it get some, and it don't all go for nonsense."

Regina nodded, her head filled with somber thoughts. To go off to a strange land, to be abruptly a grown woman, married, without love, without friends— it was a formidable task she faced.

The back door banged, and a girlish voice called, "Mom, are you home?"

"Yes, Jessie, in the front room," Molly called.

Regina stood up gracefully, wiped her eyes one last time, and turned to smile as the girl came in. Jessie was startled to see her there. "Oh, Miss Regina. How grand you look!" she said in awe. Regina looked back at the girl. Her cheeks were rosy, her eyes bright, her hair streaming down her back, caught in a wide green ribbon. She looked young, blooming, free and graceful.

Regina looked at her, and envied her. All her life was before her. She had a beau who was fine and good, and who loved her.

"I must be going, Aunt Molly. Thank you for the talk. You will write to me?"

"I will, me dear. And you write whenever you can."

Regina kissed her cheek, was hugged fiercely hard, and then went out to the waiting carriage. She got in, and gave the address of the hotel. She must go back now, and make the best of it. With Molly's encouragement, she thought she knew the path she must take. But it would be a hard one, and rocky, with many thorns, and all uphill, into a misty distance she could not yet fathom.

Chapter 26

Jacob studied the handwriting on the envelope, then ripped open the letter. He read it, scowled, cursed under his breath, then read it again.

Dear Jacob,

Before Regina left for Europe, she told me that Vincent might get into trouble because of his writing letters to her which her mother took and burnt. Now Vincent tells me he got one week's notice at his job, for all he was doing good, and the editor-in-chief had mentioned that he would get a raise soon. Regina made me promise to write to you and remind you of what you said. Vincent is all puzzled about it, and mighty hurt, and it hurts me to see what he feels.

You been so good to us, I hate to ask more. But could you see if you could maybe talk to that editor and tell him that Vincent is not pestering Regina, and won't write to her no more? I think that is behind the matter, though I did not say so to Vincent.

Yours gratefully,

Molly O'Neill McKenna

Jacob swore again, and his clerk winced. It usually meant that someone was going to catch hell. He only hoped to God it was not him.

Jacob said abruptly, "Put off all my appointments today. I'll be out for a while."

"Yes, sir, Mr. Van Rhyne," the clerk said, in great relief.

Jacob went out, called for his carriage, and set off for the *New York Times* building. Once there, he went directly in to see the editor-in-chief.

He was bowed into the large office, and the man stood up from behind his desk to greet him nervously. "Mr. Van Rhyne, I am honored, sir!"

"Good day, sir," Jacob said, shaking the offered hand. Then, wearily, he set down his cane, removed his bowler hat, and seated himself in the chair opposite the desk. He eyed the editor narrowly. "I understand you have been wanting to have an interview with me over the railroads and what is going on with them."

The editor was stunned. He sank down into his chair. What did this mean, Van Rhyne's coming to him? What did the great railroad magnate want? Was he going to grant an exclusive interview?

"Ah—yes sir, that is true. Ah—will you? I will interview you myself if you wish—"

"No, no, the most knowledgeable reporter you have, on business affairs, is Vincent McKenna. He can do it," Jacob declared simply.

"Ah, ah, Vincent McKenna?" The editor looked about, as though to find him pinned to the wall. "He, ah, he's not here any longer. You know, he left us."

"Left you?" Jacob jumped on that sharply. "Left you. No doubt he got a better offer. You ought to have

374

offered him a higher salary, you know! He was the smartest man you had!"

The editor shrank into his chair, looking utterly miserable. "Well, frankly, Mr. Van Rhyne, we had a letter. That is—"

"My wife didn't write to you, did she?" Jacob asked, helping him along. This was going to be easier than he had thought.

"Actually, she did." The editor reached into his desk, and drew out a heavy, cream-colored envelope, with Antonia's copperplate handwriting on the face of it. Jacob held out his hand, and the man gave it to him without thinking.

Jacob opened the letter and read it, keeping his face smooth to conceal his rage. That bitch, Antonia! Regina had done as her mother had asked, had gone through with the wedding. Was that not enough? Must the woman now hit out at everyone Regina loved?

"I'll keep this. I wouldn't want it to get around," Jacob said, stuffing the letter into his pocket. "You see, my wife is getting older, and her mind isn't what it was. She imagines all kinds of things. Actually, McKenna and his family have been close to us for years. His mother was a maid in our household before she married Evan McKenna—the politician, you know. Fine family. I wouldn't want them in trouble because of my wife's ravings."

How Antonia would scream if she could hear him! Jacob derived a sardonic pleasure from imagining the scene.

"Ah, really? Her mind isn't—terribly sorry, sir. Really very sorry," the editor said, wiping his forehead. "I could not but believe what she said . . ."

Jacob leaned forward and tapped the desktop with his thick fingers. "Confidentially, don't believe a word my wife says," he said quietly, staring straight into the man's eyes. "You can't trust her—not a word. She's gone a bit dotty, with the strain, you know, of the girl's wedding to a British duke, and all that. It got her upset and raving a bit. No wonder, all that strain. I've got to get her away on a vacation and calm her down. Women are fragile things, you know."

The editor did not share his opinion. He had a tyrant of a wife who bullied and browbeat him, so he would come into the office and do the same to all around him. Nevertheless, he nodded his head sympathetically.

"Yes sir, I understand. Ah, I believe McKenna is here." He stood up in relief, and beckoned through the plate-glass window. McKenna, who had come to the office to collect the rest of his belongings, came in, glancing from one of the men to the other. His face was thin and worn.

Jacob held out his hand. "Ah, Vincent, how are you?" McKenna shook it mechanically.

"Mr. Van Rhyne has graciously consented to an interview with you, McKenna," the editor said.

"Indeed? How kind of him."

"I was telling him you are the best reporter on his staff, and that he should give you a big raise to keep you on," Jacob said, smiling.

McKenna swallowed. So did the editor.

"Five dollars more per week," the editor said weakly. At a glance from Jacob, the editor raised his eyebrows, and added, "Make that ten dollars more per week. You do excellent work, and we must manage to keep you from all those fellows who will want you on the other newspapers."

"Thank you very much, sir," McKenna said, looking as though he had been struck over the head. Jacob stood up, gathered his cane and hat, and put his hand in McKenna's arm to usher him out of there before he had a chance to say anything more.

"We'll go out, have a drink, and talk. I must set you straight on what is going on in the Southwest, McKenna. You had a couple of wrong impressions in that last article," Jacob said, as he steered the reporter toward the door, leaving the other reporters gaping after them.

At the stairs, McKenna halted. "What *is* going on,

Mr. Van Rhyne? Did Mother tell you—you know I am being fired—"

"Nonsense, all a mistake. Now, keep on walking unless you want all of New York to know what we are saying!" Jacob said sharply.

Jacob got him downstairs, and out to the saloon three blocks away. There, they sat in a corner, and talked for three hours straight. McKenna scribbled in his notebook and fired question after question at the great man.

Jacob talked to him freely, encouraged by the reporter's quick, intelligent questions. He outlined for him the current situation in the railroads—how some lines were trying to freeze others out, and take them over, and how the banking house of J. Pierpont Morgan was trying to make peace between them, and settle it all.

"That's our one hope, that he can make peace, and settle the rates. If all the lines keep to it, we can show a profit and not cheat the farmers and cattlemen either. It would be good for all concerned. But some rascals in the railroad business, who would rather see everyone go bankrupt but themselves, sweep a huge profit into their own pockets," Jacob said savagely.

"May I quote you, Mr. Van Rhyne?"

"Go ahead! Might as well be hanged for a sheep as a lamb!" Several drinks had loosened his tongue, but he was still in command, as he always was. "Tell the people how it is. I am tired of being the villain. The farmers are being squeezed between the railroad profiteers and the cattlemen. For the future, I see—" And he went on talking for another hour until his voice was hoarse.

When they had finally exhausted the subject of the railroads, McKenna laid down his little notebook and pencils, and said, "Did my mother come to you?"

"She wrote. Antonia was making trouble. Regina warned me before she left that her mother might pull something like this. A bitch, my Antonia."

"How is—Regina?" His voice broke over the name. His eyes seemed sunken in his head. He must truly love her, Jacob thought.

"Thin, tired. It is hard on a young girl, having such a big society wedding."

"But the duke—he treats her well?"

Jacob studied his glass as though he had never seen it before, turning it in his big fingers. "Well enough. You know how royalty are. It's an adjustment for her. Regina never went for the social doings. Has to learn to dress up more, go out and dance."

"She might like that," Vincent said. He drained his glass. "She never answered my letters. I was worried about her. I wanted to be sure the wedding was what she wanted."

"It wasn't," Jacob said bluntly. "Her mother pushed her into it. She said she wanted to marry you. Antonia stopped your letters. She'll get over it, but you'd better not write to Regina. Her husband will be furious, and she'll get the worst of it."

Vincent was staring at Jacob incredulously. His face was white and his strong jaw was tensed. "Stopped my letters? Regina never heard? That's why she didn't write. Oh, God."

Jacob clasped the lad's hand, and remembered him as a boy, so tall and sturdy and grave, so responsible, like his father, like his mother. Yes, he would have made a fine husband for Regina.

"I'm sorry. Her mother wanted it, and I—I was worried about Bernie, and all that business this summer. Regina will be all right. She will face up to her responsibilities, and she married well. A duke, and all that."

"And marriage to me would not have been suitable," Vincent said bitterly, his mouth hard. "I see that. Yes, I see that. The son of Irish immigrants—"

"Not that. It's the money, lad," Jacob said with a sigh. "Money marries money, that's the way of it, so Antonia says. She is pushing Errol to marry money. I did, so did my father. And the money grows and clings to one like moss, until you don't know what you look like any more, all covered with moss . . ."

Vincent was not listening to him. His vivid blue eyes were staring into the distance, his chin grim. Jacob said a few more things, realized there was nothing more to say, said goodbye, and left him.

But Jacob could not return to the office. He had the coachman drive him down to the docks. He would often go there when he was troubled. He found the ships and their busyness comforting. He sat in the carriage, watching as the sailors climbed on the ropes, loaded the stores, and painted the sides. The warehouse clerks were running about, and the owners were rushing down to see what was happening, and shouting orders to everyone. Jacob got down from the carriage and paced around to his own warehouses, barked his own orders, then left as suddenly as he had come.

He returned to the carriage, but still he could not go home. He kept thinking about Vincent and Regina. Would it have worked? She had been raised in luxury. She thought she loved Vincent, and he was a fine man. But he had no money. No, it would not have worked. She was better off with her English duke, he finally told himself.

He ate dinner down at the dockside with one of his chief clerks, and finally, reluctantly, returned home about nine o'clock that night. The Van Rhyne mansion was ablaze with lights.

"What's going on?" he asked his coachman.

"Dinner for about fifty, cook says, sir," replied the coachman.

"Drive me around the back way then," Jacob said with a sigh.

He entered the house through the back, startling a maid into dropping a dish of gelatine, which quivered like something green and slimy on the kitchen floor. He went up the back stairs to his room, and paced the floor for a while before retiring. The music and laughter reached him only dimly.

He departed for work early the next morning, but returned home early. He had made up his mind.

Antonia was in the front parlor, some guests having just departed. She lay elegantly across the chaise longue in her new cream silk brocade with the gold trim.

When he entered, she looked at him sullenly. "You ignored the dinner last night, Jacob," she reproached him. "And the guests thought—"

He cut her off with a wave of his hand, and shut the door behind him. He stood over her, looking down at her with disgust. She moved uneasily beneath his gaze.

"Have you seen the *New York Times* today?" he asked abruptly.

She crinkled her brow. "Jacob, I never read the newspapers until evening," she said. "What is wrong?"

"You might have been interested in the financial pages. I gave a long interview to Vincent McKenna yesterday. He wrote it up well—five columns in the *Times*. He got all the facts right, too."

She flushed slightly, and turned to stare at the fire burning brightly in the fireplace. "Oh—is he still with the *Times*?" she asked vaguely; she seemed indifferent.

"Damned right he is, and he'll stay there, with a hefty raise," Jacob said firmly. "I went to see the editor. He gave me your letter." He took it from his pocket, waved it before her eyes, then replaced it. "Antonia, if you ever, ever, pull such a stunt again, you will be bitterly sorry. I have warned you not to interfere in my concerns. You have gone too far."

She went pale, and sat up straight. "That damned editor—he *told* you. I'll see that he is fired!"

"No, you won't. You don't have the power in this family, Antonia. *I* have the power, *I* have the money, *I* have the stock, and don't you ever forget that! You interfere with Vincent McKenna or his family ever again, and I'll see that you regret it to your dying day, and that is a solemn promise!"

There was a brief silence as she stared at him, shaking a little.

"How dare you—" she sputtered, but he cut her off.

"I told the editor that all the planning and work of the wedding had gone to your head. I told him you had gone mentally ill, and he was not to pay any attention to what you said. I told him that my wife is to be ignored, because she is not mentally competent. And I gave

380

McKenna a damned long interview and got him a raise as big as he deserves. So that's your scheming, gone for naught."

Antonia struggled with her rage. "You told him—I was mentally ill? How could you—oh, oh,—how could you!" And her lips curled up as though she would weep.

"I think you had better take a six months' vacation, Antonia," he said, striding up and down the room. "I think you had best go away for a time, and rest. You're worn out, and ill. I shouldn't be surprised if you *are* mentally ill. This is the action of a peculiar mind."

She pressed her lips together. "Vacation? I could go to England—"

"Damned if you will! You've done enough to Regina. Let her alone. You'll go to one of your aunts, and be quiet. The social season can get along without you."

She eyed him rather fearfully. She had never seen him so quietly angry, so furious to the core. "Jacob, let me go to England. I swear I won't trouble Regina, but I could help her—"

"You will not go near Regina! You will go away to one of your aunts, I don't care which one. Tell your maid to pack for you, and be gone within a week. I don't care to see you again this winter."

He turned to leave the room. The significance of what he had said began to dawn on her. "Jacob! For the love of God, don't send me away! It could be my biggest season! My daughter is a duchess. I'll be asked everywhere! My party last night—everyone was curious, and so respectful—"

"You'll go. Within a week," he repeated, and slammed the door heavily behind him.

He could not go back to work in his study. He was too full of rage and weariness. He got the carriage out, and drove to Evan McKenna's house.

Molly met him at the door, beaming, clasping both his hands. "Sure, and ye're a miracle worker, Jacob Van Rhyne," she said, in a low tone. "Vincent has been promoted to city editor this very day! And his fine interview with you in the papers, and your name on every lip! It's grand, that's what it is!"

He squeezed her hands, smiled down into her frankly happy face, and came in to shake Evan's hand. Jessie was there, with her beau, Padraic Cassidy, and he shook their hands too, and looked them over keenly. By the glow on their faces, he could tell they were courting seriously.

"Well, now, that was a fine thing you did for Vincent," Evan said heartily. "Giving him that interview, and everyone quoting from it today. Did you mean what you said about the unions?"

And they were off into politics, while Molly went off to the kitchen and brought back great steins of cold beer, and some German pretzels. Jacob settled back to enjoy the evening.

Molly said presently, "Now, have ye eaten, Jacob? If not, ye'll share our supper. Vincent won't be home until ten, if then. And he'll want to be thanking ye."

"I'll accept the supper, and thank you, Molly," said Jacob. "But then I'll be off. Vincent does a fine job. He doesn't need to thank me for the fact that he has a fine father and mother, and takes his job so seriously. He's a good, hard-working lad, and you must be very proud of him."

Molly's smile was blissful. "That we are, that we are! And Muir is doing well at the shirt factory; he was promoted to foreman last year, you know. And Molly with her two wee bairns, making me the proudest grandmother on the street."

They laughed and teased her, and she laughed with them, and bustled about setting the table for supper. The food was simple, but delicious: corned beef, cabbage, onions, potatoes, raw carrots, apples, and a raisin salad. And for dessert, apple pie, hot from the oven. Young Molly stopped in with her husband and her two children, to join them. It was a noisy, happy, warm family, and tonight they made Jacob feel as if he were one of them.

He left at eight, but did not head home. What was there for him? Antonia's cold rage? An empty bed? He wondered what had gone wrong between them. All those years, and three children, and tonight he despised her.

His carriage turned automatically in another direction, and he found himself at the apartment of Deirdre O'Callahan.

Deirdre opened the door to him, a warm smile on her face. "Come in, come in, Jacob. It's been a long time."

The sitting room was spilling over with patterns and cloth. She swept them to one side, and brought him coffee.

"And what has been going on with the shop, Deirdre?" he asked, not caring much, but wanting to watch her face light up with enthusiasm.

"There now, we have so much to do I've hired another woman to work this winter," she said with satisfaction. "In the mornings we have fittings, and in the afternoons we sew like we was crazy. How do ye like this hat?"

She held up a creation of blue felt and orange feathers with a butterfly stuck on the brim, larger than life and quivering.

"My sainted aunt," Jacob said. "That is a hat?"

She burst into bubbling giggles, and had to set down the hat and wipe the tears of mirth from her eyes. She spoke of the article in the newspaper, and talked intelligently about the railroad men and the union, and the hopes they had.

Presently, Jacob asked her permission, and got out his portfolio of papers. "I couldn't work at home, I was so upset," he said, spreading them out on the table she used to cut her sewing.

"There, now, ye can work in peace here, Jacob—you know that," she said comfortingly, without asking what the matter was.

Because she did not ask, he told her, finally, what had happened. She shook her head compassionately.

"The poor girl, the poor girl, she must have been torn," Deirdre said. "I hope and pray her marriage will work out well. Is he a good man?"

A good man? Jacob did not know. They had talked about horses and railroads, and about Regina's dowry, and about the drains at the duke's castle. Thinking of the tight, thin mouth, the long, supercilious nose, and Regina's misery, all made Jacob feel very uneasy. He went to work on his papers, and worked until midnight. Deirdre sewed in silence, on an elegant dress of green silk brocade, in a golden chrysanthemum pattern.

He finally finished going through the stack of papers he had brought with him, and leaned back and yawned. "Do you mind if I stay the night?" he asked, purely as a matter of courtesy, for she had never refused him.

"Sure, I've already turned down the sheets, and run the warming pan over them," she said placidly. "Your robe is on the chair, and your pajamas are warming in the kitchen. I'll fetch your slippers."

He grinned, a little ruefully, after she had left the room. He felt more at home here than at home! He got up and stretched, then blew out the lamp on the table.

He went into the kitchen, and she found him getting the pajamas from the chair near the stove. "I'll just turn off the stove now, unless you want something hot before you go to bed."

"No, nothing more." He turned and drew her into his arms. She rested against him, her plump body moving against his, her head on his great chest. He stroked the red-gold hair, which she had unwound. It hung in a long plait down her back. "Sometimes, Deirdre, I feel I don't know the right answers anymore."

"Land, who does?" she asked. "But you do, if any man does."

He thought of the terrible depression of a few years past, the crash of the market, the way the railroad men had fought until several of them were ruined. One of his friends had killed himself by jumping from a tenth-story office window. And still the race for money went on and on, relentlessly.

She felt the shiver that went through him. "Come to bed, Jacob, and get warm. It's a cold night."

They went to bed, and lay together comfortably, warmed by the blankets over them, and the presence of each other. She was a good, warm woman, Jacob thought, a motherly woman, a wifely woman. He wished she were his wife instead of Antonia.

Deirdre stroked his bare body with her gentle hand, and aroused him. He turned over in the bed, pinned her under him carefully, and began to move with her. He needed her warmth. He needed to bury himself in her and forget everything.

Her arms closed about his body, and her hands moved over his bare back, up to his neck, smoothing away the tension, then down over his back and thighs.

He closed his eyes, and pressed his face into the soft, warm curve of her throat and breasts, pressing his mouth to the roundness of her breasts, moving his lips against the hard nipples. No words were necessary now. They moved together, faster and faster, enjoying each other in the closeness, the warmth, the gentleness that shut out the cruelty of the world.

He felt the tension giving way inside himself, the hatred melting into a haze of love and quiet happiness. He relaxed into Deirdre's arms, and moved with her, and finished in a blur of heat and passion.

He rolled over, then, and drew her into his arms, her back toward him, spoon-fashion, his hands on her, stroking her. He nuzzled his face against her tousled hair, and drew the blankets up around them. He felt her stir, snuggle comfortably against him, and drift off to sleep.

He cupped one hand around her breast, held her to him, and finally, he slept.

Chapter 27

Castle Kildare was a huge, rambling, drafty monster of a medieval fortress looming on a hill overlooking two thousand acres of forests and fields. Five villages were strewn about on the slopes and in the valleys, and all of them looked to Kildare for work, support, and help. But few people got more than token help from the Duke of Kildare.

He gave some of them employment in the castle, as cooks, maids, butlers, footmen, or grooms. The fields took another few hundred, for the planting, reaping, and cattle-raising. There was also a large poorhouse, where some of the elderly and crippled lived out the remainders of their dreary lives. Kettles of food were sent down to them from the vast kitchens of the Castle, and they were given piecework to do, those who could still sew or knit, and sometimes they sent back little tokens of gratitude to the duke, and his new duchess.

The duke's mother came to call promptly, one month after Regina had arrived in England. Regina was received in state, and she trembled before her mother-in-law's blue stare. But she soon found the woman a comfort.

Lillian, as Regina soon learned to call her, carried her chin high, but her eyes were sad and lonely. She had led a miserable life. Her husband's infidelities had been notorious, even in that Victorian age, when much was hidden under a prim surface. She had had one son, then her husband had gone his own way, leaving her to raise the boy until he went off to school.

"I almost went mad here at the Castle, until I took up embroidery," she confided quietly to Regina, finding a kindred spirit in the girl. "I was young, shy, and very timid in those days. I thought it was some fault in myself, that my husband left me alone. It was only in later years, as I observed others, and read much, that I realized it was not me he left, but the duties, the responsibilities, the sheer toil and drudgery of the work here. He was never one to work."

Regina listened, then asked some shy questions about the work, and the estate. Her mother-in-law told her everything she could. "You will find your own way, I expect. With your money," she said frankly, "you can do much more than I was able to. I understand Alastair is repairing the drains and the roof. I am glad of that. He is not as reckless with money as his father was. Sometimes I wished one of my husband's mistresses would have given me one of her diamond bracelets. I could have used the money to pay the bills!" She laughed lightly, but her face was sad.

"I have no money of my own," Regina finally confided. "All my dowry went directly to my husband, His Grace. I do not wish to ask him for funds. He always asks 'what for?' and is so cross. But the people sometimes need food, and I wish to help them. What shall I do?"

Lillian told her, advising her warmly. Food could be arranged, and the bills sent to his secretary. They would be paid without question. "Just don't ask Alastair beforehand. He hates to be asked for money."

"And my dresses? He said I should get more, but I have wardrobes full—"

"Get them in London when you go there, or send for patterns and materials and hire dressmakers. Then send him the bills. Just never ask!"

Regina thought about it. She felt uncomfortable about going behind her husband's back. She also did not like having to ask him for money. Oh, if only she had some money of her own. Hadn't she done as her parents had wished, and married well? Her brothers had money of their own, why not she?

She wrote to her father at his office, and asked him

bluntly. She had learned not to use Antonia's wily ways with him; he hated that.

"I want to be able to do what I wish now and then, Father," she wrote, bluntly. "Alastair controls all the money you gave him. I know you gave money to my brothers; will you not allow me some to handle as I wish? I don't mean railroad stock, I know you have invested some for me.

"I do not know how it can be handled, but I want to have some money that Alastair would not know of, if possible. At least, I do not want him to control it. Can that be arranged?"

To her amazement, Jacob responded at once. His conscience had been hurting badly, and he was only too glad for the chance to make it up to her.

. . . I have sent a draft for a million dollars to an account opened for you in a London bank. Antonia knows nothing of it; do not mention it to her, or to your husband, unless he insists on knowing of it. I have directed the money to be for your own investing and use. No one else can touch it, not even with a written order from you. No one can bring pressure on you to make you sign it over. Only by your check or personal presence in the bank can anything be done with the funds. I advise you to invest some in sound English stocks. The rest can go into a savings account and into a large checking account. Then if you wish, you can hop over to Paris or down to Italy, without asking anyone for permission. . . .

Regina stared at the letter, unable to believe her eyes. Her father said nothing of his supicions about her husband, but she could read between the lines. He knew that Alastair might be tight with money, and that she might wish to escape for vacations, and have money without begging for it. She felt somewhat warmer and less bitter, knowing that he understood.

Lillian remained with them, over Christmas and New

388

Year's. When she prepared to depart, to return to her London town house, Regina asked to accompany her.

"I should like to learn the shops, the best dressmakers, something of society," she told her husband calmly, concealing her anxiety over his response. "Your mother has kindly offered to introduce me about. Would you like to come?"

He hesitated, then refused. "No, you go ahead. But do not remain long. A month should be sufficient. After all, we are just married," he said. "People might talk."

He was cold and indifferent to her, personally. He came to her bed about once a week, and had relations with her. Otherwise, he scarcely spoke to her. At dinners, he was abstracted, and spoke more to their few guests than to her. She was beginning to prefer that, for they had little in common.

She went to London with Lillian on the train, in a private carriage, much more luxurious than any she had found in the States, except for her grandfather's private car. Jacob rarely used that now, preferring to ride without pomp. Regina wondered what he would have thought of this car, with its velvet upholstery, mahogany furnishings, and gilt-edged windows.

In London, she went to the bank to which her father had directed her. She was received with low bows, and the personal attention of the president of the bank, a friend of Jacob's. He vowed secrecy, confirmed her father's advice about investing, and set up accounts for Regina to which no one else would have access. With a relief that made her sigh deeply, she thanked the man and left the bank.

Now there was but one more urgent matter to attend to. Before she had left for London, she had begun to suspect she was with child. That night she confided in Lillian, who recommended an excellent doctor. "After all, the child will be the heir of Kildare," Lillian said with satisfaction. "Does Alastair know yet?"

"I was not certain," stammered Regina. Actually, she had been afraid to tell him.

She went to the doctor, and was examined by him,

with her maid present. Phyllis, an experienced English maid, was stiff, proper, black-uniformed, and had an English accent that Regina could not even understand at first. Gradually they became acquainted, cautiously, until Regina found the woman a font of wisdom and gentleness.

Regina said to the doctor, "I am very slim, and have been in fragile health at times. I feel, during my pregnancy, that my husband—should not have access to me. Do you not agree, Doctor?"

He cleared his throat, tapped his lips with a forefinger, and nodded, not looking in her face. "Of course, Your Grace," he said formally. "I quite agree. You must speak to him, or I shall come with you to Kildare, and speak to him myself."

"Oh, I will tell him—that is, ask him," Regina said. "If he should question it, I only want you to confirm what I say."

"Naturally," the doctor said. With Molly's advice, Regina had used creams to good effect. But he had still been able to see what Kildare had done to her: the torn flesh, the scarcely healed scars. He fumed inwardly, but said nothing to his patient.

They returned to the Castle one week later. Lillian, worried about her daughter-in-law's condition, thought Regina should be getting back to Kildare. They did not send word to the duke about their early return, for they thought to surprise him with Regina's good news.

It was a gray afternoon in early February, and Alastair was out hunting. Regina went to her suite, bathed off the grit of the train tracks, and rested for a time. She must have fallen asleep on her wide plush bed. On awakening, she heard sounds coming from her husband's bedroom next door.

She put on her robe, and went to the door joining their rooms. The noises had stopped. Without knocking, she opened the door and walked into his bedroom.

In the dimly lit room, with its drapes drawn against the gray dusk outside, she could not see clearly at first.

When her eyes grew accustomed to the darkness, she was unable to believe what she saw.

Alastair lay on the bed, his crimson robe parted at the legs. Beside him lay his male secretary, Gilroy Ericson, a tall, handsome, blond young man, who had always smiled mysteriously at Regina and disappeared discreetly whenever she entered the room. He had fluttery hands, and was always well-dressed, with rings and studs of rubies and diamonds. She had wondered vaguely why he worked for Alastair when he must obviously be so well-off.

They lay together, intertwined, holding each other. As Regina stood there, silently horrified, Alastair brought Ericson's face to his, and kissed his lips.

Something in the man's face must have warned Alastair. He turned around and sat up abruptly, staring at Regina. Then he blazed, coldly, "Whatever are you doing here?"

"Alastair—" she whispered.

"Get out of my room! Never enter again without knocking!" he shouted. She backed out of the door, and shut it after her.

In her own warm room, she began to shake. She put her hands over her face. The scene she had witnessed kept flashing before her eyes. She would never forget it.

Phyllis tapped, entered quietly, and saw her. "Oh, Madam, whatever is the matter?"

Regina staggered over to a chair and sat down limply. "I can't believe it," she whispered. "I can't believe it." Phyllis glanced toward the door to Alastair's bedroom, and her mouth set grimly.

She brought Regina a glass of cold water, and poured a little brandy into it. "Drink this, Madam," she insisted gently.

Regina drank it, and shuddered violently. But the brandy made her feel warmer, and finally burned down to her stomach, heating her, stopping her shaking.

Phyllis stroked back the hair from Regina's face, and held the glass for her. "I expect you saw something, Madam," she said finally.

Regina nodded. "Does—does everyone know—but me?"

"Some know, Madam. Others—well, it don't get around. He's a duke, you know. His mother knows. She asked me if you knew. Not yet, I told her. So she said not to tell you. He might change his nature, she says to me."

"Oh, my dear God." Regina felt sick. She drank more of the brandy feverishly.

Phyllis helped her to bed, and soothed her tenderly. She waited until she thought Regina slept, then tiptoed from the room. But, though Regina's eyes were closed, she did not sleep. She lay awake, trying to make some sense of what had occurred.

She could not believe it. She scarcely knew what a homosexual was; she was not aware of ever having met one. They were people who lived alien lives, people in other worlds. Not in her world.

She wondered, that night and afterward, if her mother had known. She finally decided that Antonia had not known, nor her father. He would not have permitted the marriage, had he known.

But she was married to the duke, and expecting his child. There was nothing to do but confront him with her condition, and wait for his reaction. She would see how he took the news of his coming child, and then decide what she must do.

She found Alastair in the drawing room, sucking mechanically on his pipe, staring absently off into space. He did not look up as she entered.

"Alastair," she said firmly, "we must talk. I have something to tell you."

"Yes, Regina, what is it?"

She was amazed. He did not sound the slightest bit angry. He obviously did not wish to bring up the subject of what had taken place last night. Encouraged, Regina continued, telling him that he was to become a father—that Kildare was at last to have an heir.

"Why, that's wonderful. Yes. Wonderful." He seemed

genuinely pleased. Still, he made no mention of the scene in his bedroom.

That was it, then, thought Regina, later that night, in her warm bed. She would have her child, remain for a time at Castle Kildare, and make herself useful to the village folk, as Molly had advised her. She thought of the money in her private account and blessed her father for having sent it. At least, she would not have to depend on her husband for that.

Gilroy Ericson, Alastair's lover, hung around, and Regina tried not to shrink whenever she passed him in the hallway. But she never spoke to him. Once she thought she caught him smirking at her as she walked by, but she could not be sure. Just his presence was enough to send a shiver down her spine.

Her son Peter was born later that year. He resembled his father, and Alastair was pleased. The christening was a huge social event. Lillian came, and many members of lesser royalty.

No sooner had Peter been born, than Alastair insisted on coming to her again. "I need two sons," he told her. "Two children will ensure the line."

She endured it grimly. Harold was born the following year—1890. He and Peter were adorable boys, blond, and quiet of disposition—almost too quiet. They would play in the nursery with sturdy Nanny Jones in charge—an older, understanding woman, who kept them away from their father and from Ericson, at Regina's request.

After the second birth, Regina was ill for two months. The baby had been large, and she had been much torn. Antonia wrote, saying she would come to visit. Regina wrote back that she was going to Italy for a few months with her mother-in-law.

Lillian was very kind to her. She took Regina to Italy, and showed her Florence, Venice, and Rome. They lived quietly, unlike some of the British who took the Grand Tour in winter. They talked, embroidered, and visited museums.

Regina returned in the summer, much healthier. She

became acquainted all over again with her babies, and looked after them as much as her social duties permitted. She refused to be presented to royalty. It would be such a mocking gesture, she thought, to be presented as the Duchess of Kildare. And she had made private plans.

She helped on the estate, quietly, but thoroughly. The townspeople in power were told to come to her for aid, and she would see that it was given. She increased the food allotments to the charity homes, and made sure everyone in the five villages had enough work, food, blankets, clothing, and wood for the winter. Alastair grumbled angrily at the bills, at times, but was too well-bred to make much of a fuss. Besides, he was having a fine time, going to Scotland on shooting trips with his lover, and taking a long journey to Greece with him, leaving Regina in charge at the Castle.

Regina hired a governess for the boys when they began to walk and talk. Later, she looked long and carefully for just the right tutor for them. She eventually found Mr. Richardson. He was an older man, a widower with three sons of his own, who were now grown and in college.

She had a long, frank talk with him. "I want the boys raised away from any homosexual influence, Mr. Richardson," she told him. "With his father the way he is, there is danger that his sons might be influenced. Also I understand that at school they are subject to all kinds of—unhealthy influences. I would rather they were tutored at home. If they must go off to school, I want you to go with them, to counsel and guide them."

He understood, all too well, judging by the sadness in his eyes. "I will always do my best for them, Your Grace," he said. "You may believe their well-being will always be my first concern."

With that settled, she began to consider ways to obtain a divorce. Alastair would never willingly consent to one. She knew she must force him to it. She studied the English divorce laws, and thought for a long time. She had to lay her plans well. Alastair had discovered that she had her own source of money, and had been coldly angry. He had tried to make her turn over control of the funds to him, and she had refused. "My father would not allow it," she said simply. "The money is for me." Now it would be her means of escape.

Antonia had been bitterly disappointed by the contents of the few letters Regina had sent to her. Jacob would not permit her to visit Regina unless the girl invited her. And Regina did not. Instead she wrote brief epistles:

Dear Mother,

I hope you are well. The boys and I are fine. The roof has been repaired at last, even that over the wings. I hope to get the final work done on the drains next summer. The greenhouse needs improvement. We are very busy about the harvest; it looks good this year.

Antonia fumed and fussed, but there was nothing in Regina's letters she could quote. Nothing she could use to impress her friends. She thought, desperately, to make things up, but could not come up with anything that sounded authentic. And when Regina refused to be presented to the Queen, Antonia blew up.

"The girl is mad! My own daughter, completely mad! To refuse a presentation! I could have gone over there . . ."

Only twice had Antonia had occasion to be proud of her. Two charity balls had been held, at which Regina had been a sponsor. Her photos had been in the newspapers and glossy magazines, one showing her in a dress of lace and silk, creamy and fitted to her slim body, the dog collar of pearls and diamonds adorning her swanlike neck. The other showed her in a black Spanish-type gown, with a black fan, and her hair piled high. Antonia showed them proudly to all her friends, until the clippings were faded and torn.

Antonia turned her attention to Errol. She could not

concentrate on Bernard, for he practically lived out West, in dingly hotels and boardinghouses, working hard. Privately, she was relieved that she did not have to see much of him.

Errol was now past thirty, a handsome bachelor. He had been introduced to every eligible female in New York City, and twenty states beyond, also to several from England, France, and Italy. He escorted them about, was courteous to them, flattered them, and forgot them. But now Antonia was beginning to hope.

His blond head was bent this evening toward beautiful, young, and bubbling Marilyn Grey-Vaughan. She was but twenty-two years old, and a little in awe of the wealthy bachelor. Yet she was wealthy herself, the daughter of a steel king and a British lady. She was spirited, amusing, amazingly unspoiled. And Errol did seem to enjoy her.

They went to the opera, attended by his mother and Marilyn's. At intermission, they strolled in the foyer, and bowed to their friends and acquaintances. During the next act, Marilyn kept turning to Errol and whispering to him. He smiled.

Yes, it might be, thought Antonia. It might be!

"Oh, I do enjoy opera," Marilyn said, when it was over. She turned to Errol again. "I do thank you for taking me! I adore seeing all my friends!"

Errol smiled, bowed, and escorted her and the other ladies out to their waiting carriage. He was thinking seriously about marriage for the first time in his life.

Marilyn was charming, amusing, beautiful to look at. She had luscious strawberry-blond hair that she sometimes let free, to fall in graceful waves about her neck and shoulders. But most important, she made him laugh. She could make him forget about work for hours at a time. And she was quite a modern young woman, independent and original, with a sparkling wit that was not malicious at all.

Then, Aunt Frieda came down from college for the Christmas holidays, and brought her current favorite pupil with her. Frieda had made a splendid career for herself. Now graying, plump, a little absentminded, and too much absorbed in English literature, she could be lively and interesting when she chose.

The friend and pupil she brought with her was a young lady named Sarah Nicollet. Errol was present in the drawing room when they entered, still speaking of the concert he had attended with Marilyn that afternoon. On seeing the drawing room full of strangers, the young lady stopped abruptly, and a shy, pink color stole into her cheeks.

Errol stood to be introduced, and came to kiss Aunt Frieda, and shake the hand of the young lady with her. "Miss Sarah Nicollet," said Aunt Frieda. "A very clever young woman who is going to teach with me."

Sarah gave her a warm affectionate look, and smiled. Errol could not get over how beautiful she was. She had a face like some Errol had seen on Greek coins, with sculptured features, an olive complexion, and straight black hair in a thick chignon at the base of her slim neck. She was tall, slender, and regal, with a softly accented voice at which Antonia frowned. Errol learned later that her mother was Greek and her father French. Antonia contemptuously called her an immigrant.

She came from a scholarly family. She spoke— besides English—Greek, French, Spanish, German, and Italian. She could translate Hebrew and Aramaic, and was considering a career as a teacher of languages, or as a translator.

She also played the piano with more than ordinary skill. Next to her, Marilyn looked like a frivolous child, with her shorter skirts, her white kid boots, her wide lace hats, and her fluttering hands.

Sarah stayed with them for the holidays. Her parents had gone to Greece for the winter, to care for her elderly grandparents. Her brother was a professor in a university, her older sister a teacher.

For a few days, Errol watched Sarah from a distance. He saw her coming and going, busily, with his Aunt Frieda. One day, he stopped them. "Where are you going today? You go out constantly, even in the coldest weather." He smiled at them, noting the bright color in Sarah's cheeks from the chill winds.

"Oh, we already went to the archeological museum today. It was so splendid," Sarah said, and Aunt Frieda nodded, her eyes bright.

"And do you go to the opera with us tonight?"

"Yes, Antonia invited us," Aunt Frieda said. "You shall not mind having more in your carriage, dear boy?" Sarah caught the "dear boy," and smiled slightly to herself.

He assured them that he would not mind, and they talked for a few minutes about the opera that night—*La Traviata.* Aunt Frieda excused herself, and drifted on up the stairs, probably to explore the library once more. Errol caught at Sarah's arm as she started to follow.

"Come and tell me why you are laughing at me," he ordered, and drew her into the unoccupied drawing room.

"Laughing at you? Oh, no, Mr. Van Rhyne," she protested.

"Yes, you are. I can tell by your eyes." Her eyes were large and black, fringed with incredibly long, curly, black lashes that shadowed her cheeks. Her black hair was mussed slightly by the small toque on her head, and by the winds she had walked through. She brushed back a lock with a white-gloved hand. Her hands were large for a woman, her fingers long and graceful.

"I only thought—well, Frieda called you 'dear boy,' and you are not a boy," she apologized, her eyes glimmering.

"She thinks of me as a child in skirts, as she once knew me," Errol said, the corners of his mouth twitching. "It is hard to remain dignified with an aunt who once changed your diapers."

She *did* laugh then, and it was soft and pretty. Color had risen attractively into her cheeks.

"Will you enjoy the opera tonight?" he asked.

"Oh, yes, *La Traviata* is one of my favorites." She hummed a few bars of one aria, then stopped and shook her head. "Dear me, I act as though I am home! My

398

father would burst into song—he always does, and we join in, and it is loud and we all go a little mad, when we get ready to go to the opera." Unexpectedly, tears were brimming in her large, black eyes.

Errol thought of Marilyn, whispering and giggling through a death scene at the opera. "Do you miss your parents very much?" he asked gently.

"Yes, yes, we are all very close. But they will come home in the spring."

"I shall look forward to the opera tonight," he said, unable to think of any excuse to detain her longer.

She appeared that evening in a plain gown of rose-colored silk. It was, Errol thought, a striking contrast to the layers of lace and brocade, with jet fringes, that his mother wore.

Sarah wore a cloak of a deeper rose hue over her gown. Her hair was piled up in coils, beautifully black and shining, with only a rose scarf over them, which she removed later, in the opera house. Her only jewelry consisted of a pair of gold earrings, round and swinging. "Barbaric," Antonia had whispered, seeing them. She did not like Sarah, and she did not like the way Errol looked at her, or the way everyone else looked at her. For when the Van Rhyne party entered the opera house, all eyes were on Sarah. People turned and whispered to each other, "Who is she?" "Who is that girl?" "Is she Errol's new *amie*?"

The opera was beautiful, although Antonia was restless, and wriggled about. Sarah and Aunt Frieda sat rapt and motionless, all their attention focused on the stage, the singing, and the orchestra. Errol sat in the shadows and studied Sarah's profile.

At the death scene, Sarah took out a white handkerchief and dabbed at her eyes. Antonia was looking about, trying to find someone she knew. Aunt Frieda was sniffling, searching for a handkerchief. Errol leaned forward and gave her his. "Thank you, dearest boy," said Aunt Frieda.

Sarah turned her head, saw them, and smiled. It was a sweet, gentle smile, a little abstracted, a little mischievous. Then her attention returned at once to the stage.

Antonia spoke to Errol the next day. "You know, Marilyn Grey-Vaughan is such a lady," she said hopefully.

"Yes, she seems to be, Mother," Errol said, sitting warily on the edge of a pink damask chair in her bedroom.

"And wealthy. Such a good match." She looked at him over her coffee cup. "You do like her, don't you?"

"Oh, quite well. But I'm not thinking about marriage," he said, and knew that it was not true. He was thinking about marriage. "You'll have to wait for more grandchildren, Mother!"

She flinched. She hated to be reminded about her age. "I'm sorry Frieda brought that foreigner with her," she said plaintively, still watching him alertly. "Such a wrong feeling—the wrong tone, you know. I am sure people wondered at seeing her with us. But Frieda was set on seeing the opera. We could have left Sarah at home. She is perfectly content with the library."

Errol studied the toe of his gray boot. "She is an American, I believe, Mother," he said, with no expression.

"Well, well, you know what I mean. She *looks* foreign. Those earrings! Well, would anyone else wear something like that?"

He left for the office, glad to escape Antonia's prying questions. He worked until late that evening, and missed an elaborate dinner party his mother had planned. Antonia had retired to her rooms, furious that he had not come, and had left poor, dear Marilyn without an escort.

When he arrived home, he walked quietly into the drawing room. It was past midnight, and only the fireplace lit the room. Someone was at the piano, playing arias from *La Traviata*. He went to a big chair, and sat down to listen. The music was lovely and soothing to his frazzled nerves. He leaned back his head, and closed his eyes. Then he opened them, to see Sarah's silhouette against the dimly lit blue walls of the room. Her head

400

was bent over the piano, and her large hands moved over the keys with precision and passion.

She did not seem to know he was there. But presently, the music died to a murmur of sound, a trickle of notes from her fingers. She said, "I think you are very weary, Mr. Van Rhyne."

"Yes, very. Would you mind continuing to play?"

She smiled, not looking toward him, and her fingers picked out another melody, something beautiful and restful.

Jacob came in quietly, and sat down. He kept looking at the girl seated at the piano, and at Errol in the big chair. Finally she stopped and stood up.

"Good evening, Mr. Van Rhyne," she said to Jacob.

"You play very nicely, child," he said. He liked her.

She bade them good night, and left them, drifting up the stairs like a shy ghost. The two men were silent for a few moments after she left.

"I think we've got it licked," Jacob said presently.

Errol nodded. "Bernie will take care of his end. We'll get out of the West eventually. It's turning nastier."

"I'll stay a couple more years. Hate to give up there," Jacob said. "Antonia says you're thinking of getting married."

"I might," Errol said.

Jacob stirred restlessly. "Be careful," he said heavily. "Marry someone you can live with for a whole lifetime. That's a long time. Don't rush into anything. That Marilyn child. She's cute, but sometimes, when she gets shrill, she reminds me of your mother."

"I thought that the other night," Errol said meditatively. "Her voice kept going up and up."

"Have you ever seen her angry?" Jacob asked.

"No."

"Try getting her mad as hell. See how she acts. It would be worth the risk," Jacob said, then got up to go to bed. Errol remained for a time, his eyes half-closed, picturing Sarah's feminine classic profile against the pale blue walls.

Chapter 28

Antonia and Jacob both received letters from Regina on the same June day in 1895. Jacob received his at his office, and opened it with eager anticipation. Regina wrote good letters, but had warned him not to show them to her mother.

He sat back, jolted by the first line:

Dear Father,

I have left Alastair. I can bear the situation no longer. I should like to get a divorce, but an English divorce is difficult to obtain. I hate to trouble you over the matter, but there is no one to advise me. I am staying with my mother-in-law, who is most kind. However, she is in an awkward position, as you can imagine. I should like to obtain the divorce, then return to the United States. I am very homesick.

My mother-in-law advises me to obtain a separation, and to set myself up in a town house in London. I do not wish to do this. I want to come home, not to Mother's house, but to a little house of my own. I am very weary.

Please, Father, could you come and help me? I am so lost and bewildered. Please let me know if you can come.

If you cannot come, may I return home for your advice? Alastair threatens to have me stopped from leaving England. He says I am pouting, and will get over it, and that he will not be disgraced. Believe me, it is far more serious than that.

I cannot have the boys, but I have provided for them.

Please, Father, can you come soon?

Your loving daughter,

Regina

Jacob studied the letter, then went directly home. He found Antonia in a raving fury, watched curiously by Cecil Meryon. Jacob came into the drawing room and ordered Meryon to leave at once.

Antonia stopped raving and sat up furiously. "Jacob, you *will* be courteous to Cecil! He is so helpful and kind to me—"

Jacob turned his head, saw the man smirking, and ordered him again to leave the room. This time Cecil obeyed. He left hastily, closing the door after him.

Antonia stared at her husband, her eyes ablaze. She started to say something, but Jacob spoke first. "Have you heard from Regina?"

Antonia blinked. "You heard also? The girl is insane! A little quarrel, and she is ready to risk disgrace and social banishment."

Jacob took Antonia's letter and scanned it. It said merely that Regina had left Alastair, and that her mother might correspond with her in care of the duke's mother in London.

"I know very well what has happened," Antonia said positively "The duke is repelled by her coldness, and has turned to a mistress. Regina found him out and is furious. I warned her—"

"Has she written anything of this before?" Jacob asked, not offering to show her his letter.

"No, not a word. That is why I am sure she is pouting. It will blow over. Write to her, and tell her to behave herself like a lady! Oh, the disgrace of it," Antonia moaned. "I hope no one gets wind of it here in New York."

"If you don't talk, no one will know," Jacob said

dryly. "And muzzle that tame puppy of yours." He left the room quickly before she could scream after him.

He booked passage on a steamer leaving shortly for England, and told Errol what to do in his absence. He would have to talk personally with Regina. The tone of her letter had been reasoned and mature, but he sensed a quiet desperation beneath her words. He had to find out what was responsible.

From Jacob's own experience with society under Queen Victoria, he surmised that Antonia might be right for once. Alastair probably liked to kick over the traces from time to time, and Regina must have found him with some bit of fluff. He would have to persuade her that it was nothing serious. After all, there were the two boys to consider.

He arrived in London two weeks later, and made his way to a capacious town house on a smart street. He knocked, and was answered by a middle-aged maid in a black uniform. She let him in, and went to summon Her Grace, the Duchess.

Jacob stood uncomfortably in the middle of the pink-and-white drawing room, wondering how one sat on such small chairs. Then he heard a sound at the door, and turned.

For a moment, he did not recognize the lady who stood before him. She was tall and slim, with her hair done in a stiff blond coronet. She wore a lilac silk gown trimmed in jet braid. There was no jewelry on her neck or wrists. Then she smiled tremulously, and he recognized his daughter.

"Papa, you came!" She moved forward into his open arms, and put her head against his broad chest. His arms closed about her fiercely. He was more touched by the sight of her than he could express. Her face was thin and lined, her eyes sunken in hollows, their blue-violet color washed away into a lifeless gray.

She was shaking. He held her tightly, then sat her down beside him on the pink brocade sofa. They talked with the door closed.

"What is the trouble, my dear child?" he asked gently.

Having seen her, he no longer doubted that the matter was indeed serious, as she had written.

She looked up at him, her lovely, slim throat moving as she swallowed. She clasped her thin, white hands in her lap. "I must tell you all of it, Papa. For the divorce will be so difficult, and I don't know what to do. The duke is furious, and says he will come and drag me back to Kildare. He will not have his reputation smeared, he says. That is so ironic."

"Ironic, Regina? Tell me," he said quietly.

"I will begin—at the beginning," she said wearily. She spoke as though she had rehearsed it in her mind. He realized, with his business sense and experience, that she had gone over and over it, in an attempt to make it understandable to herself.

She began with the courtship. "I did not want to marry him, he was so cold. I loved Vincent—I still think of him, though we have not met nor corresponded at all." She looked at her father. "You do believe me, Father? I do not even know whether he is married. I expect he is, he is such a fine man."

"He is not," said Jacob. "I talked with him at Molly's, last week. He is still a bachelor."

Her eyes lit up briefly, then she gazed down at her hands again. "On our wedding night, Alastair told me that he had married me, knowing I loved Vincent. He said that he, too, loved another. I asked him why he had not married her." She smiled sadly. "It was only months later that I realized why. We came to Kildare, and started a child. I went to London for a month with my mother-in-law, and we returned earlier than expected. I found him in the arms of his—love. His secretary. A young man. His name is Gilroy Ericson."

Jacob was staring at her incredulously. She spoke in a monotone, quite unlike her normal, musical voice. She recited the facts automatically, as if they were engraved on her memory. He could not doubt them.

She told him of her two sons, and her efforts to keep them from her husband and his lover. "I have done all I can. I know he will not give up the boys, but I cannot

405

endure to remain, even for them. Lillian, my mother-in-law, will keep an eye on the situation for me. She knows her son for what he is. If there is any trouble, I can go to court. But Papa, I am reluctant to do that, for the sake of the boys. It would disgrace them, and they are such fine, handsome young boys."

She swallowed, and clasped his hands firmly. "I shall miss them," she said in a subdued voice. "I could not bear to leave them. I wept for a week. I had kissed them for the last time, put them to bed in their lovely rooms, and said their prayers with them, not telling them I should never return."

Tears were in Jacob's eyes. Regina did not weep. She looked as though all her tears had dried in her long ago, leaving her empty.

"What is the English law about divorce? Why is it so difficult?" he finally asked her.

"I spoke to several lawyers. They did not, at first, believe my story, but eventually I convinced them it was true. In England, a man must prove unfaithfulness in his wife. A wife has to prove not only unfaithfulness, but also physical cruelty, or else nonsupport and desertion. How can I go to court, Papa? It would all come out."

He patted her hand, kissed her cheek, and said briskly, "Don't worry, Regina, there is always a way." Already, his keen brain was setting to work on the problem. There was always an answer, and it was usually money.

Just about anything in the world could be bought, as Jacob knew. He had already bought Alastair once. The second time should not be difficult.

The maid brought tea, and a bottle of Scotch whiskey for Jacob. He remained for luncheon, and met Regina's mother-in-law. He was relieved to find her bright, sensible, and kind to Regina. However, Lillian was troubled about the possible disgrace of a divorce, and the effect it might have on her son, as well as her grandsons.

"If only Regina would consent to a separation. They could go their separate ways," she mused, after the maids had left the room. "It is done here. Everyone knows they do not get along, but everyone is polite and genteel about it. It is the social way."

"I do not want to remain in England, Lillian," Regina said gently, as though she had said these words many times before. "I have never belonged here. I want to go back to America."

"And so you shall," Jacob said. "Would you like a home in New York, or elsewhere?"

For the first time since his arrival, she smiled openly and happily at him. "Oh, may I choose, Papa? I have been thinking about Connecticut. It is so pretty, with the apple trees in bloom, and lilacs. I remember one summer I spent with Aunt Frieda. All the lilacs were sweet under my windows, and the stars at night were so bright, out in the country, away from the city lights."

Lillian looked very troubled, but said no more. Jacob lay awake that night in his comfortable room on the second floor, and thought and thought. Aunt Frieda was fond of Regina. They might live in the same college town, and be comfortable together, visiting often. Yes, that might work. He hated to think of Regina completely alone. From the looks of her, she had too often been alone.

The following day he spent visiting with some of his old cronies. He found Tweedy, now quite aged and hobbling about, and they reminisced about the old days.

"The fellows today are soft, soft," Tweedy grumbled, and Jacob agreed. Except for Errol. Errol was tough as they came, for all his smart townish appearance.

The next day, Jacob took a train down to Kildare. He was shown into the duke's study, where Gilroy was taking notes and going over accounts with him.

"Oh, I am glad to see you," the duke said, rising to greet him. "I hope you can put some sense into Regina. She's run off, you know. Some bee in her bonnet."

"I'd like to speak with you alone," Jacob said curtly. He seated himself, and looked pointedly at the young blond man at the desk, who grinned back at him amiably.

"Gilroy Ericson, my secretary," Alastair said. "Mr. Jacob Van Rhyne, my father-in-law. Mr. Ericson knows all about my business; you may speak freely before him."

"About your divorce?" Jacob asked, and both of them started.

Alastair frowned, turning chilly and aloof. "Nonsense. No divorce is warranted. Regina is jealous that I am gone so much. I have promised to remain at home more. Some woman's whim—"

"How much?" Jacob asked.

Alastair froze. "You cannot *buy* her a divorce, Mr. Van Rhyne! I will not have the disgrace of it! I have a position of importance to maintain. None of the Dukes of Kildare have ever had a hint of scandal—"

"Not what I hear," Jacob said. "How much do you want?"

"Just like an American!" Alastair dropped all pretense of courtesy. "You think you can buy anything! I told Regina I would not give her a divorce, nor can she have access to the boys if she gets a separation. The sooner she gets back here and settles down, the better."

"She won't be coming back. I am taking her home to America," Jacob said. He rose. "I'd like to see my grandsons. You have no objection, I hope?"

"Not at all." Alastair rang for a footman, who showed Jacob upstairs to the schoolroom.

He spent two pleasant hours with Harold and Peter, now five and six years old. The boys were handsome, quiet, and intelligent, and took to their new grandfather from across the Atlantic Ocean without much difficulty. He had brought them toys, and he knew how to talk to them. Yes, Regina would miss them sorely, Jacob thought.

He talked for another hour with the governess and the tutor, who took turns caring for their charges. Regina had chosen wisely. A smart brain under the blond curls, her father thought proudly.

The next day, he met Alastair in his study again. His

secretary hovered nearby. Jacob ignored him, and pulled out his pipe.

"Well, I've been thinking it over, Your Grace," Jacob said, with barely concealed sarcasm. "It looks like it all adds up to one thing. You'll have to provide the grounds for the divorce. We might hire someone to pose with you, some bit of fluff who'd be glad for the money."

"Are you *mad*?" Alastair snapped. "I shall do nothing of the sort!"

"I understand that a man can obtain a divorce if his wife is unfaithful. Regina isn't that sort, and I won't have the disgrace on her," Jacob said thoughtfully, puffing away, eyeing the duke through a cloud of smoke. "A woman has to prove unfaithfulness, physical cruelty, and so on."

Alastair smiled. "She can't do that. No evidence."

"No? I think if we take you into court, there'll be no problem, Your Grace," Jacob said. "What with your affair with this young man here, there's ample proof of unfaithfulness. And as for physical cruelty, I believe the doctor can supply evidence there."

Alastair turned a sickly shade of green under his tanned skin. "What are you saying?" he whispered. Ericson stared at Jacob; his smile had faded.

"And England being the way it is, I suspect that the fact that you have been unfaithful to your wife with a young *man*—well, a hint of scandal, I think you said? Think it over, Your Grace."

Alastair's long, slim fingers tapped on the desktop. "You would not do that. Your grandsons—"

"They'll have to be tough. Regina was worried about them. I'm not. They're both good, solid boys. They'll grow up fine. The thing is, if all the facts come out the court will probably give Regina custody of them. She'll take them to America, and bring them up as Americans. Do you want that to happen?" He leaned back, and waited.

Alastair looked at his secretary, and away again. "How long until you have to have my answer?"

Jacob pulled out his gold pocket watch and consulted it gravely. "Maybe one hour. I'll go up and talk to the boys. Nice chaps." He rose to his feet, strolled to the door, and walked out.

When he returned an hour later, Alastair said, "I'll have to have more money. The repairs and all took much more than I had dreamed—and Regina was madly extravagant."

Jacob ignored that. "How much?"

"Ah—three million pounds?"

"Nope. Make it three million dollars, and it's a deal."

Jacob came away satisfied. Alastair would arrange for the lawyers, the setting up of a fake affair with some woman, and all the evidence necessary. It would be a formality, for it would never go to court.

It took another month to set the wheels turning. Then Jacob booked passage on a liner and took his daughter home. During the crossing, she was so exhausted and weak that she frightened him. She spent much of the voyage lying on a deck chair, half asleep, bundled in blankets against the cold wind. Phyllis had remained in London, to work for the old duchess. Regina had insisted she did not need a maid for the voyage.

In New York City, Jacob settled his daughter in a good hotel, then sent for his lawyer. "I want you to find a nice house in Connecticut, near my sister Frieda. Something with about a dozen rooms, in a decent location, with an apple orchard nearby."

The lawyer was used to Jacob's idiosyncrasies, but this was a bit whimsical. "Apple orchard, sir?"

"Right. And some lilacs about, if you can manage that."

The lawyer managed it.

Antonia wanted to see her daughter. Jacob arranged for them to meet at dinner, in his presence. He would not allow her to see Regina alone. Regina was so weak and thin that even Antonia was shocked, and said little.

Errol drove his sister up to Connecticut in his carriage, with blankets and cloaks wrapped about her against the autumn chill. Then Jacob saw to it that

Aunt Frieda came over often, with Sarah Nicollet, and introduced her to their college group, the artists and musicians and literary buffs.

There was one more chore to do. Jacob sent for Vincent McKenna, and he came at once.

He sat down in Jacob's office without immediately pulling out pencils and his "wee notebooks," as Molly called them.

"Regina's divorce is going through within two months," Jacob said, without preamble. "I think she wants to see you, but is too shy to ask."

"If I see her, I shall ask her to marry me," Vincent said gravely. "Do you approve, now?"

"Yes. I'll handle her mother," Jacob said. "You just make sure you and Regina know what you want. Ah— she's changed, Vincent. Don't show your shock too much. She's thin and pale and wan. But," he added, smiling, "I think she'll pick up now."

"How soon may I go?"

"Whenever you like," Jacob said, and gave him the address and his blessing.

Vincent went home, packed a small case, and took the evening train. He arrived in a hired carriage from the station, and looked at the white-painted house with its green shutters, and the late lilacs around the porch.

A country girl with blooming cheeks answered the door, stared at him curiously, and finally let him in. "I'll just see if Mrs.—I mean, herself—will see you," she stammered.

Vincent managed a smile. He set the case down in the hallway, and went into the small parlor. It was one-tenth the size of the one on Fifth Avenue, he thought, gazing out of the window at the night sky with its brilliant stars.

"Vincent?" At the familiar voice, he turned to see Regina, tall and stately, her delicate, wistful beauty all the more poignant for the hollowness of her cheeks, and the lines engraved about her lovely mouth. She wore something soft and creamy, with lace spilling over her wrists.

411

He had meant to be calm, to talk quietly. But seeing her so mature, so poised, with the suffering in her violet eyes, dashed all his plans to bits.

He put his arms around her. She sank against him, and he closed his hands around her waist, sliding his fingers over the fragile bones of her hips.

"Oh—Vincent . . . " she whispered.

"My darling—my lovely love—oh, Regina—" She raised her head, and he bent his, and their lips met tentatively, and then warmly.

He felt a great rush of passion swell up in him. But he gentled himself, fearful that she might break in his big hands.

His lips caressed her forehead, the fluff of her hair over her white temples. He could not believe he was holding her, after the months and years of wanting and needing and loving.

"Vincent," she said, dreamily, against his breast. "I am asleep, am I not?"

"No, my love. This is real. We are here together—at last."

"I thought of you so often. When the pond at Kildare froze over, I thought about ice skating with you and Errol and Bernie and Muir."

"And I thought of you, my darling. Always. Oh, how I love you."

They kissed deeply. Their mouths knew each other, though they had rarely touched. Their arms, their bodies fit together as though meant for each other, two halves of a whole, long separated, together again.

He sat down in a big chair and pulled her down to sit on his knee. "How soon can you marry me?" he asked seriously.

"The divorce must go through. Father thinks it won't be final until December or January."

"As soon as it is, we'll get married."

"And move to New York?"

He sensed her reluctance, and had thought about it on the train up. He had made up his mind.

"I've gone as far as I want in New York. I'd like to

get a place on the newspaper here. Maybe start one of my own. It's nice up here, not so frantic. I could write that book I want to write."

"Oh, Vincent, you must not give up your life in New York for me. Father says you are such a success—"

"Give up? Without you, I gave up living, I gave up breathing. I was nothing, I moved and slept and wrote, all without feeling. For all those years," he said passionately, trying to keep calm for her sake. "All those years. Now nothing matters in the world but you—just you—"

He stayed at a boardinghouse next door for the remainder of the week. He had told his boss he was finally taking his vacation, which he had put off for some time.

For a week, they talked, walked, discussed the past, settled the future. The autumn crispness suited them, the smell of apples in the air, the brilliance of zinnias and asters, the scarlet smoke of fires as wood burned. Their world had taken on color again, after years of gray endurance.

Errol came up that week to see Sarah Nicollet, at her little house near the college. Together, they visited Regina and Vincent, and the four of them had a merry picnic, sitting on the grass in the yard, alternately talking, laughing, quiet, as the mood struck them. The light in Regina's eyes made her beautiful as she had never been beautiful before. Her violet eyes sparkled. She seemed to have bloomed like the late roses in the garden. Vincent could not take his gaze from her.

"They are so sweet, so touching," Sarah murmured to Errol as they went indoors for more apple cider. She filled the pitcher in the cool room, and he took it from her. "Happiness after long troubles—there is nothing more healing to the heart."

"No woman is so beautiful as one who is loved," murmured Errol.

She flashed him a look from her great black eyes. "You understand? Yes. A woman needs to be loved, to be at her best. The radiance then comes from inside her. The loving and the loved, they are the color of life,

413

the red of blood, the blue of the sky, the brightness of the sunshine, more beautiful than gold."

"How do you know all this?" He set the pitcher down on a chopping block in the pantry. "Experience?"

"Oh, no." She flushed furiously. "Oh, no, it is my parents, you see. They love each other, they are only half alive when apart. They must go everywhere together, or they do not live."

There was passion in her, under the cool control, thought Errol. On impulse, he put his arm around her slim waist, and drew her toward him. She caught her breath, and looked up into his eyes. He pressed his mouth to hers, tentatively, then more fully. Her lips were warm, ripe, rosy, half-opened in amazement.

She pulled back. "Oh, Errol—" she reproached him. He put his hand behind her slim neck, with the heavy chignon pressing against his fingers. He kissed her again. It was sweet and heady, like brandy, apple brandy, he thought in a daze, with the smell of the cider in his nostrils. She was warm, rounded, tempting against his long limbs. He lost his head for a moment, and his lips went exploring about her slim throat, probing beneath the deep crimson collar of her dress.

"You—must—not!" She pushed in vain at his chest. He finally drew back, and reluctantly released her. She picked up the cider pitcher with trembling hands.

"I'll take that. You may drop it," he said, cool once more. Then he smiled down at her, impishly. "You'd better get used to that, Sarah. I intend to do it again."

Errol came up often with Vincent. They found they had much in common, and would talk away the hours on the train, discussing the future of the railroads, electric engines, the rate wars, the horrible depression of the past few years, and Vincent's decision to stay in a small Connecticut town and start a newspaper there. Errol thought Vincent would do well anywhere, but how would he feel, married to an heiress? Regina had plenty of her own money now, Jacob had seen to that.

Vincent seemed to have no doubts. He was radiant and confident. "Regina has been so unhappy. It shall be my life's work to make sure she is never unhappy again. I mean to make her the happiest woman in the world."

Vincent's optimism began to rub off on cynical Errol. He had seen much of Sarah that winter. In contrast, Marilyn Grey-Vaughan seemed a shrill, spiteful child. He had now had his chance to see her angry when the pressures of work had made him late for several of their appointments. She would fret and pout, tossing her pretty head, reminding Errol far too much of his mother. Finally he dropped her, to Antonia's bitter disappointment.

Vincent and Regina were married in January, as soon as her divorce came through. It was a quiet wedding, in the parlor of the house they would share. She wore a silk gown the color of Parma violets, and at her waist were real violets. On her blond head was a short white veil, held with a small tiara of diamonds, a gift from Jacob. Jacob came, but Antonia stayed away, at Jacob's orders. She was cross with Regina anyway, and Jacob would not have the wedding spoiled.

After the wedding, Errol drove Sarah and Aunt Frieda back home, to the little house they shared, near the college. Aunt Frieda went upstairs to change her elaborate gown—and get out of her corsets, she announced frankly. Sarah led Errol into the parlor, and poured him a drink. She was still somewhat afraid of being alone with him. He had tried, on another occasion, to kiss her but she had pushed him away.

He took the glass of whiskey she held out to him. "You know, weddings are contagious," he said solemnly.

"They are?" She looked doubtful. "I have not noticed that."

"I have. All this winter, while Vincent and Regina were courting, I got the strangest notions in my head. You know, I have avoided marriage—too many bad examples before me," he told her.

"I suppose so. But you are a most eligible bachelor, I have heard. You could marry as you choose. One of the pretty debutantes, I expect?"

"Oh, no. What crashing bores they are, all of them. I mean to marry someone with depth," he said earnestly. They had seated themselves in the straight-backed parlor chairs. He noticed her hands. They often gave her away. Now they were twisting together nervously, her fingers pulling at each other.

"You do?"

"Yes. I'd like someone intelligent, someone I can talk to about railroads and my work, without having her yawn in my face. Someone I can take to the opera without having her giggle over the death scenes. Someone who could play the piano for me when I am weary. Someone who won't drag me to parties when I am tired and discouraged. Do you know anybody like that?"

The fingers twisted and twisted.

He stopped his teasing. He got up and pulled her into his arms.

"*I* do," he said, a little roughly. "I haven't been able to forget you for nights at a time. Your face comes between me and the pages of my accounts. I close my eyes, and smell your soft perfume. Sarah, I want you, I need you. You have to marry me."

The great black eyes gazed up into his. "But your mother calls me—" He put his hand over the soft, rosy mouth.

"I love you," he said. "Will you marry me? Right away?"

"I think marriage is—"

He stopped her mouth with kisses.

He finally relaxed his hold when she stopped pulling away. His mouth traveled from her lips to her soft cheeks, over to her earlobe, and he bit it softly above the golden circle of her earring. She trembled in his hands.

"Tell me you love me," he ordered her.

"Oh, Errol, it is not suitable. It will not do—"

"Tell me."

"Oh, I do love you. I have since the first—oh, Errol, but I am not—"

He closed her mouth again with his, and felt a response rising in her, a passionate warmth that enveloped him and captured him, and made him want to make love to her right there and then. He held her tight, kissing her again and again, pressing her even more closely to his hard body, feeling the length of her rounded form, melting into his.

"Oh, my goodness gracious me," Aunt Frieda said from the doorway. "*Whatever* in the world are you doing?"

Errol laughed, and told her, "We're going to be married, Aunt Frieda."

She stared at him in her nearsighted way. "Of course you are," she said, mildly surprised. "I thought so all along. Have you set the date? I hope it will be soon."

And soon it was. They were married in February, just three weeks later. Antonia wept in private. Jacob forbade her from meddling, threatening to cut off her allowance. She had done enough mischief for one lifetime, he said.

"But a schoolteacher! When he could have married Marilyn!"

"I like Sarah," Jacob said. "She's a damned nice girl. I think I'll settle some money on her for the wedding. And some jewels. Do you think she would like emeralds?"

Antonia did not hear him. She had already fled the room, her heavy silks rustling behind her.

Jacob smiled. For the first time in years, he felt like singing.

Chapter 29

Jacob went often to Connecticut to visit Regina and Vincent. They were so quietly happy they made his heart ache. Both were mature, having suffered through bad times. Now they had happiness together.

A child was born to Regina the following year, a small, precious girl with bright blue eyes and blond curls, a doll-baby of a girl, whom they named Mary Cecilia.

"After Aunt Molly," Regina said, smiling radiantly over the blond head of the baby in her arms. "She has been so good and kind. I could always talk to Aunt Molly."

Regina was in her final month, when Molly came up one day with Jessie, to pay a visit. Molly ended up staying for a week when Regina confided to her that a nurse had taken care of her two boys from birth on. Now Regina wanted to care for her child herself, and Molly patiently taught her how.

Regina still worried about her two small sons, so far away. The birth of her daughter only made her more anxious about their welfare. Jacob arranged another business trip to England, and talked to the sullen Duke of Kildare. Briskly, he told the duke that he wanted monthly reports sent to Regina.

"I am too busy to write," the duke said. "I go up to Scotland for the shooting next month. Then to the Riviera . . ."

"Get someone to do it for you," Jacob advised him cunningly. This was what he had wanted all along. "How about that tutor? What's his name?"

"Richardson."

"Ah, yes. Tell him to write once a month. He isn't

swamped with work, is he? Get him to write and inform her how the boys are getting along. Make it part of his job."

So it was arranged, and Jacob came home again, feeling quite pleased with himself. Regina welcomed the tutor's scrupulously detailed letters with great pleasure. As the boys began to learn to write, he included letters of theirs along with his, letters that touched her to tears.

"One day we will go to England and visit them," Vincent promised her quietly, as she smiled over the latest letter.

"Oh, how can we?"

"Easily. Your former mother-in-law could take the boys for the summer, or on a holiday. We could go over then, and stay with her. I think she still likes you, and understands."

"Oh, Vincent, you would agree to this?" She hurt his heart sometimes when she was surprised by his goodness. It pained him that she had become so unused to kindness, and he vowed again to himself to make her the happiest woman in the world.

"Of course. And one day they can come to us here. After all, the divorce was amiable, and the duke is happy in his life."

Her violet eyes shone. "Oh, I was so afraid I would never see them again, unless it was after they grew up," she said. "If I could only see them from time to time, assure them I love them, and try to get them to understand why I left." She bit her lip. "I could scarcely bear to leave them, so young and vulnerable."

"Mr. Richardson takes good care of them," he assured her.

"I am so glad Mother did not have her way with Errol," she mused after a time. "I do love Sarah. If only Bernie would marry someone like her . . . "

Bernard was in trouble. He wrote to Jacob, and Jacob groaned and cursed. He had left Bernie out West for several years, and he had thought the young man had matured. Now he was not so sure.

419

Dear Father,

I have killed a sheriff, and am now in jail waiting for the trial. Some folks are mighty mad at me. I think you better come quick.

Love,

Bernie

The letter was postmarked from a town in the Arizona Territory. It came in an envelope that was filthy and torn. Jacob sent for Errol.

He showed him the letter. "Do you want me to go, Father?" asked Errol. "I could take Paul Malone. He's been wanting to go West again, and he looks damn tired from that infernally busy practice of his. Ever since Sunny died last year, he's been burying himself in his work."

Jacob was saddened at the mention of Sunny's name. He still could not believe she was gone. "Not a bad idea. But I have a better one. You stay here and mind things. With Sarah expecting, you won't want to be gone indefinitely."

Errol's smile was sweet. "No, I don't," he agreed quietly.

"I'll go, and take Paul with me. I'll have a look at the situation out West. It may be time to make a move there. I'm not getting any younger, and maybe Bernie should come back home to live."

They understood without discussing it what Jacob meant. The rate wars were maniacal, and destructive to all the railroads. Few could make any profits at all. For years, Jacob had hesitated to give up all his holdings out West. He enjoyed the vast country, and loved to go out there, where he could see wheat, golden yellow from horizon to horizon, or desert cactus in bloom after a sudden rainstorm. He loved riding with the drawling, laconic cowboys, talking with Leigh Sheldon, taking great whiffs of the spicy air of cedar and pine and desert sand. A man could breathe out there without choking to death.

But maybe it was time to pull up stakes and get out, before they too were destroyed, and eaten up by the giant railroad mergers. Time to sell out, pull back, and concentrate on the Eastern road they owned entirely. Time to improve the engines and the tracks. Time to invest in luxuries: parlor cars, sleeping cars, and dining cars.

"What do we tell Mother?" Errol was asking.

"Nothing, damn it. She would have hysterics, then tell everybody in New York about the shooting. You can't trust her to keep anything secret."

Errol looked at his father thoughtfully. Jacob remembered that look later on.

He left the following week. He couldn't stand the idea of Bernie in jail. He wondered if perhaps the lad was too quick with a gun. Years ago, it had amused him and made him proud that the boy had the keen eye of a huntsman. Now—well, he was not so proud. Jacob winced as he remembered the shooting of Clinton. That had been a bad business.

Lodewick had stopped all pretense of work, and had moved to Florida to a summer home where he and his wife lived all year round. He had taken up golf and yachting. Their daughter Annette had married down there.

Hans and Blaine had left the railroad business, and gone into a small shipping business of their own. Just as well. Jacob wanted his business for his sons. He had bought out his brothers' stock. They were pleased to be out from under his thumb, and they did moderately well on their own.

Elisabeth still enjoyed coming over to visit. Her husband had died years ago. She had no children, and enjoyed telling Antonia how to raise hers. Katrinka was a motherly woman, and her lawyer husband wasn't bad company. They often came at Christmas or for summer holidays with their sons Philip and Jon, also lawyers. So it goes, thought Jacob, wondering where the years had gone.

Jacob and Paul enjoyed their long trip west, in Jacob's private car. Both were getting older and, for such a long journey, they liked the luxury of the private parlor car, though they joked over it as Jacob's valet served them.

"We are getting soft," Paul said, stretching out his long legs. "My bones creak at nights. I can't believe how old I am."

Jacob ran his hands through his hair, now entirely gray. "My God, I'm over sixty," Jacob mused. "What a surprise. Where did the years go? Only yesterday, I turned forty, and thought Father was elderly. And now I am over sixty."

The parlor car was upholstered in red plush, with mahogany walls and fittings of silver. It rode so smoothly that they could drink their whiskey without its sloshing over the edge of the glass. They could gaze out at the changing countryside, glance at the towns whisking past, grimace over the filthy coal yards and the small, gray houses with laundry hanging on the clothes lines in the yards.

"I never thought it would look like this, the years I was helping to lay track," said Jacob.

"I remember, in the gold towns," Paul said, "how clean everything was. The air sparkled like gold itself in the morning, and the snow on the mountains was clean. We would go out and pack snow in a bucket, and make ice cream with vanilla and sugar. Or pour molasses over it, and eat it fast before it melted."

"Vanilla ice cream in the restaurants never tastes as good as that," Jacob mused, remembering.

The scenery changed as they passed the Mississippi River. There were long stretches of country on either side of the tracks, dotted with a few cattle, yellow wheat fields, a slim sliver of town flashing past, as the train sped along faster and faster.

They came to the desert, and both men peered with interest at sights they remembered from the old days.

Jacob remembered the long days of work, from sunup to sundown, swinging a pick and shovel, directing the work in the sun, wiping the sweat from his forehead; the dry desert wind blowing against wet shirts; the tents on rainy nights; the open sky above a campfire on warm nights; the approaching winter, and the hurry to get a last stretch of track finished before the snows.

Several times the train stopped. Their parlor car was unhitched with great groaning and bumping, and was attached to another train. Finally they were heading south, into the great Arizona wilderness.

Once they saw some Indians near the tracks, sitting their horses like statues, not waving, not moving, until the train had gone past.

"I thought they were on reservations now," Jacob said uneasily.

They had not looked peaceful. They had looked gaunt and savage, as though driven back to the bare bones of existence.

At midnight, the parlor car was unhitched, and left on a siding outside a small town. Jacob looked out, saw the darkness, and said, "It'll wait until morning. I need some sleep first."

He was thinking about Bernie, locked in a small, cramped jail. He had seen those jails when they were built of adobe and straw, with iron bars across the tiny windows, and hot as Hades.

In the morning, Jacob and Paul left the railroad car. They earned a lot of curious looks in that small town, the two well-dressed men in frock coats, with guns buckled on. They strode through the dusty streets, heading for the jail.

"Gamblers?" muttered a woman, not intending them to hear her.

A grin slashed Dr. Paul Malone's thin face. "If my patients could hear that . . ."

They found the jail and sheriff's office. It was in the center of town, a square, uncompromising block of adobe, with space all around. Not much chance of breaking Bernie out, Jacob thought grimly.

They stepped into the office, and glanced about. A man, sitting with boots up on the table, stared at them. He pushed his dirty sombrero, and took the straw from his mouth.

"Whatcha want?"

"I'm Jacob Van Rhyne. Have you got my son Bernard here?" said Jacob.

The man's eyes widened. He took in the smart coat, the striped pants, the shining boots, the holster and gun. "Who'd ya say?"

"You heard. Where is my son Bernard?"

"Father!" A man in a dirty white suit got up from his cell bunk, and came to the bars. A grin lit his unshaven face. His hair was streaked with gray. "You came!"

Jacob went over to the cell and put his hands over the hands clenching the bars. Bernie was thin and worn, but the vivid light in his eyes was the same—bright and mischievous. Yet he had matured, he was older, his gaze direct.

"Hello, son. I came to get you out," Jacob said.

"You cain't talk to no prisoner without a permit!" said the man in charge, striding toward them. "You cain't—"

"Then get a permit," Jacob said, without turning back to him. "I've come to get my son out of this filthy hole. Where's the judge?"

"Ain't no judge here."

"When is he coming?" Paul asked quietly. The man swung around to talk to him.

"The judge, he comes ever' two months. Cain't come now. This man has to be held for him. It's a serious charge; he done killed our sheriff—"

Jacob said quietly to Bernard, "What happened?"

"The sheriff was pestering some girl at the dance hall, wanted her to go to bed with him without his paying, or he'd throw her in jail. I interfered. She seemed so frightened—"

Jacob got the whole story out of Bernard while Paul held the attention of the deputy.

424

"Could you get me some food, Father? They feed me only when they feel like it," Bernard said simply. "And fresh water?"

The deputy heard that. "Cain't bring him no food," he protested.

Jacob looked at him in a way that would have sent his clerks scurrying for cover. "We'll be back. You look after him, and don't let any harm come to him," he said sharply.

"He's a prisoner," the deputy said sullenly, with an ugly look to his jaw. He was a tall, stringy man, with hamlike fists. "If he tries to break out, he'll get in trouble, he will." He touched the holster of his gun.

"He isn't breaking out," Jacob said levelly. He looked at Paul. "You stay here. I'll be back."

"Right," said Paul. He took the other chair, and sat down, crossing his booted feet as though meaning to stay for hours. The deputy glared. Paul smiled back serenely.

Jacob went to find the dance-hall girl. She had a bruised face and was sullen about talking. He promised to get her out of town, and send her a hundred miles away to where her sister and brother-in-law worked in a restaurant. Then she opened up.

Bernard's story was true. She wanted only to dance. She had a steady fellow, but he had been scared away by the sheriff, who fancied her. When she had tried to fight off the sheriff, he had struck her. Bernard had drawn his gun, and so had the sheriff, only Bernard was faster and more accurate.

Her sullen eyes lit up a little. "I never seen anybody so fast. We figured he was a gunfighter. Is he?"

"No, he's a railroad man, my son is," Jacob said rather grimly, remembering Clinton, and remembering some of Bernard's other escapades in the West. Too fast with a gun, too quick with his temper. He had better get him out of the West, back to civilization, and make him hang up that gun for good.

Jacob then tried to find out who the law was. Everyone was vague about it, the dance-hall girl, the stout

425

madam, the greasy bartender who knew everybody in town. The bartender brought Jacob a neat whiskey, from his best bottle, and volunteered some information.

"That judge, he won't come back soon. He's skeered of that deputy, he is. That deputy, he's mean. He likes having a prisoner in jail, because he collects on the food, you know. Then he keeps the money. I slipped a plate of food to Bernie a couple of times when the deputy went out. Otherwise . . ." His eloquent shrug told the rest.

Jacob got the picture. He collected the bartender, the owner of the local seedy hotel, and the manager of a dry goods store, and went back to the jail with a plate of food and a canteen of water.

The deputy got up when he saw them coming. "*I* feeds the prisoner," he began to protest.

Jacob cut him off. "I have the whole story, Deputy— Wills, is that your name? You don't have any reason to hold my son, because he killed in a fair fight. You haven't made any attempt to hold a trial."

He gave the water and food to Bernard. The other men stood around uneasily, waiting.

"So we'll have a trial now," Jacob said evenly. "The way I figure it, in the West you can have a trial, when citizens come around, listen to the evidence, and decide on a verdict."

"Now, see here, you can't get high-handed with me," said the deputy, advancing, his hand on his gun.

Jacob moved so fast, he had the deputy on the mud floor of the adobe jail before you could wink, as the bartender said later.

Jacob had the bartender give evidence. He repeated what the dance-hall girl had said. Then he had Bernard tell his side of the story. Finally, he turned to the three citizens, and asked gravely, "Now, does my son get held, or does he get turned loose? Was it murder, or a fair fight that the sheriff lost?"

The men looked at each other and nodded briskly. "Fair fight. He gets turned loose."

"You can't do that!" cried the deputy.

Jacob took his keys away from him and opened the cell. Bernard stepped out.

He was filthy. His once-white summer suit was black with grit and grime. He had not shaven for weeks. But his eyes were bright and happy.

"Now we're going over to the hotel and clean up," said Jacob. "Tomorrow morning, Mr. Wills, after you have had a good night's sleep, you can come out to the street in front of the hotel, say about ten o'clock. If you feel you've got a beef about this business, you and I will settle it. At ten o'clock tomorrow morning."

The deputy had turned green under his tan. He stared.

"If you haven't got a beef, or want to forget it all," said Jacob deliberately, "I reckon you'd better get on a horse tonight, and get out of town and far away. Or I'll start remembering how you treated my son. And I've got a very good memory."

They left, and at the saloon, the bartender stood drinks on the house, grinning at everybody impartially. Presently the stableman came in, and told them the deputy had just saddled his horse and ridden off.

Everyone cheered, clapped Bernard on the back, and had another round of drinks. Then Bernard went up to a room and soaked in a tub of hot water for an hour, with an ecstatic expression on his face. Jacob's valet came and shaved him. The hotel staff was dumbfounded. They had never seen a real valet before. Their respect for Jacob increased even more. They had heard vaguely of the Van Rhyne railroad, and thought Jacob must have some money. But a valet?

"What now?" Jacob said the next day, as the bright sun burned away the mists of the night. They were sitting in the crude dining room of the hotel, eating a huge breakfast of ham and fried eggs, potatoes, and thick slices of bread with butter.

"Let's get away," said Bernard, in a low tone.

"We'll go back East, son," Jacob promised. "But let's take the little dance-hall gal home first, then go down and see Leigh Sheldon. I want to get this dust out of my throat."

They packed up and left, taking the girl with them in a second car Jacob had hired. She was terribly impressed, and very grateful.

"You go straight, now, gal," he told her. "You're young and pretty. Find yourself a good man, get married, and have kids. You're not tough enough for this life."

She promised. They left her at her sister's farm, in a little town a hundred miles away. Then the parlor car rolled on down the miles of track, toward Spanish Pass, through lush, green mountains and valleys.

They left the parlor car on a siding, locked up, with the valet in charge. They mounted horses and rode to Leigh Sheldon's ranch. He welcomed them heartily, a beaming smile on his face.

He, too, had aged, but not as much as Jacob. He was gray, and his sons were grown and married, except for the gunfighter, who had disappeared into the Far West. He might come home one day, Sheldon's wife said hopefully, a distant look in her pretty eyes.

Jacob thought of the Bible, and the shepherd with the one sheep that had strayed. She had these others, but she could not rest, or be completely happy, until her stray lamb came home.

Sheldon rode with them over his vast ranch. They spent nights in the open, with the smell of sagebrush and pine in their nostrils, driving out the dust of the desert and the dirt of the Eastern cities. They ate heavily, rounded up calves, helped in the branding, and broke in a couple of horses. Jacob laughed to see Bernard working a wild mustang, hitting the side of his leg with his sombrero, as he yelled and hollered at his mount. He looked like a kid again, his father thought.

Jacob and Leigh sat up nights, talking at the campfire, while the others slept. They drank coffee and talked of the old days.

"Ever go back to Virginia?" asked Jacob once.

A shadow crossed Leigh's face. "No, that's another

428

life, another time. I put it behind me long ago, thank God. I could not have lived with that grief. I had to begin again."

"I'm too old to begin again," said Jacob, making marks in the dirt with a stick. Leigh gave him a sharp look.

"Too old? Never too old to start again, if you really want to. I did. Though I was sick, felt old as the mountains, and fed up with life. Found a new life. You're not old, Jacob, and look at your sons. Fine sons. And Regina was able to start over."

Jacob nodded. "Yes, but she was young. She could begin again. She had to begin again. She could not have stayed there."

He had told Leigh the whole story earlier. Leigh's face had been shocked, and his eyes had burned with the old fierce anger of the gunfighter, as though he would have liked to have that Duke of Kildare in his sights.

"She had courage, guts. A true daughter of yours, Jacob. Direct and honest with herself, as well as with others. With honesty, you can go ahead. Know yourself, what you want, then go out and get it."

"Courage, honesty," Jacob muttered. He drew a deep sigh. "Well, I'd better turn in. By the stars, it's past midnight."

They looked up at the bright stars that hung over them, so close it seemed as if they could reach up and grab one. In the blackness of the night, near the mountains, where the air was clear and cold and stung with the scent of cedar, the stars were very close.

Autumn came, and they decided it was time to go back home. Paul Malone had put on weight; he was tanned and hearty, and ready to go back to his beloved practice. He had tied up broken legs and treated panther-scratches and knife wounds. "Quite a change from my city work," he had said, laughing.

Leigh Sheldon and one of his sons rode with them to the town where they had left the parlor car. The two men strode into the car to see it. "My God, it looks like a brothel," said Sheldon's son, grinning.

Leigh cuffed him gently. "And how would you know what a brothel looks like?" he said.

They were laughing and joking. They had a final drink of whiskey, a last cigar, and then it was farewell—until the next time. Jacob watched them riding away, the father and son, free and easy in the saddle, riding close, like friends.

They hitched up to the next train and went north, then to another train, and went east to St. Louis. Then to Chicago, and toward civilization again.

Bernard was quieter as they approached New York. He was thinking. "Father, do you want me to go out West again?"

Jacob shook his head. "We'll talk out plans later," he said gruffly. "I've got a lot on my mind. We'll talk it over with Errol."

Bernard looked him over thoughtfully. Usually Jacob made up his mind and then told him what to do. "You mean, I'll have a say?" he asked, half-jokingly.

"You will now," Jacob replied. "From now on."

Bernard smiled, and so did Paul. Bernard had matured. He had become a man, not as tough as Errol, not as smart, but smart enough. It would work, Jacob thought, satisfied. He drew on his Havana cigar with pleasure.

They got into New York late in the day, and hired a carriage to take them home. They dropped off Paul Malone at his house, empty for him since Sunny had died. He should have married, Jacob thought. Maybe not, though. Paul's life was his work.

They went into the big Van Rhyne mansion, tiptoeing through the back door, into the kitchen, and up the stairs. Only a sleepy footman saw them, and a night guard outside, and the stable boys.

Bernard went to his wing of the house. Jacob went up to his bedroom, but hesitated before entering.

He would see if Antonia was awake. He would tell

her Bernard was home for good. She would be pleased, he hoped.

He went quietly along the hallway to the front of the mansion. There was a light under Antonia's door. He opened the door quietly, and stepped inside.

Later, he thought now he knew how Regina must have felt. The shock, the disbelief, the humiliation. He might have believed it if someone had told him first. But seeing it like that, coming upon it suddenly, there was nothing that could make him believe his eyes.

Yet, there it was. Antonia lay in the bed, in that great, wide bed where her three children had been conceived. With her lay a man, his back turned to Jacob. At the sound of the door, they both turned from their locked embrace. Antonia sat up with a squeak, her aging body rising from a froth of pink and violet silk and lace. The man rose up nude, his face turning an ugly shade of red.

Cecil Meryon. Antonia's tame puppy. The sharp-nosed, clever man who had wormed his way into society clinging to the lace-trailing skirts of women.

Jacob stared at them in silence. Antonia, for once in her life, was utterly speechless. She held the covers up to her aging breasts, and stared back at her husband with frightened eyes. Her blond hair stuck out in disarray from beneath a violet net. That blond hair he had caressed. Jacob felt sick.

"I'll leave you," he said, in a voice he did not recognize as his own. He felt strangled, choking with nausea. "I'll talk to you tomorrow. In my study. About the divorce."

He closed the door, and went back to his own bedroom. He locked the door after him, and was violently sick in the washbasin. Then he went to bed. He lay awake for a long time, thinking, planning.

He had thought at first, he would leave her the house. Then he decided savagely, why give it to her? It was his home, and Bernard's, until the lad married. Why give anything to Antonia? She had taken and taken, in her clever way—enticing him, pleading with him for jewels and clothes, and for the social life she loved. She had taken Regina and given her to a— Jacob could not think about that, and closed his eyes.

He thought hard about the open air of the West, the smells of the sagebrush and pine. He thought of what Leigh Sheldon had said to him.

Tomorrow, he would settle it for good. He was finished with her. Finished. It was over.

Chapter 30

Jacob sent Bernard to the office when they got up late the next day. Antonia was still in her room, the housekeeper said.

"Send her to my study when she gets dressed," Jacob said.

"Yes, sir, Mr. Van Rhyne."

Antonia came down about noon, dressed in a soft, blue silk gown with lace trailing behind her on the Persian carpets. She had made up lightly, setting off her still lovely face, her violet eyes. But she was frightened.

She sat down, lounging back in the big chair opposite his desk. Jacob glanced at her, then down at the papers on which he was writing.

"I should like for you to leave the house at once, Antonia," he began, without preface. "Would you like a small house, a flat, or an apartment in a hotel?"

She started, and sat up. "Now, Jacob, don't be hasty! I can explain. And it isn't as if you haven't been doing the same thing, sleeping around—"

"Did I complain?" Jacob asked evenly. "I don't like you any more, and I want you out of here. Our lawyers will settle on the terms of the divorce. I'll pay you enough to live on, though you won't be able to spend quite so madly as you have. The money will be tied up

432

in trusts for you, so you won't spend it all on tame puppies. I imagine Cecil Meryon will run off to a more promising prospect, now."

Her face went white. She recovered only with great effort. "Jacob, I am the mother of your children. I am not going to be discarded! You know quite well that you seized on this chance to discard me now that I am old. You haven't slept with me for years."

"You didn't miss me," he said. "But we are not going to discuss that. I don't even want to know about the men in your life, or about how you amuse yourself. The only question is, how soon can you get out? If the children want to see you, they can come to you."

"I want this house!" she blazed, losing her temper as she realized how harsh and cold he was determined to be. "I deserve it! I'm the one who decorated it, and made it famous with my parties, playing the gracious hostess even when you refused to come! I am the Van Rhyne name in New York City! You won't discard me! I'll live in this house until I die."

"There are several mistakes in that statement," Jacob said curtly. He thought of Errol, the cynical bachelor who frowned upon his mother's social life. He thought of Bernard, hiding out West from the consequences of his overindulgent upbringing. And he thought of Regina, her chin up, in that house in London, telling him bravely of her years of agony. Her children, indeed! "The Van Rhyne name is railroads, and I am that name. Your father died almost broke. He left you nothing. Other women will take your place in society. The changeover will be painless—for them. I am sure there are many waiting to take whatever social standing you still have."

Alone, in New York, stripped of her name and position? It would be a living death. "Jacob, you would not, you cannot do this to me. Oh, you must not torment me so." She began to whimper, and an artful tear rolled down her rouged cheek.

He looked away, toward the opened windows. The autumn chill came in, and he felt suddenly weary of all his sixty-plus years. He thought of more years of them together in this great house—with the chatter in the drawing room, the clatter of teacups and whiskey glasses, and the wild laughter at some scandalous gossip. No, no, he would not endure Antonia, trailing about in tea gowns, her made-up face more and more lined, applying more and more rouge in a frantic effort to keep her appearance, adding more and more tint to her blond hair.

"When can you leave?" he asked, his pen making aimless marks on the page. "Tell your maid to pack what you want. Leave the amethysts for Regina. I want to give them to her. You can have the diamond set— you always liked that—and the ropes of pearls. But leave the emeralds for Sarah; she'll like them."

The jewels were locked in his safe, except for a few gems she kept in her dressing room, beside her mammoth bedroom. She began to weep genuine tears now, out of sheer fright.

She wept, and he could get no sensible answers from her. He gave up, sent for her maid, and ordered her to pack some of Antonia's clothes. Then he reserved a hotel room for a few weeks, until Antonia could decide upon a place to live.

She was out by late afternoon, having stepped into the carriage he had ordered for her, looking shocked and dazed. The household was soon buzzing with the news, and Jacob had to order the housekeeper, the butler, the grooms, and the stable boys to carry on as usual. Bernard came home and wondered what all the commotion was about. When Jacob finally told him, he did not seem very surprised.

"Oh, you finally saw her with that Meryon," he said mildly, with some relief. "The way they carried on was something. He's such a fawning whelp of a dog."

"Did everyone know but *me*?" Jacob asked in disgust.

Bernard shrugged. "Errol put me wise. He thought you would find out in time."

So Antonia could keep a secret after all. Jacob took a carriage and went out, driving himself. He headed for the McKenna house, remembering too late that Molly had gone up with Jessie to visit with Regina in Connecticut. The house was shut and dark. He stood there, muttering impatiently in front of the house.

Then he drove on down the street to the corner saloon. He wanted a drink. He tied the horse to the hitching post, and went inside.

"Hey, there, Mr. Van Rhyne!" He looked in the direction of the voice and saw a hand waving to him from a small crowd in the corner. Evan McKenna stood up and came to him, beaming.

"Well, now, Jacob, it's good to see you! I thought you were still out West."

"I got back last night," Jacob said, sitting down with Evan and his friends. Last night seemed a thousand years ago. "How is everybody?"

"Molly is fine, and so are the children. Little Mary Cecilia is trying to walk." Evan flashed his best smile at the other proud grandfather. "Cute little button she is."

They had a drink on it, and another. The talk turned to politics, and Evan and his friends briefed him on what was happening in New York. Jacob listened carefully. He knew that if a man wanted to find out what was going on, he talked to a laboring man, and got plenty of information. And Evan always knew the inside stories.

"And will there be work on the railroads this year?" a man asked Mr. Van Rhyne. "There's talk that they'll be laying off."

"Not Van Rhyne's," Jacob said with assurance. "We're going to need more men. We're going to add some more trains. We might go in for some of those new electric engines. My son Errol wants electric engines. He swears they're the coming thing."

The faces brightened. They talked about Van Rhyne's plans, cheerfully, hopefully. Unemployment had been high for several years, and the prospect of more work sat well with Evan and his friends. Maybe the bad years were over, one of them remarked.

"They may well be over," Jacob agreed. "Times are

looking up. The railroads have to settle their differences, straighten out the lines, and decide who owns what." He would talk to Errol this week. Yes, and Bernard, too. Bernard should come in as a junior partner. Maybe that would encourage him to marry and settle down.

They would talk about selling out in the West, and concentrating on their Eastern roads. And they'd talk about the new inventions. They might get better railroad carriages. They might specialize, some lines carrying freight and others carrying passengers. People wanted more elegant ways of traveling. Well, Van Rhyne would give it to them.

He left them after a couple of hours, and several beers. The talk had lifted his spirits and left him feeling more like himself again. He went out to his patient horse, got into the carriage, flicked the reins, and soon found himself on the street where Deirdre lived. He smiled to himself. Well, it was where he wanted to go, wasn't it?

He went up to her apartment, and knocked on the door. She peered out, then opened the door. "Well, Jacob, you're home," she said with pleasure.

"That I am." He stepped inside and kissed her.

The apartment was warm and cozy after the chill of the autumn night. She felt warm and plump and welcoming in his arms. They moved over to the couch, and he sat down, pulling her gently down beside him, still holding her. Her head came down naturally on his shoulder, her graying, red-gold hair brushing softly against his cheek. She snuggled against him.

"There, now, I was thinking about you tonight, and thinking you would be home soon," she murmured against his chest.

"Were you, now?" He stroked his hands over her dress, and felt her yielding warmth beneath it. She was wearing a green dress, with black braid smartly sewn on the hem and down the front. He was sure she had made it herself. He thought of Antonia in the trailing silk and lace, and shivered.

436

"You're cold, honey," Deirdre said. "I'll get you a warm drink."

She got up and went to the kitchen, and returned shortly with a china pot of coffee, a bottle of whiskey, and two cups. They drank, and talked a little about the West. He told her about Bernard, and she listened intently, with wide green eyes.

"Well, I never. It sounds like a story in the papers," she said, marveling. "And he shot the man over a little girl. What did she look like?"

Jacob grinned. "He wasn't interested in her, Deirdre. Just the principle of it, this time." He told her about Leigh Sheldon's place. He could describe how the night sky looked purple, and how brightly the stars blazed, and how the smells of cedar and pine got into your blood and made you long for more.

She listened and listened. He said finally, "When I got home, I told Antonia to leave. I found her with someone."

"Antonia?" she gasped.

"Yes. She moved out today, to a hotel. We'll get a divorce."

Now she did stare, her cheeks growing flushed. "But, Jacob, she is the mother of your children—"

"Mother? A stray dog is more of a mother to its pups than she was to our children!" he said violently. "The children were raised by nannies and housekeepers and governesses and tutors. She only showed them off when they were all dressed up. You know, Errol used to go out and fall deliberately into a mud puddle, to keep from going to those damned parties and having to show off for her? And she shoved Regina into that damned marriage."

Deirdre was never shocked at his language. "There, now, I always said Errol was a clever one," was her only remark.

"And he married a nice girl, too," Jacob said, his anger simmering down. "Damned nice girl!"

"I like her, she sounds so sensible and right for him."

He looked at Deirdre, sitting there so calmly, pouring

out his coffee and adding whiskey to it, her hair shining under the lamplight. She never asked for anything. If he gave her something, she thanked him and said, "Now, no more, Jacob, you're doing too much. I've got the shop, and thank God for it, and I can make my way."

She was sweet and gallant, and she gave without stinting, and she had been more loyal to him than his own wife. Never did she go out with any other man. She belonged to Jacob, quietly, behind the scenes, but she belonged to him, and no man had her heart but him.

He found himself saying, "Deirdre, I want to marry you."

She started, then shook her head. "No, Jacob, you don't mean that. It isn't suitable."

"Yes, I do mean it. It would be fine. The boys like you. Regina will love you."

She tried to smile, looking rather distressed. "It won't do, love. You keep on coming here, as long as you want. You know you're always welcome. But I can't marry you. What will people say?"

"To hell with that!" The more Jacob thought about the idea, the better he liked it. Deirdre had worked hard all her days. She deserved a life of comfort and ease. And how nice for him, to have her always about. He felt soothed in her presence. She could calm him and help him, just by being there.

"You are a wealthy man, Jacob," she said gently. "And I am not of your social class. The conventional approach—"

"To hell with conventions! What good is money if you can't have happiness? Conventions be damned!"

It took Jacob several weeks to convince Deirdre. However, by the time he had his divorce, she was shyly agreeable to "try it out," by first becoming engaged to him. He said some forceful words about that, and they were married in a quiet ceremony two weeks before Christmas.

Deirdre moved into the great mansion on Fifth Avenue. At first, she had her quiet qualms about it. She dreaded the servants, the gossip of Antonia's friends, and most of all, that she might make Jacob miserable because of the differences between them. What if people were to laugh at him? She could not bear it.

Her fears were groundless. The servants came to her for orders, and were only too happy to be relieved of Antonia's temperament and Meryon's dictatorship over them. Antonia's friends did not come; most of them had even deserted Antonia. As Jacob had predicted, there was some new society queen, waiting in the wings for her chance. With Antonia's fall from grace, she had taken over, and everyone flocked to her parties.

Bernard had known about Deirdre, and he welcomed her. She was a decent woman, he thought, tender and loving. And she seemed to make his father so happy.

At Christmas, Jacob decided to have all his children and grandchildren present. Sarah had presented Errol with a son, and young Donald Rowan had already won his grandfather's heart. He was a sturdy lad, with dark hair and vivid blue eyes, and a face that reddened when he wept, which was whenever he did not get his way. Sarah would not have him indulged. She fed him, kept him dry, then said, "No fussing over him. If he cries, he will get over it," and he did.

The house seemed to overflow with Christmas spirit. The huge tree stood in the drawing room, surrounded by gaily wrapped packages. Fat, red candles were set in silver holders on all the mantels and on the big mahogany table in the dining room. Deirdre liked all the Christmas customs, and had even tied red stockings to the mantels for the grandchildren.

Regina and Vincent came down from Connecticut for a week. Mary Cecilia was toddling about, falling down on her plump bottom, but staggering up again with an engaging, toothless grin. Her blond curls were always ruffled by someone's loving hand; she was the kind of baby everyone wanted to hug. She was enchanted, in turn, with baby Donald. When Sarah brought him in and unwrapped him from his blanket, Ceci, as she was called, toddled over and stared at him. "Baby," she said, very clearly, and patted his toes.

Errol had already welcomed Deirdre into the family with a frank smile and a big hug. Sarah was pleased about Jacob's new wife; she had never liked Antonia. But Regina? Deirdre wondered if she would accept her. She, a former duchess! And how must Deirdre act? Must she curtsey?

Regina came in, having removed her outer mink coat, and showed herself in a slim violet wool suit trimmed in mink. She was radiantly happy at last, her lovely heart-shaped face hauntingly beautiful, her eyes sparkling with new joy. She came over to where Deirdre stood and held out her hand. Deirdre extended her own hand, and Regina squeezed it warmly.

Then Regina leaned toward her and kissed her cheek. "Papa looks so much younger already," she whispered. "Thank you for making him happy at last." And Regina won her stepmother's heart.

Jacob was feeling fine. He had never had a Christmas like this. Antonia always avoided family Christmases; she would plan many activities, none of them including the children. Now, at last, the family was together, and Jacob sat with baby Donald on his knee and beamed proudly. Ceci tottered over to him, clutched his arm, and steadied herself. She gazed up into his eyes, with Regina's own clear eyes.

"Gran—pa—pa—" she managed.

Regina clapped her hands. "Oh, good! I have been teaching her for weeks, but she would not say it right!" She laughed.

On the day before Christmas, Molly and Evan McKenna stopped in "for a minute," Molly said firmly. They were persuaded to stay for the day, and to join in the merrymaking. Molly slipped some presents under the tree, and sat down, with Ceci on her knees, beside Jacob and the baby. They smiled at each other over the babies' heads.

"I heard you and Deirdre were married. I'm so happy, Jacob," Molly said, under cover of the laughter and merriment.

"I've made some mistakes in my time," Jacob said quietly. "This is not one of them."

"I know. She's a fine woman." Molly bounced Ceci on her knee, and chanted a rhyme to her.

The butler and a maid wheeled in a silver trolley of tea, cakes, and whiskey. Errol jumped up to help hand around cups. Deirdre poured, though she tried to get Regina to do it. Regina only smiled serenely and shook her head. "I'm on holiday," she said happily. "This is your house, Mother."

Deirdre was so startled at the word, that she almost dropped the coffeepot. She glanced at Errol; he was smiling down at her. Bernard lounged against the mantel, surveying them all, his tanned face calm.

The tree glittered with ornaments. Sarah had helped Deirdre choose them and had helped her decorate the tree. Aunt Frieda was coming down that night. Elisabeth would drop in tomorrow, as would Katrinka and her family. Family, Jacob thought contentedly. The big, stately mansion felt like home for the first time since he had moved in. The laughter, the smell of pine and candles, the chatter of baby Ceci, even the roar of Donald when he wanted his bottle, only added to his pleasure. A family. He was a father and grandfather, and all present loved him.

Only Bernard did not seem to be happy. Jacob had made him a junior partner, and he and Errol were making decisions, selling out the western lines, consolidating their possessions in the East. Together they planned the great future of the Van Rhyne railroad.

Vincent McKenna went over to Bernard, and started talking to him. Presently they sat down in matching chairs by the fire, and began discussing politics. Bernard's face lit up. He leaned forward and talked to Vincent about his ideas on unions and shorter work weeks for railroad men. Vincent was a good man, Jacob thought. He had changed Regina from the thin, overwrought creature he had found in London to the radiantly serene young matron she was today.

441

And lovely Sarah, holding Donald now, her face like a beautiful madonna's as she bent over the child to give him his bottle. Her black hair was smoothed into a chignon, and her plain, scarlet silk gown set off her olive face and her great dark eyes. On her shoulder was a spray of emeralds in the shape of an olive branch. One look at her, and Errol would forget everyone in the room, Jacob thought, and chuckled to himself.

The children were put to bed, and the family went to the dining room for dinner. The great, long table was groaning with platters of hams, a mammoth turkey stuffed with sage bread dressing, a huge tureen of pea soup, bowls of sweet potatoes, cranberry sauce, and oysters in a delicate cream. Even the footmen were beaming discreetly as they handed around the platters, and left the family to enjoy their dinner, and to talk and laugh.

Champagne was served. Jacob lifted his glass to them all and began to sip.

"No, no, no," Molly McKenna cried, her flushed face radiant, her graying hair spilling over her forehead in rebellious curls, the way it had when she was a girl. "Let me make a toast. Or Evan. Or someone."

"What toast, Molly?" Jacob asked indulgently. "Come on, girl, give us a toast."

She laughed, and stood up. She lifted her brimming glass of bubbly, clear wine high in the air. "To the Van Rhynes," she said. "They rescued me and Rowan on the dock. They gave us shelter and a home. They gave us work, and we built a railroad, we did, and made our homes here in this new land. To the Van Rhynes. Long may they prosper and work in the great land of America!"

She sat down, abashed by her own eloquence. They stood up, one and all, and drank to it, and to Molly, and to Jacob, and to everyone they could think of. Giggling and laughing, their faces flushed and glowing from the warmth, and the candles shining on them, they talked, ate, and drank.

After dinner, so stuffed they could scarcely move,

they adjourned to the great drawing room, to gaze sleepily at the Christmas tree and to talk about the past. But to Jacob, the future was more important—the future of those two children upstairs, the future of the Van Rhyne family, and the future of the Van Rhyne railroad.

Ecstatic, Jacob looked about, fondly observing them all, his family, his dearest friends, and thought what a fortunate man he was. He had his wife, Deirdre, with her sensible, loving warmth; his sons, with their new responsibilities, settling down now to the task of running the Van Rhyne railroad; and his daughter, with the man of her choice, happy, finally. And Errol had darling Sarah with her gentle ways.

Presently Sarah went to the piano at their urging, and began to play Christmas songs. They joined in singing then, some standing around the piano, some from their chairs.

And the firelight flickered on them, and the candles shone redly, and the closed, heavy drapes kept out the cold of the Christmas evening. Tomorrow was the celebration of the Birth of the Christ. What a marvelous event, Jacob thought. The birth of a Holy Child. Symbolic of a family, of a father and a mother and a child who drew all together, the links between the past and the future. The logs crackled in the fireplace, the clear voices rose in song. Deirdre slipped her hand into Jacob's, and squeezed it hard.

He leaned over and kissed her cheek. Her eyes were wet, though she smiled. "We're a family," she whispered happily.

"That's right," Jacob said.

Errol was standing behind Sarah at the piano, his hands resting on her shoulders as she sat there, her clever hands moving so beautifully on the keys. Regina and Vincent were close together on another couch, hands clasped. Bernard sat alone, leaning forward, his hands clasped together.

"We must find someone nice for Bernie," Deirdre whispered.

"Someone nice," Jacob repeated. Very nice, for a fine lad, who had somehow grown up in spite of the difficulties. He looked across at Molly, sitting with her hand in Evan's, singing with the unself-conscious joy of the Irish girl she had been. Someone nice, like Molly— or like Sarah. Yes, they would help Bernie find someone nice.

And he would start a family too, and Jacob would have more grandchildren. How splendid it was to have grandchildren, Jacob decided. You could enjoy them, and leave the worrying to their parents. A splendid thing!

The Van Rhynes would go on. Old Pieter would be happy, if he could see them tonight. Pieter would have liked being here among them, surrounding himself with their joy and their laughter. Maybe he was here, Jacob thought, and glanced involuntarily over the mantel to where Pieter Van Rhyne's portrait was set into the wall. Was it his imagination, or was there a smile on that austere face?

THE CLIFTON HERITAGE

by Louisa Bronte

PART I

1880–1910

Chapter 1

"Hey, Sam, you done plowing yet? I finished an hour ago!"

Sam Clifton raised his head from his gloomy contemplation of the uneven furrows he and the heavy wooden plow were cutting into the rough, brown earth before him. He scowled as he recognized the taunt in the voice of his best friend.

His lips tightened, and with an effort, he refrained from throwing back a retort. Art Verlaine was quick with his stinging tongue. Sam enjoyed matching wits with him sometimes, but today he was too tired and discouraged to try.

"About done," Sam shouted back curtly, and pushed again at the heavy plow. Damn it all, he thought. A man wasn't a beast of burden. There ought to be some easier way to push a plow through the thick, stubborn earth—a way that utilized something a man could guide and direct with his brain, rather than pushing and grunting behind a plow like a weary horse.

Art hung on the fence and watched for a time, until Sam finally reached the end of the furrow and began to unhitch himself from the thick leather reins. Then he came to help.

They were much alike, burned by the sun to a reddish, leathery tan, and stringy as bean poles from long hours of work all their young lives. There was only a year of difference between them. Jacques Arthur Verlaine was the eldest child of his French family. The Verlaines had emigrated to the Michigan wilderness ten years before Sam Clifton's father had abandoned his failing factory in England and moved his entire family across the ocean. Both boys had gone to the same school, and had sat side by side on wooden benches and recited the tables, poems, and spelling exercises in monotonous chants that were designed to drill knowledge into their young minds.

Verlaine was handsome, though, and fond of girls, which Sam was not. "You going to the barn dance tonight?" the young Frenchman asked eagerly, as he helped unstrap Sam from the harness.

Sam grunted. "I have a watch to repair—old man Burns's watch. That should take me half the night."

"Does your old man know?"

Sam shook his head and scowled. "He thinks I'm wasting my time. Why, I bet I know more about watches and clocks than the jeweler in town!"

"Sure you do." Art was silent as Sam scraped the mud from the heavy plow with a stick, and began to turn it back toward the barn. "Come on, Sam, forget it for tonight, and come on. There's going to be two fiddlers."

Sam hesitated. He did love to dance, and when he put his mind to it, he could jump in the air and crack his heels together with the fastest of them. Yet he felt depressed, somehow. It was spring, he was twenty years old, and his father thought he should be working six days a week on the farm.

"What's wrong?" Art asked, as he helped Sam with the heavy plow, and they pulled it between them back to the barn. "You've been grumpy for a week or more."

"I wish I could go into town and get a job I'd like," Sam blurted out.

Art stared at him. "Doing what? Before you're married?" he gasped.

No young man of their acquaintance ever left home until he married. Then his parents would help him set up in another farm, and get him started with cast-off furniture, tools, and such.

"I could work for the jeweler," Sam said moodily. "Except that he can't pay me."

They walked on in silence. Jacques Arthur Verlaine had all the quick-changing moods of a Frenchman, so

448

he could well understand the depression of his friend. But this was a new thought. Sam was always coming up with something different.

When they had been boys together, Sam had often led Art and other boys in sneaking off from school, tramping through the woods, hitching a ride on a railroad, or going bird-watching. Art's mother said impatiently that he was as full of ideas as a pot was full of beans. But this was different. Going off to town and getting a job away from the farm! Art thought about it seriously, and shook his head over it. Sam was in for trouble.

"You'd best come with me to the barn dance," he said finally, "and work off your bad feelings. It always works with me. When I hear the fiddles working, and see the pretty girls . . ." He laughed, and flung back his head with its handsome, black, curly hair, and his black eyes danced. "That makes me forget everything!"

"Come on in and have supper with us. We have plenty," Sam said in response. They put the plow away neatly, with the mud carefully scraped off. His father never held with careless ways. The equipment must be well cared-for. "Take care of your tools, and your tools will take care of you," was one of his many solemn old saws.

They walked into the house through the kitchen door. Enticing aromas came to them at once, of dried apples cooking on the stove, and of pork bubbling in a pot, with cabbage covering it. Sam's mother turned to see them, and gave them a straight look. She was tall and thin, and her cheeks were always flushed from the heat of the stove, or from making soap, or from doing the laundry in a big kettle in the back yard.

Mr. Clifton was already sitting at the head of the long table. "Did you finish the rows, Sam?" he asked.

"Yes, Father."

"It took you long enough," Mr. Clifton said dryly. "Sit down, Sam. Good evening, Art."

"Good evening, Mr. Clifton. Good evening, Mrs. Clifton," Art said, then gave Sam's mother the kind of graceful bow that betrayed his French background. Sam felt a sort of sour pleasure at seeing how the ladies fluttered whenever Art bowed to them. Even his sedate mother would blush a bit, and Lucy, his oldest sister, would gaze back at Art with wide, solemn eyes.

"You'll join us for supper, Art," Mrs. Clifton said, lifting the huge pork roast carefully onto a serving plate.

He eyed it hungrily, but said politely, "I don't want to be a nuisance, Mrs. Clifton. I just came over to ask Sam to go to the barn dance tonight. Would you all be going?"

Sam's mother looked at his father. He might go, as long as they were home before midnight, which marked the beginning of the Sabbath. Mr. Clifton nodded.

"We'll be going," Sam's mother said, smiling. "Do sit down and have supper with us. Lucy, set another place."

The short, plump girl had already risen, her face flaming red. She avoided Art's gaze as she went to set another place for him, at her mother's right. She set it neatly, with the napkin folded just so, for she was a neat, quiet girl. Despite her plainness, she would make a good wife, Sam thought. She was also a good cook, had a sweet disposition, and always helped look after the younger ones.

They all sat down in two rows, one on either side of the long table. There were Lucy, Sam, Philip, Arnold, Jessie, and Sarah. And Annie, who had been a baby when they had first come to Michigan ten years ago, in 1870. Now she was a slim, pretty little girl of ten, with shining brown eyes.

"Are you going to the barn dance, Sam?" Annie piped up, after grace had been said.

"I don't know," Sam replied uneasily. He hated for it to be brought up before his father's stern gaze.

"It might do you good, Sam," his mother said, as she placidly ladled out the vegetables while his father carved the roast. "You've worked hard this week. It's been four weeks since you went to a dance. And you know you like to dance."

"Sam's a good dancer," Lucy said softly, and flushed rosy at Art's look.

Art grinned. "Sure he is. Girls fall all over themselves trying to get his attention."

"He might do well to look at a girl, instead of staying up all night with his watches," his father said with a frown. "You've got all that work up to date, haven't you, Sam? Don't take on any more. I don't like to see you spend so much time fooling around with things that don't make any money for you."

"I'm about caught up," Sam mumbled into his plate. If Art betrayed him—! He shot Art a fierce look across the table. His friend met his gaze with innocent black eyes.

"That's terrific," Art said. "Then you can come tonight."

Sam was caught in a bind. He didn't much want to go, but if he said no, everyone would want to know why. He knew why Art wanted him to go. It was easier to hang around the door at a barn dance with a friend, laughing and joshing, than by one's self, looking lonesome and not knowing what to do with one's feet. If you didn't get a girl to dance with you, you could always go outside and swap yarns with a fellow. If you were alone, all you could do was stand around, trying not to twiddle your thumbs. It was awkward.

"I might as well go," Sam said grudgingly.

Lucy brightened up. She looked at her mother, who nodded. "We'll all go," Mrs. Clifton said. "It'll do us good to get out and have an enjoyable time with our good neighbors."

That was the decision. When his mother spoke like that, it marked the way it was going to be. They would all go. Usually his father had the last word, but sometimes his mother would step in, and say what was to be done, and his father would go along. It was interesting, and Sam thought about it for a couple of minutes. He wondered if that was the way marriage was. The man made most of the decisions, but sometimes the wife said something, and the man went along, as though they had

451

quietly discussed it in their bedroom, away from the children, and had made up their minds together—like two parts of a good whole.

Maybe that was a good way to be. Sam was something of a loner, but he liked to talk things over with Art, or to confide in Lucy, who would listen well and sympathetically. A wife? If he could find a girl who was like his mother and his eldest sister, Sam thought, he'd marry her! Only she would have to like engines, and take an interest in his inventions, and not ridicule him all the time, the way his father did. Yes, the girl he married would have to be truly interested in inventions, and not just be fooling, or bored, the way Susie had been last winter when he had taken her out a couple of times. He had caught her yawning when he had described a locomotive's works to her, and that had finished her with him. He never took her out again.

After supper, Art went home to wash and change. Sam helped with the cows, all the while reflecting gloomily that if tomorrow wasn't Sunday, he would probably have to muck out the barn *again*. He had hated that job most of all, ever since they had come to the farm. As the eldest and strongest boy, he always seemed to get that job. It seemed to him that it was time one of the others did it once in a while. He hated the filth and the smell.

It took two hours for all the family to wash, and change to their best clothes. The parents, along with the three youngest children, rode in the buggy, while the others walked alongside. Lucy carried her good shoes, and walked in the dust along the side of the road. Her round, good-natured face was thoughtful.

Sam spared a thought for his sister. She was a good soul. Here she was, twenty-two and not married, when all her friends had been married for years and even had had a baby or two. What would happen to her? She was plain of face, but her heart shone through her eyes, and when someone fell sick, nobody was kinder than Lucy. It was a pity some men couldn't see beyond a pretty face, Sam reflected.

452

When they got close to the schoolhouse, they could hear the fiddlers. The party was in full swing. Sam's steps quickened as he abandoned his earlier gloom. He enjoyed dancing, and he wondered if he would find a good partner tonight. If not, he would stick to Lucy, who could dance as well as the best.

As his father tied up the buggy, and Sam helped his mother and the young ones down, they could hear the caller. "Swing your partner, take her round the square! Under and over, and don't you care! Claim that lady and swing her once again . . ." Yes, it was going strong.

Sam paused in the doorway and looked for Art. He had thought his friend would be hanging around the door, waiting for him. Instead, he was out in the middle of the floor, dancing up a storm, grinning all over his darkly handsome face. Sam stared at the girl opposite Art. She was a looker! He hadn't noticed her before. Maybe she was new.

He took another look, then decided it was Patricia Reuter, with her hair done up in a smooth bun at her neck. She was growing up. She must be sixteen by now, since in school she had been about four grades behind Sam and Art.

The dance ended. Art bowed low with that studied grace the ladies liked, and took Patricia back to her folks. Her father, a German, had white hair and a bushy beard and an accent the boys made fun of. Her mother was large of build, and pacific of temperament, in contrast to her volatile husband. Sam looked at the big man. He was an inventor, and he knew an awful lot about engines. Their two sons, both much older than Patricia, the last one in the family, had set up a machine shop in town, and some said they were very smart.

The music started up as soon as the fiddlers had had a drink of cold cider. Sam's parents took to the floor. Lucy had found a partner already, which made her smile and glow. Sam headed for Art, who was at Gerhard Reuter's side, talking to him. They swung around

453

when Sam approached. "Good evening, Mr. Reuter," Sam said respectfully.

" 'Evening, young man!" Mr. Reuter seized Sam's hand and shook it vigorously. "It is warm here, no?" he said, and wiped his perspiring forehead with a big red handkerchief.

"Yes, sir. Hello, Art."

"You're late." Art grinned, significantly. "I came an hour ago. The dance is half over now."

It wasn't, but that didn't prevent Art from gloating. He was sticking close to Patricia Reuter's side. She was certainly pretty tonight, Sam thought. He liked the rose-colored dress she wore. It set off her light brown hair and hazel eyes, and her oval face. She had a serene look, with a glow in her face and eyes, but with a gentleness like Lucy's. He gave her another look. She was growing up. "Good evening, Patricia," he said.

She smiled at him, and he felt a funny sensation under his breastbone. " 'Evening, Sam," she said in her soft voice.

"Did you hear about my daughter?" Mr. Reuter asked proudly. "She's got the job to be the new schoolteacher come September! Smart, she is! Only sixteen, and a schoolteacher yet!"

"I wish I was still in school!" Art said with a smirk. They all laughed except Sam. Patricia's cheeks took on a rosier hue. Why did he have to come out with such wisecracks?

"May I have this dance, Patricia?" Sam asked abruptly, ignoring the way Art held tight to her arm.

"Why . . . yes, of course, Sam. I'd be pleased." She stepped forward, and Art had to let go. He gave Sam a flinty look, but Sam could not have cared less what his friend thought. He led Patricia to another square just forming, and they joined in right away.

She was light on her feet, like a feather on his arm. He was pleased about that. He enjoyed dancing so much, he couldn't have tolerated it, had she been a clod. He let himself go, and kicked up his heels, and did fancy steps between the other calls, just to see her laugh and to watch her cheeks grow pinker.

He didn't take her back to her parents when the calling stopped. "Would you care for a cool drink?" he asked. She nodded, and he led her over to the lemonade stand. They stood in a corner, out of the way, by themselves, and he pleased himself by gazing down at her. She had truly bloomed during the past couple of years. She was fully grown now; her mouth was serene and softly smiling. He liked the way the lanterns made her brown hair glow golden.

"Father said you're an inventor also, Sam," Patricia said unexpectedly, gazing up at him over her cup of lemonade.

"I'd like to be," he said honestly. "But I can't say I've invented much. Did your father hear about my tinkering with watches and engines?"

"No. He saw one of the tools you made, to pick apples more easily." She spoke precisely, in a clear tone. He liked her voice. "He said you had a future, if you wanted it."

"Really? I wish I could talk to him. My Pa, well, he said it was a waste of time, always trying to make work easier. He said man is born to work hard, and it's foolish to try to get around it."

She gave him a thoughtful look. "Father likes to invent." She sidestepped the argument neatly. "He thinks up new ideas in his sleep, he says. Do you?"

"Yes. Or while I'm lying wakeful, trying to sleep, and watching how the moonlight falls on the wall. I think of things then, and I get up and try to draw without waking up my brothers."

She smiled slowly, and he watched, fascinated, as dimples appeared in each of her cheeks. "That's what Father does, drawing all night, then sleeping all day."

"Doesn't your ma mind?"

She laughed a sudden, low laugh that enchanted him. He wanted to hear it again. "No, she is used to it, she says. They've been married more than thirty-five years. They met in Germany, when he was already rather well-known as an inventor. So she knew what to expect."

He could have talked to her and listened to her all night. But Art Verlaine came up at his elbow, glared at him suspiciously, and asked Patricia to dance. Patricia went right with him. Sam gazed after them.

Because she was popular, she danced only once more with him that evening. Even Art was having trouble claiming her. Her cheeks got pinker and her eyes more sparkling. Sam danced with his sister Lucy, and introduced her to another friend. He danced with his mother, whose steps matched his, and they enjoyed it. At other times, he hung around the door, and watched Patricia. She hadn't ridiculed him because he wanted to invent things that would make life easier. She seemed to respect her father, and not to view him as an old crank, absent-minded and shabby.

He thought a lot about her the next day, as he hustled about doing the Sabbath chores, and as he sat on the hard seat in church, listening half to the sermon and half to his own mind. He gazed up at the candles in the wall sconces, and wondered how it would be if a light source could be invented that wouldn't burn down and go out. And as the April warmth seeped into the church, and made him stir restlessly, he wondered how it would be if man could control the weather, and make it fine and sunny and cool on the days he set aside for rest and recreation, and rainy when he needed it for the crops, and dry when he wanted to plow.

If his father could have read his mind, he would have taken a strap to him, Sam thought wryly, and tried to straighten his shoulders and pay attention.

That afternoon he took his young brothers fishing. He had two reasons: it was a fine day, the fish were biting, and he wanted to present his mother with a change, with something different, for supper, and the whole family liked fresh fish; and if he gave his brothers a good time, they would keep their mouths shut tonight when he burned a candle late to repair the watch.

It worked. They brought home a dozen fine carp,

456

and had fried fish for supper with new potatoes and canned beans. And later that night, he stayed up past midnight, fixing the watch, while his brothers slept peacefully, worn out from the day outdoors.

He got five hours of sleep before his brother Philip woke him, and said his father would be mad if he slept any longer. Sam yawned, got up, and started to dress. His mind was so busy reviewing the events of the weekend just ended, that he had nothing to say at breakfast.

That was all right. His father did not encourage chatter. Then they all went out to do their chores, and Sam got after the plowing in the west field. The corn had to go in soon.

He was kept very busy all week, for the weather was fine, after a brief wet spell. They wanted to put in corn, wheat, and the rest of the vegetables as soon as possible, so they would have a good crop this summer. All the boys worked—the younger ones after school. Even little Annie helped prepare the sacks of seed for planting. In their family, everyone worked. It was necessary.

After supper on Saturday night, Sam washed and dressed in his best suit. When he came out, his father was reading the weekly paper. He looked at Sam over the edge of the newspaper.

"Going out? There's no dance tonight," he said.

"Going to Reuter's," Sam said.

"Ummm," his father said, and his mother glanced up from her sewing. Lucy looked over at him, from where she sat making a dress for Annie, and her eyes were troubled, but she said nothing.

Sam got the use of the buggy, and went out. His heart was light. Somehow he had the feeling that his life was changing, achieving purpose, taking a new direction; and the feeling was good, after all the years of boredom and frustration.

The Reuter parents were home, and welcomed him. But among the children, only Patricia was left at home; the boys were in the city. Mr. Reuter was willing to ramble on about the boys, and about the work they were doing—something about making tools for the

457

farm. Patricia was sewing something white and feminine, but she hastily put that away, and got out a square embroidery piece.

Sam kept glancing at her, and once she smiled at him. Mrs. Reuter asked him in a friendly fashion about his work, and he talked enthusiastically about mending watches. The sound of a buggy drawing up outside interrupted him. He peered through the lace curtains at the windows to see the shadowy figure of a man coming up the front path. Art Verlaine!

"Expecting company?" Sam asked Patricia directly. She flushed and shook her head.

That settled it. He sat squarely in his seat and vowed to remain. Mr. Reuter answered the door, saying, "Well, Art, come in, my boy. Nice to see you tonight."

Art came in, stopped short, and glared at Sam. "You here?" he snapped.

"Right you are, Art," Sam said pleasantly, not moving from his seat, in the chair nearest to Patricia. Art had to settle for a seat on the horsehair sofa next to Mrs. Reuter.

Nothing fazed Art Verlaine for long. Soon he was chatting away about his plans for the future, ignoring Sam, and directing his talk to Mr. Reuter, who smiled and puffed on his pipe, and stroked back his long white hair. Occasionally he would put in a comment, "Is that so? Well, now . . ."

And his merry eyes kept taking in Patricia's demure face, and Sam's scowl, and Art's determined, ingratiating smiles.

All the while, Art went right on talking. "So I'll be going to the city. I'm going to get myself a job like your sons, Mr. Reuter," he announced, very respectfully, with his little bow. Damn it, how could he bow sitting down? Sam watched him closely, but couldn't figure it out. And what was he yammering about getting a job in the city? His father would have a conniption!

At ten o'clock, Mrs. Reuter folded away her sewing. So did Patricia. They got out a jug of lemonade and

458

some cakes, and served them in pretty cups and plates of thin china decorated with a floral pattern. Sam was almost afraid to touch his saucer. If he broke it, would Mr. Reuter throw him out of the house? He studied the cup intently. One day, he would have a whole set of these pretty cups, with white backgrounds, and with wildflowers on them, and with a rim of gold all around. They were mighty pretty things.

They ate and drank, and talked some more. Mr. Reuter started talking about Mr. Thomas Edison, who had invented an incandescent lamp, and had shown it at Menlo Park, New Jersey. Mr. Reuter had gone to see it, and was enthusiastic. "It will revolutionize lighting," he said, his accent guttural in his enthusiasm. "Chust think! Chust think! A light that will burn without tending, for many, many hours. By electricity! Imagine!"

Fortunately Sam had been reading the newspapers. "Yes, I saw that Wabash, Indiana, is going to light its streets with electric lamps. It will be safe to go out at night then!"

Mr. Reuter looked at him approvingly. "Many inventions will come about, young man, in the future years. We shall harness this electricity and put it to many good uses—to make labor more easy, to make our streets safe, to improve living in many ways."

Art was sitting steadfastly on the horsehair sofa. Sam sat on determinedly in the hard chair. He would not be out-sat by Art Verlaine! And from the determined look on his face, Art felt the same way.

Eleven o'clock came. Mr. Reuter still spoke of inventions, of the marvelous Mr. Edison and his ideas. Mrs. Reuter began to stir. Patricia stifled a yawn.

Eleven-thirty arrived, and the clock chimed. Mr. Reuter stopped talking, and peered at the clock. "So late, it is?" he said, and shook his white head. "Soon it will be the Sabbath. You boys must go home now, yes? You can come another time, and we will have a good talk."

Firmly, he stood up and marched to the door. Art

459

and Sam had to get up also, but each sought politely to be the last out the door. Art won, and shoved Sam ahead of him, with mock-politeness.

Sam, fuming, went to his buggy, but hesitated. Art was still at the doorway, talking to Mr. Reuter. The longer Sam waited, the angrier he got.

When the door finally closed, and Art went to his buggy, Sam was already there.

"You think you're smart, don't you?" Sam said. "You thought you'd outstay me!"

Art turned on him in a fury. "You've got no business calling on my girl!" he hissed, and his fist lashed out and struck Sam on the chest. Sam at once shot out his fist and hit back. Art sprawled on the dusty earth, but came up fighting.

They traded blows; they were rather evenly matched. They had fought for fun over the years, down behind the woodshed or out in the woods. But somehow this was different. Sam felt a hard anger as he flailed away, meaning to hit Art's handsome face that had been grinning and grinning all evening. He connected, and saw blood spurt from Art's nose.

"Damn you!" Art flashed, and struck Sam such a blow that Sam felt the world spinning around him as he reeled back against Art's buggy. The horse shied, neighing in alarm. The door opened, the light shone on the path, and Mr. Reuter came out, his white head shining.

"Boys, boys, what are you doing out here? Shame on you, fighting! Come on, give over! Stop this, you are big boys now, you do not fight!"

Somehow he got them separated, and held them apart. He gave each of them a shake with a powerful fist, and glared at them. He shook his head ponderously.

"Go home now, and be sorry! First, shake hands, and say you will be friends again! Come on now, shake hands."

But Art would not shake hands. He pulled himself from Mr. Reuter's grasp and got into the buggy, still bleeding all over his face and his woolen shirt. He

Sweet Love, Bitter Love
By Anna James

Towering passion, unquenchable lust and undying love as America rebuilds after the Civil War.

Breathtaking Bethany Winfield, a honey-haired Carolina beauty, sought haven—only to be brutally violated; knew fiery passion—only to seek gentle love; gained tenderness—only to crave burning desire. Initiated into savage island rites, she yearned for respectability. Forced to submit to captivity, she longed for freedom. She tasted love, shame and humiliation before she could find safe harbor in the arms of the one man whose love and strength were destined to hold her turbulent, vagabond heart.

HBJ JOVE

$2.25 12046975

Available wherever paperbacks are sold.

NT-32